DANCING WITH DEATH

WHO WILL DIE? OR DISAPPEAR?

AN AUBREY GREIGH MYSTERY

GK JURRENS

eBook ISBN: 978-1-952165-28-3
Print ISBN: 978-1-952165-29-0
Audiobook ISBN: 978-1-952165-33-7

v.221015
R.24090524_0700

Note the list of major characters in the appendix.

Also, please write and post a brief review or email your thoughts to gjurrens@yahoo.com. I read every single review and comment with gratitude. Thank you.

Subscribe at GKJurrens.com

CHAPTER 1

MORE THAN A FEW YEARS FROM NOW….

Late Evening
Monday, August 10th
City Lux Executive Apartments
Suite 3-16
9 Tietgensgade
Kobenhavn (Copenhagen), Denmark

Something is very wrong…. The thought prickled Aubrey Greigh's every nerve ending. In contrast to the warm hallway, a chill breeze funneled through the crack between the lavish suite's entry door and its jamb. Perhaps an omen. *The door ajar? Not good.* He whispered a curse as he stood with his back to the opulent hall. A gust of cold air caused a momentary whistle as it puffed out from inside the suite. His skin crawled as goosebumps sprouted all over his body, confirming his fear that something indeed was very wrong.

On instant alert, he peeked in and eased open the door with one knuckle, his face a mask of concentration; if he carried a gun, it would have been out in front, held low and ready. Not a master of mixed martial arts, but Greigh managed to take care of himself in a fight better than most. "Peter?" Nothing. Louder. The same. He had expected Peter Fontera to meet him at the door, flashing his dazzling white dental implants. He was a force of nature at any gathering; a man who elicited both admiration and exasperation with his quirks.

Greigh had never been here before. As he stepped into the suite, a rental, he noticed a portrait in the dim light of the foyer - a framed headshot on the only table. It was as though someone had placed it there with deliberation, to catch the bright recessed spot overhead. The whole room was lit with the dim glow of that single light focused on that one picture.

The atmosphere of the place felt eerie and uncomfortable. Greigh struggled to identify why—something about that photo, and the silence, unsettled him. He couldn't wait to leave. That portrait—an oil painting?—was small enough to fit into a suitcase, but large enough to broadcast professional vanity. It featured the tools of Peter's trade: a Botox'd face and perfect hair too good to be true. His movie-star smile and dimpled chin hovered over a wild bowtie. The light achieved its purpose at just the right angle.

Peter was famous for those hideous bowties. Even the characters he portrayed in every movie all wore them. The entertainment media loved to report that those ties were the subject of an ironclad provision in his every contract. Made him appear a tad wonky. Only Peter could pull it off. Greigh didn't care. He didn't know Peter, other than as a source. Most said Fontera was the nicest bloke ever. Greigh allowed his set of ever-present antique brass knuckles gripped in his right hand and a small but powerful flashlight in his left to guide him.

AND THERE HE SPRAWLED. STUNNED, BUT IN ORDER TO GET to him, Greigh had no choice but to track through a spreading pool of blood that surrounded the international celebrity who now lay at his feet. Peter appeared either already dead, or close to it. The body was unrecognizable except for that silly tie. Greigh's stomach flipped, but he had already envisioned this horrific scene in his mind's eye. Didn't make it any easier. He swallowed hard, mopped his brow. *Sweating despite this cool breeze? To business, then.*

The night air caused the white curtains to billow inward at the balcony's French doors open wide to a starry sky and the heavens. *How bloody poetic....* Before tonight, everyone in the western hemisphere would have recognized Peter Fontera from stage and screen. His popularity had soared as the most prominent Chicago studios satisfied a sudden retro demand. Windy City Productions led the way with stars like Peter Fontera and Stacy Michaels. A few years ago, the public once again hungered for skilled human actors and real-world settings in their entertainment, versus the industry standard—those that were computer generated or enhanced. C.G. and A.I. had been all the rage for decades. It had grown old and Greigh agreed.

So handsome in life, Peter himself now seemed artificial. Like a staged corpse in a horror flick. He was still alive, wasn't he? Or was that just incorrigible optimism? Though repulsed by violent and messy death, Greigh went to work. *All right, then. I must try. Pulse at the carotid? Inconclusive. At the femoral artery? Weak, but there. Mouth-to-mouth? Out of the question. Not much left of the poor bastard's face. Like that was one of the killer's targets. Likely no killing wound there, but no chance for a controlled airway. Chest compressions, it is.*

These high-velocity thoughts swirled like errant dust devils through Greigh's parched consciousness, along with the gruesome spectacle of Peter's exposed crotch area that had been reduced to soupy kibble. *Oh, bloody hell!* Another gut lurch. He focused on Peter's chest. Straightaway, he started cracking Fontera's rib and sternum cartilage a hundred times per minute until he accepted it was all too little, too late. Still, he kept at it. No stranger to violence, Greigh nevertheless abhorred it. Well, he avoided it. Most of the time.

With Fontera's blood and other fluids now everywhere, including all over Greigh's own hands, arms, knees, and the soles of his sandals, he discarded any concern over leaving fingerprints and distinctive tracks. Couldn't be helped. He had not worn gloves, much less waders. Did not expect to slog through a bloodbath and drop to his hands and knees into the thick of it. After less than two minutes, he gave up, already huffing like he'd run a race. Most can't appreciate the exertion proper chest compressions require. He mopped his sweaty brow. *Did I just smear this poor blighter's blood all over my forehead? Shite! What had Peter learned that he'll now take with him to his grave? If only....*

CHAPTER 2

~

A week earlier, Interpol contacted Greigh as he ate breakfast in his suite at the Hotel Literati within Chicago's Near Southwest Loop. His presence was required in Denmark within twelve hours. Unprecedented. Until now, *he* had always done the contacting. *And* he'd be traveling incognito? Another first. False papers—passport, international driver's license, credit cards, deep background with a very authentic criminal history, should that be required—the works. It would all be waiting in a locker at O'Hare, they said. This was also new. Nobody creates a complete legend—a deep cover identity—in twelve hours. Pre-meditated, then. Interesting. He'd talk to Freya about that.

Now, he stood in a murdered man's apartment. Earlier today, Peter Fontera had contacted him. He'd refused to talk over comms. Under his cover, Greigh had posed as a colorful entertainment reporter covering the latest Windy City movie project,

Dancing With Death. He'd shared coffee with the actor at the waterfront movie set the last few days during breaks in the shooting. They'd hit it off—two creatives. At least, that was Peter's perspective. Greigh could be a chameleon.

Tonight, not knowing who to trust, Peter said he had vital information to share, but only with Greigh. Too little, too late, which apparently, was to be tonight's theme. Greigh liked the lanky but dashing fellow. He now cursed himself for burning two precious minutes administering useless chest compressions to a corpse. Even under less dismal conditions, he knew the failure statistics behind CPR—cardiopulmonary resuscitation. Here and now, they were *far* worse than that. There was always room for hope until… there wasn't. That time—measured in a few dozen seconds—had come and gone. *Well, then, right so! Face obliterated, chest wound still pumping, but… no defensive wounds? Unconscious, unresponsive. Shite be on the saints!*

Time passed Greigh by in a fog of futile optimism—his Kryptonite. If there was *any* chance…. Now, the police couldn't be far. After failing to raise a good pulse, Greigh got to his feet. Almost slipped and fell in the wet mess. Even his toes stuck together in a stinky soup. He'd worn his *thinking sandals* despite the nip in the air. If only he'd known….

Time to beat a hasty retreat until the team could sort all of this. He turned to bolt out of the suite's door on the sixteenth floor of the ultra-contemporary City Lux condos. He needed to brief his handler. No sooner had he crossed the threshold than a gazillion-candlepower beam stunned him.

"HÆNDER, HVOR JEG KAN SE DEM. NU!"

Bloody brilliant! Just what I need. But then, maybe I can learn more as a suspect than as a witness. Greigh's working knowledge of Danish made it clear the cop had said, "Hands where I can see them. Now!" He complied. No sudden moves. Not now. Street cops in any country made Greigh's left eye tick. The voice behind the light reported over comms. Translating in his head: "One in custody."

Four rough hands shoved him face-first against the wall to his immediate right, in the hallway just outside the suite. Not his first rodeo, as the Yanks might say. Three other tactical-clad human tanks slid by to clear the rest of the massive suite with their artillery at the ready. *Who had called them in? Were these lads the Lux's concierge cops? Nope, these boys were Tactical Squad—or whatever they called them here. Copenhagen's finest.*

From deeper inside the apartment, one cop said, "Body!" And then three seconds later, a different voice shouted, "Clear!" Then one more. A softer voice, likely the first bugger again, almost inaudible from the hallway, spoke with, what? Horrific awe? His response translated to "Holy Mother of God…." Greigh didn't even need to mentally translate.

Yup. That was the first one who had discovered Peter's remains. Is that wanker now vomiting in their crime scene? Sure sounds like it. A "tank" with a sensitive gut? The bugger must be a rookie. One of the Tacs? That is, a member of a highly-trained elite tactical squad like those in the Chicago Enforcement Department? This certainly isn't Chicago!

Before being told to do so, Greigh piled both palms on top of his head, leaving two smeared handprints on the wall in front of his face. Two hands—not his—turned out his pockets, while two more held a compact H&K 9mm pistol to his left temple in a white-knuckled grip. They discovered his wallet, US passport, a few Danish and American bills in his favorite money clip—a relic from when cash was king. They dug deeper for some loose change, an A-bus pass, a folding knife, his old brass knuckles (he imagined trying to explain *them*), and his miniature high-lumens flashlight. He winced. The officer handling him bruised the boys—the family jewels—exploring the depths of his jeans' front pockets, perhaps hoping to root out some homicidal lint.

Bollocks! Greigh stared at his own shadow through slitted eyes. It stared back at him from the lavender wall, an inch from his nose. The cop-strength body spot lit his backside with his hands still on his head. Not his best pose for the official body cam recording of the arrest. His elevated elbows gave his sharp-edged shadow a shape that reminded him of a bird of prey. *Someone bloody well preyed on poor Peter tonight.*

Greigh heard the cuffs clink as they snicked away from an equipment belt behind him. He anticipated the need to bring his right hand down to get hooked up. But not so soon or so fast that the arresting officer would think he was making an offensive move. He swung his arm out to his side in a slow, wide arc, always keeping his hand open and visible, until it was low enough. With one hand now cuffed—pinch-tight—he lowered his open left palm behind his back in the same fashion.

After pinning him harder against the wall, the cop grunted the Danish equivalent of an appreciative, "Huh," like it was a relief dealing with a professional. Textbook hook-up. But the poor fellow's breath broadcast yesterday's garlic. Caused Greigh's stomach to lurch. Again. He'd bet this edgy officer was likely into his second or third shift in a row. The guy could use a change of uniform and a shower. Bad breath and BO—the universal labor language. *Exhausting, all this scurrying about.*

One officer read the Danish equivalent of Greigh's rights to him. Since Greigh had yet to utter a single syllable, they still assumed he was a local, despite the passport. *Hmmm… they're not as sharp as I thought. Or….*

Another stout fellow escorted him to a waiting paddy wagon outside, a high-security panel van out on Tietgensgade. Looked like they assumed he was a very dangerous guy—like an airborne tornado biding its time to drop from the clouds and strike without warning.

It was mighty uncomfortable to be so wet and sticky. He was a mess, face to feet, stinking like yesterday's sewage. Like he'd been rolling in the stuff. Not just blood, either. Smart cops. They'd thrown a plastic sheet over the seat toward which he was being guided in no uncertain terms. They forced him down onto a bench in the van's cage just inside its rear door on the driver's side, but the doors remained open.

After a while, old blood ripens and reeks before it scabs or scales.

And that's just the blood. Even rugged Naugahyde upholstery is not immune. Not even in this snazzy Volvo EV van—high security law enforcement edition. They seemed to have sent the first string—except for the projectile vomiter. Nothing but the best for the suspected killer of a celebrity victim—McQ would call poor Peter a *vic*.

CHAPTER 3

A battalion of media vultures already flocked in force out on Tietgensgade Boulevard, even this late on a Monday night. Must be a slow news day. By the time the tac squad led Greigh out for his perp walk, the night burned brilliantly from all the spotlights out on the Tietgensgade. Serious battery power pushed *megawatts* out there. They dappled the caravan of police cruisers and "his" van-slash-mobile cell in high-contrast through the dried leaves that still clung to the trees lining this exclusive neighborhood's sidewalks.

A veritable media circus had already set up behind the portable barricades beyond the Lux's circle drive. Felt like an old-fashioned movie premier in Old Hollywood. Somehow, the media always got the word, almost before the cops. This might be a brilliant scene for a reality series called "Star Killers."

But the *Men in Black* surprised Greigh. He smiled at his private quip. He spotted the pair of suits near the van's still-open rear doors. His sharp eyes zeroed in on tiny lapel pins adorning these two well-tailored hulks. Each pin bore a white cross on a field of red inside a thin gold border. Hard to miss on those custom-fit charcoal suits.

DDIS agents? Their international colleagues referred to them as the Danish Defense Intelligence Service. After all, who in bloody hell accurately pronounced their agency's real moniker in Danish—*Forsvarets Efterretningstjeneste*. Or who'd remember what the acronym *FE* meant? The agency was enigmatic enough to be known by other names, too.

Greigh had spent time in Denmark. While researching one of his earlier manuscripts, he learned that DDIS responsibilities included collecting information about national political, financial, scientific, and military interests. Maybe even UFOs, for all he knew. So, why would DDIS be interested in a common homicide—even that of a celebrity? What might they know that he didn't? Had they already discovered Peter's intel? Most curious. He'd ask Freya Ecklund, his Interpol handler.

Fontera had been in Copenhagen for the last three weeks on location for his starring role in *Dancing With Death*. Although he couldn't have foreseen *this* scene as his finale. And nobody had captured the murder on video. Some cold-hearted prig of a producer would no doubt lament *that* more than their star's violent demise.

Celebrity victims always nipped the best coverage—especially homicides with a salacious theme. And if that theme involved a bizarre modus operandi? Even juicier. Was this personal vengeance, or something else altogether?

GREIGH WORRIED ABOUT THE NEWS CREWS. HE HOPED THEY were far enough away.... *Vultures have a job to do, too, I suppose. The same everywhere. Nobody seems to have recognized me. So far, at least.* Greigh kept his head lowered, just the same. Why on earth had Interpol asked him to travel under a false identity this time? Made no sense. If anyone recognized him, he'd be famous for yet another reason. *Bloody brilliant, this.*

He could not afford such exposure. He imagined his publisher stroking out. Besides, all of this was inconsistent with the damn mission. *And* he had screwed up. It was stupid to attempt triage with that much blood loss and soft tissue damage. *But I had to try, hadn't I?* Precious minutes lost needed to make his escape. A leopard can't change his stripes, as they say. Or some such rot. *American idioms!*

There'd be hell to pay, and he'd be the one paying. But these cops were the least of his worries. He'd try not to think about all of this until after they'd cleaned him up. If he was lucky, they'd subject him to a good night's rest in a holding cell, and possibly even a state-sponsored breakfast. He hadn't eaten or slept since, what, yesterday? *Shite!*

Not easy to switch off the mind of an investigator. Despite his best efforts to do so, Greigh reflected during his bumpy van ride to Tårnby—he'd heard the driver mention their destination while chatting with his dispatcher. Greigh imagined Fontera's luxury rental suite before all the blood on the floor, damaged walls, ceiling and furnishings, not to mention the contents of Peter's vacated bladder and colon soaking into the grout between the Italian Travertine floor tiles. Someone had rented that apartment almost a month ago for the movie star—probably his studio. It was every bit as spectacular as his famous high-rise on the *Mag Mile* back in Chicago. That's what the locals called it—Mag was short for Magnificent. They called it that or the *Miracle Mile*—a bunch of overpriced apartment buildings and concierge businesses inside the West Loop. That patch of ground was once quite the tourist trap.

The best apartments boasted the most splendid lake views. But Fontera preferred the river side. They "re-gentrified" that entire area on the Chicago River about twenty years ago so they could justify the "exclusive"—that is, bloody inflated—prices for that rarified real estate.

These days, most stars and other celebrities huddled near each other on Celebrity Row out at the southeastern shore of Lake Michigan. That portion of Chicago—the city now a massive regionplex of fifty million souls—was recently part of Western Indiana before bored politicians redrew invisible state lines. The lake now stunk like shite, but... "The Row" *was* lake shore. Everyone said The Row made Hollywood Hills look like a shantytown by comparison. They even featured their own mag-lev limo train from out there into all the major studio lots north of the Cicero district. And the rolling parties between The Row and Cicero were the stuff of legends. No doubt Fontera's suite on the Mag Mile, as well as his mansion out on The Row, would fall to his heirs, if he had any. *Shite-for-brains idiots with money. I'm different, though… aren't I?*

Fontera never had a chance, the poor sod. IN THE FEW MINUTES Greigh had been in the celebrity's suite near Copenhagen's city center, he concluded the killer was not a professional. Too messy. Too personal. Or it was just meant to appear that way, as if someone was sending a message. A brutal one. It appeared the movie star had expired from exsanguination. Greigh's cop friend in Chicago—the lovely Detective Chance McQuillan, a.k.a. McQ—would say he "bled out."

A pro hitter would have delivered decisive strikes—two or more in the chest, one in the head or face—just to make sure. But it appeared the killer's blade hit no vital organs. Sloppy, unless… for appearances….

Greigh speculated Fontera might even have still been *survivable* as the killer fled. *He'd* assumed so, hadn't he? It's possible he even interrupted the kill. And that would beg the question of how he missed the murderer. He'd ponder that.

Further, Peter's door was ajar when Greigh had arrived. No evidence of forced entry, either. And that high-end apartment featured a sophisticated security system with a video monitor. Yes, Peter knew his killer and had let him or her in. He'd pass all this info on to Freya at his earliest opportunity. And possibly to the local police at the appropriate time.

THEY SAT IN THE TÅRNBY STATION TWENTY MINUTES LATER. The veteran street cop with the bad breath and body odor sat behind a small steel desk with chipped corners and dented sides. He stared at Greigh's passport. Still covered in drying blood from head to every toe

—no doubt that was by design—Greigh squirmed in the bolted-down guest chair with his right hand cuffed to its frame. The cop must have construed his squirming as post-homicidal jitters.

Tac guys doubling as intake processors? Interesting. Not Chicago, for sure. This squad room, though smaller, vibed very much like McQ's at the ninety-ninth precinct house back in Chicago; that is, before they placed her on administrative leave for getting a civilian killed and he lost his access through her. Like McQ's squad, this one stunk of burnt coffee and something more foul. Like week-old sweat socks dipped in rancid cooking fat. He glanced up at the stained ceiling. Lots of dents in the acoustic tile, like this guy's desk, only more holes than dents up there. Under his feet, most floor tiles had long ago defeated their underlying adhesive and lost their corners. Raucous dregs of humanity acted out minor flurries of boisterous drama all around them. Yup, much like the nine-nine.

Officer Halitosis said in accented English lilting with some volume over the din, "So, Mr. Arthur Granville, is it? What kind of name is that?"

The very Scottish Aubrey Greigh said, "Irish, laddy. Grew up there. Now a naturalized American citizen, proud to say. Dual citizenship, you see."

"So, Mr. Granville, why did you kill him? Mr. Fontera? Did you use those old metal knuckles?"

"What say you just process me in, Officer? I'd be delighted to chat with your detectives."

"You'll then be spending the night in a holding cell, *røvhul*." Greigh knew that was the Danish version of smart-arse—paraphrased for polite company.

"'That'll be quite alright. What are your meal options down there, then, boyo?"

EVEN THE DANES ALLOWED THOSE INCARCERATED ONE phone call. "Freya, a complication in the mission plan, dear. I'm calling from Tårnby station. Fontera is dead. It was personal, not a hit. Or at least meant to appear that way. I'm a suspect and in custody."

"Keep your mouth shut and sit tight."

He just adored his Interpol handler's accent—less lilt, more growl. And he loved her black American Express Card for bail money even more. They did that here, didn't they?

CHAPTER 4

As the clock ticked off eleven PM local time, Greigh slid into the front seat of Freya Ecklund's ancient Volvo station wagon that sat waiting for him at the curb of the wet cobblestone street outside Tårnby Police Station. Must have been a cloud burst. The jalopy's heater didn't work. Greigh was used to the cold. It appeared by her shivers and bulky wraps that Freya was not.

"You stuck to your cover, yes? Is that your blood on your clothes?"

"Freya, I am ever enthralled by your charming accent and your sumptuous ride. This is not my blood. Fortunately, the cops allowed me to clean up a bit. But alas, I'll look forward to changing." He swiveled around to peek into the back seat after adjusting his feet around and on top of myriad fast-food wrappers on the floor. He didn't have to say anything about that. Though she was tall at a willowy five-ten, his six-two would still tower over her. Both their heads came close to kissing the headliner. She must have her seats as high as they go.

"Cut the crap, Greigh. What do they *know?*"

"And your knowledge of American colloquialisms? Truly impressive, my dear." He wrinkled his nose at the rancid fried-food odors rising around him in noxious waves, not all that different from inside the station.

"Greigh!"

"Sorry." He grinned. Rubbed his nose with vigor, using the back of his right index finger. Re-smoothed his mustache with his right forefinger and thumb, stroked his beard. Her impatience was legendary. At least with him. He tested it, although he wasn't sure why he relished doing so. "My cover is blown, as the Yanks say. Peter finally recognized me this morning while I was canvassing their set. Maybe it was something I said. But it turned out alright. He's a huge fan. Nobody else recognized me. I kept my head down, and he agreed 'mum's the word.' Some day soon, you'll have to share with me why an alternate identity was necessary, Freya. Plus, why the hell did you request *me* for this case? Smuggling isn't my sort of muck."

"Damn it, Greigh!"

"Yes, yes. Peter called me this afternoon. Said he'd picked up on something. Wanted to see me tonight. Refused to talk over comms. I walked into the grizzly scene, right on the heels of the deed. It would appear someone set me up." He muttered all this more casually than he felt as he visualized the odors, the blood, his bitterness at the senselessness.... Peter's bowtie, half untied, askew, and... drenched. Greigh tucked all of that into a box he labeled, 'Everyone deals with shock and grief differently.' *Yeah, bloody brilliant strategy, that.*

Freya interrupted his momentary reflection. "A violent disturbance reported by an anonymous call." Not a question. The Danish lead detective had debriefed her. Freya said the man was not happy about releasing his prisoner—and still number-one suspect—to Interpol. Without an explanation. Not that the detective thought *Arthur Granville* was the murderer. It was just the idea.

"I attempted CPR, but... I was making my very wet exit when they arrived—mere minutes after *I* had arrived. Of course, they assumed the worst. I did not resist, and said nothing. Stuck to my cover. It held. With them."

"And at Tårnby station?"

"Arthur Granville answered all the detective's questions. They, too, found the anonymous call of dubious provenance. Once you arrived, and Interpol vouched for me, well, that changed everything; however, I am still to remain in town for the inquest."

"I'll take care of that. Too bad your informant didn't pan out."

"Not Peter's fault someone murdered him. Like I told you, Freya, Peter said he'd heard some things down there. Never had the chance to tell me."

"Curious who discovered that and took him off the board." She stared at Greigh.

"Yes, curious." He scratched his bearded neck, deep in thought, oblivious of her expression at that moment.

Freya said, "Who would want him dead?"

"Well, the man *was* full of himself. He was a brilliant actor, but had become a pariah on the set, some said. Everyone either hated or loved the guy; however, his demise might have nothing to do with our case. Or everything."

FREYA SHARED WHAT SHE KNEW. "DANISH AUTHORITIES called Interpol when they got wind of an international arms deal. They had arrested a low-level courier who cut a deal for leniency, I'm told. But whatever was happening eclipsed local police jurisdiction. They just didn't know it yet."

And that would explain the "Men in Black" from DDIS—one arm of Denmark's 'feds.' They weren't at Peter Fontera's crime scene because someone had committed a homicide. They were in the loop. Why hadn't **they** *contacted the locals? Or had they? Inter-agency animosity? Distrust? Didn't matter. Something was going to happen.* As they sat there at Tårnby station's curbside, Freya tapped the steering wheel with her furious fingers while Greigh reflected on the evening's events and his long-standing relationship with this intense woman. *She is always a bundle of nervous energy, this one.*

When she could remain silent no longer, she said, "We need intel. Leverage whatever you've learned over the past week hanging around that ridiculous movie set on the waterfront, now that your CI didn't work out. We're running out of time. Since they compromised your legend, you're now worth more to us as yourself." She tossed into his lap his genuine passport, a packet of credit cards, and the rest of his real identity.

"What? Where—?"

"Your automated butler was very cooperative. I anticipated someone might recognize you. Look, you know someone. A Russian." Not a question. Almost an accusation. Freya had done her homework and had anticipated this dilemma since he did dabble in fame.

It was stupid to send me in undercover, anyway! Now, Greigh was not pleased Interpol had invaded his suite at Chicago's Hotel Literati, and with such ease. He'd bloody well have a chat with Butler, his security system, his personal attaché and confidante. He remained most troubled why the alternate identity at all if she expected him to be recognized. He'd file that one away for later.

"Oh, well, right, then. A Russian. You're referring to my friend, Captain Galkin. Didn't know he was in town. Yes, we have a history. Andrushya loves American movie stars... and the bottle. He grows chatty once in his cups. Wouldn't surprise me if he'd heard something, too. And they say Peter always liked to mix it up with the local chaps."

"Get down to Nyhavn, again. The *Marya,* his boat, is in port for at least another twelve hours. Find out what in hell is going on. The agency says there's been yet another uptick in chatter of a WMD in the region."

"So *they* are in a sharing mood, are they? There's always chatter about weapons of mass destruction."

"Something *is* happening on the Baltic, Greigh. My contact says the noise about a black shipment from the east is likely within days. We need intel. *I* need intel. Other assets are working different angles, but you're on this one."

"I'll deliver a bottle of Andy's favorite sixteen-year Lagavulin."

After a beat or two, Freya wrinkled her humorless brow. "Is that not a Scotch? Not vodka?"

"A single-malt, and one that is so smokey many purists shun the stuff. Andy has always been a contrarian."

"Well, whatever is effective. Now go."

She almost shoved him out the passenger door of her beat-up Volvo wagon. "Always a pleasure, my dear. You should get that heater repaired." Freya's fluency in hand-to-man signals also impressed Greigh. She possessed some razor-rough edges. He suspected that she contrived most of them—a woman in a man's world.

CHAPTER 5

The next day, Freya Ecklund arrived late for her appointment with Copenhagen's top cop at their police headquarters building on Polititorvet, southwest of the city's center. She'd had trouble finding a parking space.

Freya's meeting with the pompous Rigspolitichef Fjorkeld Dagde wasn't going well. The Danish police commissioner fumed. "Why are you investigating in my front yard and failing to coordinate with my department? Also, what good reason is there for one of your agents to be apprehended at a murder scene? Using a false identity, no less?"

"Sir, I—"

"You need to listen and not talk in this moment, Frøken Ecklund. I am told this isn't the first time you've operated in… how do the Americans say it… in gray areas? And we expect more cooperation from Interpol than this." He circled both his sausage-fingered hands in front of him to encompass their relationship. "*Now* you may speak."

Freya loathed being dressed down like this, especially from this… petty politician. But he had every right to be upset. She'd take her lumps. For now. "Herre Dagde, you are within your rights to be angry.

And I apologize, with all sincerity." Even though she was rolling her mind's eye as she spoke, she continued in an almost contrite tone of voice. "Our investigation started abroad, and events moved ashore quickly—"

The commissioner interrupted her. "If that is the case, am I too bold in assuming you have already engaged with our intelligence service?"

"Yes, sir, that is happening as we speak. DDIS is assisting us with a smuggling operation that is rumored to involve Danish civilians. We are tracking an active operation at this very moment. But we've involved only a few personnel for security reasons. Of course, we'd share anything we discover with you that would shed light on the murder of an American citizen in your jurisdiction. And a celebrity, no less. Interpol and DDIS will share relevant intelligence with your department."

Freya was lying her ass off. She knew DDIS—the Danish Defense Intelligence Service—did not play well with their police. So, this pompous ass was likely clueless, and she needed to keep it that way. Upon hearing this, Hr. Dagde softened his tone. He was smart enough to recognize big things happening beyond his jurisdiction. "Very well, then. Please do so. And now, if you will excuse me, I will say goodbye and thank you for your time, Fr. Ecklund."

"Thank *you*, sir. We'll keep you apprised." The little man with his enormous head atop his fancy suit nodded, not entirely ready to shed his gruff demeanor, also had to know he could not afford to alienate a mid-level Interpol official, either. Freya marched out of this ass-hat's office. He could not see her self-satisfied smirk as she tromped out like an imperious storm trooper.

Greigh's Interpol handler began her career in law enforcement after changing her name to Freya Ecklund. Through her adoptive father's connections and because of her stellar academic record, Interpol recruited her. Her father encouraged her to develop her own sphere of influence, even though Russia's reputation within

Interpol was often maligned. And not just because they were often less than forthcoming. After four years, she started building her personal reputation as a firebrand in Russian Interpol. Publicly, she decried their use of that organization's influence to prosecute political and business enemies.

As recognition for her stance against misuse of this prestigious law enforcement organization, senior agency management recruited her at Interpol's European headquarters in Lyon, France. She jumped at the chance. Not that she believed the rubbish she peddled about Russian Interpol, but like Papa said, expanding one's circle of influence often meant employing duplicitous methods.

Freya viewed herself as a dedicated agent with little time for the nonsense of life outside of work. At least, that's the persona she projected. She'd requested Aubrey Greigh to investigate this worrisome case, even though it comprised rumor and innuendo more than anything. But it meant a great deal to her.

All lauded Freya to be a talented and respected field agent for Interpol. She moved between countries and cultures with ease. Her job as a handler for contracted field agents gave her flexibility and free time, with which she maintained a low-profile on a day-to-day basis. Why had she asked for Greigh? Interpol had long leveraged the man's unique combination of investigatory skills and his minor celebrity status. Plus, he possessed the ability to connect with people in ways that eluded most Interpol agents who were more law enforcement types.

Aubrey Greigh was a good-looking, arrogant son-of-a-bitch who only dabbled in international law enforcement investigations. She considered him a gifted amateur because he found things out. Maybe better than most. As a reflex, she rubbed the bullet on the chain that hung around her neck. She wished to discover how much he'd unearth on this smuggling case.

FREYA'S PERSONAL LIFE WAS IN A STATE OF CONSTANT disarray. Or so it seemed. As a very private person, she made no time for a social life. No need. Friends were too nosy. And messy. She could not afford that. Inconsistent with her objectives. Best just to avoid those complications—that messy part of life so many seemed to believe so important, even crucial. *Idiots.*

Greigh had already stumbled onto key clues, much faster than she would have expected. She smiled. If she were a bad guy, she'd somehow want to contain Greigh. Somehow. He pushed on all the soft spots and reported them to her.

She was one of Interpol's older supervisory field agents. At fifty-six, her vanity competed with that of a woman three decades younger, even though she had sworn off men... and women. Because of the voluminous cases she had closed over the years, even employing dubious methods, they offered her a choice of assignments. The agents she ran loved her. She could be charming, even with her rough edges. Freya left Lyon. As a gifted multi-linguist, she then moved around to various Scandinavian countries and found she preferred Copenhagen. It was convenient and fit her lifestyle. Especially at this point in the Autumn of her career. But she did not plan to retire with a whimper. *If they only knew.*

CHAPTER 6

The Encinal Bluffs beachfront neighborhood in Western Malibu, California near the Ventura County line appealed to the ultra-wealthy who proclaimed their need for solitude. Its remoteness created one of Malibu's most secluded, private, and tranquil enclaves.

This setting was also ideal for those who could afford any real estate on the planet, but could *ill*-afford nosy neighbors. The large estates here perched on the hills above the Pacific Ocean, each with stunning panoramic views of the coastline, Catalina, and the San Nicolas Islands.

Lionel and Angelique Hollowell made their millions as real estate magnates. Their empire stretched from Paradise Cove Bluffs on the Malibu beachfront to the Hollywood Hills. They also held the choicest properties in Doheny Estates above the Sunset Strip. Each estate lot boasted jetliner views of the Los Angeles Basin to Beverly Hills, all the way from The Flats to the crest in the Santa Monica Mountains.

The Hollowells sold, rented or leased mansions, lofts and everything in-between to Hollywood royalty. They owned or held majority interests in hotels, restaurants, and a variety of other commercial establishments, all in the finest of venues, of course. Location, location, *and* location! Yet they were as inept as they were rich. It seemed they possessed the Midas Touch despite their ineptitude. But this pretentious duo fancied themselves inspired visionaries. They admitted, without shame, to manipulating the American Dream to their advantage. In their minds, being geniuses in the methods of unadulterated greed made them masters of *all* things. Of course, they didn't know what they didn't know or could not see.

Lionel and Angelique were stunning narcissists who always got their way—blundering orchestrators of the long con. Other sycophants flocked to their sides as wannabes, and that was fine with them. They had nothing to do with the entertainment business, other than pandering to celebrities—their real estate clients. This mob was composed of like-minders who spoke their names in reverence, and wanted to be their friends, to be like them. The Hollowells were royalty among the washed few—the sleazy elite.

"This is absurd, Lionel. Look at this." Angelique tapped her three-quarter-inch acrylic nails on the platinum and glass desktop. She stared at her husband and business partner. "This is reasonable only to uncultured buffoons who have no appreciation for true talent."

"Don't blow a gasket, dearest." His expansive gesture with one arm while cradling his oversized Manhattan in the other seemed theatrical, but contrived, like he'd seen too many old movies saturated with over-acting to make up for the lack of sound. He couldn't take his eyes off his wife's perfectly crossed and waxed legs. "Our time will come. And when it does, those buffoons will be clueless what demolished their artificial little fifteen minutes of fame."

"Oh Lionel, you say the sweetest things. When? This is just intolerable. You'd think *Variety* would not pimp for those cretins at Windy City and Miracle Mile. You've heard what they say about Midwestern actors, haven't you? All they think about is corn and cattle, for pity's sake. Nothing of *genuine* show business. You can't blame them, way out yonder 'n all." She uttered this last phrase as if she were auditioning for a 1950s Western.

Lionel said, "Reading that rag has become as toxic as watching politics. Just say *no*, my pet. Lovely sunset tonight. Another?" He nodded down toward her nearly empty birdbath martini while gesturing with a sweep of his right arm toward the magnificent wall of glass. Those windows isolated them from the odious salt air of the Pacific. Waves broke a hundred feet below their living room which was cantilevered over the breakers crashing far below.

"Magnificent, as always. That was my third..." she glanced down at the mammoth stemmed glass on her desk with faux regret, "oh, what the hell. Let's get crazy. Make the next one extra dirty, sweetheart." She flashed her outrageous perma-lashes and winked her tattooed mascara. Never having to re-apply it was such a blessing of modern science. *And,* it never ran. "Let's drink to Chicago's demise!" The glee in her slurred voice caused Lionel to experience a delicious involuntary shiver.

CHAPTER 7

Greigh sat at the desk in his room overlooking Nyhavn—pronounced *NOO-hown*—Harbor on The Sound, one of Copenhagen's most picturesque neighborhoods. The concierge called. Greigh had received a message to call an old friend who said he'd learned his author buddy was in town. They had not spoken for many years. *Andy Galkin is calling **me**? Interesting. On Freya's orders, I was about to call **him**. Serendipity?* In the past, he and Andy had shared a camaraderie forged between two people on the run together in fear for their lives. Not unlike brothers who have shared the field of combat and survived.

Both he and his friend were in town—at the same time. Since Andy navigated the Copenhagen waterfront with ease, Greigh expected some local scuttlebutt relevant to Interpol chatter about possible smuggling operations in the area. Captain Andrushya (a.k.a. Andy) Galkin was a Russian fisherman—code for smuggler. He was a likable sort who loved his Scotch almost as much as his little ship, the *Marya*. Instead of vague rumors or hearsay, the unusual little mariner provided Greigh with his first solid lead.

. . .

CAPTAIN GALKIN HAD ALWAYS BEEN A MAN OF FEW WORDS. Ironically, the origin of the name *Galkin* meant *talkative.* Greigh guessed his "friend" hated the sound of his own voice. Couldn't blame him. The man sounded like sandpaper with lungs, and an octave higher than he might have wished. So, he coarse-whispered when he spoke. But the high velocity of his well-structured chatter when he did speak revealed a sharp mind. If he needed to shout the occasional command to one of his crew—four grim young men—all would wince, including Andrushya himself. Reminded Greigh of a Russian leprechaun held hostage by what sounded like a damaged voice box. Smart as a whip, and a good businessman whose sometimes honorable ethics impeded more than helped his chosen profession as an unapologetic smuggler, he knew the sea. And he knew people. But with tradecraft—the finer points of spying—Andrushya could be naïve.

Andy had said on the phone, "It is never good news when we visit same town at same time, my friend." The wiry little sea captain loved all things Western, especially American movies. In private, he insisted that Greigh call him Andy. "So American," he'd say.

The elevated pier was high enough to accommodate Copenhagen's two-meter tidal range. Greigh peered down at the large boat's midship deck, but up at its towering bridge farther aft and cargo-loading gear forward. The *Marya* was a small ship more than a large boat.

As Greigh walked down the pier, he spotted Andy alone just aft of a foredeck festooned with derricks. The ninety-five-foot fishing vessel hadn't seen a fish in a decade. Nobody seemed to notice. Greigh recognized the vessel was a combination purse seiner and pelagic trawler, a normal sight in both coastal and offshore waters in this part of the world. Like a taxi in New York.

The gun-metal sky threatened snow, rain, or something in-between. Andy's glance around and nod confirmed he was alone on the little ship at that moment. Then.... "Today, I come bearing gifts, Captain. Well, just one. Permission to come aboard, Andy?"

"Da, Greigh. You come. I am glad you are here. Let's have gift. Maybe we enjoy together. Long time, old friend." The shape of the brown bag all but announced its contents. The fierce little man with the fiery red goatee grinned. His teeth were almost as reddish brown as his well-trimmed mane. Greigh handed the bag down into the smiling Russian's up-stretched hands. No sooner had Andy clutched the bag in his grasp than he pulled out its contents and held it at arm's length to read the fancy label.

"Ah! Scotch from a Scot. Like a joke, da? And Lagavulin. Not all Russians drink wodka. *You* know! Many do not."

As he stepped aboard, Greigh listened hard. The man's husky whisper revealed that he might have damaged his larynx in some violent encounter. He guessed this was the persona Andy wished to portray—not that of a little man with a scratchy voice that also annoyed. The elevated foredeck festooned with cranes and other equipment obscured the pier ahead of the little ship. And the multi-story pilothouse and bridge farther aft hid them from the opposite direction.

"Andy, I need information, and I am not talking about seamanship."

"Good. Because I need your help, too, Greigh. I take a job that pays off my *Marya*." He swept his arms out to take in the entirety of his beloved little ship. "But with big pay, big risk come, too, I think." His furtive expression communicated a sense of dread. "I may be under the water on this job."

Greigh smiled. Andy's clumsy turn of phrase reminded him of his own unique relationship with one impertinent police detective in Chicago. "You mean 'in over your head'?"

"Da, that. We talk while drinking smokey Scotch." He down-nodded at the bottle and empty sack now both in his right hand.

Andy, my favorite smuggler, is in over his head? Interesting. Greigh just expected to collect dirt on Peter Fontera's murder after all the time Peter had spent on Andy's waterfront. This new and unexpected info might be a lead on their arms smuggling case to which Freya had assigned him. And if Peter had pressed his ear to the right conversation, this could go to motive. Possibly even a suspect. But Andy's dilemma might just as likely lead him in another direction. *Why am I just now learning that Andy is in town? Curious.*

Greigh shared a unique relationship with this little man. The two of them had crossed the embattled Crimea Peninsula together many years earlier, escaping capture... or worse... more times than either could recount. They were brothers-in-arms. At least, they were between Kerch in the east and Sevastopol to the west, before making a harrowing escape on the Black Sea in a boat very much like Andy's *Marya.*

Andy turned and walked aft to an already open hatch in the bulkhead below the bridge tower. He hustled, either in a hurry to dip into the Lagavulin, or he was burning off nervous energy. Most likely, Andy did not want to be seen with this American. He also exercised discretion while nestled in the awkward cradle of sobriety. After all, it was already close to noon. Greigh followed at an equally brisk pace. After stepping through the hatch's high threshold, they climbed up a short flight of narrow stairs. Made a quick right turn toward the ship's centerline to Andy's combination stateroom and office. It was quieter amidships and higher above the waterline.

Greigh guessed they were below the bridge. The door looked more household-ish than the rusty steel hatch with dogs—locking levers to make such openings watertight—on or below the weather deck. The air inside the stuffy little ship, even up here, was at least twenty comfortable degrees warmer than the outside chill, a musty stench notwithstanding. He could hear the throaty hiss of the diesel boilers somewhere beneath them. Powerful fans circulated dry heat around them. The ship, though closed to the late summer climate, did not smell offensive. More like a log cabin closed against a prolonged winter. Felt nice in the small compartment. Greigh detected a hint of diesel fumes, likely from the exhaust of the boiler somewhere beneath them that supplied the heating system popular on such vessels. Such a boiler exhausted outside, but there were always leaks.

The mariner grabbed two squat glasses with heavy bases off a shelf surrounded by a low fiddle to keep things from sliding off in a seaway.

He set the glasses on his desk. In a single fluid motion, Andy opened, dispensed a generous pour for both of them, replaced the cork, and handed one glass to Greigh. Extended his glass for a wordless toast. *Clink.* They sipped. Manly sips. More like noisy slurps. Greigh knew that was a Russian thing. The two men explored each other's eyes as they drank. Then, after each mini-gulp, they both drew in a crisp breath between puckered lips to enjoy the Scotch's bouquet and sharp, almost dangerous, finish.

"Andy, why don't you tell me about this job that finds you in over your head?"

The wiry sea captain scuffed his forehead, jostling his faded Greek fisherman's cap. "They offer much money, Greigh. I not sure who. I am quiet, reliable and competent captain. I wish to keep it that way. I also wish to survive, so you may buy me more Scotch."

"The job?"

"Transport a metal box and four men. The box weigh ninety kilos, they tell me. The size of two sea chests, I am told. In crate."

There it is. "Source?"

"I pick up in the south harbor—cargo harbor—of Paldiski, south of Tallinn."

"Estonia. When?"

"Three days. Friday."

"Destination?"

"We cross Baltic. Transfer case and men to freighter at sea in Kattegat Sunday night."

Why is it Russians don't use articles like "the" when they speak? "The straight between Denmark and Sweden." A simple statement. Greigh made it a habit to study maps and charts of any area he visited. Old writer's habit—research.

"They not allow questions. Armed men accompany this cargo, for safety, they say. Men transfer to freighter with 'valuable cargo.' Pay right after transfer. Cash. Greigh, *so* many rubles. Takes *so* many credits to stay afloat these days. I take job. Now I regret. What should I do, my friend?"

As Greigh listened, he grew conflicted. While he feared for his friend's safety, this was the profession he had chosen. Now, committed to what sounded like the job of a lifetime, his probability of survival would diminish if he backed out. Plus, they needed intel. *Shite!* "Do the job, Andy. Pay your crew well. Tell them to keep their mouths shut—before, during, and after. But *you* observe. Everything: the vehicle or vessel that delivers this cargo to you in Paldiski; whether they deliver a cargo manifest; the precise dimensions of the container, if possible; the name and class of the freighter to which you will transfer your cargo; take note of how the guards dress; types of weapons they carry; their clothing; the language and dialect they speak. What shoes do they wear? Tattoos, scars, and accents? Remember what they eat or drink; any labels you see; any names you hear. Everything. Since you've already committed to this job, it is best to see it through. Just be their invisible captain. Ask no questions and do not initiate any conversation. Do not appear too curious. And other than your ship's business, engage in no comms. Can you do that, Andy?"

The little man took to drumming his calloused fingertips on his desktop strewn with papers stained with water spots and coffee rings. They'd been there a while. Though it was warm in that compartment, the cheap fluorescents and the mood chilled Greigh to the bone. The Scotch helped. "Mmm, da. I will heed your guidance in this matter, Greigh. Thank you for that. And for Scotch." Andy shrugged and grinned. He tried to look rakish, but only shivered.

"Good. I will know when you make port here again next weekend, but still, you call me, okay?" Greigh jotted his private number on a scrap of paper from the desk between them. "I will bring another bottle, and we will celebrate burning your ship's mortgage. And Andy, allow no one to see this number. Especially the guards. They likely will be watching every move all of you make. Don't put it past them to search anything and everything. Best if you just memorize and destroy it."

Greigh decided not to ask Andy about Peter Fontera. The smuggling case took precedence. Besides, Andy already squirmed in his seat. Despite his smile, his furrowed brow revealed his profound consternation. After pouring two more generous drams, he set the bottle down harder than intended and winced at his own over-reaction. Hoisted his glass.

Greigh hoisted his as well. "Bóo-deem zda-ró-vye!"

"Na zda-ró-vye!"

CHAPTER 8

The next day, Greigh needed to talk with some of the Windy City cast and crew at their warehouse movie set in the harbor. Through Freya, he discovered the executive producer of *Dancing With Death* was also the studio's senior executive and general manager, Lance Bowman. She provided his photo and profile. That seemed a great deal of horsepower to bring to one movie project's location so far from Chicago. This tickled the back of Greigh's consciousness. He'd get more out of this guy if he showed up on the waterfront warehouse set as Arthur Granville, entertainment reporter. If that didn't yield results, he'd reveal his true identity as an Interpol investigator. And failing Bowman's cooperation at that point, he'd get the locals involved in a more controlled setting.

There he stood, pretending he knew what real actors on a proper set needed. Greigh listened to Lance Bowman pontificate. He saw a few of the veteran extras roll their eyes now and then. He spewed lots of talk about vision and opportunity and the future of their industry. Greigh heard one actor in costume who had grown impatient say, "All due respect, sir, we're not getting anything done. Your director is afraid to tell you that. Why not let her direct? Sir?"

Bowman looked like something odious had just been hung under his nose. He turned on the nobody, about to rail on him, but thought better of it. Instead, he said, "You have balls, kid." He pointed at the young extra who, in retrospect, might have decided he'd just cratered his fledgling career, and dropped his chin without losing the certainty of his comment. Then, the studio GM said, "You're absolutely right. Guess I'm nervous about how important this project is to our future. I'll shut up, now. Jessica, you're the director. You know my vision. So direct, already! Thank you, all."

Bowman backed away as he bowed, like he had just completed his magnum opus. As he drifted away from the center of the set, his sheepish expression faded. He took a seat nearby in a canvas chair—a high chair with a footrest—with his name emblazoned on the back. He planted his brilliant Italian loafers on the footrest. His right elbow rested on the armrest supporting his chin with a loose fist. As an afterthought, he brushed a piece of non-existent lint from the sharp crease on the thigh of his pressed blue jeans.

Greigh considered it odd he said nothing about their murdered star, Peter Fontera, in his little speech to the cast and crew. Peter had been found dead and brutalized less than twenty-four hours earlier. But he might have missed that part. The director's sheepish expression turned into a grateful nod as she awaited final confirmation that the top studio exec had indeed relinquished the set to her. She tugged at the headphones hanging around her neck and laid them down onto a collapsible table next to Camera One. They went to work. She addressed the company with words like "We'll miss Peter," and "we can't let this stop us," and "let's get this done for him. Alright, let's prep to roll one!"

That was more like it. Greigh had already formed an opinion of this Bowman character. He was Ben-Affleck-handsome with premature gray in both his hair and well-trimmed beard. More like a manicured four-day growth meant to casually soften a granite chin. But he seemed to wear a certain asymmetry with pride. Heavy tattoos covered his entire left arm and were only visible because he shoved up only one arm of his long-sleeve t-shirt with a two-button slit at the neck. The tats and jeans and t-shirt all seemed in conflict with those shiny loafers. Were they *Ferragamos?*

Everyone else wore light jackets. Some wore gloves. And everybody's breath was visible in the open-door warehouse on the chilly pier under a gray sky. Propane post heaters offered some respite as they hissed away until production assistants turned them off before each take with audio. But the temperature was dropping along with the sun outside, now low over the concrete pier. Bowman's right sleeve was pushed up only a bit. Greigh could see no ink on that arm. Or he was hiding... what? A tat that embarrassed him? Something that now offended? An unfortunate artifact from an impetuous youth? Looked more like a cameraman or a grip than an exec. Except for those costly patent leather loafers. Like a guy who was trying too hard to fit in with a rough crew and a bunch of dilettantes, but failing in epic fashion.

At the risk of interrupting a reflective reverie, Greigh approached Bowman. Stood off to his left, so they could both observe the director do her job as they prepared for a take. He muttered, "You have a tough job, Mr. Bowman, in your single-handed attempt to reshape your entire industry." Greigh figured he had lucked into one of this man's vulnerable moments. He was wrong.

"Who the fuck are you?"

"Sorry, I write for Entertainment Weekly as Arthur Granville. I'll leave you to your task with apologies, Mr. Bowman." Greigh turned to leave, knowing he wouldn't be allowed to do so.

He could almost read this wanker's mind. He was betting a switch flipped. The press? From Chicago, no less? Now behind him, he heard this guy turn on the charm. "Mr. Granville! Of course. Sorry. A bit of business, here. You understand. What can I do for you?"

"Well, Mr. Bowman—"

"Lance. Please."

"Lance, I was to interview Peter Fontera, but it's all over the set. He was murdered?" The man's face dropped on cue. Or did it?

"I'm so sorry. Yes, that's hit us all hard. We're like a family here at Windy City." Greigh cast his eyes around. Most folks looked relieved that their micro-managing executive was distracted by his favorite topic—the media. But they did not look at all like a family.

"I *am* sorry for the loss of one of your *family*... Lance. Peter mentioned he was having some trouble with someone on the set. Had you heard that as well? You seem to have your pulse on the entire location."

Greigh caught a quizzical look from Bowman, but the man answered. As if it was too soon in their relationship to make waves. "He had words with Stacy Michael's production assistant—"

"And that is...."

"Um, his name is Ted something-or-other. Stacy can point him out. I don't see the lad anywhere about right now. It's been quite a morning. The local police have been all over us. Treating us like *suspects!* And then, like magic, they all disappeared. After that, well, nothing. Very odd." The prig issued a gratuitous chuckle. Could not have been more inappropriate. Off his game. Greigh filed away this factoid about Fontera's case. He'd inquire with Freya. Had the locals closed the matter?

"I see. So, your vision... I couldn't help but overhear. Plus, you're the talk of Cicero and The Row, Lance. Bold. Can it work?"

The man lit up, but bore some immense emotional burden. "To create movies without the crutches of CG and AI? The challenges are monumental, Arthur, but I am confident. Movie-goers are tired of all the computer-generated actors, scripts, voices, and sets. They've grown weary of super heroes and immortals. Don't even get me started on all the plot holes that are dismissed with magic or with paranormal trickery. And as good as artificial intelligence programs are, their work products, particularly on longer works, just don't feel... *organic*. Audiences want to get back to what's real and relatable, Arthur, the very human but extraordinary experience that could happen to *them*. That's what escapism into cinema is all about. Movie goers tell us they feel bloated with *only* make-believe. We're losing their suspension of disbelief and the gem of human drama, comedy and mortality."

"And what does losing a major star like Peter do to your plans?" Greigh waved one hand to encompass the set.

"Oh, we're writing him out of *Dancing's* script, of course. But we're early enough in production that—"

"No, I'm referring to your business model. It must take some time to groom an actor to perform CG-free, or nearly so, does it not?"

"Oh, yes it does. Thankfully, we also have Stacy here to step in. Time never stops as it tromps over us mere mortals, does it, Arthur?" His second ill-timed chuckle in as many minutes stopped short when he realized he was joking about one of his *family* member's brutal murder and its consequences.

Greigh chalked it up to nerves. "Lance, were there any hard feelings between Stacy and Peter?"

"What? No! That is an odd question for a reporter to ask, Arthur. That's the sort of dribble with which the Danes pummeled us before they evaporated."

"Yes, well, wouldn't it be marvelous if an empathetic American reporter from Chicago solved Peter's murder for you? For the police? Thank you so much for your time, Lance. And it was a sincere pleasure chatting with you. Good luck with your studio's transformation." Greigh thrust his hand forward, still standing as Lance sat there on his imperious little wood and canvas throne. He did not like this man. And despite his press credentials, Greigh sensed this Lance Bowman felt the same way about him. Surprised by the abrupt end of their interview, Lance hesitated with his head cocked to one side with a startled look frozen on his chiseled face. But then he clutched Greigh's hand in both of his with what now was sure to be artificial gusto. Especially that pasted-on Ben Affleck grin. No doubt well-practiced in front of a mirror.

"No worries, Arthur. A pleasure, I'm sure."

Greigh hustled off, grateful for his escape without being discovered. And, he thought, now in a morose mood, without discovering what Bowman wasn't saying. He sought the only other major star on location at that moment—Peter Fontera's principal rival.

LANCE BOWMAN THOUGHT ABOUT THE UNUSUAL INTERVIEW and its abrupt conclusion. He watched the too-handsome, too well-dressed reporter wander off to talk with his backup star. He thought of Peter. *Well, none of us lives forever. And we each serve a purpose, don't we?* Still, he wasn't sure about the Copenhagen police closing Peter's case as a home invasion gone bad. They seemed to throw their hands in the air as if it were unsolvable. Or they thought something else, but kept it to themselves. *That's* what worried him.

Lance clearly had little to say in the matter. They said Interpol was involved. But it wasn't clear if that was just pro forma when a foreign citizen was involved in a crime. Or whether they considered a serious investigation beyond the local police department's scope. But Lance knew he had bigger fish to fry, despite his personal relationship with the victim. So be it. Now, he'd need to do what was necessary to save this project without Peter as his star, as well as his over-arching strategy.

He allowed himself just one self-indulgent smile hidden behind a cupped palm. He had earlier decided to take action based on a brainstorm inspired by an online acquaintance in "the biz." *Why not book passage on a slow boat back to the States for myself and the entire cast and crew of this project?* He could think of a lot more reasons to do just that than not to do so. There were risks, but that might just be the least of his worries.

CHAPTER 9

It was obvious to Greigh that Stacy Michaels hoped to fill Peter Fontera's star-studded shoes, and then some. Could that be sufficient motive for a brutal murder? Where audiences loved Peter, they loved to hate Stacy. He was a natural villain, both on screen and some said in real life, too.

"Goddammit, Bricker, where's my tea? Bricker?"

"Mr. Michaels? A word, if you please?"

Michaels swiveled only his head to grimace at Greigh as the actor perched on his own wood and canvas chair, not as fancy as Lance's, reviewing several pages of script. He frowned and slapped his pages onto his thigh. "And who the fuck are you, now? Too old for a PA, too good-looking to be an extra. And too polite to be my boss. Wait, don't tell me. That asshole Bowman saddled me with more competition. Am I right?"

"Sir, I'm not a production assistant. I *am*, however, a senior reporter for Entertainment Weekly—"

The actor's eyes lit up as the grimace evaporated, and he projected his most convincing baritone. "You're from *Chicago?* Not this Godforsaken Scandahoovian backwater? Well, why didn't you say so at the get-go, man?"

Like Bowman, Michaels lit up at even the most remote chance at an opportunity for publicity. It was obvious the guy didn't get as much press as he craved. Unlike Fontera, who had found it necessary to shy away from the paparazzi. More motive?

"Mr. Michaels—"

"Stacy, *please.*"

Bloody hell, this character sounds needy. Greigh knew this wasn't the case for all actors. He wasn't sure about studio executives, however. Especially general managers like Bowman. "Ah, yes, well then, I'm Arthur Granville, and I insist you call me Arthur—"

One beat. Two. Now, an even bigger smile. Not too quick. He looked ludicrous. "As in *King* Arthur. Fitting. Especially with your accent. What sort of interview do you seek, King Arthur?" His contrived laugh not only sounded skeevy, it displayed this buffoon's considerable lack of social skills. The obvious sort to shy away from *live* TV interviews—if his agents had any wits about them. Greigh had seen him act. Thankfully, he was better when handed a script under the iron-fisted supervision of a strong director. *I wonder if this bloke knows what a douche he is....* "So tell me, Stacy, how does it feel to be the new star of *Dancing With Death?*"

For effect, Greigh extended the fist that clutched a recording device. Its tiny but bright blue flashing light made it a tacit request to record their "interview." Michaels glanced at it, and after a momentary hesitation, he blurted, "I'm looking forward to delighting my fans with what I hope to be the best perf—"

Greigh interrupted his string of self-aggrandizing platitudes. Time to shake his cage. *Did this guy kill Peter to get this role?* "Sorry, Stacy. What I meant to ask is, who would you consider had motive for killing poor Peter?"

Shaken, the actor whose villainous giddiness of a classic Peter Lory in baritone eclipsed his dashing Harrison Ford features and sculpted a confused, but semi-hideous Alan Rickman (he-who-must-not-be-named) leer into his otherwise handsome face. "I'm sorry? What did you just ask me, *Arthur?*"

"Other than you, who else had a motive to murder Peter Fontera?"

"You're a reporter, not a cop, right? Why would you ask such a question?"

Since he wished to ask this character more questions, he threw the ass-hat a life ring. "Better me than a cop asking you this, right, Stacy? Think of this as a dress rehearsal. It is obvious, even to a humble reporter, that you benefit from Peter's death, perhaps more than anyone. How will you answer that question for the local *Scandahoovian* cops? I'm just here to help, you see. What would you say to them?"

Now confused, which seemed to happen to this pitiable sod more than most, Michaels said, "Well, um… hey, I know! Listen, on screen, everybody loved Peter. Off screen and off stage, though, the guy was a real dick." He chuckled at his own tiny joke. "Get it? Peter? Dick? Anyway, he was the butt of a running gag among the PAs. They had a pool, betting when somebody'd hang him by one of his cute little bowties. Besides, the local fuzz already asked me all this."

Greigh had now led this puddle of conceited pudding in the direction he wanted to go. *This guy is no more capable of a brutal homicide than he could win an Emmy. Obvious the local "fuzz" thinks so, too.* "So who should I talk with, Stacy? Should we consider one of the PAs a suspect?

"Could be. They're all a bunch of conniving, attention-seeking weasels. They are not to be trusted."

Describes every single person I've met on this set so far, including this prig. "Stacy, do you know if the police questioned any of the PAs?"

Michaels droned on, finally spewing something relevant. "Not sure. Don't think so. They're just grunts. The only PA I trust is my own, Todd Bricker. He's around here somewhere. Never where I need him, of course. Now, about my interview."

"I'd like to watch you in action for a bit and then we'll continue. Okay by you, *Shawn?*" Greigh was buttering the muffin now by using the moniker of *Dancing's* hero, Shawn Butterfield. *Buttering Butterfield? This shite-for-brains buffoon isn't the only bad comedian on the set today.*

CHAPTER 10

Todd Bricker, PA—Production Assistant, a.k.a. go-fer extraordinaire—appeared young, ambitious, and one-hundred-percent affable. The personable young man wore a ball cap backward. An almost-invisible walkie-talkie microphone nestled underneath his short beard and clipped to his t-shirt collar, obviously paired to an earbud. His energy was palpable. His eyes darted around to see if anything on the set needed attention.

"Excuse me, Todd?" The kid looked like he was one paycheck away from homeless, but oozed good cheer and enthusiasm as he rushed from one seemingly trivial task to another. He spun around with a smile, ready to deploy, when his face lit up the entire room.

"Aubrey *Greigh?* Oh, my *gawd!* I *adore* your books. And we're neighbors! I live in 4F at The Lit! So! What can I do for you, sir?" The kid almost left the floor in his bubbling and fizzing before he turned helpful with a serious expression the very next instant. The kid was quick. Greigh smiled. So much for operating undercover.

"Lower your voice, please, Todd. It's just Greigh. I'm traveling incognito." The kid contained his jittering, as if slipping into a role. "Oh, of course, but… well, yeah. Wow! What name should I use?"

This kid was really good. "Arthur Granville. I suggest Mr. Granville, for now. I'm a reporter for *Entertainment Weekly* and I'm looking into Peter Fontera's murder. You understand, Todd?"

His jaw dropped. As soon as he recovered it, he grinned again. "You shitt—you kidding me? An undercover gig with the mystery master himself?" His face petrified as he said more loudly with his eyes darting around, "Look, Mr. Granville, I'm pretty busy here. What happened to Peter was terrible. How about you tell me what's on your mind?"

Gotta have the heart of an actor to love any job in this business, I guess. Greigh took an instant liking to this kid. "Very well, Todd. Maybe later you can give me the name of a screenwriter you trust. But for now, as a PA, I imagine there is little you don't see, correct?"

While they were talking, almost to illustrate the point, while Greigh heard nothing, Todd held up his right index finger. He reached up with his left hand to grab the drooping collar of the limp shirt he wore open over his t-shirt. No doubt from being grabbed and pulled upward toward his mouth. He squeezed something and spoke into the lavaliere microphone at his neck. Todd responded to an invisible inquisitor who spoke into his earpiece, "Copy that." He excused himself, promising to be right back. And thirty seconds later, true to his word, he hustled back, answering Greigh's question as if he'd never left.

"That's a fact, sir—Mr. Granville. Very little we PAs don't see and hear. The AD—that's the Assistant Director—is my boss. He works with the director to organize the entire day's shoot. We PAs are the eyes and ears of the entire set. Somebody's asking, 'anybody have eyes on Stacy?' And they expect all the PAs to find Stacy, especially now that he's *the* star, even though he's *my* primary charge."

"So, PAs are a general resource on the set, but they also assign you to a specific actor?"

"Well, *I* am assigned. Stacy is sort of a special case. He needs lots of attention." The kid smirked and winked as he said, "if you know what I mean."

"I can guess, yes. I've already spoken with the bloke. What else must you do?"

"Everything. I work with all the departments across the production, which makes it a great training ground for the aspiring director. That's me!" He grinned big, but his eyes drifted up and to his right as his attention once again focused on a voice in his ear. He focused on what he was receiving on the walkie. "Copy that. Bricker's on it." He turned back to Greigh. "Sorry. One moment, okay?" And without waiting for a response, he scurried off, but returned less than a minute later with his grin refreshed. "Stacy needed his nose wiped and a bottle of water that he made me taste. Like a royal taster, ya know?" The kid shrugged and smiled his apology as if to say, *It's the job!*

Greigh wrinkled his brow. *So the bloke is a paranoid douche.* "Here's the deal, Todd. Peter was a friend. I discovered his body, and I'm going to find out who killed my friend. Can I count on your help… *and* your discretion?"

The young man blinked his round eyes in rapid succession as his head shivered from side to side to ensure he heard correctly before he responded in an exasperated, but conspiratorial whisper. "Mr. Greigh, it would be my honor, sir. I'm your man. And hey, introduce yourself to Josh Carver in Sherwood at The Lit." *Sherwood* was a tight neighborhood on the lower floors of The Lit. Folks camped there in the rough until they caught their break and moved to the upper floors. The folks in Sherwood called the floors above them *Camelot*.

"Josh is an extraordinary screenwriter who needs a break and will work his ass off for you." In a louder voice that broadcast he was annoyed at the disruption to his sacred tasks, Todd said, "Look, Mr. Granville, all due respect, I'm really busy. You should be talking with one of the stars, like Mr. Michaels, or our GM, Mr. Bowman. General managers know everything. Now I gotta get back to work. One of the PAs needs a fresh battery pack for his walkie, and I'm carrying. Have a nice day, sir."

A few nearby heads turned. But nobody saw the playful wink Todd tossed in Greigh's direction before he wheeled on his heels and spoke into his walkie as he hustled off. "This is Bricker, copy. Eyes on Ash. Carrying a hot brick. Will get it to Ash." Then, he turned back to Greigh, pointed to the invisible speaker in his left ear and said, "First AD just said, 'we're about to go for picture. Lock it up.' That means be real quiet, Mr. Granville, or you'll get kicked off the set. Understand?" Another endearing smile. Todd said to no one in particular loud enough for those around them to hear, repeating his boss's pronouncement, "Okay, thirty seconds, and we're gonna roll!"

Greigh stood there, not seeing what was going to "roll," but savvy enough to understand that movement generated noise. So, he froze in place, hoping for a few more insights from being on the set, even at its periphery. Half a minute later, Todd repeated for those not privy to walkie talk. "Rolling, rolling, rolling!" *This nice kid? Quite the pro. I've recruited a confidential informant, and got a lead on a screenwriter for 'Voodoo Vendetta.' Not a bad day's work.*

Several minutes later, the word *Cut!* echoed down from the Director, the AD, and all the PAs stationed both inside and just outside the set where Greigh now stood. Still frozen in place, Greigh studied the surrounding activities. Todd returned to him for a few additional minutes with the famous mystery writer, now his handler. He said, almost under his breath, "Is this your first experience on a sound stage, Mr. Greigh?"

"Just Greigh, Todd. Yes. Fascinating. Quite the ballet of specialties, is it not?"

"More like a liquid puzzle. And while everyone considers my PA job an entry position, I've been called back enough that they trust me to babysit—I mean, support—a major star like Mr. Michaels. Must be doing something right, huh?" That charm-stuffed smile again.

Greigh knew the first rule of recruiting and keeping a CI—a confidential informant—was to build trust and a rapport. "So what else does a PA do, Todd?"

"What *don't* we do? Gotta keep the set clean, especially after the picture wraps. Then, we prep for the company's move to a different set, like when we head back to the studio. This one will be a big move

—back to the Windy City lot in Chicago. International moves are the most complex." He grimaced, but his enthusiasm for everything in "the biz" could not be suppressed. "When the AD needs something, he walkies to certain PAs. I try to find it fast, so it's *me* he or she calls next time. And if I can't deliver, I let the AD know. *Nobody* on the set wants to be the reason the camera's not rolling. That's the worst. I have to be present on the walkie *all the time* if I hope to keep getting called back. And that's what it's all about if you want to work in this business—getting callbacks. The one thing you do *not* want to do on the walkies is not respond. Even when I'm taking a leak, I *always* respond with 'Bricker is currently 10-1.'

"I make myself indispensable. Best case: I satisfy a need even *before* it's needed without expecting any acknowledgement. I anticipate and act. That gets noticed. Being a PA leads to everything else. Hang on—" Todd relayed to those standing around, "Okay, Take Three is coming in!" That same phrase echoed from another PA on the other side of the room from where they stood. That unheated warehouse contained the entire current indoor set. But they stood just outside the actual set itself. A flurry of people and equipment moved past them into a temporarily walled-off area. "Mr., ah, Granville, this will be a short take, after which I'll be real busy with breakdown and setup for the next take. Anything else for me, sir?"

"Todd, would you be willing to debrief with me in private this evening?"

With round eyes still inflating, Todd said without hesitation, "Hell, yeah! I mean, sure. Name the time and place."

"How about Sporvejen, 9pm?" The kid looked like Greigh had just gut-punched him. "Whoa! Only if you're buying. Like an American diner at Danish prices."

"Of course. On me, Todd."

CHAPTER 11

The sun had set over the city's center. Shadows came first to Nyhavn on Copenhagen's southeast side, just west of the canals. Greigh arrived at Sporvejen a half-hour early to wait for Todd Bricker, Stacy Michael's PA. The diner's name—Danish for *tramway*—originated with its first dining area built in what looked like an ancient street car. The outside dining area sat empty. Too chilly after dark.

And there he sat. Todd hunched in a dark-wood booth, fidgeting, with his shoulder against the diner's orange interior wall. Greigh had eaten here a few times whenever he missed American cuisine, which wasn't often. But he liked the intimate ambience and sparse patrons this time of night. Plus, they were not likely to see anyone from Windy City here. The food was good and not outrageously priced. Not that Greigh cared about the money, but he felt Todd might be more at ease in a place like this. "Todd, you're early."

The kid lit up. "So are you, Greigh. Can I just say, this is awesome."

"If you still have an appetite after we talk, we'll order a feast. Fair enough?"

"Sir, just ask away. My life is an open book—that nobody has read. *Yet.*" The kid chuckled at his own dour but optimistic humor which sounded more like a thin-breathed huff through his teeth.

Greigh settled in across from this bearded young man. He laid a menu on the table, but didn't yet look at it. "Todd, did the police question you or any of the PAs about Peter's murder?"

"Not me. Can't speak for the others, but I don't think so. We saw them ganging up on Mr. Bowman, Stacy, and a few others, but they didn't seem interested in us grunts before they all just disappeared."

Fascinating that the cops wouldn't talk with the best sources of unvarnished info on the set.... "Who would kill Peter, and why?"

"Oh, ah, well, you said Peter was a friend."

"More of a casual acquaintance."

"Okay. Full disclosure. Unlike his lovable on-screen persona, Peter was an arrogant prick in real life. He could be a flaming gas ball of fury. Pissed off more people than Stacy Michaels. That's a long list. But to kill him? Short list."

"Stacy?"

"Naw. He can be a jerk, but he's all bark."

"Bowman?"

"I don't really have much to do with Mr. Bowman. He tries real hard to be liked, but I'm guessing he plays a lot of hardball. Not sure."

"Anyone else?"

"Well, last Sunday, something happened. Peter seemed fine on the set Saturday, but Monday, he was off. Agitated. Didn't remember his lines. Not like him at all. He was a real pro. But all day Monday, he was a frickin' mess. I asked him if he needed anything. He grumbled something about 'nothing is as it seems.'"

Greigh scratched his own closely cropped beard, burrowed his gaze into Todd's eyes. "Monday afternoon, he called me, said he had something important to tell me. And Monday night, someone murdered him before we could speak."

Todd's eyes floated up and to his right, even as they widened in horror as they swung back to meet Greigh's penetrating gaze. "Oh, shit."

"Any idea what might have happened Sunday?" Were you shooting?"

"Only in the morning. We wrapped after lunch. But Peter liked to drink. And he loved the attention he received from locals. That's all I can tell you. Didn't see him after lunch on Sunday until Monday morning around six."

"Could this be a drug buy gone bad?"

"Oh, man, there was no straighter arrow than Peter. He was a real John Wayne type, ya know? Except for those stupid bowties, of course,"

"Had to ask. Other thoughts, Todd?"

"Not really. He'd hang around those waterfront bars beyond the nicer Nyhavn 'hoods. Those cobblestone alley dives serve cheap booze and cater to the salty dogs. Yeah, workers from the boats down on the canals. Dunno...."

Greigh sensed the kid drifting, and said, "Don't worry about it. This has been helpful. What's next for the company?"

"Well, I think we'll wrap the location real soon. Like in a day or two, cuz the AD told me we need to be squeaky clean by Friday noon. Says we're taking a friggin' boat back to the States. Oughta be different. We leave Sunday. I'm guessing this is one of Mr. Bowman's brain farts. Treats the cast and crew like we're on a corporate retreat. He might be a good studio GM, but as a director or producer, well, he kinda sucks."

"Todd, if it's okay with you, I'd like to check in with you once we're all back in Chicago. Would that be alright?"

"You kidding? Yeah, that'd be awesome. And don't forget to call Josh. He really is one helluva writer. I have this fantasy that some day, I'll get to direct one of your movies with Josh's screenplay, Greigh. How sick would *that* be?"

"Yes, that would be sick, indeed. Sick is good, is it not?"

Todd laughed out loud. "Greigh, you crack me up, bloke." He tried on a tame Chicago'd-British accent for size with a side of Scottish. It didn't fit. Greigh joined in the kid's laughter.

Sick, indeed. Am I inquiring into a case that's already closed? But what did poor Peter want to tell me? And why me? Was he "going public" for reasons of personal safety, but failed? And is there a connection to Andy's smuggling job? Shite!

CHAPTER 12

~

The Industrial and Logistics Park outside Paldiski, Estonia on the rocky shore of South Harbor bordered the Gulf of Finland that fed into the southeastern shore of the Baltic Sea. The town had grown to become a major gateway between East and West. Especially since Obelisk Prime located their headquarters in Paldiski's South Harbor three years earlier. Mika—pronounced *MEE-ka*—Kuzmin was President of OP, one of Europe's largest import/export enterprises. At least it appeared so.

Mika paced behind a mammoth ebony desk in her expansive fourth-floor corner office suite. Though her office in the squat black-glass OP building was dimly lit, it was not for a lack of windows. They comprised most of her sanctum sanctorum's southwestern exposure. She kept the window's insulated drapes closed. Occasionally, however, she'd spread them wide to the magnificent view that was Paldiski's South Harbor.

Today was such a day, an important day. Only an array of ship-loading derricks and the squat field of liquid natural gas storage tanks broke her viewscape of the gulf. She glanced at the ever-present mirror on her massive desk, the only item on its surface other than the single sheaf of papers she worked on. Mika practiced not sneering with that mirror. Not an easy task.

It was a crisp September day. Some would say beautiful. This did nothing for Mika. On speaker and while signing various papers, she barked, "Yes, you'll get your money. Just ensure they stay on schedule... that is correct. No complications... yes, you understand very well." She punched off and continued working through the raft of papers. Though she commanded a vast enterprise, and she was a master delegator, a handful of matters required her personal touch. Mika jabbed a speed-dial button on her desk panel. "Captain, be ready to disembark in sixty minutes." She punched off. She was not looking forward to the short hop from nearby Tallinn to Kastrup outside Copenhagen. Mika made it far too often in her—Obelisk Prime's—Gulfstream G500. Mika used this eighty-million-Euro jet like most used a commuter car, but with an annual operating budget of over three-million Euro. Big numbers, she was told; however, the only important number? Two—being in two places at once. Almost.

Mika's office represented a blatant dichotomy, an amalgamation of two opposing styles. Both Russian. Dominant was a curdling scream for an emotive return to pre-Soviet architecture and design. That stylish and ornate grandeur could still be found in the old Romanov palaces, similar to the Terem Palace in the Kremlin. She did not miss Moscow, even after three years. She hated that city, but she loved what it stood for—raw power sublimated only to global expediencies.

This first style of the old emperors flaunted trappings of aristocratic whimsy that seduced the eye. As part of that heritage, she inhaled the pungent odor of priceless first editions stuffed into the built-in bookcases on the expansive wall just behind her ornate one-ton desk. These volumes filled the room with the odors of musty leather and old paper. The imported bookcases themselves were striking, adorned with Italian and Ancient Russian heraldic patterns sculpted in the seventeenth century. Mika never read those fanciful volumes, of course, but they looked quite handsome on those intricately carved shelves. She glanced over her shoulder to make sure she was still fond of them.

But a comely rectangular table with sharp corners and straight edges dominated her twelve-meter-square office-slash-library-slash-conference room. Twenty austere chairs—places to sit in comfort, nothing more or less—surrounded it. On the far side of that table against her eastern wall stood a mammoth two-meter-long Soviet-era sidebar festooned with bottles of vodka and quadruple-size shot glasses known as buckets. Its oiled walnut surface was at chest level. She inhaled the stale odor of old walnut oil, even from behind her desk. This proletariat-inspired ensemble clashed with, well, everything else in Mika's complex office. She adored the visual collision that raged against conventional aesthetics.

Memories of Romanov-era emperors cowered behind the desk to her west. Stalin-esque utilitarianism—all in muddy hues, clunkiness, and severe angles—stood plain and proud in front, to her east. She was almost erotically hyperaware of both styles, their orientation, and how incompatible they must seem to everyone but her. Or how critical they both were in defining her very essence.

Like her office, Mika was a walking and breathing enigma. Few knew her as a spymaster—most as a businesswoman—who was aging well, an erstwhile femme fatale of considerable repute in certain circles. Only a handful saw this side of her and still lived in that silent knowledge.

Despite her role as the leader of a gargantuan publicly held multinational enterprise, she treasured her privacy above all else. She remained an enigma. Mika chose her trusted minions with great care —and utility. Most, however, saw her only as a consummate professional, beautiful and successful. Meticulous. Fanatic. And *nobody* that still lived was aware of her privileged but troubled childhood.

Mika excelled at crafting and practicing her public persona. She was now fifty-six. Age could not diminish her natural beauty, or, at least, the perception of it. Especially to men who appreciated women of great power and influence. In fact, her allure grew with time—and with periodic adjustments. Enormous eyes enhanced her charisma. A slender frame and her subtle femininity with its harsh edges belied an iron will and controlled ferocity. Without makeup and constant effort, however, her full lips tended toward a slight sneer that she controlled —at least, when in the company of lesser mortals who could not understand. She softened her angular cheekbones and other sharp features with the artful application of cosmetics and well-practiced exercises to control her facial musculature. Sometimes, her expressions seemed contrived; she had been told by those brave enough to comment.

A soft knock interrupted her. She stole a compulsive glance into her mirror before anyone appeared behind that knock.

SECONDS LATER, MARGUS, HER ASSISTANT, MADE HIMSELF visible in her dual doorway, which was three men high. It dwarfed his muscular six-foot frame. While the mammoth doors always remained open, he was smart enough to knock before appearing. Though he'd been employed by OP for six years, he'd only been trusted to work this close to Mika in the last two months. It was learn fast, or perish. He knew that and relished the challenge. He adored being this close to OP's seat of raw power. To Mika. And he'd already learned more than he'd bargained for.

SHE THOUGHT, *THIS ONE JUST MIGHT WORK OUT.*

In the tone of voice and posture she favored, Margus said, "Mika, the foreign minister would have a word." She preferred that first-name salutation. Made her feel less like a spinster. This new young man had only called her "Madame" once. And she had warned him. Once."Of which country, Margus?"

"It's Comrade Kashinski from the Kremlin."

"I am not available," she responded in a flat tone without hesitation.

"Understood. I suggest you leave for Tallinn soon. As always, your Danish papers are all aboard the Gulfstream. Captain Magnussen assures me you've already spoken." She nodded toward her assistant without looking up from packing her ancient top-loading briefcase grown limp with age. The old leather favorite smelled musty, too.

~

MARGUS WINCED, TURNED ON HIS HEEL, PASSED BACK through the tall doors, and disappeared without a sound. He hoped he would survive longer than his predecessor. He thanked the god he didn't believe in that he held an insurance policy. The ambitious young man had observed and learned. He initiated an encrypted call and waited. After Margus had spoken once the proscribed words and the connection was secure, he said, "She's on her way."

~

DOCTORS DIAGNOSED MIKA EARLY IN LIFE WITH MULTIPLE Personality Disorder, or MPD. But like all obstacles, she had wielded her condition as one of her most powerful weapons in an already formidable arsenal. Unlike most who suffer from MPD—some call it Dissociative Identity Disorder—she did not experience memory *gaps* so much as personality *translucence*. She reveled in one very different persona dominating over another, depending on the point in time. They were seldom in irreconcilable conflict. Considered herself blessed.

Mika chose not to use much make-up, only just enough to disguise who she truly was—a vicious heart with too-severe eyes, too-hard lips and a molten disposition. She didn't feel a flaccid world could accept her for all of that without subterfuge. So, she became someone else. After all, she'd done that her entire life. It was not only a part of her, she relished it. She reveled in keeping those around her in everlasting ignorance. Some in fear. Maybe more than "some." She always smelled almost fresh. Raw power that pulsed beneath her skin never emanated the sweet odor of a bathed and powdered virgin. There was always a delicious hint of death and rotting. That's why she allowed no one too righteous to get too close. They might discover that dimension of her lethal spirit. She would protect *that* advantage at all costs.

This formidable woman was an underworld figure of considerable repute. In addition to running a profitable shipping fleet with broad international reach, she nurtured a loose federation of self-serving criminal figures who did her bidding on occasion. Inherited wealth and influence from her father's questionable enterprises in Russia served her well on an international scale. She buried her father with more than a smile.

Like her love of two unique styles, she reveled in being two very different people. They knew each other, of course. But they were adversaries, not friends. And as of two months earlier, the feared and revered Mika possessed a new purpose. It consumed her, above all else. Beneath her tectonic exterior, she pulsed with seismic vibrations. She exuded endless energy and hungered for even more power and influence that were means to a new end—a bold plan some called insane. All would look back at this moment as the genesis of that plan. She sent a message to the international team she called her *angels*. Just one word. "Go."

CHAPTER 13

Sunday night, August 16th, Windy City studio executive Lance Bowman reflected on his plan. He felt the deck of the old ship heaving and vibrating under his feet on the open seaway between Sweden and Denmark they called the Kattegat. He had booked passage for the entire cast and crew of *Dancing With Death* on this freighter from Copenhagen back to Chicago. This tub looked like the modern equivalent of a tramp steamer. But it should provide the movie's company ample opportunity to rehearse and to bond. At least, that's what he'd told everyone.

They had departed early evening—a lengthy process for a three-hundred-foot ship. Once on open water, a small boat had pulled alongside to return the harbor pilot to shore. The local pilot was necessary to navigate the ship clear of Copenhagen's tricky waters. But then, they no sooner attained cruising speed than the captain announced that all non-crew personnel were to remain in their quarters for a "routine" man-overboard drill. To be conducted by the crew. At midnight. Lance was awake, anyway. *They wake all twenty-three of us up with an announcement over the loudspeakers to tell us to stay in our cabins? Idiots.*

The engines wound down. A steady vibration coming from the steel deck no longer tickled the soles of Lance's slippered feet when he got up from a tiny desk to peer out of his cabin's porthole. The ship drifted to a dead stop on the calm sea. A gentle heaving motion reminded him they were offshore. He knew this was as calm is it got out here. Even though his only experience with ships had been aboard luxury cruise liners, he knew something unusual was happening. Did freighter operation differ so much from passenger ships? No frills aboard this tub. Fine with him. Fewer distractions.

He paced his tiny stateroom. Six feet, back and forth—that's all the crappy little space allowed. He blamed his hypertension on stress as he gambled with the future of his studio. *And* possibly his personal survival. As one of the youngest general managers in the history of Windy City Productions, he needed to make his bones fast. He battled time. Transitioning Windy City from the standard and cost-effective business model using CG and AI to a more costly approach of using live actors in real-world settings and tempestuous writers killed his financials. He was betting big. And that wasn't even his biggest bet, nor his motivation. But it *was* the job.

Computer-generated actors, sets and venues, not to mention dialogue scripted by AI—artificial intelligence—systems, were much cheaper and faster. But the public hungered for a return to what he called organic productions. So did his writers. And his studio jumped first—back onto live sound stages outside of cyber space. That was *his* script, and all home-grown. The subtext—that which isn't spoken, but adds layers of meaning—would take him to the next level. *I am a true visionary. In more ways than one.*

He knew his own financials would suffer until a stable of new stars cranked out a couple of mega-hits. The grand promise—the long con. Windy City had yet to produce its first full-length HG—human-generated—production for the big screen: *Dancing With Death.* The fly in the ointment was that old snake-oil salesman Toby Stiler over at Miracle Mile Studios. Toby was sniffing up his skirt, and Lance did not like it.

Rumor was that Stiler was close, too. Both risked a lot chasing this payday. *Big rewards require big risks, don't they, sport?*

So far, the Windy City board of directors, composed of his executive team and six major investors, screamed he was squandering studio resources. They said he was pampering prima donnas, and developing their individual brands with TV pilots. But it *was* working. Sort of. He was as surprised as anyone. *So sayeth the ratings based on PR promises, anyway. Now, I just need the freaking financials to follow. But whether they do or not... payday for yours truly.*

Most everyone now knew and identified with quirky (all-too-human) celebrities like Peter Fontera and Stacy Michaels. Every woman in the world—the straight ones, anyway—dreamed of spending a night with either of these bozos.

Lance Bowman had made commitments. To some very committed characters. That's why he had stayed personally involved with the *Dancing* project, including traveling far away from his studio back lot and the Chicago area—the mother ship. He had already slashed his CG budget and pounded the money back into Fontera and Michaels. Some of it, anyway.

Since everything seemed to move beyond the speed of light these days, he fought the clock. Still, this passage on a slow boat back from Denmark to Chicago was a stroke of genius, inspired by his new friend. They would still maintain a rigorous production schedule during the voyage, but without most of the distractions of the city and the Row, that slowed progress. Fewer watchers out here, too. Of course, he maintained almost constant contact with his board. They wanted updates. But now, they sucked him into far fewer bitch sessions and incessant interruptions. He could hide behind shipboard issues.

He now needed time to think about the future of *Dancing* without Fontera. At the very least, he needed a plausible strategy for the board and for the press. Peter was a decent actor, a pro. But he could also be adorable. They had made plans. He would miss the big lug who broke his heart. But business was business.

Lance had demanded action from the Copenhagen police over

Peter's brutal slaying. But his demands fell on deaf ears, maybe because of recently stuffed pocketbooks. Yes, he suspected industrial espionage. In public, anyway. The young executive proclaimed he would put nothing past his chief competitor, old Toby Stiler, over at Miracle Mile. That bastard came across as even more ruthless than him. But something else even more nefarious nibbled at his consciousness. And that was his other reason for booking passage on this piece-of-shit tub. At least he had fewer trust issues out here on the open sea. And it would be easier to see someone coming.

CHAPTER 14

Meanwhile, Todd Bricker couldn't sleep—his first time at sea. He knew they'd be rehearsing at six AM in what they called the ship's *ballroom*. More like a converted cargo hold with the slightest veneer of civility inside a gigantic steel box. Shitty acoustics, even worse lighting, and forget amenities. Didn't matter to Mr. Bowman. It was more about the craft. Real acting, he said. Todd liked that. They'd clean up what they could in post-processing back home, as challenging as that would be.

Just past midnight, though, this stupid crew drill meant he'd feel like shit in the morning. *So* not a cruise ship from stories others told. This was a hardcore working vessel that tolerated civilians. *Do they call us land lubbers among themselves—or just lubbers—like in the movies? Or something more profane?*

Even though forbidden to leave their cabins, Todd needed to go for a walk. And if he stumbled onto something that might prove useful to the production, he'd be sure to score more and better gigs with Windy City. Being this close to the studio's GM was a rare opportunity. And Todd was an opportunist. One deck below what the old salts called *the weather deck* toward the front of the ship, far from the "ballroom," there was a lot of activity. Todd was a good PA. He knew when to be seen, *or* how and when to stay invisible.

He crept along a narrow hallway on the right side of the ship, what the salts called the starboard side. Small round windows—portholes—at his right shoulder lit up with a dim glow. They cast shafts of dusty light upward that reflected off the ceiling and the wall to his left. *What the....?* There was another ship out there! The portholes were high on the wall, meant to let light in, not for sightseeing. In the hallway up ahead was a latched box under one porthole. It contained life jackets according to the sign in four languages above it. He stood on the box to peer out the porthole. Yep, a smaller ship had pulled alongside their own. A few lights blazed—enough so a half-dozen crew out on deck could see what they were doing. Curious. *I wonder....?*

At that moment, not far away, Todd heard several big men breathing hard, and grunting. They carried something heavy. Sounded like they were getting closer. He slipped into a darkened compartment to his left, closer to the center of the ship, away from the portholes. But they weren't coming down his hallway at all. They were in a large open space at the end of the hallway. Voices echoed off these metal walls. The crew called them "bulkheads." *Really, guys? Why don't you just speak plain English? Or even American?*

He crept to the end of the hallway and snuck a peek through the metal door with the rounded corners. It was only open an inch or two. They spoke English. But they weren't from England, were they? From a previous colony, like India or something? Their darker complexion? From one of those sand countries? The next voice, though, came not from the ship's hands who were bitching about health issues handling this cargo. He'd keep his distance. The voice came from some monster's gravelly voice, the owner of which he couldn't see.

"Silence! You will be fine as long as the crate is not opened, and you spend no more time near it. You will get what you deserve once the next transfer is complete. Now, back away from the crate."

That accent sounded... Russian, maybe? Eastern European, anyway. When that guy spoke, Todd cracked the door open a hair wider to get a peek. *Holy shit! Four huge white guys with automatic weapons? What the —?* He backed away, eager to put some distance between him, that crate, the monsters talking about risks and yet another cargo transfer. But the hand warming pocket on the front of his oversized sweatshirt caught on one of the handles that surrounded the door he'd had his cheek pressed against while he listened and watched.

Todd stumbled, made a creaking noise as the handle tried to turn. He broke free and took off at a full run back to his cabin. Shut the door, and oozed with gratitude for his escape from some unknown fate. Like a child afraid of the dark, he slipped out of his jeans and sweatshirt, threw on some lounging pants and a t-shirt, and slipped into his bunk. Joey, the PA in the upper bunk, never knew he'd been gone. He'd gotten away clean. At least he thought so.

He felt more than heard the ship's engines turning up. A few minutes later, the deck rumbled and shivered. Todd closed his eyes and pulled the blanket over his head. He didn't want to know. Not anymore.

CHAPTER 15

The next day, Greigh worried. He sat at a long table with other customers, not eating the late breakfast in front of him. More like brunch. Less inhibited by the ozone layer over this part of the world, the sun blazed through the cafe's front windows at the southern perimeter of a huge square near Copenhagen's city center. He looked up at a railing and the sidewalk outside as he sat a half-story below street level. He studied busy people bundled against a chill wind, hustling to something important somewhere else. Waves of smoked eel, buttery eggs, the scent of maple syrup and strong coffee embraced him like a warm blanket on this chilly morning. Yet, he worried.

Captain Andy Galkin was to contact him after the previous night's mysterious cargo transfer on the Kattegat, somewhere on the body of open water between Sweden and Denmark. He had received a breathy voice message from the trawler captain. The man's words tumbled out, oozing with adrenaline and exertion.

He had double-tapped his right temple to activate his communications implant and said "Replay voicemail received at 1 AM this morning." The message chilled him to the bone. Why hadn't he receive this call live? Or had he, and failed to wake up? *Shite on a bloody pike!*

"Greigh, this your friend, Captain Andy. Transfer made. Including four guards, all armed. Scary men.

Me and crew pull away, now. I will moor in Nyhavn by four AM. Money is good, my friend. Very good. I tell you all about what I see and hear.

Just before we pull alongside one-hundred-meter Liberian-flagged cargo vessel Maltana, one guard say 'Windy City' to another and he spit on my deck.

Pretty sure he not know I was in shadows. Not sure what that mean. Bring more Scotch tonight to celebrate, and—"

The connection ended. He had received this voicemail via satellite comms and it ended with the *signal lost* tone. Not willing to dismiss it as a simple connection issue, Greigh waited. His level of anxiety escalated. Blood pounded in his temples. He tried calling back, but still *no signal.*

Greigh had checked *Marya's* berth at the waterfront. Empty and appearing forlorn, all mooring lines remained coiled, awaiting Marya's return.

Less than two uneasy hours later, Greigh sat across from Freya Ecklund, his Interpol handler. They sat at a corner table in his new favorite eatery in Copenhagen. Not because it stood out as a culinary Mecca. Rather, its familiarity bred a certain brand of comfort. And the truth be told, he preferred the food served by the quasi-American diner style of Sporvejen. The endearing clatter of dishes and flatware trumped the clarity of other customers' voices.

Greigh had just told Freya of his suspicions concerning the *Maltana* —the freighter now sure to be involved in his smuggling case. Freya had been quiet at first. That was uncustomary. She drew in a sharp breath, as if recalling some hidden memory or associated factoid. He shared his fear for his friend. Disappeared, along with his boat—in the middle of the night at sea. "Someone paid my friend, Captain Andrushya Galkin, in cash. Further, four heavily armed guards accompanied that bit of cargo."

Greigh suggested both incidents may also tie back to Peter Fontera's murder two days earlier, less than a mile from where they now sat. He waited, listening to Freya's soft but measured breaths that sounded like a staccato jackhammer on mute inside her chest. Her expression shifted from cautious to something akin to fear. Or was it anger? "What is it?" he asked.

Freya's gaze shifted away from him to the busy sidewalk outside the window next to their table. "The *Maltana*," she repeated, her voice trembling. "What cargo?"

"Unknown. But they packed it in a large metal box encased in a wooden crate framework the size of two sea chests believed to weigh ninety kilos. It originated in Paldiski, Estonia, according to Captain Andy, but neither he nor I know of their final destination. But it might be Chicago." Greigh noticed her hands. They had clenched into tight fists. When he prompted her for an explanation, she seemed to shake off her unease and changed the topic of conversation. Dropped her hands below the table.

"We should focus on ensuring I understand the facts of the case as you learn more," she said. She cleared her throat and summarized what Greigh had told her. But Greigh sensed an unspoken dimension to this case lurking beneath Freya's words; one that he would need to uncover if he wanted to get to the truth of the matter. Her subsequent silence and thousand-yard stare broadcast her worry, too. No smart-arse remarks from her this morning. None. "Go to Chicago."

"Freya, it seems you're trying to get rid of me. I still—"

She responded with a single word. *"Now."* Without another word, she buried her untouched plate of food under her napkin as she stood and turned to leave. Her abrupt departure from the diner further deepened Greigh's concern. What wasn't she telling him? Was she protecting him? Or setting him up for something? Surely not. He shivered at the way she said *Now*. Freya sounded different. And her features had also sharpened in a way he had never seen.

The connection between Peter Fontera's murder and the smuggling op seemed tenuous, yet his gut screamed they were intertwined somehow. The Copenhagen police had closed Fontera's homicide as a simple robbery and home invasion with unintended consequences, even though that conclusion was contrary to the forensics. Nobody believed it. Especially him. Now, Freya had just booted him out of the country. Implied she wanted him in Chicago when and if the Libyan-flagged *Maltana* made port, even though Greigh felt he had unfinished business in Denmark.

He envisioned Freya fingering the bullet she carried on a slender chain around her neck, as she did again before her abrupt departure. She kept it close to her chest, strung from a delicate gold lasso. It was a dark blue-gray lump, the approximate size of a small misshapen plum. Yet it seemed to want to bulge outwards, as if it were just one tiny step from bursting. Every time she seemed anxious or worried, her fingers drifted towards it - as if its mere presence could provide some comfort. Greigh wanted to understand why that piece of deformed lead was so important to her, but he also knew he wasn't prepared for whatever Freya's answer might be.

It would be nice to return to his apartment at the Literati in Chicago's Near Southwest Loop less than a mile from the western shore of Lake Michigan. But to what would he be returning?

CHAPTER 16

She remained unemployed. Well, not really. They called it compulsory administrative leave that had extended from days to weeks. At least she still received her paycheck. *Jeez, this sucks.* Sitting on her tiny sofa in her tiny apartment in the pre-dawn hours on a Monday morning, ex-Detective Chance McQuillan, a.k.a. McQ painted her damn toenails. Again. Boredom had driven her to this absurdity. Couldn't sleep, anyway. She slid from being the Chicago Enforcement Department's youngest detective lieutenant to America's worst pedicurist in five short, but eternal weeks. Plus, her sensible loafers gleamed more than they had any right, considering their age and mileage. *Damn shoes must be older than me. Wait, that's not right. I'm only twenty-seven.*

She had helped that putz Johnson at the ninety-ninth precinct, *her* precinct, solve three complex homicides—on the down-low. Spoon-fed him after he had slipped her case files to review in her ghetto-chic one-room apartment above Harrow's, the oldest cop bar in the city. Even now, she could smell the joint beneath her studio apartment on Dearborn, a couple of blocks down the street from the nine-nine. But the chow at Harrow's filled you up. And his drinks were cheap. Not that she drank. Much.

After solving a big case last summer with her witness-turned-friend, Aubrey Greigh, he'd invited her to ditch her badge and join him as some sort of international cop-slash-spy. He shared with her that on occasion, he worked for frickin' Interpol. The guy surprised her. Non-stop. Told her he contracted for an on-demand investigatory group within Interpol called ADR, or Advance Defense Regiment, although he might have been jerking her chain. Didn't seem like it, though. Apparently, ADR was a small, specialized covert arm of Interpol. Independent contractors from around the world investigated sensitive cases—a small, specialized subset of crimes that spanned international borders.

Greigh had wanted her to commit to a confidential contract. But she couldn't process all of that fast enough before he was called away. He'd been gone for weeks, now. Said he was on one of his month-long writing retreats. *Right. Whatever.* Now, as her compulsory leave dragged on from days to weeks, she wondered if she should have just thrown caution overboard and leaped into the unknown with him. McQ liked the guy. Maybe more than she cared to admit. Maybe even more than that. Didn't matter. She wasn't ready to toss her badge now that she was almost seven years into her twenty. Or was she?

Her implant buzzed. She tapped her right temple. Before she said anything, she heard, "Hello, Detective." He sounded out of breath.

"Greigh? Where are you?"

"Copenhagen."

"Denmark?"

"I'm coming home, and I may need your help."

"Oh. Will I be breaking any laws?"

"Probably."

Shit. He usually attempted to mask that unbelievable Scottish brogue. Not now. He gasped, "I've missed ya, lass." Blood pounded in her temples. The line went dead.

CHAPTER 17

Five days later, on August 22nd, Lance Bowman had spent more time online in his cabin than normal on the freighter *Maltana.* And tonight, Saturday night (the discussion was always livelier on the weekends), he'd entered into a fascinating give-and-take with a couple of users in the *Hollywood or Chicago* chatroom from somewhere in the middle of the Atlantic Ocean.

He hated Chicago. Windy City Productions promised to be one of his meal tickets. Maybe enable his early retirement. If so, Hollywood might make a nice post-retirement gig. And a little networking hurt no one. These consortium folks smelled like money. The star *makers.* As a studio exec, he recognized that sort of friend makes *their* friends wealthy. And influential.

It had been a few weeks since the online chatroom's moderator had okay'd his entrance into the "room." He was in—all the way. Until then, they granted him read-access only to a small percentage of the general posts, but he could post nothing. Folks in the room entered one heated debate after another, worse than opposing political parties. These were fanatics. But he needed to be there.

Today's chat revolved around the hypothesis that a major natural disaster in Chicago might result in Hollywood's comeback. Intriguing. Some heavy hitters postulated two choices. Throw aid Chicago's way, or throw Chicago away, at least with respect to their entertainment industry and its infrastructure. He knew where this foreplay was headed. His new friends softened others to one possible alternate future, inevitable sooner versus later.

Lance relished being on the inside of this thing instead of the poor ignorant schmucks who would fall by the wayside. Yes, one needed important friends. Time for an encrypted direct message—one-on-one with the man himself.

"LACC1, is everything okay at your end?" He waited for a response. The head of the Los Angeles County Consortium just *had* to be a very busy guy… or gal. Then….

"Of course, WC1. Soon, we reap the rewards, my friend. M1 says to be ready. "

"Can't be soon enough!" Once again, Lance gushed with gratitude. These were *his people!* This is how opportunities were *made.*

TWO DAYS LATER, SOMEWHERE OFF THE US COAST, LANCE Bowman, studio general manager, found it encouraging how the cast and crew of *Dancing* had come together on this voyage. The fruit of a marvelous brainstorm. Not that it would matter for long. But for now, it was all about the craft.

It seemed like everybody was performing with passion, despite the loss of their star, Peter Fontera, their diverse backgrounds, and lack of unity prior to putting to sea. They were generating great footage with excellent production value while underway despite the noisy soundtrack. They'd fix that in post-production at the studio. Maybe. Depending on his Plan B.

Now, there was something funny about yet another rendezvous and cargo transfer about to happen, with yet another smaller vessel. He'd discuss this matter with the ship's captain. He smelled his opportunity materializing. The wind whipped around the deck of the mighty freighter. Bowman leaned against the rusty rail, his eyes trained on a smaller craft that approached twenty feet below. Looked like a large private yacht, maybe eighty feet, or a little longer. Hard to tell. It was big for a yacht. He watched with a mixture of excitement and apprehension, trying to reconcile this moment with all his expectations for the voyage.

They'd been underway for a week. Must be close to the US coastline by now. It was clear the smaller vessel meant to come alongside. As planned. It left Bowman underwhelmed with uneasiness. Their compact captain interrupted his swirling anxiety. The wiry little man approached him in silence from behind. "You're observing something closely," he said in a gruff voice.

Bowman spun on his heel. The man in uniform said, "What brings you out here tonight, WC1?" *WC1? Oh, my.*

Bowman turned to face him full on and smiled: here and now *the* opportunity began to unfold—a chance for adventure, discovery, and fortune, if all went according to plan. With newfound enthusiasm, Bowman listened as the captain explained a daring course of action—a plan so audacious that it would alter history. Now it was time for them both to put their plans into motion.... Much depended on its success. The unthinkable hinged on its failure.

CHAPTER 18

Four days later, on Friday, the 28th of August, the *Maltana* moored at the Port of Chicago's Iroquois Lakefront Terminal eleven days after departing Copenhagen. At just over one hundred meters, the approximate length of a football field, she blended in as one of the smaller seagoing commercial vessels in the Port of Chicago. What experience Hans Flughler lacked in berthing at one of the largest seaports in the United States and the largest inland port in the world, his well-paid veteran crew and first mate compensated for.

It took the crew most of two hours to moor the *Maltana* at the Iroquois Terminus per their float plan. They were now just twelve miles from downtown Chicago. A normal landfall in every respect. They were all but invisible. A low-priority cargo status further diminished any interest harbor management might otherwise have in this ugly little ship.

By design, Captain Flughler and Lance Bowman had not been seen together by anyone during the entire voyage, even during their only late-night rendezvous at the railing on the weather deck. Bowman now walked up onto the pier at a slight incline via the gangway from a lower deck. His cast and crew of two dozen followed him. He turned and looked up at the starboard bridge wing where he saw the captain relaxing, smoking a cigar and leaning on the railing. Bowman then cast a vacant gaze from the captain down to the water between the ship and the weed-infested concrete pier encased in a corrugated steel seawall. The water was a muddy green—the color of toxic baby shit. Oh, how he hated Chicago.

The limo bus awaited near the foreboding terminal building, less than a hundred feet distant. Cranes towered overhead. The concrete pier underfoot had fallen victim to decades of frost heaving, spills of various liquids, and... he didn't want to know. He shivered in the afternoon shadows of buildings and cargo loading gear. A commercial operator would truck their equipment to the studio later in a steel container that would occupy half of a full-size eighteen-wheeler. Bowman decided sea voyages were too pedestrian for his taste, but this one had served its purpose.

THE NEXT DAY.... "THIS IS DONNA MATTHEWS REPORTING for Entertainment Exclusive from the executive suite of Mr. Lance Bowman, General Manager of Windy City Productions, the largest movie studio in Chicagoland. Stay tuned for an exclusive interview with Mr. Bowman right after these important messages from our sponsors."

Bowman's office was not exactly spacious, even with sparse furnishings. But he now felt claustrophobic with all the portable lighting, reflectors, screens and camera equipment stuffed into the space. And the show's production crew turned his office into a downright stuffy space. He could *smell* Donna's camera operator!

Bowman had disembarked from the open air of the *Maltana's* rusty decks the day before and jumped right back into the media fray. No rest for the oh-so-wicked. Channel Thirteen insisted on bringing all their own equipment and personnel, even though he bragged they had twenty-seven *spacious* sound stages on the Windy City lot in the Cicero area of Chicago. But since Thirteen was an affiliate of one of the four major networks, he had agreed to do this interview on their terms. Plus, Donna Matthews and EE were a hot streaming and podcasting commodity at the moment. He'd not say it out loud, but he needed this press.

Makeup primped over him and the gorgeous Ms. Matthews as they sat facing each other across his desk. She cooed, "Lance, I am *so* happy we could feature your studio on EE. And your brilliant idea of covering a bit of history will remind the country how important the Chicago movie industry has become in recent years."

"Thanks, Donna. I am *so* tired of hearing about Hollywood and Broadway. They had their time in the spotlight. Now it's our turn."

"I couldn't agree more."

The producer interrupted, "Thirty seconds, guys."

As they settled into their positions, each facing two separate cameras, Donna pasted on her most alluring on-air smile that also broadcast her depth as a serious reporter. "We're back with Lance Bowman, General Manager of Windy City Productions. This is the same studio that brought you such superb entertainment as *A Love to Die For* and the entire *Dragons and Gods* franchise. Congratulations on those amazing successes, Lance. Your mega-hits are just too numerous to list."

"Thank you, Donna. We place a premium on offering the entertainment our audience most desires."

"Lance, your studio led the revolution in bringing your industry to the heartland. Is Chicago the new Hollywood?"

"Absolutely not, Donna. Hollywood served its purpose, but time and fate changed all that. Our audience demanded this industry's transformation. Windy City and the other remarkable studios recognized the wisdom of centering their efforts here." He swept his arms and swiveled his gaze. "Now, they define our industry in its new mold."

"Why do you think that transformation was necessary? And why Chicago?"

"Well, two primary motivators. First, movie fans demanded a different style of entertainment. They've grown weary of computer-generated actors, voices and locations. Our audience votes with their box office and pay-per-view dollars. They want studios that produce more... organic entertainment, with human actors, real-world settings, and better scripts with more depth... that's what people want. And that's what is now central to all our newest offerings instead of CG and AI."

"CG? AI, Lance?"

"Sorry. Instead of real actors and settings, folks have signaled they're tired of CG, or computer-generated actors and settings—essentially little more than high-tech cartoons. Movies have become little more than single-player video games that players—audiences—can't control. And instead of solid writing, the AI, or artificial intelligent computer systems rehash canned scripts with tired variations."

"Ah. And why has this all become staples in the movie industry over the last few decades?"

"Simple. It was fun when it was new. Now, it's just that the computer-generated stuff is a cheap production technique. We at Windy City spare no expense in our productions because our audience demands it. They buy tickets and pay-per-view. We invest that revenue back into the entertainment they demand.

"Which brings me to my second point, Donna. You asked, 'why Chicago?' Simple. Cost of production. California suffers from constant tremors, quakes, slides, tsunamis, flash floods, wildfires, and as a result, astronomical costs in general. All of this translates into unaffordable production delays and physical relocations, no more so than in the mercurial entertainment business, and especially in movie production.

"Besides, technology has severed the our industry's geographical tether. Remote collaboration lowers costs. So motion picture sets, or locations, can be computer-generated, anywhere, anyhow. Most now are. So can any character. AI even provides sound effects, music, and voices for machine-generated characters and settings, not to mention prompt-generated scripts. Artists everywhere have lamented that creativity is now AI's domain. Well, Donna, not at Windy City."

Bowman's enthusiasm was infectious, and he knew how to work the cams. Donna said, "But why Chicago, specifically? They had rehearsed this line of questioning.

"Many of your viewers may not know this, Donna. Ever hungry for economic growth that rivals both coasts, the State of Illinois offers insane subsidies—financial incentives—to tech startups and multinationals alike. Much of the Silicon Valley culture has since migrated to the *Quantum State*." He watched Donna's forehead pucker despite her obvious Botox regimen.

He explained. "This pun characterizes the collective culture of the growing group of bleeding-edge AI, and quantum physics research and development organizations. These advanced businesses have clustered around our very own local and area university campuses, private research academies, and government-sponsored think tanks. So, regarding organic entertainment *and* AI or CG? This part of the country is now king."

It was time for her voice to be heard in this interview that was becoming a lecture. Donna blurted, "So, all of that has contributed to this regionplex's growth, right, Lance?"

"You are precisely correct, Donna. The common denominator of this ground swell? Audiences lust once again for human actors who speak their own lines from their own faces in natural settings—flawed and messy and, well, natural. Organic. But guess what, Donna? All of that increases production costs. Audiences do not want to absorb those higher costs, organic or not, nor should they. That means every penny must count. That also means not spending those pennies on recovering from natural disasters and a century or more of expensive traditions.

"For example, do you know what a *key grip* is? Or a *best boy*? These are traditional movie production jobs that still exist only because unions maintain a stranglehold over our industry. Other jobs like the *dolly grip*, are also no longer necessary. Instead of using wheeled camera dollies and booms for rolling or high camera shots, we now use aerial drones with integrated cameras. Those are just a few simple examples among many. We leverage technology to reduce our costs *behind* the cameras, but *not* to replace what the audience wants to see on their screens.

"As a result, we are not hemorrhaging cash spent changing locations because of mudslides. We've eliminated traditional jobs that are no longer necessary, and we invest more in pre-production jobs like selecting real-world locations and casting actors. We're putting most of our pennies into paying actors, writers, and shooting in real-world locations. Audiences are loving it. So that's what we'll continue to do."

Thoughts swirled through Donna's mind. *Jeez, this guy loves the sound of his own voice. But this interview will pop EE's ratings! Time to wind up this Ben Affleck wannabe.* "So, Chicago is cheaper, and you're using real people in real places. What else, Lance?"

"For whatever magical reason, Chicago has become *the* melting pot for every flavor of talent. The area offers authentic seasonal changes, an inland seashore—Lake Michigan—and a robust cultural hub. Since Chicago has grown to be the nation's largest and most diverse city, we can also brag about the largest movie-going audience in a single geographical area. The perfect *local* audience that's representative of a *global* one."

Donna and her viewers knew of Hollywood's diminishing cries that it remains the movie capital of the world. But with every passing year, those cries were falling on more deaf ears. And so, the money poured into studios like *Windy City*, *Deep Dish*, *Lake Hollywood* and *Miracle Mile*. With *Windy City* leading the way, they all grew to be the new titans of entertainment broadcasting and distribution. But now, it was time to inject the real reason Donna wanted to snag this interview—to appeal to her more patriotic viewers. Time to go all journalistic. This unrehearsed approach would surprise Lance Bowman and could be risky. *Here we go.*

"Lance, while nobody really says this out loud, many might suggest movies are now the new international space race, the ultra-nationalistic rallying cry. From what you've just shared with us, cost is a primary driver, but so is national pride. As production companies migrate across borders, disputes have taken on warlike dimensions. Mediation companies offer a militaristic component as a distasteful necessity. How does *Windy City* view this dimension of your industry?"

Yup. I caught him by surprise.

"Donna, unfortunately, I am not at liberty to discuss that."

"Oh, of course. My apologies. But it's my understanding that—"

"Thank you so much, Donna. I've really enjoyed our time together."

"Ah, yes. Thank *you*, Mr. Bowman. *The slimy fucker!*

Donna Matthews was already planning her next episode, now that she'd squeezed all she could out of this arrogant turnip. Production companies for stage performances flourished in Chicago, too. The movie studios grew up in and around Cicero farther south—closer to Celebrity Row. But the Loop closer to the city's center had become the new Great White Way, the new Broadway. New York had suffered many of the same maladies as America's "Left Coast."

Chicago's theater district leveraged its long theatrical tradition and fame. The area between Randolf and Lake Streets, west of Clark and east of Wabash, experienced explosive growth. Much like New York's Broadway in the 1950s and beyond. Plenty of proof in that pudding, like the Annual Playwright Festival, the Gene Siskel Film Center, Nederlander Theatre, Joffrey Ballet, The Chicago Theatre, Goodman Theatre, and Broadway in Chicago.

Domestic production and entertainment companies elsewhere struggled, too. The desert had reclaimed most of Las Vegas as Lake Mead dried up, while the sea had reclaimed much of Atlantic City. Most companies there were moving to Chicago, too. Despite its escalating crime rate, Chicago had also captured the titles of *New Vegas,* the *Lakeshore Strip* and *New Atlantic City,* a.k.a. *Boardwalk 2.0.* Only the tourists and pulp journalists called them that, though.

There would always be international players in India, China and elsewhere. But Chicago had grown to be the global entertainment nucleus, unlikely as that would have seemed even a decade earlier. Besides, few would risk venturing to casinos in Macao or Kuala Lumpur unless they had a death wish or quick access to ransom bucks for a chance at survival. *Or* if they traveled with their own private security force. The world had become a very dangerous place.

CHAPTER 19

~

Early afternoon that same day on Windy City Studios Sound Stage 7, Stacy Michaels screeched, "Todd! Where's my mineral water? And don't forget the damn lemon this time! I need a read-through and I'm hoarse from all that horrid sea air."

Todd chirped, "Coming right up, Mr. Michaels... here ya go."

They had arrived back in Chicago less twenty-four hours earlier, now having been on the studio's back lot almost non-stop ever since. This after endless rehearsals for twelve days aboard that tramp steamer, or whatever the hell it was. Todd grew tired of Stacy Michaels. But Todd was a pro. A production assistant—a PA—never gave up on the job, his star. The PA version of *the show must go on.* Managing arrogant and temperamental actors with minimal drama was a fundamental part of what would make him a successful director some day. Besides, he now worked undercover with the famous mystery writer, Aubrey Greigh. Things were looking up. He had *so* much to tell Greigh after that weird voyage home.

Nobody was in costume for this scene's final read-through before performing it for the Assistant Director the following morning. Street clothes only. No props. The scene was set. This was to be a firearms shooting scene in a small but exclusive dance club. During some dialogue between Stacy and his dance partner, a wealthy debutante, an armed extra would appear from off-camera, from "the club's" alley entrance.

The gunman was to enter unseen by Stacy, but would be spotted over his shoulder from the dance floor by Stacy's on-screen love interest and dance partner playing the VIP debutante, and in real life, a newcomer to show business. Jeanette Lang was young and pretty, but she struggled to memorize lines. Stacy would observe the shock in Jeanette's eyes as she'd spot the gunman over his left shoulder. Without warning, the gunsel was to shoot and kill the actor near the glitzy bar. He was one of Jeanette's on-screen bodyguards, an extra.

Her second bodyguard would engage the shooter and get shot in rapid succession before getting off a shot of his own. Just sound effects, no actual weapons. They'd mouth the sounds: *Bap! Bap!* With both of her protectors down, the bad guy would pistol-whip Stacy who would then fall to the dance floor, unconscious. The bad guy was to grab Jeanette by the arm and hustle her out of the club's alley entrance. That would be the end of the abduction scene.

At that moment, with everyone in place, Stacy had yet to signal the start of the action. Todd noticed *three* men—not one—enter the club set's "alley entrance." They all wore bizarre pull-over masks. *What the hell?* Todd said, "Excuse me! This is a closed set. You can't be here." He tried to sound authoritative, but his voice broke. He disappointed himself, sounding like a damn adolescent. This surrealistic turn of events shook him. With no warning, one intruder shot one of Jeanette's two on-screen "bodyguards," the one closest to the trio of intruders. The shot sounded like a loud *SPIT*.

Oblivious, Stacy blurted, "No, no, no! We aren't using guns tonight. And who taught you how to act?" He stared down at the fallen actor who had crumpled to the floor, not moving. "Where's your sense of drama, man? You don't just drop. You spin or throw out your arms! No wonder you're just an extra!" All three gunmen looked at each other as if confused or incredulous. The one who pulled the trigger first shrugged and aimed straight at Michaels. He fired. The clueless star folded like wet origami.

Now in shock, Todd rushed to Michaels' side, as if there was something he could do. Todd got shot in the back for his effort. He didn't see what happened to Jeanette, but as the last scene of his life faded to black, he could imagine… *The End.*

~

SEVERAL HOURS PASSED BEFORE A CLEANING CREW discovered the five bodies. They called the CED first, and the studio's executive offices second. Per studio protocol. Patrol officers from the ninety-ninth precinct arrived first on the scene as the shooting happened at the southern perimeter of their jurisdiction.

Detective Aidan McKenzie—Mac—drew the case and arrived less than forty minutes after the officers secured the scene and called in their initial report. It looked bad. His temporary partner per Captain Granger, the new guy Tony Santos, tagged along. Mac got the sense Santos thought such calls were beneath him. He didn't like the guy. He seemed arrogant. But business was business. When they arrived on the sound stage, their crime scene, five corpses had bled out. They all laid near one another—four men, one woman. One man had fallen on top of another. Techs awaited the go-signal from the two detectives before descending on the secured scene, searching for trace evidence.

Mac had seen slaughters before, but this was his first mass shooting as a detective. "Jesus. Looks like they dropped where they stood."

Santos said, "No sign of any defensive wounds. Looks like somebody just chopped 'em down."

Mac saw some almost middle-age guy trying to stay young standing nearby in the area that was set up to appear like an upscale dance club. Could have sworn it was the actor Ben Affleck, at first. The guy came charging over when he spotted their gold shields clipped to their belts. "Are you the police?"

"Yes, sir. And you are…"

"I'm Lance Bowman. This is my studio. What can you tell me?"

"Mr. Bowman. Not sure you're aware of how this works. We're the detectives. We ask the questions. Now, why don't you tell us what *you* know?"

"Yes, well, one of my cleaning crews called this in." He tossed a distasteful nod toward the bodies on which he'd turned his back. "And then called my office up the street. I've asked around. No one heard anything, even though other personnel were on the sound stage just south of this one." He offered another nod over his right shoulder to the adjacent building just a dozen yards away.

Tony aimed a meaningful glance to his right, toward Mac. "Silenced weapons? A professional hit?"

"Probable. No brass casings. Clean escape." Mac swung his gaze from Santos to this suit—even though he dressed down to fit in. Either that, or he came right from the gym. "Mr. Bowman, what were these people doing here?"

"Rehearsing. They and others just returned to the lot from a transatlantic voyage yesterday. We were on location in Copenhagen where one of my other stars was murdered nineteen days ago. Now this! We need to find out who and why!"

"Of course, sir. We need a list of the victims' names. Any idea why these folks were targeted?"

"Must be that Toby Stiler, over at Miracle Mile, my competition."

"Why?"

"*Why?* Well, my two biggest stars murdered in the space of three weeks? He'd have the most to gain, now, wouldn't he? And he's as ruthless as they come."

"And the victims?"

Bowman wiggled two *come over here* fingers at a young woman standing nearby who looked ready to hurl at the grizzly scene, but made every attempt to remain professional. "Valerie, do you know the others here besides Stacy?" He once again nodded over his left shoulder toward the bodies and the pools of blood and other fluids—without looking. As if it were just another mess to be cleaned up: an expensive inconvenience.

"Yes, sir. Stacy, his PA Todd Bricker, Jeanette Lang, and two extras. I'll get their names." She started scribbling a list on a piece of paper captive on her clipboard while she spoke. Wheeled around to get the last two names from someone in the crowd of bystanders that the uniforms kept at bay.

Mac thought, *Paper? Old school.* He and Santos would question Valerie later. She fidgeted, and looked like she might have more to say, but not in front of her boss. "So, Mr. Bowman, you were in Copenhagen when the first murder occurred. And you are here, now."

Deep concern on Bowman's face—probably contrived—transformed into instant contempt. "*Excuse me?* What are you implying, Detective?"

"Just asking questions, Mr. Bowman. It's what we do."

"Yes, I was in Copenhagen. And the police closed Peter Fontera's homicide as a home invasion gone wrong. I trust you are better at your job than they are at theirs!"

"Trust me, Mr. Bowman. We'll find out who did this, and we'll bring them to justice. *Whoever* they are." He tossed one more accusative look at this jerk. Couldn't hurt to make him squirm. At least, a little.

CHAPTER 20

That evening in his suite at The Lit, Greigh pondered the circumstances that found him back in Chicago so abruptly. Someone murdered a Windy City actor in Copenhagen before he could talk. Someone maSACred five more Windy City personnel in a mass shooting here in Chicago. *And* on the very day he had returned to the city. That was no coincidence. Didn't smell like a serial, though. More like a conspiracy. Further, Greigh's initial inquiries upon his return revealed the Windy City's cast and crew from the *Dancing With Death* project had returned from Copenhagen on a ship the day before. Another non-coincidence.

An incoming call startled him as he sat at his desk by the window wall in his seventh-floor suite. Greigh's temple implant tickled him. He tapped it. The status call to his Interpol handler, Freya Ecklund, would have to wait.

"Hi, Mr. Greigh. This is Josh Carver. I'm—"

"Josh! You're a screenwriter down at Windy City, correct?"

"Uh, yeah. How—"

"Todd Bricker speaks highly of you, Josh. You're in Sherwood, correct?"

"Oh, yeah, that's great. Means a lot. I now have a place on four. Mr. Greigh—"

"It's just Greigh, Josh."

"Okay, well, you haven't heard—"

"What, Josh? You sound... what's happened?"

"Greigh, Todd is dead, and—"

"What?"

"I'm in the lobby right now. Can I come up? Or—"

"Come up straightaway, Josh. Please. 7D." *Bloody hell.*

Greigh waited for his visitor in the hallway outside his suite with one of his double entry doors swung wide. He spotted a handsome young man with jet black hair and brilliant green eyes heading for him, shrouded under a dark expression. Had to be Josh. "Please come in, Josh." They shook hands. The young man cast his eyes downward as Greigh motioned for him to enter. Greigh closed the door behind them and led the young man into his living room. Greigh guided him to the sofa that faced a dark fireplace, the windows across the room behind them.

"Sir, Todd said you might call me. Something about a job. He said you and he worked together in Copenhagen."

Casting an intense gaze toward this young man, Greigh said, "Josh, just please tell me what happened to our friend."

"Sir—"

"Just Greigh. Please."

"Right, well, there was a shooting on a Windy City sound stage earlier today."

"Yes, but they haven't released names."

"Someone shot and killed Todd and four other people, Greigh. The police are investigating. Big news. Todd and I were supposed to have lunch. He didn't show, so I called the studio. One of our mutual acquaintances told me the story. It's all over the lot. They gunned down Todd, two actors—Stacy Michaels and Jeanette Lang—along with two extras. The shooter or shooters got away clean."

Greigh scratched his head, then his beard, not knowing what to say. He crossed his legs, uncrossed them, recrossed them in the opposite direction. He uncrossed, stood up, tugged at his short ponytail, and pounded his right fist on the fireplace's mantel. Greigh now towered over Josh who remained seated. Took a deep breath and puffed it out. "So, no idea why?"

"No." The kid lowered his head. Sounded like he might be sniffling. Maybe even crying. Greigh sat down again beside him. Placed a paternal hand on his left shoulder after taking another deep breath. "Todd and I only chatted a few times. We had dinner together, Josh, but he seemed a good sort. I liked him very much. Had you talked with him since his return from abroad?"

Josh sniffled one more time. Wiped his nose on the back of his right sleeve before he spoke again, now in a halting tone. He seemed embarrassed. "Oh, sure. He told me he was helping you out. He was very excited about it. Said he had something to tell you about the trip home on that crappy old ship. He waited for your call. Said you promised to connect with him once you got back into town."

Greigh felt a pang of guilt for not contacting Todd the moment he arrived that morning. He spun toward Josh and held his gaze. "Did he mention the subject of this information?"

"I guess it was something that happened on that ship. He sounded scared. Like what he learned was a really big deal. Something about scary guys handling dangerous cargo. Like they worried if they'd still be able to have kids. Stuff like that. It spooked him, sir."

Greigh pondered what he knew. Everything that had happened since Copenhagen seemed connected. Peter Fontera was murdered before he could tell Greigh about something he had learned. Captain Galkin and his boat disappeared after a mysterious open-sea cargo transfer. And now, the murder of Stacy Michaels, Todd Bricker and three others here in Chicago. Six murders—all Windy City personnel. If there was ever an international case for Interpol, this was it. *What the shite is going on here?* He'd update Freya at his earliest convenience.

"Josh, do you have access to Windy City Studios?"

"Huh? Well, ah, sure. I've caught a couple of jobs as a writer. That gives me quite generous access to most of the sound stages and other back lot venues. I've spent the last four years developing relationships. And Todd had taken me under his wing, talking up me and my portfolio. Most folks don't understand how much influence lowly PAs—the good ones—wield. Not to mention how much they see. And—"

"Josh, are you familiar with my work?"

"Of course! I've wanted to meet you for a long time. You're—"

"Listen, if you want the job, from this moment on, you're my screenwriter. As long as you continue to impress me with your work, that is."

"*What?* Gosh, that's—"

"My name and reputation will get me onto the Windy City lot. But I need you to introduce me to your friends, especially other writers and PAs. All of them. As someone you trust. Like you said, your friends see a great deal. I'm going to find out who killed our friend, Todd. But I need a circle of trusted acquaintances who will be candid with me. And discreet. Do you understand?"

"Oh. But—"

"Are you with me, Josh?"

Silence. Then, the striking young man with dark hair, new clothes, and a new apartment scratched his fuzzy whiskers. "I'm not sure, Greigh. That's a big ask. I just got inside *myself*. And some of the more experienced writers have *only recently* taken me under their wing."

"Josh, do *you* trust me and my intentions? Todd did. You already know that."

"Well, yes, of course."

"Okay, well, let's do this, my new friend. Besides, I'm confident Lance Bowman will jump at the chance to sponsor my latest success. If you were the screenwriter for *Voodoo Vendetta*, that would advance your status with the other writers and the studio, would it not? And think of what it would mean if you helped solve the studio lot murders."

The kid lit up when the implication sunk in. "Hell, yeah. Let's do this!"

"There's a bonny lad!"

"Huh?"

"Attaboy!"

Josh didn't need to know that Greigh would also investigate the connection between Peter Fontera's murder in Copenhagen and his smuggling case. Its origins in the Baltic now almost certainly seemed connected to Andy Galkin's disappearance, too.

What did Peter discover on the Copenhagen waterfront that he never got the chance to tell me? What did Todd see or hear on that ship? Is that what got him killed? Or was he merely collateral damage in the assassination of yet another Windy City star? Who would benefit from killing off these celebrities? Greigh grew solemn. Forgot Josh was there. It seemed everyone he talked with about this case turned up dead. Irrational as it seemed, pangs of guilt struck him like a cold bolt of lightning.

CHAPTER 21

The next morning, Sunday the 30th, Greigh peered out of the car window as his Bentley steered him on auto-drive toward the Windy City studio gates in Cicero. Tall, imposing steel bars facing South Cicero Avenue looked like the entrance to a prison rather than to a movie studio.

A chill slithered down his spine. Despite the casual conversation he meant to have with the studio's general manager, Lance Bowman, he couldn't shake his suspicion over that prissy wanker. He stopped the car at the closed gate. His driver's window descended. Two security guards appeared. Greigh examined them; they both had an air of professional boredom about them, but also something else. No doubt they remained on edge after the shootings just two days earlier. And now, it was as if they could sense that something was amiss.

He gulped as one of them approached the car with a questioning look on his face. The gorilla carried an unsettling air of profound unwariness, the heel of his palm on the butt of his holstered weapon. "ID, please? Name and purpose here?"

"Aubrey Greigh. Appointment with Lance Bowman."

The guy held up an index finger, wheeled on his heel, entered the gatehouse to check his monitor. Meanwhile, a second guard circumnavigated his car, waving some device in the air close to his Bentley's body. A third appeared with a mirror on an extendable handle to inspect the underbody. Or was it a miniature camera and monitor? The now-trio of armed guards in full tactical gear made the entire ballet of paranoia seem almost casual, but there was nothing casual about *these* security boys.

After getting his driver's license back and being scrutinized for what seemed like several minutes, they opened the wrought-iron gate from inside the fancy gatehouse festooned with cams and sensors. The first guard waved Greigh through without further delay. But before he rolled forward, Greigh asked, "Expecting trouble?"

"Nope. Just another day in paradise. Sir." His last word punctuated gate closing immediately behind his car 's rear bumper with a note of swift finality.

Greigh couldn't help but ponder why Bowman had agreed to meet with him after the ruse of questioning him as a reporter in Copenhagen. The man had no doubt confirmed by now Greigh was no reporter at all. Rather, he'd have been told Greigh was, in fact, a freelance Interpol investigator and a successful author.

He grew increasingly certain that Peter Fontera's murder had something to do with the mysterious smuggling case Freya had assigned him to investigate. But he couldn't yet articulate why. Maybe Bowman even held answers to both Fontera's murder and his smuggling case. The executive office building itself within Windy City seemed welcoming from the outside with its warm colors, lush gardens and well-kept lawn. But beneath this peaceful exterior lay dark secrets. Greigh was sure of it. He also suspected some would unravel once he stepped into Bowman's office. He remained a serial optimist.

A perky receptionist named Dawn met Greigh at the door. She smiled as she ushered him into Bowman's office. A wave of stale cigar smoke preceded a fresh cloud. Both greeted him as he entered the room. Bowman now wore a handsome cashmere sweater, gabardine slacks, and two-thousand-dollar Ferragamo Moccasins. His pinky ring bore what had to be a 76-facet princess-cut diamond the size of a small walnut. Its sparkles lit up the entire office from the sunlight penetrating the cigar smoke and the large window to Bowman's left. And the Royal Oak edition Audemars Piguet watch worth several million on his right wrist? So much for dressing down.

An old-fashioned desk was covered with pictures and documents, all of which appeared to be related to Peter Fontera's death. There were newspaper clippings, handwritten notes and even photographs from Suite 3-16 of the City Lux Executive Apartments in Copenhagen —official police crime scene photos. This material was scattered all over the man's desk like he had collected every scrap of evidence on Peter Fontera's homicide.

But the Copenhagen police had closed that case as a failed home invasion. Nobody believed that. And no one more skeptical than Lance Bowman, it seemed. Or was he obsessed for some other reason? What then struck Greigh was how many framed photos in the office featured Bowman and Fontera together. Close together. Further, did Bowman's voice and body language stiffen when talking about his deceased actor? There was something intensely personal about it; almost as if he had some kind of connection to Peter that no one else outside his office suite knew about, or at least, spoke about. Did it have anything to do with his murder? The one meant to appear like a crime of passion?

"You're not a reporter at all." Not a question.

"I do indeed freelance on occasion and write under a pen name, Mr. Bowman, I'm Aubrey Greigh. Apologies for the ruse. I find it handy to travel incognito from time to time. Forgive me?"

The man remained sullen. But he hoisted the brave face of managed grief and said, "Of course, I understand. I know something of secret identities."

"You and Peter." A simple statement.

"We had plans. All gone. Mr. Greigh—"

"Just Greigh, Mr. Bowman."

"Call me Lance. They tell me that besides being a brilliant best-selling author, you're also an investigator for Interpol. True?"

"It is. And I'm trying to find out what happened to your Peter, as well as to Mr. Michaels and the rest."

"So, you don't believe the bullshit the Danish police are slinging, either."

"Lance, I was there in that apartment as Peter expired. I even attempted CPR, but he was already gone." Still standing, like Bowman, Greigh reached forward and tapped one of the crime scene photos. A sudden involuntary gasp escaped from Lance's lips. He dropped into his nearby desk chair. "It appeared to be a crime of passion."

The beleaguered studio exec cast his gaze up at Greigh. "I'm a suspect. I should be. I was there, and Peter and I were… involved."

"You've collected all of… this. What do you hope to achieve?" Greigh tried to interpret Lance's silence. After sitting and slumping for what seemed a long time, he moaned as the words escaped his throat, "I don't know. It's not like I can find out more than the Danish police, or Interpol. Is any of this of help to you, Greigh? Take it all. I'd appreciate…" He couldn't continue. But he refused to weep. He just stopped talking. Stormed out of the room. This guy was no killer. But he was no innocent, either.

GREIGH STEPPED BACK INTO THE SUNLIGHT OUTSIDE Lance Bowman's building. The crisp air offered him some relief from the oppressive atmosphere of that man's office. *Do blokes in profound grief smoke cigars?* Questions raced around in his mind faster than ever before, all competing for his complete attention; leaving behind lingering doubts that somewhere among all these clues lay an answer so well-hidden no one had found it. He needed to question Toby Stiler, general manager of Miracle Mile Studios—Lance Bowman's chief competition.

CHAPTER 22

Outside Bowman's executive office building, Greigh turned to his right. He walked less than a hundred yards down Windy City's version of Main Street, bound on both sides by narrow textured concrete sidewalks with a narrow band of artificial turf on both sides . He was to meet Josh Carver, his new screenwriter, in the *Writer's Pit,* no doubt named by a scribe prepossessed of self-deprecating humor. Quite a few of the more experienced PAs hung out at an adjacent lounge during rare breaks. And out front, Marco's Café—a barista's truck—parked on a semi-permanent basis. He served the best coffee in Chicago. Not free like in the studio's cafeteria, but he would learn Marco's heavenly beverages fueled creativity and supplied motivation like no other.

True to his word, before his arrival, Greigh's new screenwriter, Josh, told him he had mentioned his name to a half-dozen PAs and a roomful of other writers in *The Pit*. Josh said most were more cooperative than competitive. During dry spells, at least. Said he trusted Greigh.

The air was still and heavy as Greigh stepped into the semi-quiet room where Josh's screenwriter friends hung out, a respite from the tornado of activity everywhere else on the lot. By comparison, the silence seemed underwhelming. The room's chilly temperature surprised him. It was possible that's how they maintained focus. Some sunshine penetrated the translucent black shades covering a high wall of windows on the Main Street side of the building. Its rays highlighted the air in *The Pit* that hung heavy with free-range dust.

A dozen writers—eight men and four women—surrounded a large beat-up table covered with as many computers. Cables fed into three community printers in the center, within easy reach. The constant clatter of fingers on keyboards generated a subdued noise that sounded like a hoard of cats clawing on raw wood. The occasional subdued dialogue between writers punctuated that drone of incessant keyboard clacking. Under their breath, two of them dictated into recording devices that translated their spoken word into text on their screens. But most were old school key pounders. A lifetime of habit, Greigh guessed.

He experienced a rush of anticipation rising in his chest. Josh had told him he hoped this would be a place where his new friend could get answers. But now, standing here amongst a dozen veteran screenwriters, all of whom seemed to stare at him as an intruder, for just a moment, Greigh's confidence wavered. He scanned the faces in the room, looking for a friendly expression, or someone who might recognize him from Josh Carver's introduction prior to his arrival. But everyone in the room seemed once again occupied with their own work. Their intermittent conversations were too low for Greigh to distinguish any words. This only made him feel even more out of place —not as an investigator, but as a fellow writer outside his own area of expertise.

A scratchy baritone voice startled him from behind. "You must be Aubrey Greigh, the *author*." The last word the voice uttered sounded somehow profane. Greigh turned around to find an older man with thick white hair wearing glasses near the end of his bulbous nose. He was also a foot shorter. The duffer broadcast an exhausted expression, though he somehow resurrected a well-practiced mask of good cheer from somewhere deep inside. His skin tone appeared more gray than olive or pink or tan. An obvious vitamin B deficiency. He introduced himself as one of Josh's mentors and a fan of Todd Bricker's. Despite his tired appearance, there was a glimmer of encouragement in his eyes as he introduced himself as Farad Mastuk. He pronounced his name as fa-DODD *MOSS-took*. "Ah, yes. Of course, I recognize you from your book covers. I am a fan, Mr. Greigh. I will warn you, however, that most screenwriters maintain a love/hate relationship with their authors, depending on one of two seasons: feast or famine."

"A pleasure, Mr. Mastuk. And it's just Greigh."

"Please call me Farad. And I appreciate you avoiding the tired old saws of 'mistook' or 'mistake.' Thank you for that. Our Josh tells me you wish to slum with those of us who perform the actual work at this studio." His eyes twinkled with disarming charm and amusement as they stood there at the room's entrance.

"Well, Farad, I so enjoyed spending time with Todd in Copenhagen. Lacking experience in how a movie project works, Todd informed me PAs and writers possess the pulse of a project and the overall studio environment, perhaps better than anyone." It was Greigh's turn to twinkle.

"I understand you're looking into the shooting using your expert nose for sleuthing. What can we do to help?"

"Josh tells me the police have little to go on."

"Greigh, the police questioned only one PA named Valerie who was on the scene. She might provide more insight." Farad turned and spoke to Josh, who now hovered a respectful distance away after appearing from nowhere while the two men talked. "Josh, Valerie Schmidt should still be over on the *Dancing* set. Maybe you could introduce our new friend to her."

"Sure thing, Farad." The kid grinned big, like he knew he was helping Greigh investigate the murder of their mutual friend.

Greigh smiled back. "Yes, Josh, that would be splendid." He turned back to the veteran screenwriter. "Farad, please accept my card." He two-handed it and bowed in the Japanese tradition of great respect. Farad seemed to recognize the gesture. "If you or any of your bonny lads think of anything else that would help us help CED catch Todd's murderer, please call or text. I thank you, my new friend."

"You are most welcome. And I thank you for giving our Josh an opportunity to show you his considerable talent. If Mr. Bowman has his wits about him, he'll recognize *Voodoo Vendetta* for its obvious box office potential. If Josh does his job, that is. I'll monitor that for you."

There was that twinkle again. For an older gentleman, Farad exhibited one crushing handshake. Josh smiled and lowered his eyes. Greigh recognized his body language. The kid knew he was now on a fast track to success. *If I don't get him killed, that is.*

CHAPTER 23

Greigh had returned from Cicero in the evening. The sun penetrated Chicago's almost-September sky and threw a lovely, reflected glow into his suite's covered balcony. Its late afternoon angle dappled his painted and textured concrete deck through the artificial trees and bushes that guarded his balcony's periphery. He took a strong cup of tea outside and nestled into one of the three small but comfortable settees under his tented dais. No better way to enjoy the southern exposure when the sun made its occasional appearance. On the way back from Cicero, he had called ahead. Butler, his apartment's automated control system, had his "cuppa" waiting for him.

Comfortably seated in the crisp air, it was time to seek out this Toby Stiler at Miracle Mile Studios. But he needed to decide whether to do so as a successful author shopping his novel for a movie deal, or as a contract Interpol investigator. But first, he had approached no one at CED as a courtesy, and should do so sooner versus later. First order of business, then.

"Captain Granger. Lois, this is Aubrey Greigh. It has been a while."

"Greigh, so good to hear from you. I'm told you're sniffing around my precinct with your Interpol hat on. I've been awaiting your call."

A momentary silence registered his surprise at her insight. "I have indeed been remiss. This call is me stumbling onto my blade."

"You mean falling on your sword? That schtick might charm McQ, Greigh. I have it on good authority that you're too precise a word player to commit that sort of verbal stumble unless it's intentional."

"Mea culpa, Lois. McQ enjoys that. I indulge. Things have been moving with rapidity since my return from abroad on Friday. A case that started in Denmark seems to have followed me here. Or I've followed it." He explained both the homicide and smuggling cases to the captain, along with progress he'd made.

"So, I believe the shootings that Mac and your new chap are working on may be linked to my Copenhagen homicide. The smuggling affair is still a work in progress as well."

"I thank you for the call, Greigh. And so you're aware, I'm doing what I can to understand McQ's forced leave, as well."

"Wonderful. *Vi ses!* That's *see you later* in Danish, should that amuse you." *Click.*

With that out of the way, he made a similar call to his Interpol handler, Freya Ecklund, and assured her he was liaising with the local police. She seemed more abrupt than usual. But that was not unexpected. After chastising him for not calling sooner, she said she appreciated learning of his progress, or lack thereof.

"Get this done, Greigh. And next time, *I'm* your first call."

"Of course." *Shite!* He then arranged an appointment to visit Mr. Stiler at Miracle Mile, also in Cicero, less than a mile up South Cicero Avenue from Windy City's lot. He would do so as himself, both as an author *and* Interpol investigator. If he was fortunate, he'd confuse the man into being truthful with him.

THE FOLLOWING MORNING, GREIGH FOUND TOBY STILER AT Miracle Mile Productions in Cicero to be a complete surprise, and he couldn't be more different from his counterpart at Windy City. Stiler stood six-three, taller than Greigh by an inch, taller with his hat on. He was at least fifty pounds overweight and a sloppy dresser. The man wore a soiled white fedora that matched his suit coat, even indoors, featuring prominent stains on the front of its brim, no doubt from constant handling by greasy fingers.

Even though it was first thing Monday morning, both the slob and his office were a mess. But Greigh guessed the man had a system and could locate every piece of paper or digital storage device, despite the chaos. A table fan oscillated at high speed which fluttered nearby papers. The small and unassuming office reeked of rancid fast-food detritus. Reminded Greigh of Freya Ecklund's beat-up old Volvo's cluttered interior as she prowled Copenhagen's streets in it.

With pleasantries out of the way, Stiler plopped his generous bottom into a tired old all-wood desk chair Greigh feared might collapse. It didn't. Stiler grabbed his hat's brim, swept it off his head, and mopped his brow with a coat sleeve rolled up to his mid-forearm. Dropped that hat back onto his near-bald head before leaning forward, elbows on his desk, and aimed an intense stare at Greigh, who now sat across that chaotic desk from him.

"Let me guess. That sociopathic little shit, Bowman, is pointing the finger at me for the murders of his own people, right? Little fucker's smooth, ain't he? I'll give you this—that sum-bitch could talk a nun out of her bloomers as he's on his knees prayin' right 'longside a her."

"Why should I believe you and not him, Mr. Stiler?"

"You gawddamn well shouldn't, sir!" Came out *suh*. "Follow your mystery-writer's nose, Mr. Greigh. I'm a huge fan, by the way. You ever wanna get your work into this here business, I'd be honored to work with ya. Far as *Lance* goes, that creep'll do anything for a buck, greedy little shit."

"Are you a homophobe, Mr. Stiler?"

"Hey, I don't give a rat's turd where anybody sticks their wick, son, or who they fall in love with. Ain't the point. Bowman sweet-talked his way into that job so he could milk Windy City dry. Look at the numbers. How's he doin'—financially? I'm betting his nums are suckin' hind tit. Am I right?"

"Well, he claims his transformation from CG—"

"Blah-de-blah. Look, Mr. Greigh—"

"Just Greigh—"

"Sure thing. I'm doin' the same thing over here. But I'm usin' my noggin. Transition, right? Not an overnight transformation. He's using that cock 'n bull to squeeze the turnip. He's flippin' the switch overnight. Wanna guess why? Cuz he clamped a gawddamn tourniquet on his CG and AI budgets. Done, and *done*. Okay, but where'd all them greenbacks go? He hires two big-name actors—Fontera and Michaels—and that's it? I'd check his offshore accounts. He's funding his early retirement. Are you spongin' what I'm spillin' here yet, Greigh? But hey, don't take my word for it. Check it out for yourself. You're good at that gumshoe shit. I followed you during that Thibodaux crap last summer. Well-played, son."

Greigh tried to discern whether this Kentucky homeboy facade was genuine. Didn't matter. This big man's words rang true to his gut. And Stiler droned on.

"Pretty smart, right? Kill off his stars now, and he bitches, 'I had this big-deal vision and poor me. Some big bad man, probably that hillbilly over at Miracle Mile, kills off my stars! No wonder I failed.' That right there is Kentucky pig shit dressed up to smell like fine wine! Don't believe me, son. Follow the money."

"I will do so. Anything else, Mr. Stiler?"

"Yeah. You been to his lot, right?"

"Yes, I've been there."

"Notice his security? Little Lance is paranoid. Iron gates, security guards that would put CED's tac squad to shame, twelve-foot walls with razor wire, motion sensors, infrared, the works. The place is a gawddamn fortress. So riddle me this, Greigh. How does a hardware-toting gunman just wander onto that lot, pop six souls, and get away clean? Just sayin'."

Greigh decided he would take Stiler's advice, colorful vernacular notwithstanding. That might even lead his investigation in a new direction.

CHAPTER 24

Mika Kuzmin's pilot and co-pilot awaited clearance for take-off from the busiest airport in Canada, Pearson International in Toronto, Ontario, en route to Grand Rapids International where arrangements had been made. She asked that they leave the Gulfstream's cockpit door open. Made her feel a little less helpless. She enjoyed the strong Afghan tea prepared for her by Margus, who accompanied her. The aging executive had taken a liking to the boy.

Mika had implored her powerful adoptive father, now deceased, to find her biological family not long before he passed away. His investigators (who now worked for her) finally delivered. Certain Kremlin files had just unexpectedly been declassified (leaked). That had not been cheap. She learned she was the fifty-six-year-old twin sister of Tihomir Leonov, already a well-known American business executive.

Tihomir had been a soldier of distinction and an intelligence officer of some repute. Years earlier, and for reasons of his own, her brother emigrated to America—the Great Satan itself. He was the president and CEO of one of the largest privately held corporations in the America. Like her, he never married and claimed no children. She was his only heir.

Of late, she realized the importance of family. With no children of her own, and never having married, something stirred deep inside. She always knew a decent family adopted her, now all dead. Some things a twin just *knows*. Like she *knew* Tihomir would *never* commit suicide, as reported by the western press. And *on the same night*, someone shot his most trusted lieutenant in the streets of Chicago. *America! And if I can't identify every person responsible, I'll punish them all!* This thought became her obsession, the reason she now breathed life. It had become the razor-sharp point she'd been honing for half a century. Now she knew why.

But Mika must *prove* no other heir to Tihomir's business and personal fortune survived. She'd seize the reigns of his estate *and* his company—Watchtower, Inc. She also learned her brother had become the sixth wealthiest individual in America prior to his murder. Not without means herself, she'd acquire Watchtower's resources and influence to execute her duplicitous strategy. She would avenge Tihomir by first identifying his murderer or murderers. Tihomir's twin *would* exact revenge.

Second, she'd punish others in that city that plotted against him, including the police and politicians that conspired against him and sided with that influential Copolla family—Tihomir's competition. It was so obvious to her what needed to happen—and inevitable. That collateral damage was inevitable could not deter her.

She had developed a vast array of contacts both within and beyond law enforcement. Way beyond. She drew and erased and redrew that fine line between ethics and power until it expanded to a dirty gray smudge. Interpol and other corrupt law enforcement agencies in a dozen countries respected her as much as did vast criminal networks. She wore different faces and was a master at compartmentalizing them.

From afar during the days and weeks before his death, but before she could connect with him, Mika had admired Tihomir. Especially after learning about their biological mother. She was a heartless old bitty, and Tihomir stepped up to the challenge of ridding the planet of the old harpy. Good riddance.

It always bothered her who her real father was. Her affluent adoptive parents—Gennady and Tatyana—indulged her. Mika called them Papi and Mami. Papi was an influential retired party official and came from money. His family acquired and built their wealth after the fall of the union. Some said Gennady Kuzmin rose to power within what came to be known in the west as the Russian mafia. Some used the word *oligarch*. She was not beyond leveraging that reputation to her own even more ambitious ends. Gennady Kuzmin was a man to be feared because of the influence he peddled. Yes, he was ruthless, but also a good father who taught her well. And they doted on their only child, Mika. Tatyana was barren, but a fine mother compared to what poor Tihomir endured.

Thirty years earlier, a train accident killed both of Mika's parents. Some say it was orchestrated. Nevertheless, Mika followed in her adoptive father's footsteps. She inherited his vast enterprise, Obelisk Prime, now worth hundreds of billions of rubles. Three years earlier, however, she moved OP's headquarters from Moscow to Paldiski, Estonia. That raised eyebrows in the Kremlin. Despite the acrimony, this was a brilliant strategy. Estonia had become a strategic gateway between vast resources in the East and untold opportunities in the West. Yet the small nation remained below the political radar while surviving in the foreboding shadow of Mother Russia.

Mika was a skilled delegator, and she wielded fear as a master motivator. She needed time away from OP to pursue other endeavors of which only she and her most trusted minions were aware. Even her senior executives at OP dared not probe. But she suffered from a lifetime of pathological schizophrenia—a variation that resembled MPD, or Multiple Personality Disorder, with two dominant identities.

Before his fall from grace, her adoptive father wielded significant influence. After the Kremlin, and once unfettered by small-minded bureaucrats, his influence exploded across Europe. Nothing but the best doctors and medicine and clinics for his new daughter, his troubled little Mika. As a child, she spent months at a time in an exclusive private clinic in the Swiss Alps. They said she not only suffered from a genetic disorder, but was psychologically scarred by her home life prior to her adoption. They had rescued her at the fragile but formative age of four. Mika always took her medicines and practiced all the techniques taught to her. When her precious papi died, or was assassinated, something inside of her snapped. Despite that, or perhaps because of that, Mika Kuzmin not only survived, but thrived. That was then....

As they strapped in to prepare for their departure from Toronto, she leaned to her left and spoke to the young man next to her. "Project status?"

"On schedule, Mika."

"Well done, Margus."

CHAPTER 25

Mika slipped into the United States in her corporate Gulfstream 500 accompanied by that private jet's flight crew, her assistant Margus, and no one else. Her aircraft had slid up to the general aviation terminal at the Cicero Regional Airport after clearing into the country at Grand Rapids, Michigan International on Wednesday morning, September 2nd. Her four bodyguards, already there, met her.

The limo ride from Cicero to the Watchtower building in Chicago on East Monroe Street took a little over an hour, long enough to collect her thoughts. The four burly men knew to keep their mouths shut whenever the boss did so. And Margus spoke only when spoken to. She imagined herself the unexpected heiress to an American throne of sorts. Less than two months earlier, she discovered she had a twin brother—just prior to his demise—his *murder*. Since then, she'd been plotting her revenge. Nobody in Chicago or at her brother's company, Watchtower, knew who she was. That was about to change.

She, or rather Margus, had groomed confidential sources inside Watchtower. These sources retrieved some of Ty's personal items at their behest for a DNA analysis. They also informed her that Watchtower's Board of Directors was meeting today at their gleaming headquarters in Chicago's financial district. It was here, on this fateful day, that Mika planned to stake her claim. She would declare she was the rightful and sole heir to the company and to the entire estate of its deceased president and CEO, Ty Leonov. Her sources told her he left no last will and testament. She held ironclad proof of her claim. That would help.

Mika gazed into her pocket mirror and adjusted her octagonal wireframe spectacles that contained nothing but flat-glass amber lenses. She ensured she was in complete control of her persona. The stretch limousine rolled to a stop. She stepped out of the limo in the parking garage below East Monroe Street. Margus remained in the car. She directed him to return to Paldiski. A surge of energy coursed through her lithe body as the rear doors of the limo were flung open. Her four fanatically loyal bodyguards secured their immediate perimeter and a clear pathway to the elevator five meters distant. They were alone in the garage.

Mika ensured she was stable on her utterly dangerous Versace Pinpoint Metal-Heel stilettos as she stood. She straightened her Bespoke suit jacket and smoothed its matching skirt so sleek it required dainty strides. She drew in a deep, cleansing breath before entering what would become the next defining moment in her life.

Her ice-cold bodyguards moved without a sound on the polished marble floor of that garage with their action-ready crepe-soled shoes. But her stiletto heels clicked with every step. Heels… a Western affectation meant to objectify the female body by accentuating a woman's leg muscles and buttocks. *Give them what they desire before you take it—and more—away from them,* she mused. Mika was already tall at five-feet-ten. Those heels would bequeath her a very male power stature. She would tower over everyone in that boardroom per their intel. But not over her elite quartet of guards. All stood at least six-six, all armed under well-tailored suits, of course. Yes, she and her all-male entourage would descend upon an un-suspecting room full of cowering minions. And if they weren't cowering, they would be.

Mika wasted no time once she and her entourage had burst into the boardroom on the twenty-seventh floor—the executive suite, like an invading army. She paced in all her splendor, completing a slow orbit around this table of toadies as she spoke. Heads turned to follow her. She cut a striking and mesmerizing figure. "Good morning, ladies and gentlemen. My name is Mika Kuzmin. I am Tihomir Leonov's twin sister and his only surviving heir. You now work for me. Or you are free to resign. Those are your options." Her most trusted companion, Rolf, towered over even her three other companions. He flung a sheaf of documents onto the table after retrieving them from Mika's travel-worn top-loading briefcase that he clutched in one fist. Those papers verified her familial connection to Ty Leonov.

"My sources inform me my brother left no will or testament to contest. So, that is it. I am also President and Chief Executive Officer of Obelisk Prime, Europe's largest import/export enterprise. We are now on the cusp of merging these two vast business concerns. You are very fortunate to be a part of this ambitious endeavor. Questions?" Ten pairs of doubtful eyes darted about the room in response to her declarations, each bouncing off the gaze of the others around the glossy twenty-foot table. All avoided *her* gaze with care, however. As her papers made the rounds, one portly gentleman snatched Mika's copious documentation with obvious defiance. He identified himself as Watchtower's assistant corporate counsel. He *demanded* that the courts scour Mika's documentation.

After having circumnavigated the massive conference table and these weaklings, Mika lowered her elegant frame into what was sure to have been her brother's chair at the head of the table. With a jagged edge to her voice and a slit-eyed gaze that penetrated the soul of this marshmallow man, she said, "Of course, Mr.—"

"Dorchester."

She tossed a cursory wave toward the monster guard now standing behind her once more. "Rolf, please escort Mr. Dorchester from the room so he can get comfortable with the veracity of my documentation." Rolf rounded the corner of the table, headed for the now-cowtowed man who still struggled to maintain his adamant attitude, but failed. Rolf lifted him from his chair with a firm grasp on his left arm that still clutched Mika's papers. They hustled from the massive room. All eyes followed them.

Mika feared the sunlight streaming through the tinted floor-to-ceiling windows off to her right might cast too harshly off her carefully crafted cosmetics. She faced the remaining nine board members and three empty chairs as she spoke in a lower tone. All leaned in to hear, as if their lives depended on it. They did. "I have studied what you did to my brother's company since he was murdered—"

A younger woman—maybe in her mid-forties—raised her hand to capture Mika's attention and simultaneously interrupted her. "Ms. Guzman—"

"Kuzmin. Please call me Mika, Ms.—"

"No one murdered Mr. Leonov. He committed—"

"Silence! Whoever you are, young lady, I will grant you this one warning. If *anyone* suggests that fairy tale in my presence ever again...." It wasn't necessary for her to finish that sentence with anything other than one precision-manicured hand *slamming* with unexpected brutality onto the glossy surface of that too-long table in that too-large room. The violent gesture startled everyone and echoed around that ballroom that her brother called his office. A ridiculous space meant to intimidate or impress or confuse visitors. She liked it. Her reaction to this woman's words clearly demonstrated how she would run the company. She had set the tone. She grinned inside.

Her first order as acting CEO would be for an *independent* DNA test as evidence to confirm that she was indeed Tihomir Leonov's heir. Such a test would reinforce the one she had commissioned earlier. She would allow this indulgence to allay any doubts still harbored by this pompous set of sycophants. Her claim would be legal and above board. Certainly above *this* board.

The room remained in shocked silence. They had not expected someone like Mika—unknown within their own corporate world—to step forward with such confidence, claiming exclusive rights over one of America's most prominent companies. She suspected, however, several of them were grateful for another strong hand at the helm.

Their company floundered. None of them were prepared for what would come next, however.

Mika held evidence that the most egregious contribution to her twin brother's death came from another immigrant. Gaspari Copolla gained most from her brother's demise as his key competitor *and* the person who highjacked Leonov's most significant Chicago real estate development project after his death, according to her sources. That could only have happened with support from the city's leadership. It seemed to Mika the entire city of Chicago conspired against her estranged brother, resulting in his untimely death. She now understood why many from her motherland called America *the Great Satan.* Mika would be Leonov's avenger.

DOORS OPENED ONCE INSTALLED AS THE PRESIDENT AND Chief Executive Officer of the Watchtower Corporation. People told her things, more out of fear than any newfound loyalty. They spoke of her brother, of his few friends, and of those who hated him. Mika confirmed that Leonov's foremost adversary was indeed Gaspari Copolla. She saw Copolla as a big fish in a little pond, even though they said he was the most infamous American mobster just a decade earlier. A relic. Now, they said he was a philanthropist and a very wealthy business executive whose enterprises rivaled those of Watchtower. *Ha! Now, a flaccid penis, at best.* They also told her Copolla and his allies were the most likely to have murdered her brother. Now they'd pay for what they did to her twin. Mika would use her contacts at Interpol to influence the direction of their investigation into her plot. They would never know. At least, that was her intent.

Her brother's death had led Mika down a dark path. The more she dug into it, the more she realized just how deep the corruption ran in this city. It wasn't just Gaspari Copolla and his associates, like Rocko Bianchi, who plotted against her brother, but also prominent figures in the city's government. Aubrey Greigh and Chance McQuillan, his girlfriend detective, were involved, too.

She continued to plot her revenge. Spent hours poring over documents, maps and blueprints of the real estate project that Gaspari Copolla had taken from her brother. The more she delved into the project, the more she confirmed the extent of the corruption that had led to her brother's death. And the lack of a proper investigation into his murder by the police. *They will pay!*

CHAPTER 26

It was a Tuesday, the first of September at the Sicily Club on the corner of South Wabash and East Van Buren. Gaspari Copolla was an immigrant from the north of Italy forty years earlier, but his family hailed from the island of Sicily. America had been good to him. His oldest friends still called him "Don Gaspari." He neither encouraged nor discouraged the use of that appellation. The old man sat in the private third-floor library of his social club in front of a roaring fire, even though the room seemed quite warm. But he had little tolerance for chilly temperatures these days. He no longer used the grand staircase to reach this, his favorite room in the club, but favored an old-fashioned elevator the size of a small coat closet.

Signore Copolla's "club" was, in fact, a walled estate with a four-story mansion at the center of manicured grounds that resembled a botanical garden. Its membership was exclusive and only numbered in the dozens.

Gaspari's little Luca Donati was both Aubrey Greigh's friend and condominium landlord at The Lit. Gaspari called Luca, imploring him to contact their mutual acquaintance and friend of Greigh's, the lovely McQ. For reasons unknown, the decorated detective remained on compulsory administrative leave from the Chicago Enforcement Department. She might be hungry for work.

Copolla feared something nefarious was happening over at Watchtower, once his major competition in Chicago and elsewhere. The old Don held McQ's investigative skills in the highest regard, but suspected she would more likely agree to help if the request came first from little Luca. He suspected she held a soft spot for the man. Besides, Copolla feared his chronic allergy to law enforcement might flare up.

~

LUCA DONATI SAT AT THE KITCHEN TABLE IN HIS 15TH-floor penthouse suite of the Hotel Literati. He owed his life to one of his building's condo owners—Aubrey Greigh. And Greigh remained close to his other dear friend, a brilliant young Chicago detective, Chance McQuillan. He didn't see either of them all that often. Luca smiled. *McQ.*

Luca was the proprietor of The Lit in Chicago's Near Southwest Loop. He was also the progeny of Gaspari Copolla, the nation's most infamous crime boss. At least the he once was. Signore Copolla was a powerful man with a preposterous reach across the country. Now, the successful old man was a commercial real estate developer and a well-respected business executive. Not only that, Gaspari Copolla had become a renowned philanthropist within Chicago society. He now paid an unspoken debt to society every day he drew breath. Gaspari Copolla was a proud American citizen. And Luca loved him like a father.

~

MCQ'S COMMS IMPLANT BUZZED WHILE SHE WAS MAKING coffee and mentally preparing for another quiet day in her apartment above Harrow's Bar on South Dearborn Street. She tapped her right temple to answer. "Luca! Been a while. Everything okay?" McQ hadn't heard from the hotel impresario for months, not since Ty Leonov's hit man had assassinated his husband. Both Ty and his trigger, Teodor Raspin, ended up dead on the same night, the previous July 5th.

"McQ, my dear! Yes, well, I'm not sure if everything is okay. I have a favor to ask."

Oh, boy. Here we go. "Luca, remember I'm still on leave from CED, a civilian."

"Yes, yes. And that is why I am comfortable asking you for a favor —one civilian to another. And it might involve our mutual friends."

"Well, your help *was* key to solving the Thibodaux case last summer, and you and Greigh seem to be closer than ever."

"When he's in town, of course. He's gone a lot these days. But I actually wasn't referring to Greigh."

McQ wasn't sure where this was going. "Luca, how're you holding up without Vince? I can't imagine."

"I'd rather not...." His voice broke.

"Okay, then. Sorry. How about you just tell me why you called?"

"You remember our mutual friend, Signore Copolla, of course."

Aw, shit. No good deed goes unpunished. She focused on using a voice that sounded matter-of-fact, if not downright cheerful. She was anything but. Not sure what would come next. Copolla was out for himself, but he *had* saved Luca and Greigh's home, The Lit, by acquiring the building and saving it from demolition. "Yeah, sure. What's up?" Poor Luca was in the middle of something—divided loyalties. This could not be good.

"Gaspari is worried about what's happening at Watchtower."

Oh, great. Watchtower, again. When Ty Leonov ran that company, it was little more than a massive front for that Russian immigrant's illegal or almost-illegal commercial real estate activities. And not only in Chicago, but across the country. McQ said, "But with Leonov gone, haven't things settled down over there?"

"Such things are beyond me, my dear. Gaspari knows he's not one of your favorite people, but he needs our help. And he asked for you. He used the word "nefarious" when he referred to what's happening at Watchtower these days. I sensed he was, well, afraid. Not for himself, but for the city. I'm so sorry I can't be any more specific."

"Gaspari Copolla? Afraid?"

"Precisely. Won't you please just call him? Listen to what he has to say? He said he'd pay well. *Off-the-books cash* is the phrase he used. Said he doesn't want to do anything that would perturb your standing with CED."

Here we go, again. But not at all sure how I'll pay next month's rent to Harrow, or *this month's.* "Okay, Luca. I'll call him. But no promises."

He exhaled an audible sigh of relief. She recalled Luca was the son of Copolla's top lieutenant back in the day. Some even said that Copolla and Luca's deceased father, Tony Donati, had a thing for one another at one time. Despite the strict code of ethics against "the fancy lifestyle" in their crime family. On a personal level, the old bird was likable enough—for a once-upon-a-time mobster.

McQ REMAINED CONFLICTED, EVEN AS SHE MADE THE CALL. If Greigh hadn't negotiated a deal to personally benefit Copolla last summer, the old mafioso would have demolished Greigh's home—The Lit. All so he could erect a vast sports complex that he had hijacked from the Russians.

"Detective McQuillan! I so appreciate you calling. You—"

"Just McQ. Sir, I'm only doing this as a favor for Luca. And for Greigh." She had spent her entire career putting guys like him in prison. This fish had always been too big to haul into the boat. She had no idea whether Copolla was still a criminal. Deep down, people didn't change. Not that much. But McQ kept telling herself there could be a greater good, here. Copolla *did* ultimately protect Greigh's and Luca's home. He bought The Lit, dressed it up, and made Luca its proprietor.

"Of course, I understand. McQ, news out of Watchtower is troubling, and not just because they're a competitor. Something, well, downright, ah, un-American is going on. Despite what you may think of me, or at least, my past, Detec— McQ, I love my country. *Our* country. And especially, *our* city."

"What do you mean?" She shivered the way he said that. Not just the halting speech of this otherwise polished and confident business mogul. McQ was a trained and effective interrogator. The old mob boss sounded terrified.

"I'm not sure how to say this. One hears things. Back-channels, if you will."

"You have a spy."

"Mutual acquaintances, McQ. You understand. Ever since Leonov... expired... it's been chaos over there. And that was just fine with me. I made overtures to acquire certain of their assets—"

"You tried to buy them out." Not a question.

"It appeared they were amenable. They had little choice. Ty Leonov was a one-man show. Deplorable, but a firm hand at the helm. There has been a power vacuum since someone removed that smug Slav from our misery. But now, they're making moves all over town—well-orchestrated moves, most of which involve violence and brutality that surprise even me."

"Sir, that sounds criminal, but not un-American, whatever that might mean to you." She made a mental note to pass this info along to her friend, Detective Aidan McKenzie—Mac—at the nine-nine. And did this old mob boss just confirm that Leonov's death wasn't a suicide?

"Members of their board have disappeared. Two, at least, that we know of. And there's a new player that is rumored to make Leonov seem genteel by comparison. Some major foreign player. A woman. Even our mutual acquaintances have closed ranks. She strikes fear into everyone associated with her or the Watchtower organization. We learned several players have been smuggled into the country before our source dried up. And maybe something else. Point of origin was somewhere in Estonia."

"Where?"

"A short drive from Russia, some consider Estonia a gateway between East and West."

Oh, shit. "What else, Signore Copolla?"

"Nothing. Nothing at all. Other than these animals are killing people all over *our city*. I fear the worst is yet to come."

The emotion coming from Copolla's ancient voice box caught in McQ's consciousness, like a sharp chicken bone. The old boy cared about Chicago. He had adopted a philanthropic attitude. Worked with Greigh to get The Lit placed on the National Register of Historic Places. Gave a ton of money to a variety of local charities. Like he was making amends for past sins. But was it all just a front? His emotion seemed genuine—*our city*.

"Okay, then. Sir, this isn't much to go on, but I'll look into it." She heard a deep but raspy sigh. Of relief?

"I thank you, McQ. I know what you must think of me, and there is nothing I can do about that, other than appeal to your sound sense of civic duty. Please work with Rocko Bianchi. You know him from the Thibodaux case last summer. He will provide you with any details in our possession."

Yes, she knew Rocko. A likable mountain of a man who seemed intelligent. Also a huge fan of Aubrey Greigh's mysteries. As Copolla's nationwide businesses grew and had "gone legit" over the past two decades, Rocko played a prominent role. Gerard—Rocko—Bianchi managed all of security nationwide for Copolla's far-flung enterprises called Urban Entertainment, Inc. Rocko's organization comprised an influential division within UE called USS—Urban Security Services. USS had grown into a virtual army of security specialists, most of whom had either elite military training or a law enforcement background: soldiers. *Muscle*. They also employed sophisticated private detectives within their investigations division. And they employed a team of the best attorneys money could buy: USS's legal division.

"Signore Copolla, have Rocko call me. And sir?"

"Yes, Detective?"

"It's just McQ. Full disclosure. If I find out you're using me as a pawn in some corporate power play, or if I encounter criminal activities within your organization, I won't hesitate to—"

"McQ, I would expect nothing less. This is not about business. This is something else. I feel it in my bones. You understand."

"No, sir, I don't. But I will." *Click. Jeez. When it rains, it pours. First Greigh, now this.*

CHAPTER 27

McQ, she started digging into Watchtower on her own before contacting Rocko by leveraging Mac at the nine-nine. This all brought back a flood of memories from the previous summer. The mayhem that surrounded Tihomir, a.k.a. Ty Leonov, CEO of a huge privately held corporation, stirred both fond and horrendous feelings over a complex case—her case—that started with the Thibodaux homicide. She had worked it with Aubrey Greigh. They met and grew close during that case. That madman, Leonov—a billionaire Russian immigrant—had orchestrated a string murders. It took all of McQ's considerable investigative skills, working with Greigh, to uncover the truth, even though they came up short on proof. She almost died investigating that case. If not for Greigh....

It started with a murder down the hall from Greigh's suite on the seventh floor of The Lit. Someone tortured and killed a renowned inaugural poet laureate named Sybil Thibodaux. Greigh didn't know Sybil, but he engaged in that investigation as a favor to a dear friend of Sybil's. McQ learned much from this successful author of mystery novels. Greigh possessed acute investigative skills. She had learned he also freelanced as a part-time Interpol investigator. That explained *so* much. But then, Greigh's dear friend and neighbor, Sango Mori, was killed when she, too, got in the way of Leonov's real estate development plans. Most painful to Luca Donati, though, was the assassination of his husband and business partner, Vince. Leonov was also to blame for that.

Then, both Ty Leonov and his assassin, Teodor Raspin, died on the same night under mysterious circumstances at Watchtower's national headquarters building. The police report said Leonov killed himself by diving off his private suite's twenty-eighth-floor balcony. At the same precise moment, a vagrant shot Raspin down in the street outside that same building. No arrests were ever made. During the months since, Watchtower had vacillated between stagnant and chaotic.

AIDAN MCKENZIE, A.K.A. MAC SAT AT HIS NEW DESK IN THE homicide squad room called the bullpen at CED's ninety-ninth precinct. The nine-nine was on South Dearborn Street. Their jurisdiction included a region of Chicago known as the Near Southwest Loop. This was a misnomer because their house's jurisdiction was bigger than that. One of the largest in the city, they spanned from the lake to Wacker Drive, and from the Chicago River to the north all the way down to Cicero. He wondered whose bright idea *that* was. The nine-nine housed almost a hundred detectives—the busiest house in the city.

Mac wasn't used to this much noise. They brought in a constant chain of suspects for questioning and hauled them off to holding cells, almost always with some boisterous drama involved. Incessant banter overflowed the chest-high dividers between desks that did little to dampen the chaos, even though they were padded with anti-noise surfaces. Or some such shit. Hell, his cruiser and even the streets hadn't been this crazy when he was a patrol officer. He'd been coming in early and staying late. Not because he had a lot to prove as the new kid in Homicide, but because it was a lot quieter during those times.

Memories. Pinned to the acoustic divider at his left shoulder, he stared at a congratulatory selfie he'd snapped of him and McQ at the conclusion of the Thibodaux case. He had assisted her and Aubrey Greigh to solve that homicide last July before he scored his gold shield. He crammed down his affection for that smart-ass red-head. With gorgeous hair too long for a cop, they said, she usually wore it up in a tight pony tail or a twisted knot, somehow. Quite the looker, no matter what. More than that, she was one hell of a cop. Mac had convinced himself he was one of McQ's favorite uniformed officers back then. Even though she and Greigh grew awfully close, she still melted him. He offered to help her from inside the department, as she remained a civilian—an outsider—for the foreseeable future. Nobody had a clue why, though.

They said he had earned a well-deserved promotion to Sergeant Detective a month earlier. At least, *others* thought he deserved it. He wasn't so sure, tried to share in the blame for that poor Mori girl getting killed on an unsanctioned op last August led by McQ, with him following. But she insisted on taking all the heat. He owed her. Mac missed McQ.

Last summer, they had discovered that Ty Leonov, and his attack dog, Teodor Raspin, a.k.a. Rasputin, orchestrated several homicides. They had investigated Leonov—that ruthless Russian thug and immigrant billionaire over at Watchtower. They found no solid courtroom-worthy evidence that tied those two untouchable mooks to the murders. Became a moot point. Both Leonov and Raspin turned up dead. Deserved what they got. The official report said Leonov committed suicide by jumping from his twenty-eighth-floor suite in the Watchtower building. And a vagrant gunned down Raspin right outside that same building—with a precision kill shot from a very exotic weapon that was never recovered, only the slug. A mugging gone to shit, they said. Uh-huh.

Nobody pressed those crapola facts. Other murders—most of them—never got solved, either. With thousands of homicides a year in the city, that still was an unfortunate fact. But with a population of almost forty million in the Chicago regionplex, most thought that wasn't too bad, considering. And when two really bad guys bite it? Tough shit—chew harder. The soft jangling of his comms interrupted his stumble down memory lane.

~

SHE MADE THE CALL. HER FAVORITE BEAT COP, NOW A detective at the nine-nine, answered. "McQ! Hey, *civilian!*"

"Shut up, Mac." She knew Detective McKenzie nurtured a long-standing crush on her. She thought it was cute. Innocent enough to neither encourage nor discourage. "Mac, it's so good to hear your voice, too. And congrats on scoring your gold shield. Well-deserved, my friend." His grunt told her he didn't like her calling him a friend. *It's the real world, kid. Oops, he's my age.*

"Hey McQ, why the hell are you still on leave, anyway? It's been months."

She chose not to answer. She didn't know, either. He continued when an awkward silence needed filling. "Hey, some cases, like that damn Leonov thing, just die of their own weight. Right?"

She'd just smile whenever Mac started flapping his jaws just so he could talk to her. "Listen, Mac, I need your help."

"Name it."

"Don't get in trouble over this, but I need some info on all case files connected to Watchtower personnel." An uneasy silence ensued. A few beats passed.

"That's Leonov's—"

"Um, yeah. Hey, Mac, that whole mess cost me my job—"

"Temporary—"

"Yeah, but I got bills to pay. And my sister's care—"

"How *is* Molly?"

"Mac, without my OT on the job.... Look, I gotta make ends meet. I took on a PI-like gig. Just some consulting. Involves Watchtower."

"McQuillan, what are you getting sucked into?"

"Look, are you gonna help me or not?" That came out a lot sharper than she intended. She could hear his fingernails hammering the top of his new (to him) detective's desk. Then....

"Of course, I'll help, McQ. But I worry about you."

Her voice softened when his did. She said, "Mac, it's no big deal. And it would help. A lot. Watchtower fell into chaos after Leonov died. Now, it would seem some new players are playing rough. A client is curious about what's happening. Says some of the board members disappeared. So, I'm wondering what else is going on over there."

"Okay. Yeah. I'll pull records and send them to your comms. Who's your client?"

"Can't say, Mac. You understand." *Ironic. That's what Copolla kept saying. Mac'd flip if I told him.*

"Uh, yeah, sure. I guess."

"C'mon, Mac. What's almost a decade on the job worth if it can't earn a little trust between friends? Like... best friends?" She couldn't see Mac blush over comms, but knew he was. She only felt a little guilty about playing that card.

"Yeah, McQ. Hey, how about—"

"Gotta run, *Detective*. And congrats, again. Well-deserved. I mean it, Aidan. *Click.*

~

*SHE'S NEVER CALLED ME **AIDAN** BEFORE!* MAC SMILED.

CHAPTER 28

That night, McQ sat in her tiny apartment above the semi-sleazy cop bar called Harrows on Dearborn. She was just a few blocks south of the nine-nine in the shadow of Ida B. Wells Drive. Someone knocked on her door. It was too soon for Greigh. He was still in Copenhagen, or on his way back. She worried. Very few others had any idea where she lived—by design. She had made enemies—more than a few.

"LT, it's me—Mac. Don't shoot. I come bearing gifts."

Her beat-up old Glock G17 hung in her right fist next to her thigh. She padded in her stocking feet the nine paces from her couch to check the door cam's monitor in the short hallway near her door. She'd had the door's peephole removed after one of her vics took a bullet through the eye. She counted off her steps every time. Practiced with her eyes closed. You never knew. Mac was an ear-to-ear smile in the cam's fisheye lens.

McQ thought maybe another cop used to live here… or a gangster. She loved this apartment's security features, including a few she'd had an acquaintance install. He was appreciative of her help on a past case. Monster locking burglar bars guarded the only second-story window large enough for ingress. The brick over concrete block exterior was a hundred years old, but in decent repair, and nobody would punch a hole in it with anything less than a wrecking ball. Her laminated steel entry door in its triple-thick hollow-metal jamb pivoted on *five* steel strap hinges set into the metal and masonry surrounding it. And all that was backed up by a low-tech anti-kick crossbar she had installed that guaranteed a broken foot or shoulder if any mook were stupid enough to try defeating it. *Not on my watch.*

McQ slipped her Glock back into its holster whose belt loop hung on one of the five hooks to her right. She lifted the crossbar from its heavy retaining brackets, also bolted into metal and masonry. Propped it against the wall under her coat hooks. Took both hands and some effort, but the peace of mind was worth it. Twisted the three deadbolt knobs—top, middle, bottom. As heavy as that door was, she kept it well-lubricated. It swung open like buttery velvet.

Mac passed through the threshold into her pint-size fortress. His first time. He glanced back at all the hardware over the top left side of the box he was carrying and said, "Jesus, McQ, expecting an invasion?" She smiled and slapped his shoulder as he sidled past her in the narrow alcove of her two-room studio apartment—more like a large walk-in closet. At least the bathroom had a door. She said, "Always. Stay alive that way."

"Like anybody would be stupid enough." He chuckled as he set the box he carried on the tiny table nestled against the wall under her only window. She kept her opaque curtains drawn. He nodded toward the window while looking at her over his shoulder. "Bars?"

"Yup. Watchtower files?" She nodded toward the box half the size of a filing cabinet drawer. They left the box and wandered five feet to McQ's mini-sofa by way of her dorm room fridge. She grabbed a couple of bottled Bud Lites without asking. She knew he'd look for any excuse to hang out with her. *So cute.*

As they settled onto the sofa, angled toward each other knee-to-knee with McQ's legs tucked under her, he said, "I thought paper would be easier to sift through than digital files, and no trail, other than my signature checking them out. I raided the archives. Weird stuff, McQ. I pulled on some threads—all the open cases related to Watchtower and their employees. Two missing board members. Then, a mugging turned into a homicide - one of their senior managers. Some other strange stuff. Obviously, something's rattling lots of cages over there."

"What do you think, Mac?"

"Smells like a power struggle top down."

"Yeah. Not surprising with Major Dickwad dead."

"But only in the past couple of days, McQ. The six or seven weeks before that since Leonov kicked it, relatively quiet confusion."

McQ scratched her chin. "Huh. Wonder what's changed. Whose cases are these?"

"Most of them on our turf, inside the Loop. New guy drew 'em. Name's Tony Santos. Kinda my partner, off 'n on."

McQ wrinkled her brow. She ruffled her long auburn hair that had gone a little frizzy in the heat-dried interior of her matchbox apartment. She always tied it up on the job. "Santos? Is that the guy Captain Granger brought in to sit at my desk?" It still hurt. And nobody could tell her why she wasn't back on the job. Politics. And her union rep wasn't much help. He was out-gunned. Rumor was Commissioner Roberts feared the court of public opinion. A civilian—a friendly—was killed on one of her unauthorized ops while investigating the Thibodaux case. Hell, *most* ops were spontaneous opportunities. Turned out Ty Leonov, CEO of Watchtower, was dead center of that dirty homicide, and several others. Yeah, Roberts was covering his own ass, was all. If she hadn't felt so bad about getting Greigh's friend killed by that crazed Voodoo kid last July, she'd be more pissed than she was about still being on leave. Some PR bullshit, she was sure. It'd blow over. The commish was a good guy. Finally, she said, "So, is Santos working those missing persons?"

Mac snorted during an aborted sip of his beer. "Nothing to go on.

Even the complainants, family members, clammed up after they filed the initial cases. Both of 'em. Like I said, weird."

McQ scratched her chin. "They're scared."

"Say, what?"

"No ransom demands?"

"Nope."

"Think about it. Someone in your family just disappears. And then, what? You don't bug the cops about progress on your missing loved one? More than weird. Somebody got to them. More than one disappearance at the same time from the same company's leadership? Common denominator is Watchtower, and *two* board members, no less? Plus another? Yeah, somebody's threatening them to back off. New muscle?"

As much as Mac liked spending time with McQ, he had his own mountainous case load to worry about. And this Watchtower stuff? He wasn't sure if she was obsessed, or something else. Finally, as if he couldn't believe what he was saying, he muttered, "Listen, McQ, I appreciate your side-hustle here, but these aren't my cases. I just don't get what's going on, and Granger's working my ass to the bone. I should get going, ya know?"Almost apologetically, he got up to leave. The look of surprise on her face was unmistakable. He felt like shit.

"Mac, you haven't even finished your beer. What's going on?"

"Nothin', LT. Just that, well, you know, you and Greigh."

"What?"

"Nothin'. It's late."

"Mac, you're my friend. So is Greigh. When he's in town."

"Sure thing, LT. Hey, hope this works out. And you call me. Promise?"

"Mac, you're a brand new shield in Homicide. That's a big deal, a lot of responsibility." They both stood at her door. She patted him on the shoulder. "And you can't afford to poach cases, especially from another new guy like this Santos. I get it. Thanks again, Mac."

"For you, LT…." He smirked and play-punched her shoulder. Turned and left.

~

Mac's like a puppy, but with a gun and a badge. Poor guy's so lonely. He must think I'm nuts.

CHAPTER 29

The tickle outboard of her right eyebrow told her she had an incoming call. No ID. Wondered if—hoped—it was Greigh again. She tapped her temple. "Yeah?"

"Hey, Ms. McQuillan, Rocko Bianchi. Remember me?"

She remembered the huge man with the gentle face even though it could have been chiseled out of rock quartz. He was still capable of one of the warmest smiles she'd ever seen. The rest of him looked so rough-hewn. He showed his intelligence by being articulate and insightful. "Rocko. Sure thing. It's just McQ. Last summer's shit storm. Thanks for calling." As much as she hated to admit it, she liked this guy, even though he was a thug. But he was polite and handled himself well. Kept her and Greigh from getting assassinated last summer.

He said, "Listen, the boss says he's asked you to help out with some stuff. Looking into Watchtower, right?"

"Yeah, Rocko. Look, he's just leveraging my contacts inside CED, and that's fine. But he appealed to my sense of *civic duty*."

"McQ, Signore Copolla's heart is in the right place."

"No offense, Rocko. Deep down, I'm a cop. Always will be."

"I get it. And we'll always be gangsters, no matter how many amends we make for past sins. We all make choices, and we live with 'em. Now, how about you tell me how I can help you, Detective?"

Amends? Jeez-Louise. The old Don saved The Lit and gives a ton of cash to charity... oh, what the hell. "It's just—"

"Yeah, just McQ." He chuckled over the comms. "Sorry about your difficulties with the department. That's gotta suck. Back to business. How can I help?"

"Well, first, congrats on your organization. Urban Security Services? Sounds like a big deal."

"Thanks. I'd like to think it's good karma. We've staffed two dozen decent investigators, twice as many attorneys, and a general security staff of over two hundred specialists. Nine locations, coast-to-coast. I'm pretty proud. Sure keeps me busy, and on the move. The boss's business is good, and I got a terrific management team. The biggest branch is here in Chicago, of course. So, I got resources, and Signore Copolla says we're yours for the time being. He must be on the scent of something pretty big. The man's got a good nose. What do you need, McQ? Boss says 'name it.'"

Her eyes widened. Now *she* had resources, but wasn't sure what she thought about it. "Rocko, we don't break any laws."

"Agreed. But we have more freedom than cops. Think more like a PI, McQ. But I suggest you call yourself a *consultant,* so you stay on the right side of history, here."

"Okay. Let's start with what we know. Two Watchtower board members are missing—Maxine Newacher and Randall Cosovich. After filing missing persons' reports, their family members clammed up. They're scared. We need to know why. But even more important than that, why did they go missing? Can your investigators find out what these characters handled, and if they had a beef with the company's direction, or lack thereof? Anything that might help us understand why they disappeared."

"Well, Watchtower is privately held. But the boss has made some overtures, talks to acquire some of their divisions. That gave us some insight into how they're structured, *and* how chaotic things became after Leonov took his swan dive. He wasn't much of a delegator. That chaos is also a source of the boss's concern. Net is that we have some access. What else?"

McQ felt guilty that she had grown giddy. This was heady stuff. "How about surveillance? We need to get a sense of who the current players are, and if there are any new ones on the scene. If we can, compare those names and faces with the old-timers. Not sure what I'm asking here, but we need names and faces. Signore Copolla mentioned his gut said something 'un-American' was going on."

"The boss's gut is almost always dead-nuts on, McQ. Says he can smell treachery like a truffle pig, whatever the hell that means. Must be some old-country thing."

"We could use some recordings of comings and goings, especially of VIPs at their HQ building over on East Monroe. Something covert. How about some cams inside their underground garage? Elevators? That sort of thing. You said your guys are pretty good. And since you're not cops.... Possible?"

"I'll see to it. Anything else?"

Good Lord. What the hell am I doing here? "Let's start with that, Rocko. How about we check back in a couple of days? Do you guys have access to facial recognition software?"

"Sure. But we don't have access to official law enforcement databases to cross-reference against."

"I'll work on that. I have a contact at CED, maybe another at Interpol. Meantime, let's catalog as many faces coming and going as we can and ID the ones we already know. I'd love to study detailed dossiers on Newacher and Cosovich. Gotta be something there. And if your guys hear anything specific about new players, new agendas, new anomalies, that too. Okay, Rocko?"

"Sure thing. This is gonna be fun. And tell Greigh I'm looking forward to his next book."

"That's right, you're a big fan. Truth is, I haven't seen him in a while."

"Oh?"

She thought she'd keep to herself the case files Mac had just delivered.

CHAPTER 30

Captain Lois Granger paced in her glass-walled office at the nine-nine—her precinct house. At least it was glass from the waist up. She looked out across a sea of shoulder-height dividers that honeycombed her enormous homicide squad room in the ninety-ninth precinct. There were days she wished she was still *out there.* A lot less bullshit, working cases. Everyone called her squad room *the bull pen,* although she wasn't sure why. Her best detective only had metaphorical balls, and they were big ones. She missed Detective Lieutenant McQuillan—McQ—and her no-nonsense style. That smart-ass could close more cases than any two of her other *bulls* combined.

The turmoil died down late at night, somewhat, but with so many deadly crimes in the city, even Homicide ran three shifts. Each of her detectives shared a desk across shifts. All houses in the city operated around the clock, not only the nine-nine; although hers claimed to be the busiest. So said the stats, but the politicians didn't seem to get that when it came time to allocating resources. Especially CED Commissioner Jack Roberts, and that surprised her. Before he retired his badge to become a politician—the police commissioner—nobody knew better what serving and protecting *really* meant. Now, for some inexplicable reason, he blocked McQ's return to active duty because of that civilian's death during one of McQ's wild-hair ops last summer.

That tragic event wasn't McQ's fault, but the politicians insisted on a *full inquiry*. Fine. But an inquiry involved *inquiring*. As far as she could tell, nobody was asking shit. First, they said, "Wait for the news cycles to forget." A PR thing. Then, it was, "we need to ensure the department isn't facing any civil suits." And now, Roberts' office wasn't returning her calls. The correspondence said, "other matters are taking priority at the moment." She often thought in acronyms, and one that often came to mind on this matter was *WTF!*

She combed her mid-shoulder-length black hair back with all of her fingers and thumbs whenever she didn't pin it up, a nervous habit. The idea of a decorated seven-year veteran like McQ with a stellar case closure rate being treated like a political pawn pissed her off. Now, as she continued pacing, thinking about how she could best be McQ's advocate, her right eyebrow sang to her. Incoming outside call. Only a handful of people had access, and no civilians. But caller ID announced the name from her contact list. That brought a smile to her face as she tapped her right temple.

"McQ! Look, I—"

"Hi, Captain. Listen, Mac tells me you've been my constant advocate with the politicians. Thank you, really. But that's not why I'm calling."

Oh, oh.... Granger ran her fingers through her hair again. A reflex.

FIDGETING AT HER TINY KITCHEN TABLE, MCQ WONDERED if this might be one of those days that her boss at the nine-nine would strictly follow the book, or whether she'd be more flexible. She was about to ask for a big favor.

"Okay, then. So what's up?" Captain Granger's casual response sounded forced, like maybe this wasn't a flexibility day, but wanted to keep the conversation light and non-committal.

"Captain, I got bills to pay. No telling when I'll be able to come back, so I've taken a side job. Just informal. As a favor to an old acquaintance. He appreciates my help. Seems to think I have skills."

The captain's voice hardened. "McQ, you are not a licensed private investigator."

"No, no. He's hired me as a straight-up consultant. That's all." She hated lying to her boss, but rationalized that's all USS *had* asked her to do—offer specialized advice and counsel.

"Okay. Who hired you?"

"That's not important. But, Captain, he pays well, and I gotta pay for Molly's care. With no OT from the job, I need the money."

"I'm not comfortable with this, McQ—"

"Sir, I'm not asking your permission. I'm asking for a favor. Call it a personal favor if that helps." She didn't mean to sound so abrupt with the boss who she knew was doing everything in her power to get her back on the job—her real job. Just came out that way. Hated herself for it. The silence over the comms was deafening. Then—

"I'm gonna regret asking you this, but what do you need?"

McQ asked her old boss to green-light access to certain law enforcement databases—most all of them. She'd provide surveillance photos to Mac. *He* would then use *his* access to their confidential databases to identify suspects using facial recognition. That was all. Granger agreed after McQ alluded to the possibility of a corporate criminal conspiracy in *their* city.

I WONDER WHAT KIND OF SHIT STORM MCQUILLAN'S DRAWING ME INTO NOW! Captain Granger considered it a gigantic leap of faith giving McQ access to the gamut of criminal databases, from local to federal, even if it was through one of her guys. All her detectives had access. She wasn't really sure why she agreed to this, other than her gut and McQ's conviction. But that crazy redhead closed cases better than any of her guys. If *her* antennae were singing to *her*, something bad was sure to be uncovered. She was that good. *So, why the hell is the commissioner blocking her return to my bullpen, dammit?*

Lois Granger stuck her neck out. Again. One of those days. She dialed the commissioner's office, not to make another attempt to connect with Commissioner Jack Roberts, who was scarce as furry four-legged pets in the city these days. No, she called one of his staffers who used to work in her precinct.

"Nikki! Hey, it's Lois. How's tricks up in the ivory tower?"

"Lois? Gosh, it's been—"

"Nikki, I'll come straight to the point. I suspect you're as busy as I am. It is *so* good to hear your voice. We should do lunch. Meantime, I could use an ear to the ground. Any idea why I can't get my best detective back on the street?"

"Oh, sure, Captain... I mean, Lois. I still think of you as my boss, and your endorsement got me this—"

"No problem, kiddo."

"You're talking about the McQuillan inquiry, right? Look, Lois, everything's clamped down pretty tight around here, but I owe you. Let me sniff around. I'll call you. Soon. Fair enough?"

"Sure. Just that something doesn't sit right about this whole deal."

"Oh, shit! I gotta go, Lois. I'll call. Promise. Stay safe. Bye."

Well, wasn't that a special flavor of weird? Nikki was a good shit. She'd call. But something spooked her. *I wonder what the hell is going on down there?*

THE CAPTAIN TOLD TONY SANTOS HE HAD BIG SHOES TO fill. McQuillan was a legend. But she took chances. That got people killed. He knew what he had to do.

CHAPTER 31

It didn't seem reasonable. McQ resented still being on forced leave from the CED, and still in a quandary why. Now, doubt gnawed at her resolve. Should she return to active duty in CED Homicide once they cleared her? Or should she work with Greigh as a contract Interpol investigator? He had offered, but she wasn't quite ready to take the leap to join him on one of his month-long sabbaticals that sometimes nibbled away at a couple of months. Then, what would she do with the rest of her time? He'd been gone, and now showed up, like he'd never left. Except.... She found out through her friend, Luca Donati—as unlikely as that friendship was—that Greigh showed up back at the Lit over a week ago. *What the heck? And why do I care so much?* She called him.

"Detective—"

"Just McQ."

"Still?"

"Yeah, go figure. So, you're back from Denmark."

"That I am."

Awkward. He sounds sad. Like he brought whatever job back with him. She let her doubt hang on her silence.

"Heads-down writing," he added, as if he needed to say *something.*

"Uh-huh." But there was something else.

"Listen McQ, it is *so* wonderful to hear from you. I was about to call you."

"Uh-huh." She needed to work on her sarcastic repartee.

"I'm serious. I need a consult. If you have the time, that is. Pays well."

She sensed a hint of desperation in his voice. McQ found it hard to believe that this guy's superior investigative skills required much help from her—or anyone. But he did sound different. McQ thought of her sister, Molly, in a private institution that specialized in Bounce addicts. The word *specialized* translated to *frickin' expensive*—for ordinary working folks, anyway. Even though McQ was on *paid* leave, that meant the total absence of all-important overtime pay. Might as well have slapped her with a forty percent pay cut. That was killing her, even though her studio apartment above Harrow's was plenty cheap, and she owed nobody anything, except for back rent. Besides, she had yet to see any cash from her side-hustle with USS. She still waited for word back on the Watchtower surveillance she'd requested from Rocko Bianchi. After a full thirty-second pause, she said, "Well, I'm keeping pretty busy—"

"Shouldn't take more than a few days. Shall we say two thousand? In advance?"

Holy shit! Now, she paced her reply so as not to sound too eager, or desperate. She wondered if this was on Interpol's dime, or from Greigh's own deep pockets. Didn't matter. "I suppose I might clear my calendar for a few days." Smiles weren't visible over audio-only comms, but both knew they each were grinning like Cheshire cats. For different reasons. It was a game Greigh played that McQ tolerated. And he sounded like he needed a grin almost as much as she could use the money. McQ said, "Deal. I wanted to go over something else with you, too, but you first. Waddaya got?"

"Brilliant. I'm working on this homicide that took place in Copenhagen—"

"Denmark? That's not Chicago."

"Someone murdered Peter Fontera, an American movie star, and—"

"That handsome bowtie guy? Jeez, he was a local."

"His latest project for Windy City Productions was his last project —unfinished, obviously. They've written him out, now."

"Not a thing for the Copenhagen police?"

"They're trying—"

"But—"

"But they're still looking into it. I think. Somebody is pulling strings."

"Meaning...."

"Meaning I was a suspect, and—"

"What?"

"Wrong place, right time. They cleared me. Chalking it up to a violent home invasion."

"You're not buying it."

"No *known* motive does not mean *no* motive. Plus, their national police are involved. So is Interpol. Hence, me and my Danish handler, Freya Ecklund."

After a few beats, McQ muttered, "Is she pretty?"

"Freya? Yes, I suppose she is. Older than me, I'd guess. Relevance?"

"None. Just curious."

GREIGH WRINKLED HIS BROW AS HE SAT AT HIS DESK IN the elegant but ancient building that had gone condo a decade earlier. *McQ's jealous? She can't conceive how hard-boiled Freya is, and how wed she is to her job, that one. Let's no one in. Besides, she has at least ten years on me, as much as she tries to hide it. Twenty or more on McQ. Not that it matters what McQ thinks. Much.*

Over the comms, he envisioned his favorite smart-arse rogue cop roosted in her postage-stamp-sized apartment over that cop bar up on Dearborn. She most certainly would not be at the ninety-ninth precinct. Her by-the-book boss, Captain Lois Granger, wouldn't allow her through the doors of her elite homicide squad while McQ was on forced leave, even though she was likely their best investigator. "McQ, someone inside Windy City Productions knows something. I need someone who's local-street-savvy to work with me on this. That's you, Detective."

"Just McQ. And I'm not a fool. You wanna leverage my CED contacts. Seems that's about all I'm good for these days."

He sniggered. She clucked her tongue and issued a noisy sigh of mock disgust. "Oh, you're rubbing it in that I'm still a civilian. Fine. What's our first move?"

"Swing by my apartment. You'll sign a few forms, including an NDA—standard Interpol non-disclosure rot—and we'll be prepared to dance."

"You mean *good to go? Ready to rock?* I thought my clearance would take weeks. Wait. You knew I'd bite. So, you got the forms pre-approved." Not a question. With resignation in her voice, she added, "I'll be there in thirty."

"Minutes?"

"Shut up!" *Click.*

Just-Greigh relished seeing his favorite detective—*Just-McQ*—not that he'd speak such words to her face, although he wasn't sure why. Besides, on a hunch, he chose to only leverage unofficial channels instead of official Interpol weight with CED, Homeland, FBI and the others until the right time. He wasn't sure why he was taking this approach, now investigating murders in their own neighborhood again. Plus, something else. Was it his gut, or fear of getting someone else killed? He worried about McQ, too. But she was one of the most capable women he'd ever met. Yes, she could take care of herself.

CHAPTER 32

Upon McQ's arrival outside Greigh's apartment door, she heard the dulcimer tones of Butler, the voice of Greigh's environmental control system. Emanating from some unseen speaker in a conversational voice that sounded like the actor Sean Connery, not unlike Greigh's own voice but not quite as warm, she heard, "Detective McQuillan, it's been far too long. Greigh is expecting you. But be forewarned. He's in a morose mood."

"Thanks, Butler. I've missed you, too." She didn't bother correcting Greigh's system that she wasn't a detective at the moment. *What would be the point?* Butler announced her arrival as she rounded Greigh's entryway wall. She spotted him at his desk near the ten-foot-high window wall that separated his living room and kitchen great space from the mammoth covered tree-lined balcony she remembered so well. *This place is still knock-down gorgeous. Messier than I remember.*

Head down, he studied his inclined high-res desktop. Without looking up, which surprised her after their prolonged separation, he said, "Now, McQ, please sign these forms. Funds have already been transferred."

She approached and gave the "e-papers" on the left side of his desk-size monitor a cursory once-over. Standard non-disclosure stuff. Looked like they'd also done a deep background check on her. No surprise. She scrawled a few signatures with her finger and plopped down into one of two guest chairs on the far side of his fancy desk. *What the hell is going on? He hasn't even looked me in the eye yet.* "We can talk about it or not."

"About what?"

"About whatever it is you're so busy not talking about."

Greigh smiled, but still had not looked up. "Before we further discuss my little problem, you said you wanted to consult with me on another matter?"

"Yeah. Remember Watchtower?"

GREIGH JERKED HIS HEAD UP. HOW COULD HE FORGET? THE Watchtower CEO, Ty Leonov, had ordered Greigh's wife and daughter executed four years earlier. Leonov and his triggerman, Teodor Raspin, had killed several others, including one of Greigh's landlords here at The Lit, Vince Donati.

After glaring at McQ for several seconds, as if he were seeing her for the very first time, Greigh's expression softened. In a low tone, he said, "McQ, you look as lovely as ever. Let's sit over there." He arose from his desk, wincing at the effort. He wasn't getting any younger, and realized he'd been stationary for hours. Motioned McQ over to the large U-shaped sofa that faced his fireplace. Memories rushed in, unbidden. He pushed them aside and smiled as he walked toward her, rested a gentle hand on the back side of her right shoulder as they walked. He waited for her to be seated. After he lowered himself to sit on her left, he motioned for her to explain with an inviting, up-turned palm.

McQ said, "Okay, first, I'm doing this as a favor to Luca." She referred to their mutual friend and Greigh's landlord with an upward nod and index finger pointing toward the ceiling. Luca lived in the sixteenth-floor penthouse, nine floors above Greigh. Now he was Vince Donati's widower, thanks to the recently deceased Ty Leonov, Watchtower's erstwhile CEO.

Greigh snorted. "For Luca? Or for Gaspari Copolla?"

"Both. But not only for them. Gaspari thinks there's something, well, un-American going on over at Watchtower. His words, Greigh. My gut tells me that old man has uncanny instincts. I'm inclined to go with it. For now."

He feared old emotions would erupt. But he stuffed them. Said, "What do *you* know?"

"Not much yet. You remember your fanboy, Rocko Bianchi?"

Greigh smiled. *That big lug loves my mysteries.* "Of course."

"Well, I'm working with him. He's now not only Gaspari's top guy at Urban Entertainment, he runs a large division for UE called Urban Security Services, or USS. Has P.I.s, lawyers, and lots of muscle—a private security force. The old man put them all at my disposal. Can you believe that?" She obviously meant to chuckle, but it came out as a very unfeminine snort.

"Careful, McQ. You're getting sucked in."

"Rocko's guys are surveilling Watchtower for me. I'm expecting some intel back from them in a day or two. Not sure how much I can trust what they find, especially since Watchtower is, or was, UE's competition."

"I'll ask again. What do you *know*? Right *now*?"

"There's some kind of top-down power play going on at Watchtower. Up 'til last week, the place was in chaos without Leonov at the helm." Greigh winced at the mention of that sleazy monster's name. McQ silently acknowledged his expression and continued. "Gaspari tried to acquire some of their assets. Looked like those talks were moving forward. Then the talks stopped and Gaspari's source or sources inside clammed up. New players have come on the scene with their own muscle. Rumor has it they entered the country illegally from Eastern Europe. Nobody outside Watchtower knows who. Two board members just disappeared. Watchtower now seems more organized, has grown more violent on the streets, and they've closed ranks."

Greigh listened. Scratched his closely cropped beard. Swung his gaze from the dark fireplace to look at McQ. Playing devil's advocate, he said, "Could be they just purged some deadwood and imported leadership talent as they look to reorganize. Sounds like they needed that, given their nature and circumstances."

"I don't think so. My cop's gut agrees with Gaspari. Right after those two board members disappeared, their families filed missing persons' reports. These two top-echelon Watchtower employees *disappeared,* Greigh. *At the same time.* But within twenty-four hours after filing, *both families retracted their reports.* Here's the thing. Those two board members are still missing, and the families are too scared to even admit that."

Greigh's eyes widened. "And up pop's the devil. Somebody intimidated them to keep their gobs shut. Likely these new players to whom you allude. Yes, that wrinkles the silk, alright. What else?"

"That's it until Rocko's guys get some faces on-camera. Captain Granger has agreed to give me access to law enforcement databases through Mac for facial recognition comparisons to anyone in the system. You remember Mac, of course. He's now a detective."

"Yes, Mac. He was with us when my friend—" Both of them fell silent. Then....

"Greigh, I live with Sango's death every day—"

"McQ," he reached over and covered her left hand resting on her thigh with his right, "that was not your fault, despite what the top-knot wankers at CED might be spewing. Sango charged into the breech. That's who she was. She would have done so whether you, me and Mac had been there or not."

"Yeah, Greigh. It's just that—"

"People seem to die around us, McQ."

Another snort. More of a chuff. This time, one of derision. "Oh, shut the hell up, Greigh. We put ourselves in harm's way. So do others. We *both* need to cowboy up—"

Greigh couldn't help but half-grin despite their increasingly morose mood. *"Cowboy up?"*

She rolled her eyes and full-on smirked. "Okay, where did *that* came from? Dunno." They chuckled. Not quite gallows humor, but close. They'd both lost people. McQ paused before offering her next bit of news. "Greigh, did I mention that Mac and his new partner are assigned to the Windy City shootings?"

Greigh once again jerked his gaze toward McQ. "Is that so! Are they consulting with you?"

"Not yet. A matter of time. Let me guess. You're curious what they have."

"One of those five victims was a friend of mine, Q. I met him in Copenhagen. He was helping me with my murder case over there. At that time, the only victim was Peter Fontera."

"Wait, that bowtie guy? Jeez, Greigh. Is there any kind of trouble you don't get in the middle of?"

He chose not to mention the smuggling kind of trouble he also investigated. Not yet. "His name was Todd Bricker. Only twenty-three, Q. A young man with a bright future. I had also interviewed the star that was to replace Peter. Another victim, now—Stacy Michaels."

"I'm sorry, Greigh. I'll see what I can find out."

"I believe I'm chasing some leads that might overlap with CED's investigation. I don't want to step on any toes, but do you think Rocko's guys might inquire into Lance Bowman, Windy City's general manager? My gut is whispering to me he might be breast-feeding on his own company."

"You mean he's *milking Windy City?*"

Greigh just smiled. She swung toward him and gasped before she grinned and said, "Oh, shut up!"

"Plus, this guy has invested a king's ransom in security. So, how could a hit man or hit *team* slip onto his lot, assassinate five people, and escape without leaving a trace? I noticed the mercenaries standing at the gate keep logs of comings and goings. Might be something there if Rocko's assets have that kind of access."

"Can't hurt to ask. *Now* who's getting sucked in? Why not use Interpol for this stuff?"

"Just my gut, McQ"

"Nuff said." They grinned and knuckle-bumped.

CHAPTER 33

Lance Bowman screamed at Captain Granger over comms. "What do you mean you're pursuing leads? What does that even *mean*? Two of my stars are dead, one of those on your watch, Captain!"

She stood behind her desk at the nine-nine, squinting at the ceiling. "Sir, I assure you—"

"You *assure* me?" *Click*.

~

TWILIGHT CAME AND WENT, LEAVING HARRISON STREET IN front of The Lit—Greigh's home—cloaked in darkness. His instincts told him he was being watched, as if eyes peered at him through some unseen window. As a ten-year veteran of the city, he knew better than to be caught out after dark. But he couldn't resist a twilight visit to the food truck that parked near the entrance to Pettibone Park, just a block west on Harrison and a block north on State. He was returning from Mako's after overdosing on one of his superb Italian Ices.

Now, certain he was being followed, he quickened his pace to reach the safety of The Lit. But the telltale sound of accelerating footsteps behind him grew louder. A hand grabbed his shoulder. He spun around. Two men dressed in dark suits identified themselves. One flashed Interpol credentials, but no words. None needed. The other somber young man wore a small lapel pin bearing a white cross on a field of red with a narrow gold border—Danish Defense Intelligence Service. But Greigh pretended not to notice it.

With no further explanation, they each grabbed hold of an arm and led him into a black van waiting at the curb on the corner of Harrison and State. Only a block from home. He did not resist. The Interpol agent then explained to Greigh they needed his help to infiltrate a mysterious arms dealer's network. He would be bait to capture Fontera's killer—one who possessed information of international significance concerning weapon smuggling operations and potential terrorist attacks planned for multiple Chicago-area targets.

"*What?* Is that what we fear is being smuggled into the country? Into *Chicago?* Why isn't this coming through my handler, Freya Ecklund? And are domestic agencies in the loop?"

"Mr. Greigh, there may be a problem."

"With what? With Freya? Other agencies? You blokes must give me *something*. What sort of problem?"

"We are not at liberty to say. And we would ask that you refrain from mentioning this meeting."

"*Meeting?* More like a kidnapping."

Greigh reluctantly consented and agreed to cooperate with these new players from Interpol and DDIS. He wasn't at all sure about the nature of that cooperation, or what he had just committed to. He just wanted out of that van. The taller one handed him a card with a number on one side and nothing else. He tucked it into his jacket pocket.

Confused, but with grim satisfaction that his uneasy gut had not misled him, Greigh stepped back out of the van. He now had confirmation of the connection between at least one of "his" murders and his smuggling case—a *weapons* smuggling operation. The van crept away from the curb, and from him. Seemed his fate was now being sealed by even more strangers. It could be worse. At least, he still drew breath.

CHAPTER 34

Elijah Sooner never shied away from his image as an experienced dumpster diver. On the contrary, he excelled at what he called *living off the land* in one of Chicago's most brutal neighborhoods. He was damn proud of it, too. That's how he discovered his *little angel* with curly dark red locks and a creamy complexion wrapped in an oily blanket. On the spot, he named her Amanda Tennyson Sooner.

A month earlier, he'd come across a ragged volume, a beautiful little book in yet another K-town alley. Elijah loved to read—not that he could read all that well, but proud of what he was able. He loved the cover of that book called *The Lady of Shalott,* written by some old-time white dude named Alfred Lord Tennyson. Lord? He liked that, too. The picture on the fancy book's cover featured a young lily-white beauty with red hair.

He snuck his little red-headed bundle home to Tamra, the hard-working girl he'd called his wife for the last four years, though no preacher ever made it legal. Besides, this Tennyson dude looked to be some sort of poet, and *Amanda* sort of rhymed with *Tamra*. Tam liked that. They'd tried to have kids, but either he shot blanks, or the good

Lord plugged Tam's plumbing. Either way, Elijah figured Heaven sent this little bundle to them in that oily rag of a blanket. And sure enough, Tam had fallen in love with little Amanda on the spot. They raised her like their own. Said they had adopted her. Nobody in K-town cared.

AMANDA TENNYSON SOONER GREW UP AS WHAT SOME white folks might call dirt poor, but she didn't resent it. At all. Besides, she didn't know any different. Though her skin was the color of milk and honey, she loved her black parents more than life itself. More than she would say about the stranger who fertilized the egg carried by another stranger for eight or nine months. And then they dumped her newborn ass in a dumpster in an alley somewhere off Pulaski Road in West Garfield Park. In one of the highest crime areas in Chicago. Known for misdemeanors, felonies, homicides, suicides, drug drops, the works. But that's where a couple of saints had rescued her.

Mandy Sooner called herself MT. Kept the beatings to a minimum. She only begrudged her parents her stupid name. So, she transformed it into a badge of courage. Called herself MT Sooner and dared *anybody* to fuck with her. Nobody did. Not more than once, anyway. Not that MT was all that strong. More like a female Harry Potter. She'd seen that name with a magical pic on some white kid's t-shirt. But *her superpower?* She oozed with a lightning-fast hyper-kinetic intellect. And her powers of observation enabled her to read anyone's body language, including subtle micro-expressions. Sometimes she almost felt like a mind reader. Plus, thanks to mentorship from Elijah and his ex-combat buddy, Hamm, her street smarts and hand-to-hand skills, especially her ground fighting capabilities, were unparalleled.

ELIJAH'S POOR READING SKILLS EMBARRASSED HIM. SO HE ensured his little angel not only learned to read, but grew to love learning. MT became a sponge. He'd bring home books from dubious sources and made sure she always had a CTA bus pass when she got old enough. Ensured she could spend as much time as she wanted at the Legler branch of the Chicago Public Library. Thanks to Elijah, MT learned to adore reading anything and everything. Yeah, nobody messed with his MT. She was tough *and* smart.

AT TWENTY-FIVE, MT WAS ON HER OWN. HER PARENTS WERE gone, but she still lived in the same apartment in the same abandoned building where she'd grown up. It had been two years since those assholes had tried to rob Elijah in his own home. Big mistake. Just for fun, they'd killed their beloved Miss Tamra before he'd taken care of business, and before he bled out, himself. She'd hidden in her bedroom behind a wall panel hidden by her bed. Elijah had made her promise. She kept her promise, and hated herself for it ever since.

In K-town, which was the nickname for the West Garfield Park neighborhood, where a lot of streets started with the letter K, neighbors helped neighbors. The Sooners were squatters, like many of their neighbors. So, they dragged her parents' bodies out into the street and down the block so poor Amanda wouldn't get put out on the street. Amanda understood and helped. Another reason to seek justice for those unable to do so for themselves. The cops didn't investigate, as expected, so the coroner just hauled the bodies away. End of story. But not for Amanda, a.k.a. MT. She acknowledged it was a cruel world. So be it.

Her parents had made sure she didn't run with any gangs. Elijah was a loving father, but many feared and respected him. She only suspected. Not long before his death, he had hooked MT up with the hottest P.I. in K-town, a street-savvy investigator named Hamm Dexter. He taught her all about the gray areas of the law, surveillance and interrogation methods, not to mention how to drive a damn car.

Even helped her get her licenses—driver's *and* P.I. Hamm was like a second father.

He was a likable guy, but possessed a granite-hard edge just beneath the surface. Like Elijah. Both black mountains with snow on their peaks. Hamm could be jagged, too. The man knew everybody. Used his connections inside the Loop to help MT snag her P.I. license once she was of age. He even helped her study and practice. Yeah, Elijah was a sometime saint, and Hamm was everything Elijah wasn't. The gods of the ghetto blessed MT with both a saint and a guardian angel watching her back.

Hamm said, "Hey, girl. You're ready. Got a gig for ya."

"Yeah, old man? Does this one pay? Gotta eat."

"No, kid, you don't get it. This is an honest-to-the-good-Lord job. Ever heard of USS?"

"Urban Security? Hell, yeah. Rocko Bianchi's crew, right? No shit?"

"They're staffing. And I got you an interview. Don't fuck it up, kid."

"Yeah, no, I got this. Thanks, Hamm. I owe you huge."

"Just don't forget that when you make the big time, kid. This'll be yours to lose."

Hamm told her this two days before some street punk shot him dead for his wallet and thirty-two bucks. Just west of Garfield-fuckin' Park. She made damn-sure she got the job. *Thanks, old man, wherever you are.*

THAT WAS TWO YEARS AGO. SHE'D BEEN WORKING FOR USS since and making a name for herself. She'd learned that one job well done led to another, and got her a little closer to the man himself. Everybody who was anybody in the biz knew Rocko B. And now, she was working covert surveillance on a major outfit called Watchtower on East Monroe—inside the damn loop. MT had arrived. She'd been on the gig for two whole days. She could slide into and out of any scene without making one. Like she wore Harry Potter's cloak of invisibility. She smiled at the thought. And guessed it was about time to color her hair again, too. Everybody remembered a redhead, but black hair, or nearly so? Not so much.

Someone told her years earlier that she looked like a female version of young Harry Potter, so she had read all the books, and amped that angle. Even died her hair, wore the glasses and the 'do. Found it to be both inspiring and useful. Yeah, she was fuckin' magic, alright. And now, the man himself was personally calling for an update. A first. "Hey, Mr. B."

"Hey, kid. It's just Rocko, okay? Listen, get what you got to the client. She's getting antsy."

"An ex-cop, yeah? Wow! You got it, Mr.— Rocko. We got some good stuff, I think. And thanks. This feels like a biggy."

"You're sharp. And you got potential. What am I going to say next?"

"Um, don't fuck it up. Exceed the client's expectations. Always. And never leave a trail. Right?" She grinned over the comms. That was it, alright.

"Like I said, kid… sharp. Did I ever tell ya I worked with your old man back in the day? He was something else. The unofficial godfather of K-town. Good people. And your buddy, Hamm? Good people, too. None better."

At the mention of her poppa and the old gumshoe, the otherwise talkative MT fell silent, choked down the lump rising in her throat. "And I hid in a wall like a coward while those two assholes killed poppa and momma. And they never fingered the punk who did Hamm."

"Kid, if you don't hear nothin' else from me, you listen to this. Your pops knew exactly what he was doing—keeping you alive. He gave as good as he got. And Hamm? He died proud after a helluva life people will talk about for a good long while. *That's* what you take away. The rest is just self-indulgent chickenshit. Got it, soldier?"

"Um," sniffle, "Yes, sir."

"Good. Now, get your scrawny ass to work."

She could sense his grin over the comms, and could almost feel his virtual pat on her shoulder. Good people, Mr B. *Yeah, Rocko.*

CHAPTER 35

~

Mid-morning had come and gone. McQ glanced, again, at her kitchen sink piled high with dirty dishes. Never enough to depress her, though. She worried about Greigh. Interpol had embroiled him in so much more than a casual investigation this time. This was no favor of discretion for a rich well-connected acquaintance. This was down-and-ugly blood-in-the-mud kinda shit. More her style. Chicago style.

It seemed he now carried the weight of two continents on his shoulders, with a half-dozen homicides stretching from Copenhagen to Chicago. And all six murders—so far—were Windy City studio employees. She got the impression that Greigh felt somehow responsible. As a seasoned detective, she knew empathizing with homicide victims only victimized the investigator. McQ didn't think Greigh had yet learned that brutal lesson. Incoming comms. "Hello?"

"Hi, Chance McQuillan?"

Uh-oh. Blocked number. Bill collector or telemarketer? "Who's asking?"

The youthful voice chirped, "Yup, answered like a cop, alright. Or an ex-cop, at least."

"You wanna play that game, or level with me? Who the fuck is this? And why do you block your caller ID? You got five seconds starting… now."

"Wait. Sorry. My name is MT Sooner, and—"

"Sure it is. What's your game, whoever you are? Three seconds…."

"No, really. I work for Rocko Bianchi. Says everyone calls you McQ. My name is Amanda. Mandy. Nobody calls me that. I'm your surveillance asset at Watchtower. Okay?"

Ten seconds of silence later, McQ said, "Fine. You a P.I.?"

"Yup. And you're the client. Apparently, a pretty fuckin' important one. So, we good?"

McQ sounded embarrassed. "Sure. Listen—"

"Hey, no need to apologize—"

"I wasn't going to apologize. I was going to suggest we get together. Off comms."

"Oh. Yeah, good idea. When and where?"

"We have a common interest with a friend of mine who's investigating some murders."

"*Some?* A cop?"

"A writer. Name's Aubrey Greigh. Sort of covert. He'll want to hear this, too."

"A *writer*, huh? Okaaay, you're the client. So, when and where? Wait, the famous mystery writer? Holy—"

"Hotel Lit on Harrison. Apartment 7D. Can you be there in thirty?"

"Minutes?" Snort.

Oh, not you, too? You and Greigh are gonna get along just fine. "Yeah, minutes. What's your name again, Not Amanda? The other one?"

"MT. They call me MT. Last name, Sooner. I shit you not. I picked MT. I did not pick Sooner." *Click.*

This should be interesting.

~

An hour later, Greigh still paced on his balcony, seeking inspiration. The crisp autumn air helped him focus. The weather this time of year in Chicago could be a wild card. He called Mac at the nine-nine. After congratulating him on his promotion to detective, Greigh asked him about the Windy City shootings.

"Greigh, it is so good to hear from you. Look, you know I can't discuss an active investigation."

"I get it, Mac. But as a professional courtesy to another law enforcement official—"

"Yeah, McQ said you were working with Interpol as a *civilian* contractor, right?"

"So, how do you propose I investigate my smuggling and homicide cases without local law enforcement cooperation? Without access to the progress your department is making? I have a homicide in Copenhagen—"

"Denmark?"

"Indeed."

"Out of our jurisdiction."

"Mac, that is precisely Interpol's role, as *International* Police. I'm here to help, but I can't do that if I'm blind. Yes, I'm a civilian, but also a duly authorized Interpol investigator. That's how it works. I will also tell you I interviewed one of your local victims in Denmark, when he was still alive, and I think we can help each other. Now, do you want to delay *our* investigation by getting Captain Granger involved? I've already checked in with her. Or shall we cut to the chase, my friend?"

Greigh's tone had grown more strident than he had intended. Mac's silence worried him, so he pressed on. "Listen, Mac. What say I give you what I've learned about one of your victims *before* they killed him? Might go to motive in your case. Then, you decide how much to share. But I warn you, your case is about to change direction. Fair enough?"

"Well, okay. Jeez, I forgot how persuasive you can be, dude. I need some air. You okay if we have this discussion at your place?"

"I'd be honored, Detective. You may recall I reside at The Lit on Harrison, 7D."

"How could I forget after last summer? I need to bring my partner, Tony Santos."

"The more the merrier. See you in thirty."

"Minutes?" *Click.*

Greigh had barely hung up from his chat with Mac than he received another call. "Hello, McQ. I was about to call you. Mac's coming over."

"Um, okay," he had caught her off guard, "so am I, with one of my assets."

"One of your *assets?* Oh, it slipped my mind that you're flirting with flames. Again. To what do I owe the pleasure?" He didn't mean to sound snippy with McQ. Wasn't sure why he did.

"No need to be snotty, Greigh. My *asset,* a bonafide private eye who works for Rocko, has been surveilling Watchtower. I thought you might want to hear what she has to say firsthand. Was I wrong?"

More than a brief pause later, "Fair play, McQ. Sorry. I'm accustomed to writing about death and murder, less used to the real thing. I truly am sorry. Of course, I'd be pleased to meet with you and your gumshoe."

It was McQ's turn to express attitude. "Good, because she's on her way. Should be there less than thirty. Minutes. Name is MT Sooner, and no, that is not a joke. Talk soon." *Click.*

Twenty minutes later, Greigh's guests began arriving. McQ's P.I. got there first. She was not at all what he expected. She looked like a child. Maybe five-foot-four, skinny, short black hair, t-shirt, jeans, black round wire-rimmed spectacles, ankle-high black and white sneakers with an equipment duffel slung over her right shoulder.

"Aubrey Greigh?" She looked up at him with wide eyes and an award-winning smile, eager to please. He stood almost a foot taller.

"Just Greigh. You must be MT."

She didn't answer. Shoved past him. Her bag banged into his right hip as she charged to his right, her left, around the end of his entry wall into the living room. Greigh could hear her set her bag down as he closed the door and followed her in. Moments later, Butler announced McQ's arrival. The door unlocked and McQ rounded the entry wall into the living room on Greigh's heels. She scanned the room, as always, and spotted the young P.I. With her hand extended, she said, "Hi. MT? I'm McQ, your client." She pasted on a smile, but it didn't reach her eyes. She didn't yet know this girl. That was obvious to Greigh.

MT said, "Right. I have data for you. What should I do with it?" She unzipped her duffel and extracted a sizable tablet. "I wasn't planning for a large-scale show 'n tell." MT looked up at Greigh and offered a small smile. "Got someplace I can set this up?"

Greigh looked puzzled. "Can't you mirror it to my wall monitor?"

MT took on a condescending expression while shaking her head. "I will *not* expose this to *any* unknown network. This stays on my device until my client sees and evaluates it. No offense, Greigh, but you are *not* the client." She looked to McQ for help.

McQ said, "Greigh, can she set up her tablet on your desk? I'll want Mac and his partner to see this, too. They should be here any minute. MT, heads up, our mutual friend," she made a small motion that encompassed her and Greigh in her gesture, "is a cop. Not sure why that should concern you. Rocko assured me that we—and by extension, you—would not be breaking any laws. Are we okay there? MT?"

The girl grew more than a little jittery. "Yeah, sure, just surveillance of a public space, although that space in the lower level of the Watchtower building, a *privately* held corporation, might suggest a gray area. Um, you'll want to set that expectation with your friend. And remember, McQ, as far as your friend is concerned, I work for *you*, not for Rocko. S'just that where I come from, cops are not people you trust. Capiche?"

Some non-verbals passed between McQ and Greigh. Both nodded. McQ said, "Okay, MT. Let's get you set up."

"Yeah, fine. Jeez, I hate surprises. Okay, then, I have feeds from four non-networked cams I just retrieved." She set her small button-sized devices on Greigh's desk next to her tablet, along with a thin connecting wire. "I haven't merged this stuff onto a single device as Rocko said to get with you ASAFP. So, I'll connect each device to my tablet, in turn. We'll watch the raw data as I transfer it. Think of this as a solid chain-of-custody protocol. Once you have all the feeds, I provide you with the tablet, and you do with it what you will. Acceptable?"

McQ nodded once more toward Greigh. His eyebrows ascended toward his forehead as he bobbed his head to the right, meaning, *Whatever. You're the client, McQ*. She said, "That'd be just fine, MT. Very professional." McQ got a distracted expression back from the young gumshoe, as if to say, *What were you expecting? Amateur hour?*

A voice floated down from the ceiling. "Detective McKenzie and another gentleman have arrived. Shall I admit them?" The voice startled MT. McQ smiled. She offered MT a tiny sideways head-shake and a single wrinkled brow of smirking assurance.

Greigh said, "No, Butler, I'll greet them." His six-foot-two frame made short work of reaching the front door around the entryway wall. He swung wide-open one of the double doors."Mac, my friend! Good of you to come." They shook hands like old brothers-in-arms. They, along with McQ, had risked their lives together the previous summer.

"Greigh, this is Tony Santos. A new detective to the nine-nine."

Greigh met the new guy's eyes. He wasn't sure of this player, but smiled and extended his hand after releasing Mac's. "Detective, I'm Greigh."

"Yes, I gathered. Pleasure."

"Please, come in, gentlemen." As they entered the living room, Greigh said, "MT, this is our friend Mac and his partner, Tony. Both gentlemen are detectives from CED's ninety-ninth precinct, also where McQ here works.

Santos said, "Worked. Past tense." He never met McQ's eyes, but cast an admiring eye around Greigh's apartment. Greigh felt like the man was casing the joint, as the Yanks say. Both McQ and Greigh let the comment pass. They were here to conduct actual business, not political bullshit. McQ introduced MT as her colleague, saw both Mac's and Santos's eyebrows elevate. But they said nothing. Tension in the room had grown palpable. MT sensed it too, but pressed forward. She'd seen it before.

MT SAID, "I HAVE SOME VIDEO THAT McQ HAS ASKED ME TO show you. This is nothing more and nothing less than comings and goings in the public garage spaces beneath the Watchtower building on East Monroe. Mac and Santos glanced at each other once more, but remained silent. MT connected the first of the four miniature cams to her propped-up one-foot-by-two-foot tablet on Greigh's desk. It lit up. A live video feed appeared on the screen as it copied the cam's contents to the tablet's memory, like MT had explained, only tenfold faster than real-time. Nothing much of interest. Parked cars. Then, someone passed through the cam's field of view. And once more, nothing. MT scrubbed the video faster-forward until someone else appeared. She slowed to real-time. She repeated this tedious process until the cam had nothing more to offer.

The second cam wasn't much more productive, but several faces were clear enough for facial recognition software to work with. She captured each passing face in a still image and added it as a sidecar file to the large tablet's memory before allowing the recording to fly forward again at 10X. The third cam revealed more cars moving with no faces visible. Toward the end, however, they made out five somewhat indistinct faces at a bad angle exiting a limousine, one of whom Greigh recognized. His world was about to change. The final cam confirmed this earth-shattering fact. MT had trained it on the entrance to the underground garage's elevator. Once more, he saw the face he recognized. A woman appeared to be surrounded by four huge military types. She was obviously a VIP. But that wasn't possible. The woman was Freya Ecklund, his Interpol handler.

Freya looked different, somehow. Her clothes were not those of an underpaid and sloppy, but dedicated mid-level Interpol agent. She looked elegant, sophisticated. And her features were far harsher than he remembered from just a few days earlier in Copenhagen. *What the shite is going on here?*

CHAPTER 36

~

The morning wore on. Greigh asked MT to go through the video, frame by frame. The others questioned what he was seeing. He ignored them all, only speaking terse directions to MT, asking her to freeze the same series of frames repeatedly. He saw something, but wasn't sharing. The others grew fidgety. After ten minutes of this tedium, McQ said, "For crying out loud, Greigh, *what is it?*" Mac just waited. Santos grew more pissed by the minute.

Greigh couldn't fathom why these people in the video treated his Interpol handler, Freya, like a Watchtower VIP. He said nothing at that moment. But McQ turned to him and repeated in a softer tone, "C'mon, Greigh, what is it? You're white as a sheet." He tried to cover. Mac and Santos? They looked like they were about to leave, but wouldn't do so without some answers.

As a diversion, he blurted, "Do any of you recognize those faces?" He pointed to the four men and one woman entering the elevator. They had almost looked directly into the near-invisible cam that MT had placed above the elevator door forty-eight hours earlier. MT captured each person in a still image, added each as a separate sidecar file. Her grin at hitting pay dirt turned into a look of concern as she, too, grew impatient at Greigh's radical reaction. She said, "If those aren't clear enough images for facial recognition, dunno what is. Now I just need something to compare 'em to."

Santos muttered, "Gotta be four bodyguards and a big-time VIP, that woman. Quite a looker for her age."

McQ nodded at Santos and spun toward Mac. She caught him staring at her with affection and rewarded him with a coy smile. "Okay, Mac. Your turn. I suggest we compare these probe images with both domestic and international law enforcement mugshot databases, and liaise with the FBI for their *NextGenID* and *FACE* repositories."

Santos said, "Whoa. You're not suggesting we use official law enforcement resources to aid these *civilians*."

Still looking at McQ, Mac spoke to Santos. "It's okay, Tony. The captain gave this a green light."

Still flustered, Greigh said, "And I'll see about accessing the equivalent Interpol repositories."

Santos swung his gaze toward Greigh, but didn't say another word. Closed his eyes, dropped his chin, and shook his head in disgust.

MT said, "Would it—"

McQ couldn't resist. With thinly disguised contempt in response to Santos's body language, she blurted, "So why is that a problem for *you*, Detective?"

MT tried again. "Folks, this—"

Santos fired back at McQ. "This doesn't have a damn thing to do with our homicide case. And you, McQuillan, this is the kind of cowboy crap that got you fired—"

"Administrative leave, asshole. Further—"

"Will you *children* just shut the fuck up for *one second?* I already dug up some other stuff you need to see. *Okay?*"

McQ wheeled her glare from Santos to MT and softened her hardened expression. "Sorry, kiddo. Waddaya got?"

MT started softly, but her voice built with excitement. "I can't believe I just told a client to shut the fuck up. Sorry, McQ. Listen, as a mere *civilian*," she glared at the pompous Detective Santos, "I may not have access to all your fancy image repositories, background and criminal records databases, but I *can* search for anything in the public domain that wiggles my antennas. For example, I punched in on that big guard's wrist on the woman's left. I re-pixelated that with my interpolation software. You see that big silver watch with the teal-green face, and those red and black dots on a rotating bezel? I can do *watch* recognition all by my little old *civilian* self."

Now her whole body vibrated with excitement. MT grinned big. "Know what that is on that monster's wrist? That's a Russian-made Vostok Amphibian. My favorite search engine tells me not only that this garish timepiece was made in Russia, but it is a brand popular with their Naval Spetsnaz unit. Almost exclusively. They're like our American Navy Seals special ops, guys. Very scary characters. And they're under the operational control of the Russian Main Intelligence Directorate. That's the frickin' GRU! I've read about these guys. By the cut of that hulk, where he's at, and what his job seems to be, I think that could spell at least three likely possibilities: mercenary, spy, or Russian soldier on American soil. I wonder if he and these other goons are even in the country legally? So, is *any* of this stuff of interest to you guys?"

Everyone in the room turned to this mere child who was a great deal sharper than anyone had given her credit. She held up her tablet with two hands, now showing them all a photo of the watch and the description to support what she had just cited. Greigh suddenly looked like his namesake: gray. More than before. He thought he would be ill. *What in bloody hell is Freya doing with these people? Is she undercover?*

Mac said, "Tony, we don't know if we can connect any of this intel to our case or not, but I've worked with McQ and Greigh before. They're credible. And I *do* have Captain Granger's permission to use any and all databases—for lead identification purposes only." Mac swiveled a gentle and apologetic look toward the young lady, who looked like a hungry street waif. "MT, is it? Can you give me access to your still images on my secure device?"

"Sure, if it's okay with McQ. It's 1024-bit encrypted. I have standards, too. But it's up to my client."

She looked at McQ who said, "Do it. Something really stinks here. Leonov was Russian, but none of the other high-level players at Watchtower are. This is something new." MT picked up her oversized tablet. She asked Mac for his destination address and encryption key. Swiped it in, and Mac's tablet *dinged*—notification of an air drop. He accepted. He carried his device over to Greigh's sofa. Sat down and accessed the elevator images MT had highlighted and enhanced before sending them over, not that they needed much enhancing. He slid them into his *FaceFirst* app's window, punched in a few commands, and waited. Laid the device next to him, expecting to wait. But no sooner had he set it down than... *Ding*. Mac picked it up again, looked down at the screen. They all stood nearby when his eyes grew round and wrinkled his nose, baring his upper teeth in the process. He said, "Holy shit! You know who that woman is? She's in the FBI's NGI *Next Generation Identification*—mugshot repository as a *noteworthy foreign dignitary*. CED has a reciprocal agreement with the Feds."

Greigh was about to come clean. He would admit that the woman was his Interpol handler, the Danish National, Freya Ecklund. The same woman who drove around Copenhagen in a shitty old Volvo wagon littered with fast-food wrappers and crushed paper soda cups. The woman he'd worked with for years. But a *noteworthy foreign dignitary?* He sensed he shouldn't be divulging this dirty laundry to the CED. Especially to this Santos character. Before he could utter a syllable, however, Mac shouted, "Oh, *shit*. That's Mika Kuzmin, President of *Obelisk Prime*, one of Europe's largest import/export enterprises! A big-ass Russian company!"

At first, Greigh thought Mac had screwed up with his little tablet. But when he held the device up for McQ and the others to see, the photo of this Mika Kuzmin was a dead ringer for Freya. *His* Freya! *No!* ***This is Hell's bloody bells madness!***

~

McQ SAID, "NO, WAIT. THIS MAKES PERFECT SENSE." HER eyes darted around to connect first with Greigh, who looked like he was about to faint, then at Mac and MT before continuing. "This all started because there was a rumor that Watchtower was in total chaos after the death of their CEO, Tihomir Leonov, a Russian immigrant. He *was* the only Russian in Watchtower's upper echelon, other than his personal triggerman, before both died early in July. Then, several days ago, two of their board members disappeared without a trace. Their families filed missing persons' reports, but within forty-eight hours, they withdrew their reports, and declined any further police involvement. But a source inside Watchtower said the two missing persons never showed up again at Watchtower."

Santos said, "*You* have a source inside Watchtower? I repeat, *so what*"

McQ continued. "Rumors also suggested a top-down power play of some sort was responsible for Watchtower suddenly getting their shit together. And now, a major foreign conglomerate looks to, what? Acquire Watchtower? It fits. Nice work, MT and Mac. Let's see who these other mooks are, too."

Santos looked like he would shit a brick, but now kept his mouth shut. Mac worked his device. MT was already banging away on her own tablet as well, but she also kept to herself.

GREIGH OFFERED McQ A CONGRATULATORY BUT FORLORN grin. He leaned against his desk, rubbing the back of his now-sweaty neck despite the cool ambient temperature in his apartment. McQ stood beside and in front of him, between his desk and the sofa where Mac worked, still looking over her favorite detective's shoulder. Santos stood nearby, looking very uncomfortable, with nothing to do but look pissed, and a continued *so what* expression. He shifted his weight on restless feet, like he had better things to do elsewhere. Greigh thought, *What a wanker. <u>This</u> is the bloke that took McQ's place? No bloody imagination whatsoever.*

MT remained standing near McQ in her black and white high-top sneakers. She fidgeted as she cradled her tablet in one arm while massaging its touch screen with the other as she spoke without lifting her eyes. "Hey, you guys? Since Obelisk Prime is a public company listed in MiFID II, the European equivalent of the New York Stock Exchange, there's a lot of info on them out there. I scrounged up a couple of tidbits that might be useful while Officer MacKenzie continues his facial recognition magic over there." She nodded in Mac's direction without looking up from her tablet.

Mac winced and muttered over his shoulder also without looking up from his own tablet, "Detective, not Officer."

"Right. Well, looks like OP is *the* largest import/export businesses in the entire EU—by revenue, at least. Their HQ is in a place called Paldiski, Estonia, wherever that is. By maritime law, they need to provide real-time location data on their fleet of ships. And on their website's fleet management page, I see they have a ship at the Port of Chicago right now called the *Maltana.* Arrived last Friday. Coincidence? And does that lady look like she travels by *freighter?* I'd guess she's more a private jet type."

Greigh's head jerked around so fast he heard some small bones in his neck snap. His gasp and expression startled everyone. Didn't mean to shout, but he did. *"What? Paldiski? Maltana?"* After a half-dozen gasps in rapid succession, like he was hyperventilating, he barked, "I don't mean to be rude, people, but I need some of you to leave. This is now officially an Interpol-led investigation. I'll liaise with Captain Granger as well as other local and federal agencies. We'll be in touch." Mac still sat on the couch. He'd raised his gaze from his device with a look of confusion. Santos still stood there with his arms crossed. Santos said, "Interpol? What the fuck?" MT's jaw hung slack. Nobody moved. Greigh *screamed,* "Out! Now. Except you MT, and McQ. Please. Apologies. I'll explain later." With big arm and hand movements and exasperated wide-eyed hurry-up expressions, Greigh looked like he was an impatient cop directing traffic.

The two cops shuffled out, clearly confused, and Santos looked more pissed than ever, muttering, "Fucking Interpol? Who *is* this guy?" But he knew better than to object. This was a private citizen's home, and maybe something more. Greigh heard Mac say, "I'll explain, Tony. Let's go." Mac turned to catch McQ's eye on the way out. Gave her the *you'd better call me* sign with an expression that left no doubt. She nodded to reassure him. But she seemed as confused as the others.

After the two CED detectives closed the door behind them, Greigh motioned for McQ and MT to seat themselves on the sofa. He paced in front of them on the far side of a large glass coffee table as if he were dancing on hot coals with bare feet. McQ's patience wore thin. "What the hell is this, Greigh?"

CHAPTER 37

~

McQ suspected Greigh had been teetering on a precarious edge ever since returning from Copenhagen. But right now, he was scaring the shit out of her. She was sure it showed on her face, too. MT picked up on it and fidgeted with her device, not operating it now. Just fidgeting, looking at it. But her eyes darted up now and then to snag the latest fast-changing mood of the room. McQ just waited for Greigh to gather and share his thoughts while her legs bounced up and down as rapidly as her muscles and reflexes could handle as she sat there looking up at a very disturbed Greigh. She hoped he was about to share what had scared the crap out of him. Then....

~

Greigh gritted his teeth as he paced. Stopped and faced the two women sitting in front of him. He snarled his next words, clenching and unclenching the fists that hung by his sides. Like they needed something or someone to punch. "Ladies, I'm giving you the chance right now to back away from this case and leave the city for a time. Your lives are likely about to be put in harm's way. And I grow weary of people dying around me these days. I suggest you get up and walk out that door. Right now." For effect, he pointed at the fireplace behind him. His front door awaited on the other side of the wall behind that fireplace.

MT appeared nervous as she snorted her response. She said in a too matter-of-fact fashion, "Do you guys know where I grew up? Ever been to West Garfield Park? Try living there. Most dangerous hood in the city. I live with danger every hour of every fucking day. Besides, this sounds fun. I'm in." Her voice sounded contrived. Her sincerity did not.

McQ tried to suppress a smile, but failed despite the tension so thick they seemed about to choke on it. She said, "Greigh, I'm not going anywhere, either. Now why don't you share what you know, and what you're so afraid of?"

He took several moments to spit out the news that would change all their lives. Possibly forever. If they survived. *He* was *already* in deep jeopardy. Could be more than even he was aware. He realized that probability now. "MT, McQ already knows this. I freelance as an Interpol investigator. Are you familiar with Interpol?"

"Not really. International Police, right?"

"Yes. When crimes span multiple national jurisdictions, we assist and coordinate with and across local law enforcement agencies." He swiveled an intense stare toward McQ and said, "You'll recall I mentioned I was looking into a possible smuggling operation in Denmark when I interviewed Peter Fontera? And that it seemed pretty low-grade at the time?"

MT piped up. "The bowtie guy in the movies?"

"Yes, MT. He was to star in a movie production for Windy City Studios."

She raised her hand like a schoolgirl before blurting, "That's a local outfit."

"Right you are. Peter said he had some information for me, but was brutally murdered minutes before he could tell me."

"Holy shit! Okay, but so what?"

"A friend was helping me find out what he could. He's a Russian fisherman in the Baltic Sea. That means he was a smuggler. Told me about a mysterious cargo along with *four* armed guards he picked up in *Paldiski, Estonia,* and transferred it to a ship at sea between Denmark and Sweden. Right after he transferred the cargo *and* the *four* guards to that freighter, my friend and his boat disappeared. That was twelve days ago. The name of that freighter was the *Maltana.*"

It was McQ's turn to drop her jaw. It stayed there. All she could muster was a prolonged open-mouth moan. Her eyes blinked in rapid succession. Finally, she croaked, "This is *so* much bigger than us, Greigh. What—"

Greigh pressed on. "And that same ship now sits at the Port of Chicago docks that are, what? Ten miles north of here? I've learned the entire cast and crew of the Windy City movie project, *Dancing With Death,* booked passage on a freighter from Copenhagen to Chicago. That included all five victims of the mass shooting Mac and Santos are now investigating. They arrived last Friday. And the *Maltana* arrived last Friday. I also interviewed one of those five victims, Todd Bricker, when he was still alive, in Copenhagen. He had something vital to tell me from their voyage *on a freighter* after they moored *last Friday*. Something he'd seen and heard aboard while at sea. I learned from one of his acquaintances at Windy City yesterday that cargo might be nuclear. Hearsay only. Serial coincidences? Fat bloody chance."

MT remained speechless, her face frozen behind a mask of horrified bewilderment—eyes like saucers, hands frozen in mid-gesture, her perpetual motion on pause. That was obviously how she processed incomprehensible input until she sorted it out.

"And that's not even the bombshell, ladies. MT, the woman you captured on your elevator cam and Mac identified as Mika Kuzmin, President and CEO of Obelisk Prime? That woman," Greigh swallowed the growing lump in his throat, "leads a double life. In her other life, her name is Freya Ecklund, a mid-level Danish *Interpol* agent *and my bloody handler for the past fucking decade!"* The volume of Greigh's voice had been increasing. He now almost screamed. "She's the person who recruited me for this smuggling case. Now, it appears something worth killing at least seven people for was smuggled from Estonia to Chicago aboard one of *her* ships—the bloody *Maltana.*" Greigh stopped speaking, both because he had nothing left to reveal, but also because there was no more air left in his lungs. He gasped to regain his breath.

McQ still struggled to take all this in. After a period of stunned silence all around, she said, "If that's true, why would she get you involved in the first place? I'd think she'd want to stay below the radar, especially from Interpol."

"The only motive I can imagine, right now? She wanted to get a sense of how secure her plans were, whatever they might be. I suspect she didn't worry too much about *official* Interpol channels and agents. But I take an unconventional approach to my investigations as a civilian contractor. It's possible she wanted to see what I might discover, report to her, and she could still keep my findings off of Interpol's official radar."

"So is she Danish? Russian?"

"McQ, call Mac right now. Get him onto a deep background for Mika Kuzmin from a law enforcement perspective. She's now the key to my smuggling case, Mac's murder case, *and* your Watchtower case. They're all connected. Ask Mac to look also at the visitor logs at Windy City—video too, if they have it. The hit man or hit team on Mac's case had to get through Windy City's super-tight security somehow. They got *in and out* undetected, no doubt with help. That likely means it was an inside job. Toby Stiler, over at Miracle Mile, is convinced Lance Bowman is milking Windy City Productions dry. Bowman might be tying up loose ends."

GREIGH BREATHED SO FAST AND SHALLOW THAT HE NEEDED to pause again. After a few beats, he continued. "Regarding Freya—Mika—and Watchtower, national security might well be at stake."

McQ held up her palms toward Greigh and looked up at him, imploring him to slow down. She said, "Wait, now, what? National

Security? For crissake, Greigh, what the hell are we into here? Exactly?"

Greigh scratched his beard as he talked and paced. His gaze cast downward toward his feet—toward his thinking sandals. "My guy Todd, one of Mac's Windy City shooting victims, suspected they were shipping one or more nukes on what we now know was the *Maltana.* But I'm not sure who we can trust. Do *not* mention Freya's name to Mac, though. That official channel might tip her off, somehow. I trust Mac, but not sure about that Santos blighter. I'll need to handle the Interpol angle. Must determine who I will involve. There's now no doubt of high level corruption in play." He chose not to share his "kidnapping" by the pair of Interpol and DDIS agents. At least not yet.

After both ladies took the better part of a minute to process these shattering revelations, McQ said, "Wow.... Well... I trust Captain Granger and Mac. I agree something is very off about that Santos creep, though. Could just be a style thing, or.... Anybody else in the CED, though? Not sure. Something strange in the commissioner's office, too."

"Yes, well, I clearly have the same trust issues within Interpol, now. Let's leverage Mac and Lois. Warn them to keep the loop tight for now."

"Oh, yeah, I forgot you bedazzled *Lois*—Captain Granger—last summer. I'll keep the CED circle sphincter-tight."

MT spoke her first words in a while. "Man, you guys play big league, dont'cha? We need to get Rocko and Signore Copolla up to speed, too. I trust them. Can I assume you do as well?" Both Greigh and McQ agreed, but more reluctantly. After all, Signore Copolla's *gut* started McQ's end of things and enabled the discovery of this "un-American" activity at Watchtower. But first, they agreed they needed to know everything possible about this Mika Kuzmin. They also agreed Greigh would decide when and how to get other agencies involved after that.

"McQ, let's get Mac updated right now. Can we do that without Santos?"

She said, "I'm on it. Mac'll run Mika's background for me. And he's already looking at studio suspects. That's his case, anyway. We'll get back to you, Greigh. MT, why don't you and I talk with Rocko?"

"Sure thing. This is very cool, guys. I can do some more research on Watchtower, too."

Greigh said, "One last thing. Since we don't know if we can trust this Santos blighter, MT, do you have some good forensic accounting guys at USS?"

"Yeah, we do. Why?"

"Maybe you and McQ can put somebody who knows how to be discreet on Windy City's finances. Stiler says they make no sense. Focus on Lance Bowman personally. Can do?"

"On it."

CHAPTER 38

Late the next morning, Rocko Bianchi said, "Okay, ladies, what's so urgent and secretive that we have to meet in a place like this?" McQ and MT sat across from Rocko, head of Urban Security Services, Gaspari Copolla's security division of Urban Entertainment, Inc. He was obviously nervous about sitting in a cop bar, even though nobody else was in the place except Marco Harrow himself behind the bar a good thirty feet away. The dim light in the place directly below McQ's apartment lent not only an atmosphere of intimacy, but privacy, too. And during late morning, not twenty minutes after opening at 1100 hours, the joint was still deserted. McQ could feel the stench from last night's stale smoke seeping into her only clean top. She needed to do some laundry. Her rhythm was way off.

MT said, "Boss, this is hot, and I mean really—"

McQ smirked and interrupted with an apologetic glance toward MT on her left before she swiveled a full-intensity gaze toward the big man sitting in the booth across from MT and her. "Rocko, we've decided to trust you. That may sound funny, but we have serious trust issues both within CED and Interpol. Plus, this could very well translate into a national security issue. Involves the potential for one or more weapons of mass destruction smuggled into the country—the Port of Chicago, to be specific." McQ fell silent. *This guy must have nerves of steel. All that gets me is a wince and an intense stare?*

Rocko, former mafioso muscle, was now chief of a formidable cadre of attorneys, a small army of security specialists, and a battalion of investigators. That included MT. The big man parted the hairs of his non-existent mustache with his right thumb and forefinger, an obvious habit from a bearded past. His right hand descended from his slab of a rock jaw to his muscled neck. He scratched the stubble down there with no change in his expression. After fifteen seconds, he said, "So, Signore Copolla's gut was right on the money, wasn't it?" Almost cheerfully, he added, "Okay, how can I help?"

Incredible! I bet this guy was one scary soldier for the Copolla family in his day. Now, he is one impressive leader. "First, Rocko, we need tight control over who has access to this information. So, your discretion is critical. Second, we have a tight loop within CED, just two people we trust, working from within the department. And just one person within Interpol right now—Aubrey Greigh."

"Greigh? Interpol? Young lady, I'm confused."

"Yeah, Greigh freelances for Interpol. Something about who the man is that gives him access during investigations they can't seem to replicate with the more official law enforcement types they most often recruit. He is all over this case."

Rocko smiled and shook his head. "No wonder his mysteries read so authentic. I love that guy!"

McQ took a few minutes to explain everything they knew. Rocko took it all in stride. But then he said, "I can mobilize some of my troops for expanded surveillance of Watchtower's other facilities and personnel. I'll only hand out info on a need-to-know basis. Greigh will have to involve other agencies, but that will be difficult due to the trust issues. He'll need to manage that. What else do you need from me, McQ?"

She considered what she could ask that wouldn't screw up Mac's or Greigh's efforts. Then.... "How discreet can your lawyers be? We should try to learn everything we can about Watchtower, including their resources, facilities, structure, everything."

MT jumped like she'd just had a cattle prod shoved into the side of her neck. "Oh! Before we got tangled up in this surveillance stuff, I meant to tell you about Maxine Newacher and Randall Cosovich, the two Watchtower board members that disappeared. Newacher was Watchtower's comptroller. She maintained and audited Watchtower's business accounts. But that isn't what was most interesting. My guys did a little of their own auditing—of Ms. Newacher's email correspondence. She and Mr. Cosovich, Watchtower's General Counsel, exchanged sympathetic emails. Mr. Cosovich contracted a DNA testing lab to perform a discreet comparison between Mr. Leonov's DNA and another unidentified party. Looked like they were doing that on the QT, even within Watchtower."

Rocko scratched his grizzled throat again. "Hmmm… maybe they were looking for someone they thought might have murdered Leonov. Almost as if they didn't believe the whole suicide affair, like it was stronzata—bullshit. Or, more likely, they were looking for a familial match. Either way, what they found or hoped to find was worth killing for—or at least making two people disappear—to prevent or protect."

"Sound reasoning, Rocko. MT, any way to uncover what they're trying to hide?"

"I'll try to locate the lab they used. Might hack the report, assuming they completed one. Hey, McQ, let's not forget Greigh's request to dissect Windy City's financials with a focus on their GM, that Bowman character."

"Right. So, Rocko, your people are on Watchtower and maybe we can get one of your forensic accountants on Windy City?" He just nodded before McQ continued. "And MT, you're on the testing lab. I'll stay close to Greigh and Mac at CED. Rocko, share only what you must with your boss until we know more." Rocko said nothing, and didn't nod.

A couple of Harrow's regulars traipsed in. Their privacy window had eroded. This was a small place. After a round of knuckle bumps, Rocko left first. He still got nervous around cops. They looked like third shift beat cops even though they wore civvies. Rocko nodded as he passed them, already perched on their barstools. Their eyes followed him out the front door. MT left next. She promised to call as soon as she had something on the DNA thing. And McQ left last. Went right up to her apartment via the exterior wooden stairs in the alley outside on the back of the building. They still creaked. She needed to think. *This is huge!*

CHAPTER 39

About that same time, Josh Carver, Greigh's new screenwriter, arranged for him to meet with Valerie Schmidt. Valerie was the production assistant at the scene of the Windy City shooting when the police arrived. They were to have lunch at the studio cafeteria, but Josh told Greigh she wanted to meet offsite. So, they met at the Des Plaines Diner half a mile from Windy City's front gate on South Cicero Avenue overlooking the Chicago River. It was noisy, but nobody from the studio ever came to this diner for lunch. Its dubious reputation for questionable cuisine almost guaranteed their privacy. They slid into a booth by the windows. A waitress brought water and menus before she left them to decide.

"Mr. Greigh, it is an honor, sir."

"Just Greigh, Valerie. Thank you for meeting with me. Hungry?"

"I couldn't eat, thank you. I've told the police everything. Well, almost. If you hadn't called me, I would have called you. Todd just loves—loved—you." On the verge of tears, she continued. "But that whole shooting thing scared me to death, Greigh. I wasn't sure who I could trust. I wondered if what Todd found out on that wretched ship got him and the others killed."

"Did you tell the police about the extensive conversations you had with Todd after his return?"

Valerie snapped her gaze up to meet Greigh's. "How did you—?"

"Valerie, Todd was a friend of mine. We worked together in Copenhagen."

"You *did?* He said as much, but I thought he was just being melodramatic."

"We worked the Peter Fontera murder together. You're acquainted with Josh Carver and Farud Mastuk." A statement, not a question. Greigh didn't wait for her to answer. "Josh said you and Todd talked. My new friend Farud said you talked a lot. I was to contact Todd the moment I arrived back in Chicago, but... we never got the chance to reconnect. I only arrived in town hours before...." He honored Todd with a moment of silence. Otherwise, his voice might have cracked. "Josh said Todd had vital information for me, but could offer few specifics. I've since learned what he discovered on that ship may be information critical to the international case I'm investigating."

"Why should I believe talking to you won't get *me* killed, Mr. Greigh? Like Todd and Stacy and Peter and the others."

"Valerie, besides being an author, I'm an investigator for Interpol. You know, International Police. The worst scenario is that whoever is behind these killings gets away with it. I want to help CED and the FBI catch these monsters. I need your help, Valerie. Can you help me solve Todd's murder, and Peter's and Stacy's? Let's lock these criminals up so they can't hurt anyone ever again, including you. Todd, Josh and Farud all trust me. So...."

Greigh watched the young girl's shoulders and head slump in resignation before she took a deep breath. Then, the words rattled out, as if she now couldn't get rid of them fast enough. She talked to the tabletop, not to Greigh. "Well, Todd told me about their ship stopping not long after they left Copenhagen. They met a smaller ship in the open ocean. He said it looked like they transferred a large crate from the smaller boat to their ship. After that, less than a half hour once their ship started moving again, there was a tremendous explosion behind them. He wasn't sure what to make of that. But it scared him even more than he already was." *Andy. And his boat, Marya.* "He also saw four guards in civilian clothes armed to their teeth, like huge guys, come aboard with the crate. He said the ship's crew who loaded the crate onto Todd's ship and interacted with these men feared for their safety."

"Feared what?"

"Their cargo. And maybe those men. He said he saw a large unmarked crate that framed a shiny steel or aluminum case. The only marking was a single small sticker that looked like a black three-bladed boat's propeller on a yellow background. He saw one of those guards peel that off, crumple it up, and toss it over the railing into the sea. And Greigh, Todd said the crew members feared they might not have children or that their hair would fall out. He said he suspected the cargo on that ship was some sort of nuclear material."

Greigh nodded. "Yes, that's consistent with what we already know." He didn't say this was the first solid confirmation of what they suspected. She sounded more excited, now. Maybe more scared. "Then, after being underway for a week, they met *another* smaller boat closer to the US coastline, he figured. Todd suspected they transferred the same cargo off their ship onto what looked like a private yacht."

This is new news. Jolly good Todd had the foresight to tell someone. The poor kid must have been in constant fear for his life. So sad. Time to get other agencies involved.

THAT NIGHT, GREIGH PACED ON HIS BALCONY AT THE LIT. He remembered the two Interpol agents who contacted him. Or was that one from Interpol and another from DDIS? He wasn't really all that sure, now. Didn't matter. That mysterious encounter now made a lot more sense. Someone inside Interpol suspected Freya, and possibly others, of illegal activities, or even terrorism, or collaborating with terrorists. Would he now trust these total strangers over his own handler? It seemed he had no rational choice. He didn't know who else to turn to, inside or outside of the agency. Greigh retrieved the card with the phone number on it. Called and waited. Odd beeps and chirps emanated from his comms implant. Then....

"Monsieur Greigh. Thank you for calling." A *French* accent? This was new. "You have information. Please meet us in the same black van at the corner of Harrison and Wabash in forty-five minutes." *Click*

At the appointed time, he hiked down the street from The Lit. There was that same van. As he approached, the curbside door slid open. He stepped up, stooped, and entered. The automatic door swished closed behind him. The van rolled from the curb straightaway. Off balance, despite its smooth and utterly silent acceleration, he plopped into a padded seat on the driver's side of its cargo area. He came face to face with the two agents who "kidnapped" him two days earlier. A woman sat in the front passenger's seat that was swiveled to face the rear of the van, to face Greigh. As the only woman in the van, he surmised she was the voice on the comms. She reminded him of Dame Judi Dench, the famous British actress, but with a French accent —and nice legs for her age. *Really, old boy? God's socks!* She had yet to speak.

He swiveled his gaze. Instrumentation festooned overhead cabinets all around. A fourth person drove. The woman stared at him for a full minute as side streets glided past the cockpit's windows. She was evaluating him. Letting him sweat. Greigh recognized the technique. He kept his mouth shut. He stared back. Hoisted his eyebrows as his patience eroded. At last, she spoke in a most unexpected deep and husky voice for such a small woman. Petite, but authoritative. Sexy for an older woman. He loved her accent. In a half-whisper, she said, "You may call me Colette, Monsieur Greigh. I am from CCC—Interpol's Command and Coordination Centre—in Lyon, France. You have a problem, cheríe. We can help. You see that, yes?"

This statement unnerved Greigh. But he needed to test these total strangers. "Freya Ecklund. Mika Kuzmin."

Colette said, "Oui. A significant embarrassment to Interpol,

Monsieur, and to me, personally. Two people, one body, as we've discovered. As did you, no?"

"Oui. I mean yes. But I do not know you. What can you tell me?"

"Freya Ecklund recruited you from Lyon eleven years ago. I approved. You've worked several cases with her over the past decade. Freya requested you and only you to investigate a smuggling operation in Copenhague." She pronounced it, *CO-pn-HOG*. "That is because she shuttles between Paldiski, her Obelisk Prime headquarters, and Copenhague, where she has settled as our resident agent. You would call her your—how you say—*handler*? She felt your unique skills would unearth any weakness in her plan to smuggle weapons of mass destruction into America while keeping your findings from official Interpol eyes and ears. She underestimated us. Her, ah, ego blinded her. And you exceeded her expectations, didn't you, Monsieur Greigh?

"You drew attention to that actor who overheard a small part of her plan on the waterfront from a Russian captain with whom you are well-acquainted. She did not count on that. Your unexpected resourcefulness created a problem that necessitated a clean up by her people. And that drew attention from the local police, drawing a target on *you and her*. We must stop her and any confederates she has recruited within our agency. I could go on, but this should convince you that our agendas align. We suspect Freya has recruited others within Interpol; hence, the need for this unlikely and clandestine approach."

Greigh considered this woman's words. Accurate, as far as he could tell, and the spirit of her intentions rang true. "Do you have information on the weapon or weapons she smuggled to Chicago?"

"Our best intelligence tells us there is just one device, ready to be armed. On what timetable would only be a guess. We surmise this weapon is likely an older tactical battlefield weapon with an estimated nominal yield of ten kilotons. We believe this weapon originated from a stockpile that was thought to have been decommissioned in northwest Russia.

"Target?"

"Unknown."

"Motivation?"

"Unknown, although we suspect ideological, given her Russian family's history and a vociferous hatred of America."

"Recommendations?"

"We'll work within Interpol to determine if she has any confederates starting in the Baltic region and specifically within Denmark with help from our friends at DDIS." She aimed her next glance at the grim young man with the lapel pin. We'll also focus on containing the potential ramifications of Freya's quasi-official actions. You will represent us with your domestic agencies. Keep our contact number. We will keep each other informed. Questions?"

"Too many. Thank you."

"Until later, Monsieur Greigh."

"It's just— goodbye, Colette. Gentlemen." The van stopped and the curb- side door swished open. They had returned to the precise spot where they'd picked him up on the corner of Harrison and Wabash eight minutes earlier.

CHAPTER 40

Just two blocks from home, Greigh walked toward The Lit's covered portico, a welcoming sight with lights that burned from sunset to sunrise. Hundreds of these overhead lights once welcomed now-rare limousines filled with affluent hotel guests, but now, less than half of those points of light still burned. Money had been tight since the building converted from an aging but opulent hotel to luxury condos under casual property management a decade earlier. But all that was changing now that The Lit was on the National Register of Historic Sites, thanks to the efforts of Greigh and The Lit's unlikely benefactor, Signore Gaspari Copolla. The Lit was receiving a facelift, one more sign that Signore Copolla, the building's new owner, was making amends for past sins.

After passing through The Lit's ten-foot-high doors made heavy by one-inch-thick etched glass that had a slight greenish tint, Greigh crossed the massive lobby. He always relished the myriad subtle odors: oiled wood, musty tapestries and brass polish. The two-century-old crystal chandeliers cast shards of colored light that made the massive lobby sparkle as if cloaked in magic. He loved this place with a passion. Always had. It had been home to him and his family since its transformation. Now, he lived here alone.

Greigh entered what was known as the birdcage. He punched the old-fashioned lighted button for the seventh floor and watched the lobby disappear below him through the elevator's wire-strap framework. Visitors often grew alarmed at the cacophony of mechanical and electrical sounds the elevator's less-than-silky movement invoked. Greigh found it a comforting and predictable symphony of functional chaos in a world that had grown too symmetrical and silent in all the wrong ways. At seven, the birdcage stopped. He pushed open the metal accordion-style door, exited, and closed it behind him. Walked across the broad hallway to his apartment. As he approached, Butler recognized his presence and unlocked one of the double doors. *Snick*. It popped open an inch. Greigh entered and closed it behind him. He said, "Butler, soft music, please. Surprise me. Then, go silent until further notice."

"Of course, Greigh."

He smiled, still congratulating himself for bequeathing Butler—the system's default moniker—a facsimile of Sean Connery's voice, the Scottish actor, and not unlike his own. After all, he was Scottish, too, although raised in England. The Midwestern US had now left its indelible nasal imprint on his own accent. He almost sounded like an American.

His implant tickled the outboard end of his right eyebrow. Incoming comms. He tapped his right temple. "Yes?"

"Mr. Aubrey Greigh?"

"Speaking."

"Colette says you are a valued asset within her organization. Are you available regarding an urgent matter?"

Shite! No rest for the wicked. Or the exhausted. "Of course. When and where?"

"We'll send a car. Twenty-five minutes. You'll recognize the driver."

"Naturally."

Greigh suspected this "urgent matter" would take considerable time to resolve. He grabbed a quick shower, a protein bar, slammed a chilled triple espresso from his refrigerator and returned to The Lit's portico. Elapsed time from receipt of that mysterious call: twenty-seven minutes. A new personal best. Three minutes later, a nondescript sedan rolled silently to a stop in front of him and three steps down. Greigh descended to the car, bent over to peer into the open passenger window.

"Hello again, Greigh!" CED Detective Aidan MacKenzie. Mac's broad smile met his surprised expression. Greigh grabbed the door handle as it popped out, lifted the lever, waited for the door to rise, and hopped into the passenger's seat.

"Mac. You're late. It's been, what, six hours? Another quiet Tuesday evening for you, too?" They shook hands. Both chuckled. "So, where are we headed?"

"2111 West Roosevelt Road. FBI's Chicago field office, one of the largest in the country. They're convening a specialized cross-agency task force given the rather unique nature of what they're now officially calling a terrorist threat."

"We are late-comers to the party, then?"

"Not sure. I haven't been told all that much, other than I'm the CED rep for this party. Under normal circumstances, it would be a higher level rank than mine, but I guess boots on the ground still counts for something. Also, I suspect there's still a trust issue that's weighing heavy on the brass."

TEN MINUTES LATER, THEY ARRIVED AT THE CHICAGO FBI Field Office. Ten more to walk, get scanned, vetted, and escorted to a sixth-floor secure conference room full of suits. They invited Mac and Greigh to sit in a couple of empty chairs. All eyes settled on them. And there was Dame Judi Dench's doppelgänger, Colette. She perched on the edge of a chair like a wary canary, one place removed from the table's head, to Greigh's immediate left. Everyone treated her with a great deal of deference. Must be highly placed within Interpol. No doubt here to clean up someone else's mess within her own shop, and maybe beyond.

Greigh scanned the two dozen other suits in the large room, noticing two tiers of apparel. That of the upper echelons, he assumed were from various agencies, and that of their staff members. He mentally cataloged them *VIPs* and *support*. Colette leaned to her right and whispered into Greigh's ear, "You will now be debriefed, Monsieur Greigh."

His eyes widened. Mac overheard and offered a playful elbow jab in Greigh's right side. He whispered, "Break a leg, *mate.*" Mac's attempt at a British accent sounded more Australian-American than Brit. Greigh winced.

A regal black gentleman at the head of the table announced in a James Earl Jones baritone, "Mr. Greigh, my name is Special Agent in Charge William Spears of the FBI." Greigh thought, *Of course it is.* He stifled a grin. I'm chairing this Joint Terrorism Task Force. Represented in this JTTF are FBI, CIA, DoD, DHS, Interpol, Illinois State Police and CED. We also have DoE's Nuclear Emergency Support Team, or NEST, on call, should their support be required. We understand you will be representing Interpol." The offered a deferential nod toward Colette.

Greigh believed they expected him to be shocked at the range of alphabet soup agencies that had come out to play. Instead, he just deadpanned a simple, "Sir."

"Mr. Greigh, it would seem you've been jockeyed into a rather awkward, if not opportune, position within the sphere of our investigation. You may well play a central role when we move into our action phase. You were recruited to investigate a smuggling mission by our principal subject, Ms. Mika Kuzmin, first known to you as Ms. Freya Ecklund. You've worked with her for over a decade, off and on. Interpol has had their suspicions of your handler for some time now, Mr. Greigh. But much to Ms. Ecklund's dismay, your own rather unorthodox investigatory methods on your current mission raised several red flags. That made you a person of interest."

After a beat, Greigh couldn't help but comment on the irony. "Sir, it won't be the first time since the genesis of this affair. They suspected me of a murder in Copenhagen while working a confidential informant on Interpol's behalf. But I'm sure you already knew that."

"We did, indeed."

Under any other circumstance, Greigh would have found this entire scenario amusing, if not pulp-novel-worthy. He turned to Colette and said loud enough for the entire room to hear, "Did you know about Freya's alter-ego before she recruited me for this mission? If so, I would like to speak with you in private when we're done here." He plastered disdain all over his face. Colette just offered a coquettish smile as her response along with a nod.

James Earl Jones continued. "And when one of CIA's deep cover assets went missing after meeting with you during a subsequent fatal altercation with the freighter *Maltana,* interagency interest in your activities intensified. Since then, you've been under constant broad-spectrum surveillance. From that intel, the team has surmised your agenda aligns with those of this task force. Had it been otherwise, you would now enjoy the hospitality of our high-value detainee interrogation group. The HIG and its FBI, DoD, and CIA team of interrogators are... persuasive."

"Missing CIA Deep cover asset, you say?"

"Your friend, Captain Andrushya Galkin." *Andy? Holy shite!* Reading his non-verbal response, SAC Spears said, "Yes, that's why it's called *deep cover,* Mr. Greigh. Condolences. At first, we feared you had set him up, knowingly or unwittingly. But our intel since then guided us to treat you like an asset rather than a suspect. And here we are. Welcome to the party."

The man didn't sound thrilled about his last cold statement. Greigh suspected someone had twisted his enormous arm. *Too bloody bad.* The first thing that occurred to Greigh was this would all be marvelous fodder for the literary cannon down the road. Not the confidential bits, of course. The second thing? This would give him far more access to specifics of the case. He had moved up the food chain. Unwittingly. So be it. *Better pay attention.* Now addressing the room grown rather stuffy with twice as many bodies as the space was designed for, with standing room only, SAC Spears continued.

"Ladies and gentlemen, we must pursue four priorities in this order: detection, prevention, and failing that, containment and recovery. I wish to spend fifteen minutes on each. Then, we'll circle back as needed and discuss assignments. Let's talk about detection. I recommend we concurrently investigate the ship, other facilities, and, of course, individual personnel. Start with the ship. We search the ship to confirm our suspicions. TEDAC will scour the *Maltana* for trace evidence of fissionable materials."

A shiny young man in *tier two apparel* said, "I thought personnel from the Terrorist Explosive Device Analytical Center were called to a bomb site *after* detonation."

"That is one of their skill sets. They're also trained to search suspected bomb factories for traces of bomb-making materials. They're equipped to detect and analyze the trace signature of conventional *and* nuclear materials. We should not eliminate the possibility of non-nuclear devices."

The young man appeared chastised. But he had learned something. An eager staffer, no doubt. Greigh liked him.

"After the ship, we scour Watchtower headquarters on East Monroe. We need to find anything describing their plans. Also, any residences of their senior team, especially Ms. Kuzmin's Chicago residence. We must assume there is more than one device. We need to locate any and all potential targets. Top detection priority is all locations within a fifty-mile radius owned or leased by Watchtower. Next, recently completed or current Watchtower construction projects within the same radius....

"Second, prevention. We need to find sufficient evidence of terrorist activity. So far, all we have is third-party hearsay, rumors, and innuendo. What we possess, however, is video evidence showing an Interpol agent has undisclosed assets, entered the country on a false passport or a false identity. Either is sufficient grounds for detaining Ms. Mika Kuzmin, a.k.a. Ms. Freya Ecklund.

"I suggest a combined apprehension team brings her in for questioning as soon as possible. Since we may need to invoke the Patriot Act, DHS, supported by the FBI, will lead the way. That will be the very first assignment. Apprehend, detain and interrogate Ms. Mika Kuzmin, designated *Suspect One*."

SAC Spears nodded, and a muscular man with a military bearing stood and introduced himself as the appointed leader of the local apprehension team whose mission was Suspect One. A federal judge had already issued an arrest warrant for Ms. Kuzmin. She had entered the country with a false identity from Interpol's perspective—not Freya Ecklund. Enough to get the ball rolling. Once she was in custody, SAC Spears assured the group that sweeping search warrants for Watchtower's facilities and the freighter *Maltana* would be exercised. They hoped to thwart the expected terrorist attack. And so it went....

It was obvious to Greigh this could go on for some time, and was not the best use of his time. He whispered to Colette, "I think I would be more useful in the field. I'm still assisting CED with their homicide investigation related to this affair. Can you aid in my, ah, escape from this?" He created small circles with his index finger pointed downward at the table in front of him. This was meant to encompass the room full of suits and action that was outside his wheelhouse, far above his pay grade and equidistant below his level of interest.

Colette smiled. She said, "I agree. I'll keep you briefed, Monsieur Greigh." She caught the SAC's eye and tossed him a subtle eye and head gesture that first nodded at Greigh, then at the door. He nodded his affirmation and offered Greigh a small nod and wink before he continued issuing his analysis and assignments. Greigh couldn't make his escape fast enough after patting Mac on the back, consoling him on his continued captivity.

CHAPTER 41

~

Mika admired the late night view from the living room of her suite at the Langham Hotel on North Wabash. The Chicago River, its bridges, and the city's brilliant skyline lay at her feet. Flames roared in the fireplace. Light jazz tinkled from invisible speakers. Hotel rooms in America were so wastefully spacious. But she would not complain. She deserved it. When in America....

Beneath the veneer of her legitimate import/export/shipping business, she had spent her entire adult life building a vast criminal empire. She spread it throughout Europe to rival the biggest and baddest of underworld cabals. Through skill, luck, and the sheer force of will, she took control of such networks in France, England, Italy, Germany, and beyond that many only imagined. Few knew. Money in amounts unimaginable by most standards flowed through her fingertips.

With that power now behind her, she found it child's play taking control of Watchtower, Inc.—an illegitimate business made on the backs of honest men and women. Even before her tenure, Watchtower had become the sixth wealthiest privately held corporation in America, wholly owned by her brother, the late Tihomir Leonov. Much to everyone's surprise, an estate attorney and Mr. Alfred Dorchester, Watchtower's assistant corporate counsel and board member, provided irrefutable proof that Mika was indeed Leonov's sole heir.

Mika still faced pushback. There were those unwilling to cede their own power and influence within its walls, even as compromised as that power became after Leonov's death. But with her well-oiled organization at hand led by a battalion of expensive attorneys, it wasn't long before Mika held all opposition and petty plots at bay. Using her communications strategy, she soon inundated every corner of Watchtower with publicity proclaiming her ascension as its new head honcho—their savior.

Soon, all across Europe's darkest underworld, there wasn't a soul who hadn't heard of how Mika had become ruler of this corporate kingdom in America—overnight. And none dared oppose her further... at least not yet. For now, Mika was content with having achieved such success. But little did she know that lurking just around the corner were others who would threaten all she had accomplished with one swift move or a single well-timed command.

CHAPTER 42

Not long after he arrived at his office at Police Plaza in the pre-dawn hours of September 4th, his desk comms rang. He bellowed through his closed door to his assistant, "It's okay, Nikki, I'll take the call." Chicago's top cop, Commissioner Jack Roberts, had a relationship with Mademoiselle Colette Guibert. She hailed from Interpol's European headquarters in Lyon, France. Some said she wielded even more influence within Interpol than anyone was allowed to disclose outside of Lyon (pronounced *lee-OWN*). Probably for security reasons. Roberts knew (in confidence) that Mademoiselle Guibert nestled within the highest echelons of her agency.

"Commissaire Roberts, I thank you for taking my call."

I just love her accent. "Mademoiselle Guibert, it has been too long." He pronounced her name, *she-BARE.* "We haven't spoken for weeks and we haven't seen each other since that international law enforcement ethics conference in London."

"Bieu sûr, monsieur. I must apologize for calling instead of visiting this time even though I now am in your fair city. You will understand why in a moment."

Jack Roberts paused before responding. *She's in Chicago? What the hell is she doing out here in the trenches?* "Colette, why don't you tell me what's on your mind? What's changed?"

He abided her pause as she collected her thoughts. "Jacque, I cannot trust… I endure a messy internal problem with which I require more of your assistance. May I count on your continued discretion?"

Well, this is becoming a very interesting call. Now, we're on a first-name basis. Just like London. He paused for just one sincere beat. "Absolutely, Colette. What else can I do to help?"

"You are familiar with a certain Monsieur Aubrey Greigh, no?"

"Yes, I am, Colette. Please explain." That author-slash-sleuth and his own Detective Chance McQuillan demonstrated a brilliant collaboration. Together, they closed the highly visible Thibodaux homicide case the previous summer. Though there were many questions about the final disposition of that case, and a civilian had died, the killing stopped. Still, it solidified his tenure as commissioner of the largest police force in the world.

"It would seem that circumstances have thrown him and your own Detective McQuillan together once more—"

"Colette, McQuillan is still on administrative leave based on your earlier plea, and—"

"Please continue to keep it that way. For a while longer."

"I didn't understand then, and I still don't understand. You must give me more."

"She can help me with my problem and you with yours by working with Monsieur Greigh again. But not as a city employee."

"McQuillan is one of my best."

"And we both need her free from the constraints your detectives must rightly endure—for a bit of time longer. And because of our mutual trust issues. For now. I promise you the case on which they are now collaborating will affect your city in ways you cannot yet imagine."

"Does this have anything to do with that confidential task force that just tapped one of my detectives?"

"Ah, you know of that. Oui, it has everything to do with that, but indirectly through Monsieur Greigh. And Interpol. Your Mademoiselle McQuillan has become an integral part of a wide-ranging investigation involving homicide, smuggling, and a possible terrorist threat to your city. What is more, Jacques, these cases span at least three nations' borders."

I just love it when she calls me 'Jacques'.

Colette paused to let that sink in. The Joint Terrorism Task Force was keeping their circle small for now. "It would appear Mademoiselle McQuillan is the glue between other "unofficial" assets, my official asset—Monsieur Greigh—and the CED through her precinct and their mutual friends—trusted friends. Since my organization has been compromised, except for Monsieur Greigh toiling as one of my more innovative contract investigators, I cannot yet trust the remainder of my team. Not completely. But I do trust Monsieur Greigh, and I trust your detective. She must be free to operate, not outside the law, but not as police either. You understand, my old friend?"

"Not completely. But I trust *you*, Colette. So be it. I only ask that you keep me in the loop, and that I *will* get my detective back."

"I agree. Although, your detective has a mind of her own, as I am sure you know all too well."

The commissioner just chuffed, the way someone gestures when someone states the obvious. "Indeed I do, Colette. Thank you for the call and glad I could help."

"Oui, Jacques. Let us hope it is not in vain."

Despite his hatred of the whole idea, Roberts agreed to keep his team in the dark. He'd been warned that there might be one or more moles, even within his own department. So, he had reluctantly agreed. He knew this would create enemies, and perhaps a multitude of resentments. But Colette convinced him that his own team would later thank him for his discretion and foresight.

Nikki Larchmont could lose her dream job in the commissioner's office for this, but she owed Captain Lois Granger for getting her here. She made the call, but she did so on her lunch hour outside the *Ivory Tower*—Police Plaza. She stood on the wide Michigan Avenue sidewalk, away from passersby as much as possible. After a few thoughtful moments, she called her friend Lois, Detective McQuillan's boss, who was also that detective's strongest advocate. She hated keeping her in the dark, and she knew the commissioner did as well. Something about the greater good. She'd honor that. In the future, however, Nikki would recommend the commissioner not take such calls on speaker using his booming baritone voice. She couldn't help but overhear, even through his closed door.

"Lois?"

"Nikki!"

"Listen, Lois, do me a favor. Don't call the commissioner's office anymore about McQuillan's inquiry."

"What the hell is going on, Nikki?"

"It's not what you think. This is *not* a bad thing. The commissioner's doing your detective and all of us a solid."

"But—"

"That's all I can say, Lois. Please believe me, it really is okay. Gotta run. And we *will* do lunch." *Click*

CHAPTER 43

~

Not a day passed without Greigh mourning Mel and his little Clancy. Today was no exception as he sipped a cup of tea on his covered balcony. Most burned into his memory was the day his wife and six-year-old daughter were gunned down. He remembered every detail. It was a Sunday morning in DuSable Park three years ago the previous June 21st. Greigh had become the most vocal advocate against Leonov's development project to "re-gentrify" Chicago's Near Southwest Loop. They killed his family all because that greedy land developer needed a distraction. *A fecking distraction!*

He had never forgiven himself for not being there, maybe even to take the bullets fired from that monster's gun. From Teodor Raspin, a.k.a. Rasputin—Ty Leonov's assassin. All so that would distract him from stopping Watchtower's project that would tear down The Lit, their home. All so Leonov could build a giant entertainment complex on and around the site. Leonov and Raspin had paid with their lives, but Greigh took no satisfaction in their deaths. His Melissa and little Clancy were still in the ground, and their husband and father was not.

~

Lois Granger loved her job as captain of CED's ninety-ninth precinct. Some days were better than others. Her office was small, but it didn't usually feel this stuffy. She *still* had no idea what the commissioner's office was doing about reinstating McQuillan. And her friend in the commissioner's office told her to back off because... this was a *good* thing? *So, the commissioner's looking out for McQuillan by keeping her from returning to work? How does that make any sense?*

Plus, the new guy they'd sent? Santos? What she'd observed did not thrill her. He came with an outstanding record, some kind of hotshot from the eighty-fifth. Even MacKenzie's slow-burn body language had caught her eye. She wasn't supposed to catch the eye-rolls and head shakes from some of the other veteran detectives, either. That included a few comments she wasn't meant to overhear. All of this led her to believe this job in her house wasn't a good fit for the guy. She'd talk to him. Captain Granger sat behind her desk when Santos walked in. Even the way he walked and leaned on her door-frame got to her, like he expected her to stand at attention in his presence.

"Wanted to talk, Captain?"

"So, Tony, What's up?" She motioned for him to plant himself in one of her three guest chairs.

He remained standing by the door. "Look, Captain, since you asked, some stuff goes on here I don't agree with, but I'm just attributing that to getting used to a different house. Not sure what else to say."

"You see problems, I want to hear about them. What?"

"Well, making law enforcement databases available to civilians, for one. We'd *never* consider doing that in the eight-five."

The captain looked at him with a quizzical expression. "What's your closure rate over there? You may not be aware. I am. It's my job. This house closes a full ten points better. Wanna know why? We use our instincts here, Tony."

"And instincts get civilians killed, don't they, Captain?"

She cocked her head sideways, thought about her next words, and said, "That'll be all. I appreciate your candor. Dismissed."

Santos looked like he had more to say, but the big stick slapped him down. He wheeled, and walked. As ordered.

MIKA PACED BACK AND FORTH IN FRONT OF HER HOTEL room's wall of windows. Her mind raced as the sun rose over the city and the lights began to fade or wink out. She needed to act fast, but she needed help. There would be a new plan that deviated from the old one. It was a risky move, but one worth taking. As Freya Ecklund, Interpol case officer, Mika worried her own agent—Greigh—got too close, too fast. She had tasked him with investigating a smuggling operation. But her personal motive was to see if Greigh would unearth any weak spots in her assassination plot—including that of his own. She smiled at the delicious irony.

Mika thought she'd need to speed up her plan to eliminate Greigh and his partner, that nosy McQuillan bitch. Greigh had discovered that someone hijacked one of her own ships to frame her and Obelisk Prime for a terrorist attack on America. She now realized, however, she *first* needed Greigh to complete his investigation to clear her *and* OP of these ridiculous terrorism accusations. Mika's four "bodyguards," her assassins, had each been assigned a mark: Gaspari Copolla, Rocko Bianchi, Aubrey Greigh and Chance McQuillan. These were the four most culpable for the demise of her twin brother, Tihomir Leonov, the previous July.

But now, she placed her hitters' kill missions on hold until she figured out who hijacked her freighter, and why. The ship's crew wasn't talking. Obviously, someone made it worth their while. *Most* surprising, though, is that whoever turned them ensured they overcame their fear of her. Not a minor feat. She discovered that her four marks were all now collaborating to investigate the same thing. And they were making progress like she and her team could not, likely because of their local knowledge and specialized networks. So, she assigned her four assassins to *protect* their respective marks until they discovered her unknown nemesis—or nemeses. That would amuse Greigh, "Freya's" smug but capable investigator.

CHAPTER 44

As Greigh strolled down South Dearborn Street, he sensed he was being followed. Then he spotted the big Russian that MT's button cams had caught on video in the Watchtower garage with Mika. One of her four "bodyguards." More likely an assassin. Only a blind idiot would miss that mountain of a bloke. From that footage, MT and Mac had identified him as one Rolf Ninchkov, a Russian national.

Greigh turned a corner and doubled back to confront the big man, but someone intercepted him and prevented him from doing so. This strong stranger greeted him like an old friend and swept him away. In a subdued voice, the stranger identified himself as the member of a three-agent FBI team tasked to protect him. As they hustled away, the agent told Greigh that another member of his team "accidentally" bumped into Ninchkov and planted a tracking device on him. Greigh then joined the team in following Ninchkov from within their surveillance van, not unlike the black Interpol van, but nicer. And cleaner. After the Russian lost Greigh, they tracked him via a convoluted anti-surveillance route back to the Millennium Knickerbocker Hotel near Watchtower's headquarters building.

A six-man capture team apprehended and detained Rolf with a no-knock warrant. He did not resist. Transported him to the FBI field office for interrogation. They treated him like a terrorist, and someone who had entered the country illegally. Rolf only admitted his orders were to protect Greigh. Said he was in mortal danger. Source unknown. Greigh's heart raced as he listened to Ninchkov's terse statement through the glass panel between the interrogation room and observation rooms. Someone was indeed trying to kill him, as he earlier suspected? Why? Again, he thought, *am I getting too close? To what? Something else?*

But Mika was supposed to be the villainous terrorist here. If what this blighter said was true, why would she task one of her men to *protect* him? Were others in danger, too? He registered concern for McQ, and anyone else close to this investigation. *People around me die....*

That's all Ninchkov would say. If the man's fancy watch MT identified from the video did indeed identify him as Spetsnaz—Russian Special Forces—this guy would not crack. Unless they employed enhanced interrogation techniques—drugs and/or torture. But that was not the FBI's modus operandi, was it? The stakes involved might change that. He recalled SAC Spears's somber description of their high-value detainee interrogation group—the HIG—and how *persuasive* they could be. Not his concern. Not yet, anyway.

ALL OF THIS INTRIGUE EXHAUSTED GREIGH. IT WAS LATE. A government sedan delivered him back to The Lit. He assured the agent tasked to protect him by standing guard just outside his front door that his apartment was secure. But the grim young man insisted on stationing himself in the hallway. Greigh supposed that should offer him a degree of emotional stability. It did not.

Butler admitted Greigh without a sound. Once inside, Butler's words floated from unseen speakers: "Greigh, you have a guest, a co-worker." Before he'd even rounded the entryway wall into his living room, he wondered if McQ had paid him a late-night visit. The thought warmed him. He plastered on a grin. He thought he registered the odor of an exotic perfume. McQ didn't wear perfume. *Oh-oh....* His grin grew into a grimace.

In the dim ambient light, the ominous image of a silenced pistol met him, pointed at his chest. She clutched it in a perfectly manicured hand that rested on a long and slender set of crossed and waxed legs. He raised his eyes from that ugly silenced weapon to the woman's frigid eyes. The immaculate and costly apparel of a well-heeled and attractive woman with the fragrance of what had to be a costly perfume assailed him. Those huge, cold eyes twinkled. She looked like the American actress Uma Thurman, an aging beauty with a lithe physique, a woman who battled her age with diligent vanity. A lifetime of deception and violence masked by an innocent visage.

He recognized her in an instant, but she now looked far more alluring. Instead of downplaying her beauty as before, she now exercised every desperate measure to enhance it. She was indeed beautiful, but age was winning. The self-assured woman who relaxed on his sofa with that gun aimed at his chest was none other than Freya Ecklund. Or Mika Kuzmin.

"Hello, Greigh."

He just stood there. His arms just hung. So did his slack jaw. He had watched MT's brief video of Mika Kuzmin in Watchtower's underground garage a hundred times, but to witness this remarkable transformation up close and in real life left him stunned. And scared. This wasn't the Freya that he and Butler knew. This was a very different person. Even her voice sounded huskier, sexier. Gone were the baggy clothes of a modestly paid Interpol agent trying to disguise the remnants of her natural beauty. She must be wearing apparel and jewelry worth more than her Interpol salary would have paid for in, what, ten years? More?

"What are you doing here, Freya?"

"No, dear, the name is Mika. Kuzmin. I'm here to help you with your case, Greigh. And possibly, to save your life. At least, for now."

What the shite?

"Please, sit down, Greigh. It's rude to force me to point my lovely pistol up at you. Quite different than agency issue, isn't it?"

Even her accent is completely different. Russian? "Frey—Mika, you are a terrorist. What the hell *happened* to you?"

Mika dismissed his query as a trivial matter as if it would take too long to explain. Instead, she steered the conversation as Greigh seated himself opposite her on the horseshoe sofa in front of his fireplace that now was to her left, to Greigh's right. He couldn't help but stare at... this... stranger... in amazement. She was... stunning, and... utterly terrifying.

"Let's talk about current affairs, shall we? You and all your little government agencies pursue me as a terrorist. You are all wrong. I came to America to integrate my brother's business with my own. I am Tihomir Leonov's sole heir. He left no will. No doubt he thought he had more time. His estate and Watchtower are now mine."

It didn't seem possible, but her icy eyes grew colder as she spoke. This declaration astounded Greigh. He said, "The DNA testing lab. You were providing evidence that you are Ty Leonov's sister, and—"

"His *twin* sister."

"And you're now asserting your influence on Watchtower's board."

"That took more than a little convincing, but yes. I am also investigating my brother's murder."

"The police said he committed—"

"Greigh, stop. Never suggest that to me again." She brandished the long but slender flat-black pistol toward his face, her arm now extended, as if she were taking careful aim.

He held up his palms and continued in a calm voice. "Now, you're acquiring Watchtower into your Obelisk Prime stable."

"You know about that, of course. You are an excellent investigator, Greigh." The discontinuity between her momentary maniacal voice and now, this soothing and encouraging tone unnerved him even further.

"Then why did you transport a bomb on one of your ships?

"I did no such thing."

"But the evidence is—"

"Someone hijacked the *Maltana,* Greigh. My captain is missing. You would do well to investigate *that.*"

Once more, Greigh was stunned into silence at yet another galactic turn of events.

"Know this, Greigh. I asked Rolf to follow you for your protection. I deceived you concerning my alter ego, but I now share all of this with you as a co-worker, even though those days are now behind us." She unfolded herself from the low sofa, and in one fluid motion, that nasty weapon disappeared into her elegant wrap. She leaned forward to slip a flash drive into the front jeans pocket of the still-seated Greigh—a neat trick at which she seemed very adept. Her heady aroma filled his mind with fanciful thoughts before she backed away.

Mika somehow achieved all of that with the utmost of feminine comportment. This is *not* the rough-mouthed, junk-food-eating driver of a piece-of-shit Volvo wagon that tore around the streets of Copenhagen. All of that... just props in her one-woman show? *Remarkable!*

Now both standing, facing each other, she whispered in a lusty tone, "By the time you get to my ship, they—whoever *they* are—will have erased all the security cam coverage aboard. When I suspected something dubious was happening aboard the *Maltana,* I accessed the shipboard servers remotely and downloaded the images now in your pocket. You will find them revealing. By the way, my dear, the captain of the *Maltana* is a very tall and handsome man in his sixties with white hair and is always meticulously clean-shaven. His name is Hans Flughler. You would do well to remember that. Also, think about motives, my old friend."

She hoisted her right eyebrow and held a meaningful gaze aimed at Greigh. It took every ounce of his willpower not to shirk under that penetrating stare. As she turned to leave, she blew him a kiss with her right hand over her left shoulder. He almost missed a subtle button-press on a tiny remote between her left thumb and index finger. He didn't feel the concussive force of the blast, but he heard it. He jumped. She smiled over her shoulder, winked, waited a beat, and strolled out his front door. The FBI agent standing guard at the door had already bolted down the hall to investigate the explosion with his service weapon at the ready.

Greigh followed Freya—Mika. He stood at his still-open door and watched her exquisite backside approach the elevator across the hall. She patiently awaited its arrival, and disappeared. The distracted agent was none the wiser. *Truly remarkable!* He took his time calling down the hall to the FBI agent to alert him.

CHAPTER 45

Still stunned by the appearance of his ex-boss from Interpol, Freya—Mika—was now an accused international terrorist. It would seem she was also some sort of business and criminal mastermind. She moved and spoke like a provocative but aging chameleon—a damn charismatic one.

Greigh chastised Butler for having allowed her entrance into his most private space. But he blamed himself more for being so deceived by Mika's Freya Ecklund persona, and for so long. "My apologies, Greigh. I assumed she was a friend. You've worked with her for years. I had my doubts, but she was very persuasive. Despite earlier conversations I overheard between you, McQ and her sleuth, she convinced me she had your best interests at heart. I believed her."

After he'd settled down from the whirlwind of disturbing events over the last fifteen minutes, Greigh said, "No worries, Butler. She had me fooled for over a decade. And who knows? We might now have another lead in a very complicated case." Greigh fingered the flash drive Mika had slipped into his pocket. It was still warm from her touch. He couldn't get to his computer fast enough. Plugged in the drive and started scrubbing through more than a week's worth of raw videos from over two dozen networked cams aboard the *Maltana.* Three hours of tedium and four cups of strong black Bergamot tea enabled him to discover a brief video clip of two men standing at the ship's railing on the weather deck. One was Lance Bowman. From his earlier interviews of Bowman, Greigh remembered he was about his own height: six-foot-two. Bowman conversed with a much shorter man with reddish hair and a well-trimmed auburn beard. He wore a captain's uniform, and... no, *this cannot be.*

He punched in on the little man's chest. The name tag read, "Captain Hans Flughler," but he wore the face of... Andy Galkin? *But Andy is dead! Is nobody who or what they seem to be?* Greigh checked the metadata on the video taken several days *after* Andy was thought to have gone down with his boat. *After* he and his crew had transferred some mysterious cargo to the *Maltana.*

What are you up to, Andy? You are no simple smuggler, but are you, instead, a master of your trade? You hijacked Freya's—Mika's—freighter? You smuggled a metal case from Estonia into America? At that moment, a bolt of lightning flashed through Greigh. Every nerve ending tingled. *Andy, you are a Russian smuggler.* ***and*** *you're framing Mika for smuggling a WMD into the States, you clever little bugger!* So, Andy had hijacked one of Mika's ships, was aboard as its captain for over a week, and this is the only image of him? *Brilliant, Andy. Did you miss avoiding this one cam, you fecking git?*

Greigh jumped on his comms. "MT, a new assignment for you, luv."

"Wait. I'm here with McQ at her apartment. Some stuff about OP you need to check out. Mika Kuzmin is Russian. But we did *not* know that three years ago she transferred OP's business en masse from Moscow to Paldiski. Greigh, she became a persona non grata in Mother Russia. And guess who her most vocal and scathing critic was... still is. That crazy motherfucker—Russia's extremist president, Alexsei Domvrik. Not sure that means anything, or is relevant here, but this woman has some powerful enemies."

"She was here."

Silence. "Excuse me? Mika was there in your apartment?"

McQ piped up. "Greigh, are you alright? That bitch was *there?*"

"Yes. Mika Kuzmin left my apartment here at The Lit a few hours ago. I suggest you get yourselves over here post haste, ladies. I have news, too."

MT blurted, "Shit on a popsicle stick, old man! On our way."

Old man? No doubt McQ is smiling right now.

Twelve minutes later, Butler admitted MT and McQ. Greigh still sat at his desk scrubbing through the *Maltana's* shipboard footage. He didn't even look up as they joined him to look over his shoulder in silence. Then, after several more minutes, Greigh said, "Small world. I'm not at all convinced it is by accident or coincidence my Interpol handler specifically assigned me to this particular smuggling case. *Also,* that she happens to be an international shipping mogul. *And on top of all* that, one of *her* ships was used to smuggle a bomb into the States. *Oh, and* an old friend of mine is a world-class smuggler, and he's also Mika's nemesis *as well as* the real international terrorist here, albeit a likable little guy with whom I share a history." He pointed to his monitor. "Now, here's the most recent news. See that short guy in the captain's uniform next to Lance Bowman, our Windy City studio executive aboard the freighter *Maltana,* Mika Kuzmin's boat—?"

"Ship, Greigh. A boat leans into a turn. A ship heels outboard during a turn due to the—" He heard McQ chuckle over his left shoulder, despite her favorite mystery writer's tectonic news.

Greigh interrupted their little female Harry Potter. "MT, I love that you understand that distinction, but focus, please. This *ship* belongs to Obelisk Prime. OP belongs to Mika Kuzmin. She spent fifteen minutes chit-chatting with me *right over there,"* he pointed toward the sofa, "less than a three hours ago. Told me *Maltana's* captain is clean-shaven, six-two with white hair and his name is Hans Flughler. Plus, she said she's protecting me."

McQ rustled behind Greigh. "From what?" she said,

"I thought that odd, too. And more than a tad ominous. She used the words 'mortal danger'."

He displayed the earlier image that zoomed in on the short man with the red hair and beard, that highlighted his name tag. MT scratched her always-disheveled hair. "So, that's not Captain Hans Flughler? Who the hell *is* that, then?"

"*That's my friend,* Captain Andrushya Galkin, whom I thought was dead. I drank Scotch with Andy on his boat in Copenhagen two weeks ago. By his own admission, he took a job from some anonymous client to carry a mysterious cargo from Estonia on his little boat and transferred it to the *Maltana.* Said it was for a pile of cash. He further claimed he didn't know what it was, but that he worried. In reality, he hijacked Mika's boa—ship. I was on comms with him when we were just… cut off. As if he and his boat had been erased at sea. This salty little wanker played me! I need to swear off associating with sociopaths."

Greigh's voice had ascended at least a half-octave, and sounded strained. McQ laid a reassuring hand on his left shoulder as if to say, *It's not your fault you were played like a cheap fiddle.* MT said, "Oh, fuck me." She was a bundle of nervous energy, like always. She paced as she processed all of this. Then, Greigh continued with renewed resolve. "And now we must assume he is in Chicago. But why? Is that bomb *his*? And Mika challenged us to look at motives."

McQ proclaimed, "Jeez, Greigh, *you **are** ground zero!* But why?

"Let's think about this." He now took to pacing, too. He and MT circled each other like sharks in a puddle of chum. The cooler McQ watched with crossed arms and one thumb and index finger supporting her chin. "Mika confirmed to me she is, indeed, Ty Leonov's twin sister *and* his sole heir. She views his estate and Watchtower as *her legacies,* and is integrating the two companies—Watchtower and Obelisk Prime. Says that's why she's here, nothing more."

MT shook her head sideways and furrowed her brow. "Why would that be a motive for smuggling, much less murder?"

"Well, I collaborated with Gaspari Copolla and McQ here to take Leonov down for several murders. She might surmise we drove her brother to suicide, which she believes was a ruse to cover up his murder."

A light of comprehension illuminated MT's face. "So that might be Mika's motive for wanting to *end* you. But, then, why *protect* you?"

"Well, as Freya Ecklund, *she* assigned me to this case for a reason. Maybe she knew that with help I'd be the one to crack it, including Galkin's attempt to frame her for a terrorist plot. Now *that* makes sense to me. And that's precisely how it's playing out, isn't it? She knows I'm tight with CED—no offense, McQ." He smirked in her direction. She shrugged, he continued. "Plus, I'm betting she now can't trust anyone else inside Interpol that we know of. She wants me to see this investigation through."

"Then what?"

"Her motives will change. Until then, what the bloody hell is Andy up to? And why?"

MT said, "What if somebody is out to destroy Mika and her company?"

It was as if Greigh considered that. "Okay, but why?"

MT held her palms out, face down, as if to implore the other two to listen before dismissing her hypothesis. "How about someone resents Mika pulling billions of rubles out of Russia—out of Moscow, no less?"

McQ was used to considering outrageous assumptions, but this.... "The Russian *president?*"

MT pressed on. "Why not? Everybody says he's a vindictive prick. He's even made that central to his media presence. Like he's proud of it. Part of his political brand."

Greigh pondered that as outrageous, but then.... "Motive! It's possible President Domvrik, or someone of similar ilk, puts Galkin onto Kuzmin and OP. And what better way to torpedo OP's consolidation with an American company than to frame Mika for attacking America—with nukes, no less?"

McQ pressed the assumption. "*And* he retains plausible deniability by putting a no-name smuggler on the task."

"Brilliant! From there, it's easy to imagine a hostile takeover of OP by a Russian loyalist, or worse, by one of Domvrik's puppets."

MT paced—a crazy girl with her arms flailing like electrified spaghetti. Taking her speech to a new level of rapidity, she said, "How 'bout we assume Galkin whipped up some papers to enter the country as the *Maltana's* captain? We get your Fed buddies to search Immigration and Customs for the movement of one Hans Flughler. Could be the guy thinks he's still under the radar but will screw up by leaving an unintentional trail. Credit card, something like that."

Greigh mopped his now-perspiring forehead with a slow sweep of his left palm. "I suspect Andy's sharper than that, but it's worth a shot." He held an index finger vertical while facing MT and McQ. Tapped on his comms and said with contrived cheeriness, "Hey, Mac. How's my favorite neophyte detective?"

"Neophyte? That means new, right?"

"Indeed. Hey, I'm here with McQ and MT."

"Hey, ladies." He sounded tired. It was after midnight, and he still toiled away.

"But only I can hear you. Mac, we have a break in the case the other agencies may not have yet stumbled upon. You're still on the task force, right?"

"Blank check, buddy. What do you guys need?"

"We need ICE to check on the status of a Danish or Estonian national named Hans Flughler." He spelled the last name for Mac. "May be an imposter posing as captain of the *Maltana*. Might lead us down another probative path."

"Give me a few minutes. Shit happens real fast in this new club you and I just joined. I'll need to pass this along. McQ, you'd hate it. Too stuffy for your wild-child side."

Greigh relayed Mac's comment. She just snorted. He said, "That's fine. Also, I'll need to come in. I've met with Mika Kuzmin. Face-to-face. She just left my apartment a few hours ago."

"Holy shit, Greigh!"

"Right. They already know from the guard they left at my door. Still, I wish to present some additional facts… in person." He hung up with a double-tap without awaiting Mac's further reply.

McQ said, "By the way, you wanna tell us why the end of your hallway is all *scorched earth*?"

MT jumped in. "Yeah, I was gonna ask about that, too. Never a dull moment around this crew."

Greigh just shrugged.

MAC PICKED UP GREIGH IN FRONT OF THE LIT TWENTY-TWO minutes later while the girls walked back to McQ's apartment.

"Getting to be a habit," Mac chuckled.

"Onward, Chariot Master." Greigh yawned. Mac followed suit.

CHAPTER 46

Thirty minutes earlier, the clocked had ticked over from the 5th of September to the 6th. They arrived back at the VIP circle drive entrance in front of the FBI field office on Roosevelt Road. They left the government sedan. Spent another ten minutes navigating the maze of security and hallways before they plopped into "their chairs" in that same stuffy conference room on the sixth floor. It still contained too many suits, but now adorned by loosened ties and a few different odors. Not a terrible after-dark view of the city's skyline, though the translucent blinds on the east wall washed it out.

Greigh's new Interpol friend, Colette, was nowhere to be seen. Special Agent in Charge Spears still sat at the head of the table, although he, too, now appeared far more disheveled than Greigh's last visit a day earlier. They all did, like they hadn't left this room since the task force convened, except maybe to visit the water closet. Piles of paper had accumulated on every horizontal surface. Empty styrofoam cups were scattered everywhere. Stale-smelling plates of half-eaten food sat ignored, shoved aside. And multiple projectors displayed various tactical status reports on three of the room's four beige walls, between a half-dozen monitors on those same walls.

"What have you got for us on Mika's visit to your apartment, Mr. Greigh?"

"She claims she's being framed."

SAC Spears cocked his head to his left and crinkled his massive forehead. "Motive?"

"She jerked a business worth billions out of Moscow and removed it from the country three years ago. Possible motive: President Domvrik or somebody near the top of that hierarchy was likely enraged. Now that Mika's taking over Watchtower, we're guessing he and his are throwing a wobbly. But we're still investigating that. We could use some more eyes on that possibility."

"Interesting. And troublesome. What else? Other evidence of a frame job?"

Greigh hesitated. This would be embarrassing. So be it. "Appears her claim has merit. It seems someone hijacked one of her ships and it is almost certain to have smuggled a WMD across the Atlantic. Your team can verify that. An imposter posing as the captain of the *Maltana* is a personal acquaintance of mine."

Spears's eyes widened. He stood. His chair rolled away from him silently. Hands on hips, he said, "Mr. Greigh, it would appear that there is a nexus between the major players of this case, and you are at its center. Please explain."

There is no reason for me to feel defensive. So, why do I? "Andrushya Galkin—Andy—is an old friend, an informant. I've always known that he survived by engaging in dubious endeavors. But to my knowledge, he's always gravitated toward low-level smuggling of innocuous contraband." Greigh retrieved the flash drive from his front jeans pocket. "Mika provided me with the original video feeds from the *Maltana's* security servers as a precaution that she said now proves warranted. I've analyzed and focused on revealing still-image grabs from the videos. I've highlighted the meeting between Lance Bowman and Andy Galkin posing as Hans Flughler—the name of Mika's legitimate captain of the *Maltana*.

"Mac," he motioned toward his CED detective friend sitting to his immediate left, "is running down any information on Galkin. We're assuming he may still be using Flughler's identity while in the Chicago area. That is our working assumption. Mika claims *her* far-simpler motives are two-fold: assume the reins of Watchtower and of her twin brother's estate. We suspect that she's involved in other nefarious activities, but I now believe that terrorism is not one of them. We're not yet sure whether this Lance Bowman from Windy City studios is only a cursory player or something more. That he booked his entire cast and crew for one of his movie projects on that same freighter cannot be a coincidence. So we should plan to probe into his involvement further, obviously." Greigh winced, like a man who had been duped on multiple levels. It was plain for all to witness his pain.

SAC SPEARS CONTEMPLATED WHAT HE'D JUST SEEN AND heard. After a full minute of awkward silence and other voices muttering to each other around the table, Spears pronounced in his James Earl Jones baritone, "Well done, Mr. Greigh. Somehow, either because of your Interpol case or your personal history with at least two of our major suspects, you're in the thick of this affair. You seem to leverage that advantage well. Anything else?"

"I wish to acknowledge that credit for much of this progress has been a team effort. My thanks to CED," he nodded toward Mac, "the efforts of Chance McQuillan on leave from the CED, and invaluable support from Urban Security Services."

Spears suddenly seemed short-tempered. "Yes, yes, acknowledged. Let us focus on preventing the transformation of downtown Chicago into a nuclear crater, shall we? Thank you, Mr. Greigh. I assume you'd like to be excused?" Greigh just nodded and left with a second nod toward Mac that seemed to say, *Let me know ASAP when you learn anything more about Galkin, a.k.a. Flughler, and any of his associates.*

CHAPTER 47

~

Andy Galkin peered through the curtains at the near-empty early morning parking lot of their smelly room on South Kreiter Avenue in South Chicago. The *Four Aces Motel? Ha!* He reflected on all that had gotten him to this moment. In America! This had been a long-time coming. *I strike blow for my powerful new friends,* **and** *for myself. But I become very rich and stay here in America for all of my days!*

He simmered in the bile of his own anger. No, that wasn't right—in his seething hatred. Of *Sir* Aubrey Greigh. He remembered their many near-death experiences crossing the Crimea Peninsula to the Baltic together, escaping against all odds. How many times did they both think they would be killed? From Andy's perspective, he had saved Greigh's life—many times over. *He* did the heavy lifting for Greigh. *And what thanks I get?*

Even knowing how much Andy loved everything about America, Greigh just ghosted him instead of helping him to immigrate, to save *his* life. He had tried to reach the already-famous writer over the years, but heard nothing back. And all of this after Greigh said he would help him in any way he could to repay him for his "kindness." *Kind-*

ness? I wonder if what is said about Americans and America is true! He didn't care. He wanted a piece of that dream. He'd earned it. And ever since? He'd had to take the most horrible jobs just to survive. And now? He'd take what he could get, from whomever he could. He liked to characterize the four mercenaries as his protection detail, his King's guard. They were also to ensure the plan's success. So far, they had kept order on the ship during their entire passage.

Andy now sat in this medium-size low-budget motel room, close to the Iroquois Lakefront Terminal at the mouth of the Calumet River. He and Mika's crew had docked the *Maltana* there, where the ship now sat quarantined. Not only were each of those crew members now richer than they could have imagined, but they remained clueless. He wondered how many had been arrested. No matter. His plan was on schedule.

This place reeked of urine and mold, but he cared not. It was stuffy and hot, with five bodies in the room and just one queen bed. He stroked his thin red mustache before scratching his short reddish beard, now with gray edges. Glanced over at the blankets on the floor. Those four animals could sleep, eat, and shit just about anywhere. But they were professionals. They scared him, but he dared not show that. After all, he was the boss here. Wasn't he? Three of this foursome were covered with Russian prison tattoos. That meant they probably burned the heel of a shoe and mixed it with soot and urine before applying the mixture with anything sharp. They were professionals, but definitely not ex-military types. Just the roughest mercenaries imaginable. Their long guns leaned against the wall farthest from the door, but they kept possession of their handguns and other concealed weapons at all times. Even in the bathroom.

Andy had slowed his own discovery, gaining valuable time, by setting up that OP bitch for the fall. Amazing how many powerful enemies she had. And other interests sweetened the pot. *Da, that fine with me.* His path to fortune and US citizenship all became possible, now. All he needed to do was decimate the heart of Chicago, America's heartland. God bless America and enriched Uranium from a forgotten Cold War era Soviet missile research and development lab in the southwestern region of Mother Russia. Now, only he controlled the trigger to a ten kiloton fission bomb hidden where no one would find it. All to exact revenge for the destruction of Mika Kuzmin's twin brother, Ty Leonov. Or so everyone would believe. Until it was too late.

That this attack would deal a significant blow to what would be his new homeland was of no concern to him. He relished the irony that both this Mika bitch and he shared a common priority: the death of her Interpol employee and his "friend," Aubrey Greigh. Of course, Andy knew of Mika Kuzmin's alter-ego—Freya Ecklund. Crazy bitch thought she was so damn clever. Let's see how clever she really is.

In a single day, besides Mika and Greigh, hundreds of other souls would perish, too. Maybe thousands. He felt bad about that. But he needed these attacks to render the entire Chicago area, an important portion of the Midwestern United States and their largest city, to become uninhabitable for decades. All in the course of a single day. Just like another day with the same date, but decades earlier. September 11th would be detonation day. D-Day. *Da, symbolic.* Six days from now.

All traces of their "specialty cargo" had needed to disappear before piloting the *Maltana* into the Canadian/American canal and lake system. They had transferred their cargo to a private one-hundred-foot yacht off the coast of New Hampshire prior to entering Canadian and US waters. According to the plan, the yacht moored at an abandoned commercial wharf on the Piscatagua River, near the outskirts of Portsmouth. There, the metal box encased in a wooden crate had been transferred to an eighteen-wheeler for transport to a warehouse.

His loyal—a.k.a. well-paid and somewhat odious—team of specialists that arrived with him on the *Maltana* planned to arm and set the detonation timer on the device. They had also enabled a backup remote detonator that Galkin himself carried with him at all times. So far, the plan had proceeded flawlessly.

Galkin had also benefitted from a brilliant disinformation campaign concocted by one of his benefactors. They produced chatter certain to be picked up by America's intelligence services. The gist was that the attack would comprise ten targets, not just one, in and around downtown Chicago. All were designed to mask the plan's primary objective, at least as far as he was concerned.

Though it was pure fiction, four tactical targets would be rumored to include a major power distribution center that lit up the Near Southwest Loop. Also, Chicago Enforcement Department headquarters at Police Plaza, the Chicago Federal Reserve and Board of Trade, as well as the University of Chicago Medical Center in Hyde Park, including the Pritzker School of Medicine. Further, five symbolic targets would be rumored. City Hall and the Arch Diocese of Chicago downtown. In Cicero, the heart of the movie district. And farther north, the Great Lakes Naval Training Center. Finally, the Rock Island Army Arsenal Base out west of the city on the Mississippi River. The illusion of this latter target would threaten to carry radiation down the entire river system to the Gulf of Mexico. The symbolism would be unmistakable. It would draw law enforcement resources away from their single actual Ground Zero. But it *was* all just an illusion to mask the actual target: the Cicero movie studio district.

Galkin smiled when he thought of the care they would take to place their only device at the Hotel Literati at the very last moment. *New Ground Zero*. His personal favorite. He would direct his team to move the target from its original destination - a warehouse in Cicero. He didn't care about the added level of risk in doing so. Neither would the right people care if they knew, and the wrong people would never know. Nor would it matter. Because the bomb would take out the entire area, anyway. Nobody needed to know he'd adjusted Ground Zero.

Of course, he benefitted from a great deal of help. His new friends provided the expertise required for the selection of this illusory set of targets. They also would ensure his path to citizenship and a lifetime of personal wealth. But now, he needed to deliver results. As detonation day—D-Day—approached, he envisioned his dreams were already materializing. And since Andy was already dead—the captain who valiantly went down with his ship—Mika Kuzmin would be blamed for the entire affair. And *Sir* Aubrey Greigh would be vaporized. Da!

CHAPTER 48

~

At that same moment, Lois sat at her desk in the nine-nine and answered her comms. "This is Captain Granger..."

"Captain, this is Jack Roberts."

Granger jumped to her feet. "Yes, Commissioner, how may I help you?"

"It's how I can help *you,* Captain. I understand you've been trying to reach me for some time. I've been stalling."

"Sir?"

"You know, buying time."

"I don't understand—"

"Captain Granger, Lois, I owe you an apology. This McQuillan thing... we're wrapped up in this joint task force and Aubrey Greigh needed—"

"Sir, all due respect, what's Greigh got to do with reinstating Detective McQuillan?" Her words came out sharper than she intended. Too late to back-pedal, so she didn't try. She heard a deep sigh.

"Oh, hell, Lois, this has gotten away from us. Some have implied that there may be a mole in CED, and we weren't taking any chances."

"A *what?* Okay, well, sir, how about you tell me why you called? You must believe you can trust me, now."

"I made a commitment to Interpol. It made sense. At the time. Now, though, I wish I had taken you into my confidence earlier. But this can go no further. For now. Agreed?"

"Oh, for heaven's sake, Jack, spill it, already,"

"Yes, of course. I've been sitting on Detective McQuillan's reinstatement."

Lois didn't know what to say, so she remained silent. *He better give me more. Quick. This is pissing me off.*

"Look, Lois, this could make me a pariah. But with the city's future at stake—"

"Oh, cut the crap, sir. This is political." *Shit. Talking like this is gonna cost me my damn job.*

"Captain, there are one or more nuclear devices on the loose in *our* city. Rogue elements within the department could lead us astray of finding them. We've already unearthed one in Interpol—"

She drew in a sharp intake of breath, for more than one reason. Almost choking in shock, she said, "Nukes? Here? Mole? Not Greigh!"

"No, no. Not Greigh. But we needed McQuillan to use any and every resource available, some unconventional from the department's perspective, working *with* Greigh, out of uniform, so to speak. And she has risen to the occasion. You have as well, Captain. Yes, I do trust you. Don't let me down. Keep this to yourself. We need McQuillan out there leveraging her rather unusual relationships *as a civilian,* including Greigh, to find those damn devices before the city is reduced to a radioactive crater. Can I count on you, Captain?"

Holy shit! "Um, yeah. I mean, of course, sir. I had no idea. What else can I do?" She plopped down into her desk chair, light-headed.

"Nothing. Other than keeping this between you and me. And continue to support the task force. That is all, Captain Granger."

"Yes, sir." *Click*

~

A FEW HOURS LATER, GREIGH AND McQ CROSSED THE VAST lobby of The Lit. The cop in McQ objected to sharing information about their investigation with Luca Donati, their friend and proprietor of the building. They entered the bird cage elevator. Greigh pushed four where they'd board Luca's private lift to The Lit's sixteenth-floor penthouse where Luca lived. This was an accommodation to its century-and-a-half-old architecture. "But Luca's a civilian, Greigh, and a damn sensitive one. Why do you want to burden him with all of this?"

"McQ, he has a right to know. Maybe if we had shared more with him and Vince sooner last summer, Luca might not be living alone, now."

She chuffed out loud. "Okay, that's bullshit right there, but I understand your feelings. And he *is* the one who asked for my help after Gaspari's gut told him something 'un-American' was going on over at Watchtower."

"Don't forget, McQ, *you* are also just a civilian."

"Shut up!" She smirked and play-slapped his shoulder.

They arrived on four and transferred to Luca's private elevator. Greigh still thought of them *lifts* in his mind. As the door swished open at sixteen, Luca greeted them, gushing with enthusiasm. "Two of my favorite people in the whole wide world! Come in, come in. I am *so* pleased to see the two of you together again."

They both blushed and glanced at each other before Greigh blurted, "Luca, good to see you, too, old friend. We are not *together*, though. It's—"

"Oh, posh. Come here!" Luca threw his arms around an embarrassed Greigh who stood more than a foot taller than the rotund little man in his perennial silk and velvet smoking jacket (he didn't smoke). After a moment, though, he returned Luca's embrace before Luca moved on to hug McQ. That hug was even more awkward than the first.

As she pulled away, McQ said, "Okay, Luca, can we sit down already? We have a lot to share with you."

"Of course! It's been so long, and truth be told, I don't receive many visitors. It seems I don't have many friends. I've realized that since Vince...."

Greigh piped up before this became a pity fest. "Let's talk, Luca."

As they seated themselves on the enormous sofa down in what Luca called his conversation pit in the sunken living room with McQ between Greigh and Luca, Greigh began. He shifted to his right and leaned forward to peer around McQ. "Luca, Gaspari's gut was spot on. The power play at the top of Watchtower is real. We're still trying to understand what's happening, but we wanted you to be aware both McQ and I are looking into it—together." He looked at McQ. She glued her eyes to what must have been a fascinating spot on the top of her right knee.

"There are some new players who have taken over the board and are now in control of Watchtower—more Russians." Luca shivered, hugging himself as his eyes widened. Then he squinted and tightened his lips. Greigh issued a quick emotional back-pedal maneuver. "Listen, Luca, we're not sure what that means yet. But these new players at Watchtower might be affiliated with planning some sort of terrorist attack. A task force has convened, and the authorities are now aware of this threat. They and we are doing everything possible to contain it."

Luca shrank further in on himself as Greigh tried to simplify the situation for the little man. He now thought McQ might have been right. She slugged Greigh in the shoulder, and accompanied the gesture with a look that said, *What are you? An idiot?* She patted Luca's left shoulder.

She used a softened tone. "Luca, this is all investigatory BS. We can't confirm any of this yet. This is Greigh's way of saying we're planning for the worst while hoping for the best." She cast one more silent glance of disbelief at Greigh and added, "But Signore Copolla's gut is serving us well." Rather than making matters worse, they both fell silent for almost a minute as the poor fellow processed what he'd just heard.

"Well, I guess I should thank you for sharing this with me. Don Gaspari has always had a good nose for trouble—often how to get more deeply steeped in it versus avoiding it." He mustered a troubled chuckle before continuing. "Should I be worrying about the two of you? If memory serves, neither of you struggle to find trouble, either."

They all laughed. And that was it. Luca offered the two sleuths a glass of wine, but they declined. The memory of Luca's husband dying in Greigh's arms just a few months earlier at the hand of a Watchtower assassin still troubled them all. Now, it seemed this Autumn's *trouble* had already eclipsed that of last Summer. After a warning to keep this to himself and another round of awkward hugs, McQ and Greigh bid their lonely friend goodbye.

CHAPTER 49

Lionel and Angelique Hollowell reminisced. They were minor Hollywood business celebrities, including the funding of a few stars' careers. The couple spent obscene sums on advertising their real estate ventures all across Orange County on television, radio, outdoor (from billboards to sky-writing), streaming services, and social media. Most everyone in that county comprising a population greater than most states had heard of the Hollowells and their slogan:

Realtors to the stars! And you!

Someone even bequeathed them a pet couple's name in the press, like so many Hollywood celebrity couples. It stuck. Their tacky circle of friends and a few obscure members of the Los Angeles media called Lionel and Angelique *Lionique*. Had a nice ring to it, they thought, and did not discourage its use. This duo had obsessed for the last twenty years over making money. They surrounded themselves with others who may not have been beautiful on the outside but whose habits also revolved around amassing extraordinary wealth.

Lionique didn't hang out with stars, but with people who *make* stars. This crowd knew that money—and cosmetic surgery—bought a lot of forgiveness for genetic anomalies or a lack of social finesse, even legal dilemmas. That was a polite way of describing people from the wrong side of the tracks. But long ago, this crowd had figured out how to cross those tracks with flamboyance, now having the means to boast of their "proud peasant heritage." That was all code for rich white trash.They dared anyone to mock them with just a look or a scathing word. They even shared a familiar homily: 'Fuck 'em if they can't take a joke'. Most took it.

This circle of acquaintances called each other friends, because they were pariahs outside the circle, sharing a certain clinging desperation to one another, and especially to Lionique. They even named their little co-ed fraternity of avarice: the LA County Consortium, or LACC. They joked they *LACC'd for nothing!* Gave them a thin veneer of charitable respectability. At least, *they* thought so.

CHAPTER 50

After McQ and Greigh left Luca late morning, she dropped Greigh off at his apartment on the seventh floor of The Lit. Said he had calls to make. She and MT had agreed to meet at McQ's apartment. MT sat on the outside alley stairs, elbows on knees, waiting for her client. She wrinkled her nose at the nearby dumpster and casually batted away blowflies dive-bombing her. As McQ approached from the street and caught MT's choreography of irritation, she shrugged, nodded, and led the way up the exterior staircase that creaked as they ascended—like they had for years. That wood needed to be treated, or at least painted, before it collapsed. She'd mention it to Harrow, her landlord. Again. He was a good guy, just needed reminders.

McQ had just brewed them each a cup of strong English breakfast tea—Greigh's favorite: Bergamot. Americans called it Earl Grey. She was hooked. Sat the two cups filled to their brims on her tiny table under her only window. Muted sunshine filtered through her gauzy curtain drawn tight. So did shadows of the more opaque anti-burglar bars. McQ muttered, "Try not to kick the legs. This damn table isn't too steady.

The young PI stared across the table at McQ and wrinkled her nose. She said, "Tea? Are you kidding?"

"Hey, kid, I need some stimulation, and Greigh assures me this stuff will do the trick, even for us Yanks, he'd say. After precinct coffee, this is the only caffeine I can stomach, anymore. And sodas'll kill you dead. Here. Douse it with some honey. Good for you, too, according to Greigh." She knuckle-shoved a squeeze bottle of commercial honey a few inches toward the young PI. Not like MT couldn't already reach it on that small table. *I'm calling her 'kid' and she's only four years younger than me. Looks like a street orphan, but she is sharp!*

"Whatever you say, boss. Um, I got some intel back from our accounting guys. They've been grabbing onto whatever Windy City financials they could score, as well as this Bowman character's private accounts. I won't plague you with how they got 'em."

McQ winced. MT rushed onward. "As a cop, they tie your hands a lot more than most of us mere private citizens, even compared to us private dicks. And our methods aren't *always* strictly illegal." She tossed in a smirk with a wink, "so just roll with it. Here, check this out." She turned her tablet around for McQ.

"What am I lookin' at?"

"Focus on the line items labeled 'CG' and 'AI?'"

"Yeah. Computer generated imagery and artificial intelligence shit, right?"

"Yup. Looks like Bowman cut those two budgets by twenty million earlier this year. Like sixty percent."

"Since he's trying to back away from that stuff, right? That's what he's said."

"Exactly. Only our guys can't find out where that money went. And they are *very* good. They saw right through some half-assed attempts to bloat salary, bonus and expense accounts. All bullshit."

"But it's supposed to go for actors, locations, and such. He's also said that."

MT said, "Yeah, that's what this Bowman guy *says*, but it's like that money just moved offshore without a trace. And was *not* spent on trips to or from locations, either. Not anywhere our accounting geeks can find, anyway. That's real suspicious all by itself. The Copenhagen thing? That *all* came out of Windy City's general expense fund. Every nickel."

"Well, what are we supposed to do with this, MT? If your guys used questionable means to get it, we can't have the guy arrested."

"No, but it might make for an interesting discussion with this dude by a couple of sharp investigators, like you 'n your main squeeze." Her eyes twinkled.

McQ jerked on that trigger a little too fast. "Greigh is *not* my main squeeze." And sort of as an introspective afterthought, she muttered, "Not that I'd mind all that much." Across that little table they grinned big at each other which turned into mischievous chuckles and slantwise glances an instant later. Tea spilled over the brim of both cups.

SAC SPEARS, CHAIR OF THE JOINT TERRORISM TASK FORCE, sounded frustrated. Noon came and went. He hadn't touched any of the cute sandwiches the staff had delivered an hour earlier—only the coffee. Nor had anyone else. Spears stared down the rough-looking team leader of his FBI apprehension team, anticipating an unsatisfying answer. "News on this Andrushya Galkin, a.k.a. Hans Flughler?"

"Nothing, sir."

Spears then sprayed that stare around everyone in the room, and with volume that broadcast impatience. "Ladies and gentlemen, we must assume the fuse is lit and burning down to detonation. Other avenues? For example, there is no question this Mr. Lance Bowman was on the same ship that transported at least one nuclear device into our own backyard. And there could be as many as ten based on SIGINT. But signal intelligence chatter will only navigate us so far. We have no cause to apprehend him yet, not even by leveraging the Patriot Act.

We hold video evidence of him conversing with our primary—Andrushya Galkin—but no audio, so nothing definitive. Six of his own employees have been murdered. But we have nothing to prove he was involved, *or* that he had knowledge of what was being transported on that ship. I want CED to take the lead with this guy. He might lead us to Galkin." Spears looked down at Mac sitting to his right at the table that was now more cluttered than ever. "Shake his cage, Detective MacKenzie. Let's see if any debris rattles loose. And let's do it soonest." Mac nodded, arose and hustled out of the room without uttering a word.

MAC AND HIS PARTNER, TONY SANTOS, KEPT BOWMAN waiting for half an hour sitting at a chipped table bolted to the floor. They observed him from the far side of a panel of one-way glass that occupied most of the south wall of *Interrogation One* at the nine-nine. Greigh had joined them only as an observer, despite his good standing as an investigator with Interpol *and* as a JTTF member. Santos had made that clear. Observer *only*. Mac rolled his eyes. Greigh just smiled and nodded. They had a plan.

Greigh and the two detectives all smirked at the Ben Affleck look-a-like. The dandy couldn't allow more than a minute to pass before craning his neck ninety degrees to the right. He had to ensure his persona was perfect in the one-way mirror—that of a harried and misunderstood executive who was in over his head, but only by a little. The look broadcast that despite extending himself, he could do his job very well. But he was to be pitied, not feared, *or* exalted. Well, maybe revered for being the youngest studio GM in Chicago. And possibly feared just a little, too. That contrived look was pretty hard to misinterpret by the three skilled investigators. It was as if the mook didn't know he was being watched. Santos didn't hide his disdain for this guy's type. "This asshole is a piece a work."

"Let's see what he has to say." Mac nodded at Greigh again before he led the way out into the hallway. Turned to the left, then another through *One's* door ten feet later with Santos on his heels.

~

Lance Bowman, general manager of Windy City Studios, jumped as the two men who had brought him here swept into the room. One of them, the non-Hispanic, slapped a folder onto the table between him and them. They both held him in accusative stares, but neither said anything. "Gentlemen, what am I doing here? I am a busy man, although I'm glad to help in any way I can, of course." Lance only tried a little to hide his impatience at their impertinence. This was not how he was accustomed to being treated. He swiveled his indignant stare across that piece-of-shit table, first at the white guy, then at the Spic. Couldn't help but turn up his nose again in disgust at the room's odor. Stunk like a boy's high school locker room crossed with an undercurrent of industrial disinfectant that wasn't quite doing its job.

They were so obvious. Lance matched the tactic used by these two municipal underlings. They stared. He gave as good as he got. After all, he possessed the soul of an actor. They had brought him here, not under arrest, but as a *person of interest*. He had come voluntarily. He had nothing to hide and only wished to help—as far as they could tell. Then, the white guy, *what was his name, again?* spoke after the silent treatment had not given them what they wanted. *Score one for the Lance-man the Bow-man.* "Thank you for coming in, Mr. Bowman."

He smirked. "Didn't seem like you boys allowed much of a choice. But again, I wish to do anything I can to help with the case."

"I'm glad to hear you say that, Mr. Bowman. May I call you Lance?"

"Of course."

"Great. Just call me Mac. And this swarthy young man is Tony." Nods all around. All so polite yet informal. *Must be the warm-ups to the main event. What the hell do they have on me, or think they have? Must be something.*

Mac led. "We need to clear up a few questions that have come up in our investigation so far. For example, where were you the night Peter Fontera was murdered?"

"*Peter?* Isn't that a question the Copenhagen police should ask?"

"Did they?"

"Ask me? Actually, no, they did not."

"So?"

"Isn't that a little out of your jurisdiction? Besides, they closed Peter's case, unfortunately."

"We're collaborating with Interpol on that case. *They* have not closed it. Now, help us out."

They're treating me like a suspect! "You're asking *me* for an *alibi?* For my own actor's *murder?*"

"Lance, we ask the questions. Alibi or not?"

Without further hesitation, "That would have been a Monday, the tenth of last month, when Peter was.... I recall studying change pages in my hotel suite for the next day's scenes. Tuesdays are always big days."

Santos did his thing. "Let me guess. You were alone. Nobody to corroborate your story."

"Yes, I *was* alone. But you can check hotel security footage, or something. Can't you?"

"No alibi. How about the more recent shooting of *five more* of *your employees?* You can see why we need to ask these questions, right, Lance? How this looks?"

"Ah, of course. The Saturday none of us will ever forget. I was in my office. My assistant Dawn will remember. She was upset as I asked her to work over the weekend. She had something planned, but with all that's been happening—"

Mac jumped in again. "Lance, our forensics team verified there were multiple shooters that day. That tells me someone hired that hit." He waited, even though that was not a question.

"I'm sure I wouldn't know anything about such things. You asked for my alibi. I gave you one." *Shit! What else do they know? Sounds like they're fishing.*

THAT WAS GREIGH'S CUE—*MULTIPLE SHOOTERS*. HE JUMPED when he heard it. Grabbed a sheaf of paper, left the observation cubicle behind the one-way glass, and bolted into the hallway. He swung the interrogation room's door open so hard the knob dented the inside wall. He rushed forward and handed the pile of paper to Mac. Greigh looked over at Bowman slantwise and shrugged. Bowman just glared back at him, perplexed and angered. After handing Mac what was supposed to be news hot off the presses, as the Yanks would say, Greigh backed away from the table and leaned against the glass wall. At least, it was mirrored glass from the waist up.

Mac looked at the first page of the packet. Then, with a flourish, flipped to the next page, and the next. As he did so, his brow wrinkled ever more. He clucked his cheek, and shook his head side-to-side. Greigh thought he did so a little too theatrically. But the cheeky wanker sitting across from Mac didn't know bollocks from bee's knees about theatrics. Mac continued to pour it on. He shared what he had 'just discovered' with Santos, who then took his turn, rapid fire. "We see you've cut your CG and AI budgets by some twenty million since your second quarter. Where did all that go?"

"Well, as I've said, we're reinvesting in live actors and real-world locations. Any more precise than that would be a question for my accountant, now, wouldn't it?"

A COCKY LITTLE BASTARD, MAC MUSED. "WHO WOULD THAT BE?"

"Brad Tombaugh at Tombaugh and Leicester."

Santos took another turn. "Lance, here's the funny thing. We did ask ole Brad, and you know what he said? 'No idea.' How 'bout that?"

Mac jumped in again. Tag-teaming was a great way to fluster a suspect. "That's how our new buddy Brad started in on us, too, until we threatened to slap him with an obstruction charge in a multiple-homicide investigation. Something like, oh, accessory after the fact. He then enthusiastically checked all your biz accounts for us, and—"

"Don't you need a warrant for that?" His perfect persona cracked and his voice sounded thin and stringent. And thirsty. One cheek rippled with what might have been a momentary spasm.

Santos again, after reading that facial tick. "You mean like this one?" He waved around a tri-folded piece of letterhead-size paper. Good thing Bowman didn't ask to see it. "Look, Lance, we got six homicides, all your employees. Plus, a potential terror attack on the city of Chicago using an explosive device smuggled into America in the same ship on which you booked 'emergency' passage. And we have you on video conversing and striking some sort of deal with our primary suspected terrorist. He also happened to be the captain of that same rust bucket. We also have you pegged for a shit-ton of missing cash, which looks mighty suspicious. Maybe even enough to fund your own domestic terrorist cell. You can see how all this looks, put all together, right? So don't you think it's time you came clean so we can see what we might do for you when it comes time for your arraignment?"

THAT FLUSTERED LANCE, ALRIGHT. *HOW DO THEY KNOW ALL OF THIS?* But he smelled a fishing expedition. He said with more bravado than he felt, "But don't you need an arrest before an arraignment? This all sounds like innuendo and circumstantial to me. Am I free to go?"

Greigh came off the wall, no longer leaning, but his feet remained planted. His hands came out of his pocket, and his clamped lips parted to reveal the tip of his tongue. That was not lost on Lance. *Nope, they have nothing definitive.* Without waiting for permission, he stood as if to leave. Nobody stopped him. After a couple of beats, he puffed out a quiet strawberry of disgust and walked around that piece-of-shit table. The white guy, the Hispanic guy, and that fucking *author* all dropped their jaws. They stayed there. Lance smiled, opened the door, left it ajar, and breezed down the hallway.

~

WHAT BOWMAN COULD NOT SEE WERE THE THREE GUYS still occupying *Interrogation One* all smiling at each other.

CHAPTER 51

"Captain Flughler, the police are onto me. I can no longer wait until Wednesday to disappear."

"You fool! You call on unencrypted comms? Now we *both* need disappear early. Say nothing more. Go. Now."

"Yes, sir. Anyway, six days from today, it will all be—"

"Shut your mouth!" *Click*

THE THREE OF THEM HUNKERED IN THE SURVEILLANCE VAN on South Cicero, down the street from Windy City. "Gotcha, you slimy fuck!" Mac beamed at Santos, who said, "Saturday? Shit, man, we got a timeline." Greigh crouched across from the two detectives, *observing only,* elbows on knees, with beads of sweat popping out on his forehead. He said, "Mac, we must inform Spears straightaway. We have less than a week to find those bombs."

Santos: "No shit, Sherlock. Where did he call?"

Mac looked at a screen in front of him. "To an address on Kreiter.

Close to the Iroquois Terminal, where the *Maltana* is still quarantined." He jumped on his secure CED comms to call Spears at the JTTF. "SAC Spears, get your apprehension team to 11538 South Kreiter Avenue. Suspect One's likely location. And he's probably already on the move. Also, we now believe D-Day is next Saturday. Wait, September 11th? ***Shit!***"

"Copy. Out."

Mac said, "We're not waiting on any fucking warrant. Let's go grab this Bowman slime ball." Santos looked like he was about to object, but didn't. Greigh jumped out of the van to grab a taxi. Mac and Santos screeched up to the closed Windy City gate. One of three guards sauntered out of the gatehouse to their driver's window. Took his time. Mac flashed his shield and said, "Open that gate. Right fuckin' now."

"Do you have an appointment, sir?"

Mac could see another guard in the gatehouse reaching for the phone. He said, "Fuck it," to nobody in particular. The guard must have assumed this impatient cop had second thoughts about entering the premises and was backing out onto South Cicero Ave to depart. That wasn't Mac's intention, at all.

Sitting in the passenger's seat, Santos said, "Yeah, they're stalling." Mac backed up about ten lengths, hit the accelerator, and barreled toward the gates at speed. He hollered an unnecessary warning without taking his eyes off the gates ahead. "Brace yourself!" Those gates were as strong as they looked. At impact, the rear of the van lifted from the pavement and the impact caved in the entire front-end. But the gates gave way, along with chunks of masonry where hinges were anchored. The engine clanged in anger. A column of smoke issued around the busted-open seams between the hood and the body, but it still ran.

They roared up to the executive office building a hundred yards ahead and on their right. Barged their way into Bowman's outer office. They were confronted by a blustered receptionist. Startled, Bowman's assistant stood up behind her desk, objected in defiance as she jiggled toward them in her heels with her spaghetti arms outstretched. They pushed her out of the way and slammed open the double doors to Bowman's office. Empty. Came back out. Mac said as he huffed, "Where the fuck is he?"

"Ah, I have no idea. He received a call and rushed right out."

"Shit! We've had this place under constant surveillance." They had screwed up. Mac jumped on his comms. "This is Detective Aidan MacKenzie, badge 135622. I need a search and containment team at 33955 South Cicero Avenue in Cicero. And I mean, right fuckin' now! That is, ah, Priority Zero. Suspect is Lance Bowman. Apprehend and detain. Out."

Mac turned to Santos. "Door to door."

"Roger. I'll secure the gate."

Mac searched the building, starting from Bowman's office working out and up in the two-story structure. He expanded the search from there as Santos placed their van across the collapsed gate before the engine finally surrendered to its injuries. He quizzed the guards. No joy. Both detectives already knew they were pissing in the wind, and there was little to no chance of finding this guy on the mammoth lot. Though there was only one vehicle entry/exit, and Santos guarded that, there could be countless concealed pedestrian exits around the property's perimeter. Mac kicked himself for not containing the entire lot. But it wasn't until four minutes before they crashed through the gate they discovered this guy's true stripes. He forged ahead, building by building, but realized this guy was gone. *Son-of-a-bitch!*

CHAPTER 52

~

She tapped her temple to answer and heard, "McQ, whatever you're doing, stop! We need to meet. Now."

"Okaaaay. I'm with MT at my apartment. You're on speaker, Greigh. Where and when?"

"On my way to you. I paid a gypsy cab driver a thousand dollars to break every traffic law in the book. I'm returning from Cicero. We have a timeline. See if Rocko can join us. Tell him to mobilize his local security team. May need help with a search. I'll be there in fifteen minutes." *Click*

MT's eyes widened and she stared at McQ. "What the hell was *that?*" They sat side-by-side on McQ's tiny sofa, going over what they had on Watchtower by organizing their thoughts on the young investigator's tablet. But since they learned from Greigh that Mika was being framed by this Flughler character, or whatever his name was, they'd been looking at Windy City's financials in more detail. They'd found travel plans Bowman had made. But he had buried them under an obscure account and made in another name. The idiot had used a too-obvious alias—Lyle Betterman. *Stupid prick.* MT caught that in about two seconds once they'd discovered the account.

Bam, bam.

McQ rushed to let Greigh in. He blustered past her. Running from the cab to the alley and up her stairs had winded him. He said, "Detonation day—D-Day—is Saturday. Bloody September eleventh." Paused for a gulp of air. "Mac alerted the task force. Dunno, but what if the detonation *time* is symbolic, too? At 8:46 am EDT, hijackers crashed American Airlines Flight 11 into the North Tower of the World Trade Center. At 9:03 am, United Airlines Flight 175 crashed into the South Tower, followed by the Pentagon and Pennsylvania impacts. I'm betting it's the first one—8:46. Doesn't matter. But Eastern or Chicago time? Again, doesn't matter. Early morning." He leaned over to plant his palms on his knees to further catch his breath.

Both ladies stood with open mouths to take in this whirlwind of physical motion and the barrage of startling facts. McQ recovered first. She hustled over to her small round table. Picked up a pen and jotted down *7:46 AM CDT Sat.* She said, "Okay, then. A good working assumption. Now there's little doubt how much time we have left." She winced, not meaning it to sound like a death pronouncement. Her eyes rolled up and to her right. "It's 2PM. Daylight time doesn't end until early November. That means we have..." her eyes rolled up again in thought, "less than sixty-six hours to find as many as ten nuclear devices in and around the city of Chicago—hundreds of square miles. And we don't have a clue how to find any of them, much less disarm them. They could be anywhere. We are *so screwed.*"

Greigh plopped down on the little sofa. Beads of sweat streamed down his forehead. "McQ, one thing at a time. We now have more than we did a few hours ago. It's the JTTF's job to find the bombs. But I'm guessing they could use more arms and legs. How about Rocko's—"

BAM-BAM-BAM-BAM!

MT chirped, "Perfect timing. I'd know that subtle ham-fist anywhere!"

As McQ walked from the table to the door, she said over her shoulder, "Kid, do you gotta sound so cheerful? We're about to be nuked."

The 'kid' chuckled! "Just another day in the hood, right?"

Another whirlwind of motion as the big man hustled into the tiny studio apartment, now jammed with humanity. Rocko Bianchi, head of Urban Security Services and MT's boss, exchanged nods with the girls. He punished an exhausted Greigh with a hearty handshake. He then planted himself on McQ's bed, six feet behind the sofa, and five feet from the window-side table. Greigh stood and turned around. Standing room only now. Rocko scanned McQ's apartment. "Why do we have to meet in this closet, for crissake?"

McQ now sounded like she was in a dark mood. "MT, might as well share with the guys what you've got."

"Sure. We've been digging into Bowman, like you asked, Mr. Greigh. We found some interesting stuff. First, the guy's a rank amateur in tradecraft. He booked travel out of the country under a way-obvious alias—Lyle Betterman. Fits his arrogant ass. Booked a non-stop to London. Our guys checked it out. A false trail. Nothing else, so unless CED's BOLO picks him up, he's gone. For now. We'll find that weasel. Maybe he's not so dumb, after all. Or he's got help."

McQ said, "Tell 'em about the emails."

"Oh, yeah. Over the last few months, Bowman's been hanging out online. It's all encrypted. I picked up a couple of IP addresses. One in Malibu and one in Santa Monica, California. I can isolate a couple of street addresses, but can't read what they said. We don't have that kinda juice."

Greigh grew excited. "No, but the task force does. Text what you know to Spears, MT." He had already provided her Spears' contact info —with his permission. He then called the man at the head of the table at the JTTF. "SAC Spears, Bowman's in the wind, as you Yanks say, at least for the moment. But he's communicated regularly over the last few months with two online accounts in Malibu and Santa Monica, California. We believe the two IP addresses just sent to you by one of our investigators might prove useful in locating Bowman's confederates."

"I'll get our LA field office on it post haste. Good job, Greigh."

"The credit goes to MT Sooner on the USS team."

"Yes, well, pass on my thanks to the, ah, to the entire team." *Click*

CHAPTER 53

A year earlier, right here in their Malibu beach house, the Hollowells and their circle of friends curtailed an obscene, long-running spending orgy. It had eroded into meaninglessness, often while consuming gallons of top-shelf martinis and Manhattans. They had made a pact. The Hollywood Hollowells—Lionel and Angelique, a.k.a. *Lionique*—had sought a cause with at which to hurl themselves and their cronies—their LA County Consortium. Lionel and Angelique provided one—restoring Hollywood *and* their respective Southern California holdings, to their former glory. It didn't take long before this group of aging rebels without a clue obsessed over this cause, this… *quest*.

Their impromptu consortium had long ago acknowledged and came to terms with one harsh but provocative reality. To achieve their aim *within their lifetimes* would require unprecedented audacity. Such bold action would outpace the petty laws of mere mortals with their unimaginative morality. And by bold, they meant illegal. *That* required anonymity to avoid the unnecessary entanglement with, and tedious navigation of state and federal legal systems. Fortunately, all thirty-two righteous zealots within the consortium lacked any sense of morality. Lionique's friends included fifteen other career cocktail couples, many of whom were also business compatriots. All highly committed LA born-and-bred, they agreed with childish exuberance to this cause *because* it also required chutzpa and underhandedness. Just too delicious. But it would be costly, like godly costly. Even better.

Lionel had met Lance Bowman, general manager of Windy City Productions, in the encrypted *Hollywood or Chicago* online chatroom he created where endless debate took place twenty-four/seven. Lionel had hired the best moderator money could buy to ensure exclusive access to that online *room* only by members and vetted friends of the consortium. But Galkin's hacking skills exceeded those of Lionel's moderator and he gained entrance to the room as a member on the Hollywood side of the debate. Galkin's love of Hollywood and Southern California would honor no bounds. He was obsessed, and needed not only funding, but access to inside knowledge of the Chicago movie industry.

Thus began the international reach and influence of the LA County Consortium. Little did they know at the time this would be the genesis of their treasonous and conspiratorial career together, as well: Lionel Hollowell with his consortium, Lance Bowman with his inside studio knowledge, and Andy Galkin, smuggler and strategist extraordinaire with his underworld connections.

Now, it seemed the day of reckoning was at hand... less than a week away. Buzz in "the room" was hotter than ever; however, members only knew that something epic was about to happen, and *Hollywood would rise again.* They knew this thanks to Lionel Hollowell's inability to keep his big mouth shut.

Lionel looked forward to meeting his strategist after next Saturday's event. Of course, there would be a party even though he'd ask they remain in low profile. Whoever this dear man was, his worldly brilliance and international connections amazed the greedy real estate broker. But then he received a spy-proof email—encrypted, he was told, whatever that meant—that raised his eyebrows and caused acid to bubble in his stomach:

My dear LACC1,

A complication means I must visit you early. I trust that is not issue. But do not worry. Remote event management ensures all will happen on schedule, and clients will be very pleased with performance.

I would ask that you not mention this slight change of plan to room. For obvious reasons, I must remain very low profile, at least for now.

Your friend,

M1

Lionel hated complications. But he supposed at least one was inevitable in a plan as complex, far-reaching and bold as this one. Besides, it didn't sound like a big deal. They had foreseen every inevitability and taken all precautions, hadn't they? And without M1, none of this would have been possible. But back to the business at hand. He sent his reply:

Dearest M1,

We look forward to meeting you. Same place. We'll keep the lights on for you. :-)

LACC1

He looked forward to meeting Andy face-to-face for the first time. *I wonder what he looks like? He sounds tall and handsome. Maybe even swarthy, like a pirate. Must be, with his connections and worldly experience. And if he wants to be a star, we can make that happen! Especially in 'Hollywood 2.0!'*

CHAPTER 54

~

Less than six days to what the JTTF now believed to be D-day—Detonation Day. Few knew about the capabilities of the Satellite Vessel Recognition System, or SVRS, managed by Interpol and CIA. This constellation of surveillance satellites could identify and track vessels at sea based on their overhead physical profile. Much like facial recognition of ships at sea from a bird's-eye perspective. This system also *recorded* identification and location data for thirty days. NSA servers in Fort George G. Meade, Maryland, kept an even longer look-back. The JTTF—Joint Terrorism Task Force—tasked SVRS to look back at the *Maltana's* transatlantic track from space.

SAC Spears called out to the rest of the folks in the sixth-floor conference room at Chicago's FBI field office. "People, please direct your attention to screen number two." He pointed to a large monitor on the wall to his left, near one of the room's two doorways on that wall. "Based on publicly available fleet records and Danish Customs, we've got data on the *Maltana's* departure date from Copenhagen via their regional Vessel Traffic Service, or VTS. They monitor vessel traffic by different means, such as from required shipboard transponders, regional radar and infrared sensor systems. Plus, Danish Pilot Services retrieved their harbor pilot from the *Maltana* on Sunday, August 16th, once the ship had cleared the tricky Copenhagen waters.

"And thanks to Interpol investigator Aubrey Greigh, we also hold HUMINT, agency-speak for human intelligence, that the *Maltana* also engaged in a rendezvous with a smaller vessel. We've verified that rendezvous occurred in the open-water strait between Sweden and Denmark before beginning its transatlantic voyage. Near the other end of the *Maltana's* crossing, further HUMINT suggests a second rendezvous with another smaller vessel. US Customs and Immigration records documented when the vessel entered American waters after inspection. That gives us our SVRS surveillance window, people."

An NSA tech sat in front of a laptop near the door-side center of the JTTF's conference room table. The computer was connected to the room's secure network via a cable, <u>not</u> WiFi. They did nothing wirelessly as a precaution, even though they worked inside one of the most secure electronic "bubbles" possible. The tech manipulated a trackball on what was, in fact, a 1,024-bit encrypted portable workstation. He said, "Updated data for your search window now on screen three, sir." They identified the *Maltana* via SVRS, and confirmed that it had indeed engaged in a second unreported rendezvous with a smaller vessel, a private yacht, off the coast of New Hampshire.

THE NSA GUY, STILL ANXIOUS TO MAKE A POSITIVE impression, said, "Sir, of particular interest, OP's official fleet records don't reflect either rendezvous. Someone tampered with *Maltana's* shipboard records. That's pretty solid confirmation that someone inside Obelisk Prime, or at least someone aboard the *Maltana*, was part of this conspiracy." The NSA tech then steered the team toward two additional items of interest. First, they identified the yacht and followed its course via SVRS to a commercial dock in Portsmouth, New Hampshire. Second, via surveillance from a different low-earth-orbit geostationary land sat tasked to the mission, they traced the yacht's cargo transfer to an eighteen-wheeler who delivered that cargo to a warehouse in Cicero two days later. The truck disappeared into the warehouse and remained there, so they did not see the crate unloaded.

SAC Spears picked up the lead again. "Okay, from this sat surveillance recording, it appears this cargo comprised a single large crate. But there is no way to verify how much that crate weighed, other than that it was heavy. The team of four smugglers used a ramp and a forklift to move that crate from the yacht in Portsmouth to the truck's trailer. Guess on weight, anyone?"

The NSA guy piped up again. "Gotta be at least ninety kilos."

Spears said, "What's a ten kiloton nuclear device weigh, son?"

"At least ninety kilograms, sir—two-hundred pounds or more."

SAC Spears grinned. "Gotcha!"

CIA and Interpol agents raced against time to gather intel on the mysterious shipment to Cicero. They tasked yet another geostationary satellite to surveil that warehouse and every vehicle that came and went. But intelligence agencies picked up disturbing chatter that indicated there might be *ten* devices destined for ten different Chicagoland locations. The Danish intelligence agency paid a low-level Interpol informant in Copenhagen to provide target info. The JTTF had to assume other unknown parties had smuggled additional devices into the country undetected. Maybe months or years earlier. They deployed assets to each of the ten locations to search. Each armed and armored cross-agency search team carried detection equipment to ID nuclear material or any explosive ordnance. There were three or more expert bomb disposal personnel on each of the ten teams.

The NSA guy again. "This is a sophisticated international attack in the making, sir. We should not preclude the involvement, and even the orchestration of this attack, by foreign political actors, maybe the rogue Russian President Alexsei Domvrik, or at least some of his top-tier players. This is on-brand for that maniac."

Spears said, "But Domvrik and his operatives would know all about satellite surveillance, including SVRS, wouldn't they? No, my gut says this feels more like a well-funded sophisticated amateur op.

But who would possess the financial resources, the skill set, *and* the international reach?"

NSA conceded. "Yes, sir, you're probably right." The sharp young man appeared chastised. He was supposed to be an expert here. He sought to redeem himself. "How about Mika Kuzmin? But her motive is weak. And she led us to Galkin, who is a much more viable suspect. But what is *his* motive?"

Spears offered the kid a gratuitous nod. "Well, Mr. Greigh said that Galkin was enamored of America. Maybe someone made him promises. Galkin knows about smuggling and shipboard operation. He's been a ship's captain for two decades. And he knows that a ship's location is always tracked. But he would *not* be aware of Interpol's and CIA's classified Satellite Vessel Recognition System to identify the *Maltana* from space. *Nor* would he be aware that we are able to visually track it at sea. Galkin and whoever was backing his play made a rookie mistake."

CHAPTER 55

The sixth-floor conference room seemed a little less stuffy now that a cleaning crew with security clearances had tidied up the room while the task force continued their work. It had grown gamey with so much non-stop activity by too many people that occupied the room twenty-four/seven. The NSA tech analyst assigned to the JTTF stared at his screen. He jumped up and shouted, "Suspect using the screen name M1 just communicated with LACC1 via encrypted email. We haven't cracked the encryption yet—a matter of time. But based on info provided by your local private investigator, Mr. Greigh, we can now track the suspect's mobile device whenever it is turned on."

The tech earned two thumbs-up from SAC Spears. The suspect, of course, was Andy Galkin. They decided that was a less emotive designation than *Terrorist One,* and less cryptic than *M1*. Special Agent in Charge William Spears addressed the joint task force. "Thanks to high-priority satellite surveillance, we tracked the truck carrying *Maltana's* mysterious cargo—which we now believe is a small but deadly nuclear munition. They took two days to transport the device from New Hampshire to a small warehouse at the corner of West 32nd

Place and South 49th Avenue in Cicero. But assuming that is its final destination, *why there?* Whatever the reason, we now assume that warehouse is *Ground Zero*—the intended point of detonation—unless we witness further movement."

Their tactical plan mandated constant surveillance from a geostationary low-earth-orbit satellite. "And people, the president and her cabinet have been briefed. They are standing by in the White House Situation Room." Greigh and Mac looked at each other with worried expressions. Mac whispered, "This is getting pretty damn personal."

"I agree. Seems all the right players are engaged, though."

"Yeah, let's hope they produce results so you don't have to sell your condo and move to a non-contaminated part of the country. Oh, wait, your apartment is likely to be vaporized, isn't it? There goes resale."

Greigh raised his eyebrows at Mac's gallows humor. SAC Spears continued. "It appears the movie studio district is the primary target, but the motive for such a target is yet to be determined. This nuclear device, even if it is very low yield, is also close enough to annihilate the Chicago financial and theater districts farther north, not to mention other tactical and symbolic locations. It's also close enough to Celebrity Row farther east and south near Beverly Shores. By the way, that blast radius includes this building and all of us, people."

That obvious observation still brought the reality home hard to Greigh. He tried to swallow, but his throat was too dry, even as his hands grew clammy. Spears droned on in his James Earl Jones voice as if delivering a predictive eulogy at the city's funeral. "If our intel from Denmark Intelligence and Interpol is to be trusted, this device is likely a Soviet-era tactical battlefield weapon with a nominal ten-kiloton yield. Whatever other ulterior motives might exist, this would be a disastrous hit to the city of Chicago, its financial sector, and entertainment industry with unfathomable loss of life, not to mention the broader economic implications to the country at large.

"Confidence is high that Saturday is D-Day—detonation day—just six days from now. Too many questions remain, people. Are there other devices? If we rush to neutralize the device in Cicero, would the perpetrators likewise rush to detonate this and other still-undetected devices? We dare not take that chance. *But* we have located *none* of the other alleged nine devices. *We need answers!*" The desperation in his voice was unmistakable despite his effort to sound confident.

SAC Spears and the rest of the JTTF discussed the possibility that the other devices *could* be part of a disinformation campaign. The risky consensus was that this became a more credible assumption the longer they searched the other sites provided to them by the confidential informant in Copenhagen. What were the odds that they would find *none* of those other devices *if they existed*? They agreed that if no other devices could be located by midnight Thursday, September 10th, they would descend on the Cicero warehouse in force. That would include the DoE's Nuclear Emergency Support Team, or NEST, with FBI's TEDAC—the Terrorist Explosive Device Analytical Center. They'd be led by the nation's foremost authority on disarming nuclear devices, Dr. Andrea Bomgarten.

Meanwhile, Spears had assigned his CIA task force member to question Galkin's handler. Galkin had been a deep-cover operative for the agency before he went dark. They dived into his psychological profile, known associates, operating methods, the works. They crawled into and around this terrorist's mind. One predominant theme stood out. The guy loved America, and especially, Hollywood. No, he was *obsessed.*

So that made sense once they traced the California IP addresses in Malibu and Santa Monica. They had the contract Interpol investigator working with the suspended CED detective to thank for those addresses from which physical locations followed.

GALKIN LOVED HIS PLAN'S SYMMETRY. BUT NOW, THAT bastard Greigh and that detective threatened it all. No matter. It would all be over before they found the device. Their misinformation campaign had been brilliant. He'd be sure to thank those back home for their help, those he most worried about disappointing. The authorities were onto that fool, Bowman. And by now, they had seen through his own ruse to frame that bitch Mika, too. He couldn't take any chances. He needed to retreat to the safety of California. A few days early, that's all. But inside, he worried more. *Maybe they already discover my party popper. If so, remainder of my big payday never come. They kick me out of country where I wish to die.*

He had burned many bridges to get this far. There wouldn't be much left. One thing became certain in his mind. He would not sit in an American prison, or worse, get deported back to Russia. That *would* be the end. Fortunately, his contingency plan ensured he and his four *bodyguards* held plenty of cash in addition to the wire transfer to his Caymans account. Cash was still king where it mattered. Even in America. The plan was to make his way out west by himself, and his four companions would do so in pairs, but off the grid. Galkin took a taxi to O'Hare and stole a car from long-term parking. Paid cash for gas on the road, avoiding all traffic and security cameras as much as possible. He always wore sunglasses and a hat with a wide a floppy brim. Even at night. Best for defeating facial recognition software. Switched cars in a place called Kansas when he realized how big America was. Not like Russia, but still a big country.

Galkin ensured the third car he stole in a place called Nevada was equipped with a navigation system. He entered 28833 Selfridge Drive, Malibu, CA 90265, the address of his new home provided by LACC1. Arrived at the small but secure estate in the hills between the Pacific Coast Highway and the ocean. His benefactors provided electronic codes for both the entrance gate and the house in an encrypted email weeks earlier. The place was, of course, spectacular. He had been very specific. He'd seen pictures. *Da, this my dream coming true.*

His most trusted man had armed the device and set its timer. He would reach out to his benefactors tomorrow, *after* they all saw news of the 7:46AM explosion. Then, he would be home free, and Greigh would be nuclear ash. He would collect the remaining one-hundred-seventy-five million US dollars from his grateful benefactors. If all went according to plan, that is. But the plan was already at risk, wasn't it? It would just be too painful if that son-of-a-goat-fucker

Greigh spoiled his new life in America. He then *would* need to return to Chicago and finish the task personally. He'd at least gain *that* satisfaction. The thought retrieved a smile. The personal touch. That arrogant bastard *still* thought they were *friends!* A small part of him wished for one last face-to-face opportunity. His men all arrived within the next several hours. *Now, I wait.*

CHAPTER 56

Andy Galkin, a.k.a. Hans Flughler risked revealing the detonation date to that weasel Bowman in exchange for ensuring Aubrey Greigh would be in town on Saturday the eleventh. And near enough to *Ground Zero*. But he now realized taking Bowman into his confidence had been a tactical mistake. He himself had ensured that bitch Kuzmin would also be in town—to take the fall, and too dead to defend herself. She wouldn't be able to stay away with *Maltana's* arrival, with her name all over the smuggling of a nuclear device into the country. She would need to be there. Plus, his source on her staff had told him she would attend a Watchtower board meeting in Chicago this week.

Galkin seethed with hatred for Greigh, who abandoned him after their shared crossing of the embattled Crimea Peninsula together. Since then, Galkin had to fend completely for himself during the subsequent decades while the successful author enjoyed living the American dream. *Without him!*

And that twit Bowman killed off his own people, which Galkin did not understand. Now, Greigh suspected Bowman for embezzlement, and possibly murder, too. That caused Bowman to make mistakes. Like the un-encrypted phone call. Maybe that idiot would not survive. If the twit also made it out to California, he might make sure of that in person.

~

FOR MONTHS, LANCE BOWMAN HAD CONVERSED ONLINE with a gentleman calling himself LACC1, who vowed to help him make his dreams come true. He also cemented the deal with the captain of the *Maltana* during their voyage back from Copenhagen, the man he knew only as *M1* until that night at sea. Bowman now knew he was Hans Flughler. He had met both *LACC1* and *M1* in the *Hollywood or Chicago* chat room. His own screen name was *WC1*, short for *Windy City One*.

Bowman witnessed the mysterious cargo transfer and a murder. He had watched M1's crew place the *Maltana's* actual captain—bound and gagged—onboard a smaller vessel. They cast off all her lines, and she fell away from their own ship. Minutes later, Flughler had approached Lance at the ship's railing with a smile that seemed contrived. Even before he began a conversation, Bowman witnessed the smaller vessel they had just set adrift explode in the *Maltana's* wake that night. He recalled the conversation that followed, almost a month ago now, as if it had happened the previous night....

"*Now* Captain, I presume?" Lance had extended his hand to the wiry little man, leveling a smile of his own.

"Indeed," the man said, continuing to grin. Or was it more of a sneer? "Captain Hans Flughler at your service, *WC1*." It was immediately revealing that he used Lance's screen name in the *Hollywood or Chicago* chatroom.

A hearty handshake later, Lance said, "Very nice to meet you face-to-face at last. M1, I presume. I appreciate your suggestion to book passage on this, ah, vessel. Quite the tub of rust."

"She is low profile. No one gives her second look. You seek to retire to land of milk and honey, yes?"

Lance smiled at the turn of phrase. "I do, indeed."

"Then you on right path to make that happen. My friends need men like you. Movie makers with Chicago experience. You are top of list, my new friend."

Yes, he remembered that conversation like it was yesterday. Word for word, even the man's atrocious grammar.

BUT NOW, A CHANGE IN CIRCUMSTANCES REQUIRED A change in Lance's plan. He thought he would have held the upper hand as a movie magnate either in Chicago *or* in Hollywood until yesterday. But now he was close to disappearing forever with a false identity—at least, as a wealthy man. One must do what must be done. He had killed Fontera because Peter realized what his boss and lover was doing to the studio. That man-child felt betrayed. Peter threatened to expose him. He was fun, but business was business, even though Lance did lose control of himself that night in Copenhagen and things got messy amidst the heat of homicidal passion. That Greigh character almost walked in on that party. But he learned something surprising about himself. He enjoyed killing.

As one true sociopath to another, both he and Flughler were convinced they could both deflect blame for the fruits of their murderous—and treasonous—endeavors. And Lance didn't give a sloppy shit whatever Flughler did to Chicago next Saturday—D-Day. *Wasn't 'D-Day' also some famous holiday during World War II? Whatever.* He had done his part, and his Cayman Islands account was forty million fatter. Plus, he had skimmed another ten from his studio.

The plan had always been to fake his own death. He'd been saving his own blood for weeks, a pint at a time, prior to the Copenhagen trip. He intended to leave no doubt that someone killed him and snatched his body. All so he could start a new life under a new identity, including a new face, fingerprints, the works, born of the consortium's fabulous LA connections. Leaving a couple of quarts of his own blood pooled and sprayed all over his office at Windy City would at least leave the police with ample doubt. It should send them scurrying in the wrong direction—for a while, at least.

After Saturday, September 11th, it wouldn't matter. Instead, he would now have bought enough time to escape to a sparsely populated island in the South Pacific with no extradition treaties. He also would escape the devastation in Chicago. Funny how plans change. He'd had to use his escape tunnel when those cops bum-rushed his office. A shame all that blood in his office's mini-fridge would now go to waste.

CHAPTER 57

Hours ago, the clocked had ticked over from September 10th to the 11th—D-Day. Mac and Greigh sat next to each other in the stuffy sixth-floor JTTF conference room at the FBI Chicago field office. Colette Guibert, from Interpol headquarters, sat to their left. Still at the head of the table slumped the haggard SAC Spears. He bore the burden of leadership on his shoulders, charged with saving the city. It was four AM on the day a nuclear device was about to devastate a significant portion of the Chicago regionplex. Millions would die. Evacuation made no sense. Such a large-scale exodus from the city meant its own inevitable catastrophe.

So, they had bet on the good guys finding and disarming all the bombs. So far, however, that was likely a sucker's bet. To date, they had found concrete evidence of only one device, not ten, as the chatter and piss-poor human intelligence from Copenhagen seemed to indicate. Then, they caught a break. Members of the JTTF—at least those not already out on some frenetic assignment—watched a live satellite feed on one of a half-dozen eighty-five-inch wall monitors in the large conference room they had taken to calling the *Chicago situation room*. At the moment, everyone's eyes were glued to Screen #1. That was the feed from the satellite tasked to surveil all comings and goings of the warehouse at West 32nd Place and South 49th Avenue in Cicero. In the heart of the studio district. They also had the multi-agency "nuke killer" team, those tasked to disarm the device, just blocks away, ready to defuse the device at the appointed time. That time, as agreed, rapidly approached.

The bird locked onto the only truck departing the small structure and tracked it to 667 Harrison Street at 0600 hours. Greigh said, "That's The Lit! My home."

SAC Spears issued a tired smile. "Perhaps it was prophetic, Mr. Greigh, that I said *you* were Ground Zero on this case. It would seem to be so, literally *as well as* figuratively." Much discussion and debate surrounded exactly when they should intercept the device and attempt disarmament. The task force's experts agreed detonation while moving unlikely. They also warned that any attempt to disarm the device en route to its new destination entailed excessive risk. So their strongest new recommendations were threefold.

First, jam all comms beginning immediately until well after the projected detonation time to prevent remote detonation. Second, stand off until the bomb reached its destination. And third, once the device reached its destination, wait until those transporting it departed to preclude the possibility of premature manual detonation. Contingency: move in immediately upon reaching the device's destination at the discretion of the on-scene commander. This was a huge gamble, but Spears decided to listen to his experts, the best in the country. That also meant cutting it close. So, what was one more risk in this already insane scenario?

Those who transported the device had wandered endlessly in a convoluted route. No doubt they were trying to foil anyone who might be following. The nuke killer team remained out of visual contact, allowing themselves to be guided by the "bird"—the satellite. The device had reached its destination. The truck driver and his helper drove the truck away from the scene. A task force team followed them.

The assumption to be immediately confirmed? The device had been unloaded and remained on scene.

Yes, it was time—0603 hours, one hour and forty-three minutes from detonation. SAC Spears scrambled the cross-agency response team comprising the NEST and FBI's TEDAC, and all led by their expert on disarming nuclear bombs. The nuke killer team. Spears hated that name, but someone suggested it, and it had stuck. They descended on the Hotel Literati's loading docks.

Greigh didn't ask permission. He got up and walked out of the JTTF's conference room. He didn't know how he might help here, but he did know he needed to find McQ. In case. The car and driver at his disposal headed toward the Loop. He called McQ. She answered. She hadn't slept, either. "I'd like to come over."

"That'd be great, ya big lug."

He arrived at 0618 hours. *Ran* up the stairs. She stood at the open door. He stopped and said, "In case things don't go well in the next ninety minutes, I'd rather be with a friend."

McQ shook like she suffered from tremors. With eyes wide and fingers fidgeting as they hung by her sides, she peered up at him with misty eyes. She mumbled, "Greigh, I'm scared," afraid to say it any louder.

"Me too, partner. May I come in?" Instead of backing away to allow him to enter the narrow hallway, she eased forward, placed her hands on his hips, and drew him into an affectionate embrace. A partner's hug of friendship, wasn't it? He wrapped his arms over her shoulders, and they just stood there, rocking gently. Like slow-dancing at the senior prom under the watchful eye of a chaperone—she remembered. He dropped his cheek into her mass of wavy auburn hair.

"Smells like lilacs."

She hoarsely whispered, "My shampoo. Baby powder?"

"I like to stay dry."

They separated, and after both were inside, she kicked the door shut with her stocking-footed heel, not bothering with resetting the burglar bar across the door. They still held hands. Greigh said, "I'm sorry, McQ. I've just never felt so alone."

"Don't apologize, ya big lug. This is really good, isn't it?" She glanced sideways down at their clasped hands

"Yes, it is."

They drew together again, magnets with a natural attraction. Opposites Together. Inevitable. With their noses almost touching, McQ placed a soft hand behind Greigh's neck, just under his soft ponytail, on his clammy neck, hot to the touch. Greigh's temples pounded. Didn't care. Now so warm in such a cold world. This was no friendship hug. Something more. Much more. He wasn't even burdened with guilt anymore. Mel would understand. It had been four long, lonely years....

~

McQ's mind was a hot mess. She treasured every delicious moment. She brushed the tip of her nose against Greigh's. His hand floated up to her cheek. Cradled her chin. Their lips met, almost accidentally, until it wasn't. And his mouth consumed hers. Intimate odors embraced them: her shampoo and dry breath; his cologne and fresh sweat. Their urgency caused them both to tremble. Theirs was a comforting blanket against the end of their inhospitable world. This wasn't about lust or physical desire.

They each needed something different. She knew Greigh craved emotional closure. McQ hungered for something she'd never possessed—something she thought unattainable. But in his embrace, this lovely man tossed an anchor into the sea upon which she had been adrift her whole life. She shivered.

~

SAC Spears's assistant sent out notifications—alerts—every five minutes to all the task force members' computers, handhelds, wearables and tablets. Greigh's wristPad buzzed. He read the message:

JTTF: 0626 - Response team on site. Device not located. Eighty minutes to possible detonation.

0630 hours on D-Day came and went. McQ and Greigh sat shoulder-to-shoulder on her tiny couch. They read the alerts together. McQ's head rested on Greigh's right shoulder. They held hands. He stroked her hair. She reached across her chest to trace small circles with her right knuckle in his close-cropped beard. Nobody said a word for several minutes.

Then, Greigh spoke, hesitant to break the spell that had trickled over them. "I thought I could help the team search. That was a foolish notion. The drivers left immediately. The response team arrived on site twenty-three minutes after the truck arrived with the device. The truck was already gone. For a crate larger than a coffin, they would not have had time to hide it, just to unload, arm it, and scurry out of the destruction zone before it popped off, you know."

"I'm glad you came here instead, Greigh. Means a lot. If it ends here...."

The next alert said the same thing:

JTTF: 0631 - Device not located,

followed by how many minutes remained until likely detonation. Then, at 0640 hours, Greigh's device buzzed. They read it together, McQ's head still nestled into the crook of Greigh's neck:

JTTF: 0640 - Device located.

She raised her head to look into his piercing blue eyes. "They've got a top expert there, don't they?"

"The best. Still...."

Once more, she dropped her head to his chest, adjusted her hips so she could snuggle closer, and swung her right leg over his left shin. They just sat there. Not moving. Not speaking. Both barely breathing.

Forty-five minutes until expected detonation. McQ grew nauseous. Or was that how she was supposed to react? Now this close to the man who bombarded her thoughts ever since she met him almost three unrelenting months ago? She had almost died in his arms back then. Maybe she would again. But this time, there would be no coming back. Everything was changing. She seemed swept away in a tidal wave of new emotions, contrary to the tough cop she was *supposed* to be. Then, at 0701, *bzzzzzz:*

> JTTF: 0701 - Device disarmed. No other devices located. All members debrief at 0800.

Greigh felt giddy. He sat up board straight, but took his time to do so. Swiveled to his right on that ridiculous little sofa, and with a firm grip, placed a hand on the sides of McQ's shoulders, turning her toward him. He said, "Optimistic, aren't they? There could be nine other devices out there they haven't found. Are you okay, dearest?"

McQ leaned forward into his grip and purred like a mountain lion before she issued that hoarse whisper he found so alluring. Into his left ear she whispered, "I'm optimistic too, sweetie, and more than a little exhausted." She dropped her chin, raised only her eyes to meet his, offered a demure mini-smile, directed her eyes to her left, and nodded over her shoulder. The only thing in that direction was her pitiful excuse for a bed, still a mess from a restless night.

What the hell. we have an hour before the JTTF briefing…. He drew her in and devoured the rest of her. No guilt at all. Greigh finally came face-to-face with what he now realized was his most profound fear… that of dying alone.

CHAPTER 58

The National Security Agency contingent of the Chicago Joint Terrorism Task Force had earlier escalated the status of Greigh's smuggling case. This terrorist threat had become an urgent matter of *national* security. It had started with a murder in Copenhagen and now presented a continuing clear and present danger to the United States of America, the now-disabled nuclear device in Chicago notwithstanding,

FBI's SAC Spears had earlier tasked NSA analysts to decrypt all emails sent by Lance Bowman from Windy City Productions. Bowman, a person of particular interest in the matter, fled local and federal apprehension. Bowman's many encrypted emails to two IP addresses led to physical addresses, easy enough for the analysts to isolate. Then, the analysts cracked their encryption.

What they found of particular interest, one day before D-Day, a new Internet address popped from a third geographical location. All three triangulated to Los Angeles County in Southern California. The JTTF had earlier dispatched apprehension teams to Malibu and Santa Monica. FBI's Felony Apprehension Team out of Los Angeles, including their SWAT contingent, swept up an aging couple: Lionel and Angelique Hollowell. They met no resistance. Even if they had, the Patriot Act of 2001 gave federal law enforcement broad latitude when dealing with suspected terrorists.

The team seized their computers and their cloud accounts. They identified Lionel Hollowell as *LACC1* - the primary organizer of the domestic terrorist organization known as the LA County Consortium. They discovered a list of all the consortium's members in the Hollowell's Malibu Beach House. These amateurs tried to play the roles of big-league conspirators, but failed in comic fashion. They would all go away for a *very* long time.

The Santa Monica commercial address housed the consortium's sophisticated servers that weren't as secure as they assumed. From there, they zeroed in on a long-term lease signed over to a "trusted contractor." Odds were excellent that this was the destination address for one Andrushya (Andy) Galkin, a.k.a. Hans Flughler—someone referred to only as *M1* in the cracked emails. That address matched the origin of the third IP address in LA County that popped the day before: D-Day minus one.

Since Greigh once was Galkin's friend and comrade-in-arms, Spears directed him to join the FBI apprehension team on Selfridge Drive in Malibu for the takedown. They needed him alive. Spears still worried there may be other devices that Galkin might be tempted to detonate remotely or that were on timers, and Greigh was their best chance at taking Galkin alive. Then the HIG would get their chance to interrogate him further. They also wanted to learn if other sponsors had a hand in organizing and funding this attack.

A FOUR-HOUR FLIGHT ON AN FBI GULFSTREAM FOUND Greigh groggy and hungry as they made their approach to the Los Angeles International Airport on Saturday afternoon. He still clung to the memory of his encounter with McQ when they thought they both might die. He smiled. And tingled.

The flight crew left the cockpit door open. Just a few feet away, Greigh could hear the pilot and copilot discussing their landing procedure as they approached LAX:

> LEENA FIVE arrival order for all general aviation operators, Craig. Looks like we're headed to the south side of the airport."
>
> "Fine with me. Less traffic. I hate LAX."
>
> "Not a very professional attitude."
>
> "Very funny… 'Roger, Approach Control, cleared for runway two-five-right.'"

Greigh found the very serious trio of FBI agents that accompanied him unnerving. He wasn't accustomed to hanging out with hunter-killer types. At least, that's how he thought of them. He was told the blacked-out Chevy Suburban that met their aircraft was issued from the LA FBI field office on Wilshire. Almost before the plane rolled to a stop, the four of them hustled into the vehicle driven by a local agent. With lights and siren, they made quick work of the thirty-six miles between LAX and Selfridge Drive in Malibu—less than twenty-five minutes, hellish traffic notwithstanding. They hoped Greigh could positively identify Andrushya Galkin, and that his friendly face might get them through the gates and front door with a minimum of carnage. Optimists.

Mission objective: take the suspect alive.

Tactical plan:

1. Jam all communications to prevent remote detonation,
2. Greigh and his traveling companions would meet the LA FBI apprehension team down the road from the scene,
3. Alone, Greigh would drive the lead vehicle and attempt to get through the gates by appealing to his friend,

4. Failing to gain entrance to the estate, Greigh would back away from the gates and let the local assault vehicle containing the Apprehension Team—or AT—breach the property's perimeter,
5. If Greigh got Andy to open the gates, he was to drive halfway up to the house and stop,
6. The AT would then rush through the still-open gates (they had timed the closure rate from the live satellite feed during previous arrivals),
7. The AT pass Greigh's vehicle and secure the scene, hopefully, with minimal casualties, but Command had authorized lethal force as deemed necessary by the JTTF and the on-scene commander, except for Galkin, who was to be taken alive,
8. Once they secured the scene, Greigh would identify Galkin,
9. They'd then hustle Greigh back to LAX for his return to Chicago,
10. The suspect would be secured, hopefully alive. Classification: terrorist in possession of information critical to national security. He would be processed accordingly.

Greigh thought he might be of some value during Galkin's interrogation. Command said that would require a security clearance he did not possess. But the AT leader and on-scene commander vowed to keep the situation fluid as they saw fit. The AT was FBI's version of a police SWAT squad, but on steroids and with fancier toys. These boys, a dozen strong, weren't particularly large, but they moved like an elite military unit.

Galkin would then be remanded to the HIG—the FBI's elite high-value detainee interrogation group. At least that would be his first stop. But right now, they got word the mission was a *go*, and executed. They continued to surveil the property from a live satellite feed and 'other airborne resources.' Only three arrivals in the last thirty-six hours. No departures. Greigh wasn't surprised. *Andy has company.*

On the left side of the drive in front of the gates to the location they presumed harbored Andrushya, a.k.a. Andy Galkin, stood a pedestal encased in an ornate stucco housing. It comprised a numeric keypad, a call button, and a grill behind which he presumed hid a speaker and microphone. The top of a post that sprouted from the pedestal's miniature terra-cotta roof perched a hooded camera on a mount that could swivel sideways and vertically. Greigh got as close as possible to that pedestal with the cumbersome Suburban. Had to reach down to press the call button. A few moments later, he heard a familiar voice. But it was laden with shock. *"Greigh? What you **doing here?**"*

"Hello, Andy. I'm here with a dozen or more very serious federal agents who wish to chat with you, old friend. But before all of that, will you talk with me alone for a few minutes? Even though I didn't bring any Scotch?"

Silence. Ten seconds. Twenty. Then....

"Da, old friend. I'm afraid I'm in terrible mess. Would be good to see friendly face before unpleasantness. You come straight to house. We talk." After a few seconds, the double gates swung open on squeaky hinges. Once clear, Greigh pulled into the pebbled drive that curved as it wound up a hill. The large, modern, flat-roofed mini-mansion crouched at the summit, perhaps fifty yards away. In his mirrors, the assault vehicle appeared and roared through the still open gates. *Here we go.*

A half-dozen of the latest generation surveillance-slash-sniper drones surrounded the estate. They were armed with stabilized long-range cameras. Each drone was also the launch platform for high-tech, small-caliber, sub-sonic smart bullets. This weaponry could be programmed for heat-seeking and DNA-seeking capabilities concurrently. For this mission, however, operators programmed them to *avoid* one specific DNA sequence—that of one Andrushya Galkin, citizen of unknown nationality, but presumed to be Russian. They had retrieved five DNA signatures from the motel room on Kreiter Avenue in Chicago. Four were similar, one was not.

Nobody but senior echelons at the Pentagon had any idea this technology existed. But since this was still an urgent matter of national security, their use had been authorized. These lethal little platforms had proven effective in several high-profile theaters of conflict. However, agencies rarely used them in a civilian context on US soil. This incident would be a notable exception. Their bodies each measured thirty-four inches in diameter and less than a foot from top to bottom. Propellers extended beyond the body's dimensions. Each platform weighed less than seven pounds, powered by six small apex-efficiency electric motors, each of which powered a ten-inch variable-pitch kevlar propeller. Munitions were self-propelled once ignited.

One operator could control six of these hunter-killers (a.k.a. HKs), as they were autonomous once given their orders. The operator fed the entire swarm its operational parameters for the mission and then provided each with a specific assignment. Once on station—at high hover until engaged per their mission—they fed continuous status back to the operator's screen in a command center. To the uninitiated observer, that command center, now parked on Selfridge Drive, looked like a medium-size recreational vehicle—black, of course.

No sooner had the team's assault vehicle passed Greigh's SUV than four automatic weapons issued a fusillade of bullets from the flat roof of the house. They all targeted Greigh in the FBI SUV. When the first round hit his windshield, he dove for the floor, trying to put as much engine metal as possible between him and the onslaught.

Seeing what was happening, the apprehension team leader—Alpha Tango One, or *AT1*—changed the plan. As they say, a battle plan is perfect until someone fires the first shot. He directed his driver to place the armored assault vehicle between the source of the fire and Greigh's SUV. Once in position, AT1 ordered the HKs to engage. The drone operator pushed a red button on his console. The HKs descended from their high hovers and targeted the four gunmen on the roof. It took only six seconds. The operator reported what he saw on his segmented high-resolution screens—one segment for each HK: "four down, roof secure, but probably no longer waterproof."

With no sign of Greigh in his vehicle, AT1 radioed Greigh. "Rabbit, AT1, you still alive, partner?" Silence. "Rabbit, report status." More silence. "Command, no response from—"

"Uh, AT1, this is your bloody rabbit. Right as rain. You blokes should go take care of business, then."

"Ha! Rabbit, AT1, that's a roger. Glad you're still with us. Command, we are re-engaging."

"Copy. Go."

CHAPTER 59

~

Galkin tried to detonate his nuke now in the Hotel Literati from his new home in Malibu, now under attack. But he had no signal. He tilted his head, dropped his chin, raised his eyebrows, and opened his eyes wide. He screamed, *"Ty che, blyad?"* Loosely translated: *What the fuck?*

~

GREIGH SAT IN THE NOW-DECEASED SUV. RIDDLED WITH bullets, every window had disappeared into piles of safety glass crumbles, and he could smell hot steam coming from somewhere. He assumed it came from what now had to be the vehicle's well-perforated hood. Though the onslaught had stopped, he remained as flat as possible, face up, on the floor between the front bench seat and the firewall of this huge vehicle. He slowly uncovered his eyes.

Amazed at how the California sunshine would not be denied, it gushed in through the Suburban's ceiling, courtesy of a hundred large-caliber holes. They weren't round, more like jagged bearded ovals, no doubt due to the angle of penetration. Each resembled a rip or tear more than a hole. And each was embellished with shredded insulation and dangling headliner fabric. These perforations rendered beams of light visible by airborne dust and bits of light-as-air stuffing from the riddled upholstery. *This incident will almost certainly affect this bloody vehicle's resale value! They must not have budget for an armored vehicle to transport non-FBI rabbits.*

Why Andy would attack him with such savagery perplexed Greigh once the shock of the brutal assault aimed at him began to subside. *Seems we're no longer friends….*

Then, Greigh heard over the government-issued handheld comms unit he had taken to the floor with him when the attack began, "Command, AT1. Suspect and scene secured. No friendlies injured. Scene cleared for processing." Greigh crawled out of the brutalized Suburban. He had to twist around to position his feet toward the unlatched but jammed front passenger door. He kicked it open against its bent frame. Took three tries. He emerged as an army of support personnel, techs and local FBI VIPs made their way up the drive in an all-black caravan. *Why do the feds all drive black vehicles? Some color might lighten their perpetually somber moods.* Even though he had planned to hike the mere half-block up to the house, a suit in a sedan driving someone important in the back seat wearing a more expensive suit stopped next to him.

"Hop in. I'll give you a lift," said the spendy suit in the back seat."

"That's alright. Thanks, anyway."

"This is called a debrief, Mr. Greigh. Hop in. Please."

"Oh, ah, of course. Silly of me. You blokes have your protocols." He puckered his cheeks and launched his eyebrows in apology as he slid into the already-open rear door.

"I'm Special Agent in Charge Van Haag, Mr. Greigh, this operation's on-scene commander. I'm told you have a personal relationship with our suspect. But maybe that relationship isn't quite what you thought."

"Yes, Agent Van Haag. That attack surprised."

"You are to identify the suspect. Additionally, I am now authorizing you to engage in a cursory interrogation of the suspect. My prerogative. You approach no closer to the suspect than six feet. A simple nod will do once you verify his identity. Then, whatever intel you can glean as to motive, co-conspirators, methods, et cetera, would be useful. Touch nothing, and talk only to your *friend.* That's it. Is that all very clear, Mr. Greigh?"

"Yes, Agent. I must admit I am nervous. All this jarring violence. But so be it."

"Good. Here we are."

The house looked remarkably intact, other than the shattered front door and its frame. They had briefed Greigh that the heavy lifting would have been accomplished by automation, although he wasn't at all clear what that meant. Didn't care. Need to know, anyway, they said. As they entered a large living area, he couldn't miss six or seven members of the assault team. They still stood at high alert anticipating any possible post-action threats, while he and Agent Van Haag proceeded to a smaller room where they said the suspect—Andy—was being detained. Various techs and agents poured over the scene, Andy's house, which was lovely.

They walked down a hallway unscathed by the assault and into a bedroom whose southwestern wall faced the Pacific Ocean beyond the coastal cliffs through floor-to-ceiling glass. The spectacular view could have been a picture postcard from *Architectural Digest*.

And there sat his "friend," Andrushya Galkin, not looking too much worse for wear, other than a bruise on his left cheek, with his feet zip-tied to a stout straight chair. Greigh assumed his hands were secured behind his back in the same fashion. One agent stood on each side of Andy's chair. Their dark blue windbreakers were emblazoned with large yellow letters—FBI—on front and he imagined even larger on back, like others in the house. Their eyes alternated between staring down at Andy, observing Greigh's approach, and watching Agent Van Haag behind him in his charcoal suit. Their expressions signaled this wasn't protocol.

. . .

"HELLO, ANDY." GREIGH GLANCED AND NODDED TO AGENT Van Haag, who offered a brief nod in return. Andy said nothing, but as Greigh stopped the prescribed distance from him, Andy did his very best to launch a cheek full of spit at Greigh's face. Greigh jumped back, bumping into Van Haag. His eyes widened at the unexpected response. "Andy? What have I done to anger you so?"

The most frightening sneer transformed Andy's face into a macabre mask. His voice started low and soft but hard, like he was launching shards of broken glass from some subterranean grotto, escalating in pitch and volume as he spoke. "Anger, Greigh? This not anger you see. This *hatred.* After Crimea, you abandon me. You claim to be my friend, but I *beg* to come America, and nothing. So I find different friends. Friends who help me come America. For small favor. And I get all this." His head and eyes swirled in an arc to take in his lavish surroundings. "More than *you* give me, all these years. You only give Scotch whiskey, and only when you need something. You know what I do to survive all those years? Would curl your pretty ponytail, Greigh. All because you forget your friend." Though his mouth was dry, he went through the motions of spitting again, this time at Greigh's feet.

"Andy, I applied and appealed to the State Department for you to come to America. Six times! Each time, they rejected your application or overturned my appeals. Your background... your—" Greigh felt a lump rising in his throat. This entire episode shocked him. Hatred radiated off Andy in waves. From someone he believed was his friend. He regrouped. They needed intel. "So, you blow up Chicago to get even, Andy? How does that make any sense at all?"

"Your death is bonus." He fell silent.

"But why so many bombs?" Andy had hung his head like he was just tired of it all. But when Greigh asked that question, he raised his head at an angle, looked at Greigh with just his right eye, and... smiled. Dropped his head again. "So, there was always only one device. The rest was just disinformation." No response. None needed. "Clever. Divide resources. Your new friends have a lot of money, Andy. You always did chase a payday, didn't you?"

Andy's head snapped up once more. His nostrils flared as he

inhaled sharply through them. "What you expect? I am poor smuggler, not rich American author! I do what I must to survive. Is so bad I want this?" Again, with his head on a swivel. "So, why not attack America with American—" And he realized he was saying too much. He clammed up and dropped his head again.

Greigh jumped right back in. "But the selection of those tactical and symbolic targets. A marvelous piece of fiction. So plausible. Your wealthy Hollywood friends aren't that smart, though, are they, Andy? They just funded your little fantasy. You had help from the motherland, didn't you?" Once more, that smiling right eye, but nothing more. Except this time that tiny smile lingered. A serious tell. "And framing Mika Kuzmin, a fellow Russian, for this whole affair? Brilliant, but why? Because she pissed in President Domvrik's soup by moving OP and all its rubles out of Russia? You know, Andy, you guys act like a schoolyard gang of adolescent teenagers. When you don't get your way, you throw a fecking tantrum. Yes, that's it, isn't it? A bunch of bloody *Russian children*—Leonov, Raspin, you, Kuzmin, Domvrik.... Well, fuck you all, Andy. Just *fuck you all!* And *you*, my *"friend,"* are a tiny man with a shitty voice and a chip on your shoulder because life isn't fecking fair, you *twit!"* Greigh's voice had escalated to a near-scream. He felt the FBI suit's hand on his shoulder. But he shrugged it off and took a few steps closer to Andy, who obviously thought Greigh was about to attack him.

Andy tugged against his restraints. His eyes darted back and forth, now full of fear, to the two agents surrounding him as if imploring them for protection from this madman. Good. Greigh continued his rant. "Four years ago, I lost the love of my life and my sweet six-year-old daughter because I stood in the way of a greedy *Russian* land developer. He was also Mika Kuzmin's twin brother. And she blames *me* for the wanker committing suicide. Now she's trying to *kill me, too.* So, wait your fecking turn, you piece of shit! I am SO tired of you fecking *RUSSIANS!"*

By now, Agent Van Haag restrained Greigh from attacking the prisoner. Greigh stopped trying to advance on Andy. He just stood there. Van Haag let loose his shoulders. Greigh's voice dropped to a malevolent snarl. "And you, Andy, you are the *worst bloody bugger* of all. You'd blow up an entire fecking city just to kill me and get rich? Know what? You deserve whatever deep hole they're about to drop you into. And welcome to America where ***we*** still believe in the rule of law, you slimy little git."

Greigh concluded his "interrogation" by spitting at Andy's feet. As he walked out of the room, he slammed both his clenched fists against his outer thighs, over and over. He was mad at himself for losing control. Van Haag followed him out. "Is all that true? Jeez, Mr. Greigh, you've had a helluva run, haven't you?"

"Fuck you, FBI. Get me out of here. Please."

"Roger that."

CHAPTER 60

~

Greigh's violent encounter with Galkin and his gunmen the previous day exhausted him beyond his imagination. And almost getting shot to death? Just hours after thinking he and McQ might end up as two small piles of nuclear-incinerated ash caused him to re-evaluate how short life can be. He had faced death before, but not in such a bombastic fashion, and not twice on the same day. Not only that, but his own boss at Interpol wasn't who he thought she was, and *she still* wanted him dead. What a month. He had wasted no time getting the hell out of California and back to Chicago. Back to his home. Back to McQ. Back to some semblance of sanity. His FBI escorts thanked him for visually identifying their suspect, and for interrogating him. They assured him he had extracted valuable intel. They also told him he might be the only person who could have gotten their suspect to talk. He doubted that. By confirming that both domestic *and* international benefactors aided Galkin in their attempted terrorist attack on the city of Chicago, Greigh had performed a great service for his country. That's what they said. Whatever.

He harbored no doubt Galkin's co-conspirators included the Hollywood Hollowells *and* someone inside Russia, maybe even the Russian president himself. But the latter? Now strictly a political matter. It was late. And not like a normal Sunday afternoon. At all. Butler unlocked the door for him—suite 7D in The Lit—the aborted Ground Zero. Butler's best Sean Connery imitation announced in a sultry tone, "Greigh, welcome home. You have a guest." Greigh could have sworn those words were spoken by someone with a huge smile on his—its—face.

"Thank you, Butler. It's not Mika or Freya again, is it?" Nothing. Except soft classical music. Definitely neither Mika nor Freya nor whomever or whatever the hell *she* was. He rounded his entryway. The fireplace glowed from a low flame. The darkened room only hinted at someone lounging on the sofa in front of that welcoming fire.

"Welcome back, soldier." Of course, it was McQ in her flannel lounging pants and a long-sleeved CED t-shirt three sizes too large. Two glasses of red wine—in white wine glasses, no less—awaited on the coffee table in front of her. He smiled. She was *so*... McQ.

Without saying a word, he collapsed heavily next to her and wrapped his left arm over her shoulders as she nestled into him. Laid a hand on his leg. He laid his on hers. Their eyes met. Then, their lips. After a long kiss, they just embraced, as if there would be no tomorrow. For the longest time. They fell asleep in each other's arms, the wine untouched.

CHAPTER 61

Weeks later, a domestic cleaning crew discovered Lance Bowman's corpse at his South Pacific island retreat. A local constable notified Windy City based on personal effects found in the bungalow on Vanuatu Island, a thousand miles east of northern Australia. They, in turn, notified the authorities. Bowman's mysterious death hit the Chicago media. Said signs of torture perplexed local law enforcement. e-Records found on a device in his palatial beach "bungalow" showed that his Cayman Islands bank accounts had all been depleted—zero balance. A mystery.

An investigation confirmed the Hollywood Hollowells and their LA County Consortium funded Galkin's exploits to restore Hollywood to its former glory by removing Chicago as its competition. But who was capable of *engineering* such a sophisticated conspiracy? Certainly the Hollowells and their friends only funded it.

The World Court in The Hague, Netherlands convened an

international interagency intelligence task force to determine whether the rogue Russian President Alexsei Domvrik subsidized or abetted Andrushya Galkin—officially or unofficially—in an attack on the United States of America. Nobody held their breath awaiting the findings of that politically motivated task force that would advise the President of the United States and the US Congress with respect to sanctions, or something more… aggressive.

There was some talk of Interpol levying charges against Freya Ecklund, but nobody believed that would go anywhere. They had much bigger fish to fry, and likely wished the entire embarrassing episode to quietly disappear. And Mika Kuzmin had become untouchable. Freya Ecklund no longer existed. Not publicly, anyway.

Watchtower filed for bankruptcy amid all the scandals and the ensuing financial catastrophe. Without Leonov *or* his sister Mika at the helm, Watchtower became the corporate equivalent of a vulnerable house of cards on a windy afternoon. And Mika realized she was clearly a persona non grata in America for the foreseeable future. She would seek her revenge in a way that didn't cost her a fortune and the remainder of her peak years to achieve it. Besides, America was just too messy with too many idiotic rules. Since Interpol chose not to charge Mika with any crime—just too embarrassing politically—she had returned to Estonia, where Obelisk Prime's business was better than ever.

One of Copolla's forensic accountants from Urban Security Services came upon an obscure transaction at a DNA-testing lab while scouring all Watchtower financial transactions. They confirmed Mika's claim to Greigh. She was indeed Leonov's twin sister. But Mika was a businesswoman, first and foremost. It remained to be seen what would happen to Tihomir Leonov's estate.

Urban Entertainment, Inc, Gaspari Copolla's company, rescued

Watchtower, Inc, by acquiring it for pennies on the dollar. Mika Kuzmin still vowed Copolla would pay for his treachery related to her brother's death, along with the others—including Rocko Bianchi, Aubrey Greigh and Chance McQuillan. Maybe a few others. Just not today. She added to her list of grievances that Copolla had now stolen Watchtower from her.

Even though UE was approaching monopoly status across the US commercial real estate development market, nobody stood in the way. Copolla had transformed from sordid mob boss to revered patriot-warrior. He and his resources came through for the country when it needed his free-wheeling methods and resources the most. Gaspari Copolla and Rocko Bianchi, along with their USS agents, even received accolades from the City of Chicago *and* a commendation from US President Marjorie Cullen. In grand innocuous fashion, it read, "for invaluable services rendered to the United States of America."

Amanda Tennyson (MT) Sooner received a special commendation for her role in the case. Rocko told her, "Ya done good, kid. Your papa and his buddy Hamm would be proud."

IT TURNED OUT THAT THE LOW-LEVEL INFORMANT WHO provided the disinformation on nine targets that also never existed did so knowing that the selection of those targets would be useful in determining who had helped plan the Chicago attack. Unconfirmed rumors connected that informant to the Danish Defense Intelligence Agency. The informant had vanished.

GREIGH AND MCQ BECAME HEROES FOR THEIR PIVOTAL role in busting the potential city-killing conspiracy wide-open. By rendering justice to its chief perpetrators, Andrushya Galkin and the LA County Consortium headed by the Hollywood Hollowells, city and federal agencies applauded their achievements. Nobody outside federal agencies and a few trusted sources within the CED would ever know. For obvious reasons.

The erstwhile detective moved in with the mystery writer in his suite at The Lit. Luca Donati leaked to the media that the unlikely couple—his dear friends—were even discussing marriage. But that was only informed speculation.

NINE MONTHS LATER, JOSH CARVER'S SCREENPLAY OF Greigh's book, *Voodoo Vendetta,* was produced at Toby Stiler's Miracle Mile Studios with real actors working in real Chicago and Louisiana settings. It held the potential for becoming a box office smash, as the Yanks would say. Time would tell if audiences really did want HG ("human generated") entertainment with only limited computer-generated support.

COMMISSIONER JACK ROBERTS PROMOTED CAPTAIN LOIS Granger to commander and offered her an influential staff job in his office. Said he was impressed by Granger's tenacity in defending the rights of her detective. Even though it was only Interpol's and the commissioner's ruse to keep McQ in the field and unconstrained by CED protocol. The commissioner said the captain had earned his trust, and he owed her a profound debt of gratitude. McQ was reinstated with a promotion to captain and an offer to command her own precinct house—maybe even the nine-nine *if* her boss, Commander Granger, accepted *her* new position. McQ hadn't yet decided whether she'd return to CED, at all. Commissioner Roberts gave her time. He said he'd keep that job offer and her promotion open, but warned her not to take too long. He advised McQ to discuss the matter with her boss and most loyal supporter, Lois Granger.

GREIGH SAID, "INVESTIGATION SHUT."

McQ shook her head. "You mean, 'Case Closed?'"

He smiled. She noticed his grin and said, "Oh, you're jerking my chain, again? Shut up!"

Greigh was profoundly in love with McQ—and guilt-free about it, at last. But he just closed his mouth and kept smiling as they ate their breakfast at the large table next to the window wall that separated them from his covered balcony.

Greigh grew giddy. *Do I dare pop the question today?*

The End? Or....

APPENDIX

CAST OF MAJOR CHARACTERS

- **Gerard a.k.a. Rocko Bianchi**: Don Gaspari Copolla 's most trusted capo—lieutenant and muscle. Also Executive Director of Urban Security Services (USS) for Signore Copolla's Urban Entertainment, Inc.
- **Lance Bowman:** General Manager (GM) of Windy City Productions (movie studio), Cicero, Illinois. Screen name WC1.
- **Todd Bricker:** Production Assistant at Windy City Productions & PA to star Stacy Michaels
- **Josh Carver:** Screenwriter at Windy City Productions
- **Gaspari Copolla**: Chicago's erstwhile top crime boss who craves respect and legitimacy. Also, president and CEO of Urban Entertainment, Inc., a nationwide commercial real estate development corporation.
- **Luca Donati**: Proprietor of Hotel Literati.
- **Freya Ecklund:** Mid-level Interpol agent and Aubrey Greigh's handler (boss).
- **Peter Fontera:** Movie star at Windy City Productions.

- **Captain Hans Flughler:** Ship's captain of the Obelisk Prime freighter, *Maltana.*
- **Captain Andrushya (Andy) Galkin:** Ship's captain and Russian smuggler. Screen name: M1.
- **Captain Lois Granger**: Detective McQuillan's boss at CED's ninety-ninth precinct in Chicago's Near SW Loop.
- **Aubrey Greigh:** Best-selling mystery writer and resident/owner of suite 7D, Hotel Literati. Greigh also freelances as an Interpol investigator.
- **Colette Guibert**. Sits on Interpol's thirteen-member Executive Committee (elected by Interpol's General Assembly). She is one of nine delegates along with Interpol's president and three vice presidents. She hails from Interpol's European headquarters in Lyon, France, and is very highly place within Interpol.
- **Lionel & Angelique (Lionique) Hollowell:** Also called the "Hollywood Hollowells." Real estate brokers in LA County, California, and organizers of the LA County Consortium. Screen name: LACC1.
- **Mika Kuzmin:** President & CEO of Obelisk Prime (OP). Also, Ty Leonov's twin sister.
- **Tihomir (Ty) Ty Leonov:** Deceased twin brother (estranged) of Mika Kuzmin and ex-CEO of Watchtower Industries.
- **Detective Aidan (Mac) McKenzie**: Recently promoted detective and co-worker of McQ's at CED's ninety-ninth precinct.
- **Chance Goodwyn McQuillan, a.k.a. McQ**: Detective Lieutenant of the Chicago Enforcement Department, ninety-ninth precinct.
- **Stacy Michaels:** Movie star at Windy City Productions.
- **Jack Roberts:** Chicago Enforcement Department's police commissioner.
- **Tony Santos:** Sargent Detective filling in for Detective

McQuillan at the ninety-ninth precinct (a temporary transfer in from the eight-five). Mac's temporary partner.

- **Amanda Tennyson (MT) Sooner:** Private detective from USS assigned to work with McQ to investigate Watchtower, Inc.
- **SAC William Spears:** Special Agent in Charge (SAC) of the Chicago FBI Joint Terrorism Task Force (JTTF).
- **Toby Stiler:** General Manager (GM) of Miracle Mile Studios, Cicero, Illinois.

AUTHOR'S NOTE

As an author, I remain conflicted by the excessive use of artificially generated images, characters, settings and scripts in public entertainment. That's one of the principal reasons I felt a need to tell this story the way I did.

Now, with the emergence of astounding—some would say *plagiaristic*—capabilities by machines to write entire articles, books and screenplays as derivatives of existing works, not to mention other works of visual art, both moving and still, I wonder what the future holds for all artists.

Writers, actors and voice performers have every right to be concerned, especially when the fruits of their labors are used without their permission… or compensation.

Additionally, I empathize with writers and actors who are not fairly compensated when technology—like streaming services and unsanctioned syndication, for example—enable their unfair exploitation, even while senior executives rake in millions annually.

Meanwhile, ***over eighty percent of authors, actors and writers barely***

subsist at or below the poverty level of income (less than $30,000 annually in 2023 dollars)! [1]

I believe all artists—all creatives—should be vigilant in their awareness of such travesties of common human decency, and I support the courageous strike for fair compensation by the Writer's Guild of America, Summer 2023.

Bravo!

Now, for something very different, turn the page to read an excerpt from the first Sam Travis Outdoor Environmental Adventure: Lethal Game: Bears Under Siege

---

1. This is, at best, an anecdotal estimate.

EXCERPT FROM LETHAL GAME

BEARS UNDER SIEGE

August, 1988
Wonju, Gangwon Province
South Korea

~

A dense fog stunk like wet wool—dank and thick. Sagging strings of colored lights that hung low over the narrow street painted halos in the drifting mist; that is, those bulbs that weren't burned out or shattered. The late afternoon sun almost failed to shine through the clouds, fog and exhaust fumes.

The boy was accustomed to the pungent stench that always saturated this neighborhood. It stung his nostrils and irritated his sensitive eyes. But the urchin's enthusiasm was hard to miss even in the poor visibility. His was to be an important task for an important man —someone everyone called *Uncle*. This could lead to more jobs.

I won't be hungry anymore. Not tomorrow, anyway.

The skinny pre-teen splashed through the oily surface of a shallow puddle. Around a dark corner into an even darker alley from the narrow cobbled street, there hunched *Uncle*. That wrinkled old man drew on the long pipe in the corner of his mouth at the pharmacy's alley entrance.

The venerable old herbalist shook his head as if impatient or angry, probably both. The boy could not see Uncle's right hand as he clasped it behind him. Mad little puffs arose from his long, curved ivory pipe cradled in the crook of his crippled left hand.

The boy slid and stumbled from his dead run. The street was oily slick and littered with wet newspaper pages of yesterday's trivia. He bumped into Uncle, who stumbled back into the closed door with a soft grunt.

The boy mumbled, "Sorry, Uncle."

He looked up at the craggy face, then dropped his chin to his chest. Too close. He had invaded this important man's personal space. He shuffled back a pace under that icy stare.

Uncle's chest-length beard stunk of curry and... flowers? No, that was opium. Uncle was a rich man. He was not to be disrespected. The boy stepped back yet another pace, bowed, brought his hands together in front of his lowered face as if praying, but his eyes turned upward, pleading for leniency. He needed this job.

The venerable old man said, "You are late, Han, and you are careless."

"*Please* forgive me, Uncle." Han bowed again for good measure. The old gentleman swept one arm from behind. In his upturned palm, he revealed a small package wrapped in gold foil. With a ceremonial flourish and his pipe now clenched in between his few remaining teeth, he placed the package the size of a large pea into a small box just large enough—maybe one inch square.

"Yes, hurry, now. Hyung Gang Wa will reward you well."

Always jittery when within the old pharmacist's presence, young Han was in awe of the stinky old man. The kid snatched the box now containing the gold-wrapped pea, and offered one last bow, little more than a quick head bob. Han bolted for the mouth of the alley and the safety of the street.

The sky opened. Rain in Wonju always tasted metallic at first. Something from the factory. Han's feet were already mud-splattered, anyway. Just that when his sandals got wet, they stretched. Cheap leather, *but* he was proud they *were* leather. Made running harder and tripping easier.

He protected the little gray box containing the gold pea from the rain with his body. Surely, it shouldn't get wet. Uncle hadn't said.

As Han ran, the streets grew wider and straighter. Cleaner, too. Not that Uncle lived in a poor part of town, mind you, but Hyung Gang Wa was *very* rich.

There it was. The bathhouse. So much white—pillars, fancy statues.... Men with money always loved big and white and fancy.

I wonder if that is true everywhere, or only in Wonju.

He had been nowhere else.

Now, Japanese and American cars filled the boulevard. He dodged each of them with ease as he crossed four lanes of traffic between manicured gingko trees shedding their autumnal colors in the median. He cursed as he stepped on a piece of their stinky fruit scattered on the grass. As he crossed the southbound lanes, the shouts of angry drivers who slammed on their brakes bombarded him with words and gestures of a most profane nature. They leaned on their horns.

Trees on both sides of the street and in the median dripped with the heavy raindrops that pummeled Han's stubbled head. As he got closer to the bathhouse, he admired the cornucopia of white statues resting on its manicured front lawn behind wrought iron.

Han stopped. He knew he was late, but Uncle had told him what he carried was important. Tempted to peek at what was inside the gold foil within the little box, he resisted. Could be fatal.

He paused, then scrambled up the white wooden steps leading to the front door. Breathing hard, he knocked, waited, knocked again. The massive portal cracked open. The suspicious eyes of the huge muscular attendant flashed recognition. Swung the door open enough for his important torso to pass through to the covered landing.

Han dropped the package into the monster's outstretched right hand. It was massive. Han leaned left around the big man's tree-trunk body as the package disappeared into a pocket. He tried to sneak a look at the women inside.

The monster grabbed a fistful of Han's sturdy shirt with his left hand, raising him three feet off the white wooden landing outside the bathhouse's tall doors. The tree trunk sneered and said, "Curiosity is for cats. That can get them killed."

He slapped Han's face with such force the boy's head snapped to his right and back. Blood dripped from his nose onto both his shirt and the attendant's left hand that still held him suspended. Tree Trunk appeared both amused and angry. Laughing, he flung Han down the stairs, along with a few coins that scattered in every direction.

The bathhouse attendant shouted to Han where he lay. "Watch your manners, boy! And one day the honorable Hyung Gang Wa might invite you in. Now go!"

Face down in the puddle nearer the cobbled street, Han smiled. Tree Trunk could not see his grin. A small toss down a few stairs was well worth a fistful of coins. He could tell from their jangling as he fell this was already a profitable day. Yes, he would eat.

Han picked himself up, wiped his nose and gathered every coin before scampering off. That big man always tipped better when he got to toss Han down those stairs. A little game. Han would thank Uncle for the work on the way home.

He'd hope to catch another sweet whiff of Uncle's opium pipe.

Inside the bathhouse, nearly naked women and men lounged in dreamy contentment. A gray sun shone through skylights and reflected off tiled pools of tepid water. Exotic vapors fanned upward toward the twenty-foot teakwood ceiling.

Several of Hyung Gang Wa's customers lay on their backs atop several cushioned tables that lined the walls around the blue-tiled pool. Their bellies glistened as women applied various lotions and oils to arouse them.

A macabre carnival revolved through the big attendant's mind. The reflected light off the wavy water, the steam, the oils, incense and flaccid nudity, along with the sounds of happy endings now and then.... The big man grinned with his head on a swivel as he walked. His job was the best in the world.

He approached an oak-paneled door. Turned the knob. It squeaked. He winced. Entered Hyung Gang Wa's private chamber with the gold-wrapped package in his hand.

Large ornate carvings of wooden lions and dragons peered down from all four corners of the ceiling. A threadbare red rug covered the floor except for the three feet of glossy bamboo planks around its perimeter. Dozens of candles flickered and offered a sensual glow.

Translucent curtains dotted with silvery beads veiled the four-posted bed. Tendrils of incense within rose toward the bed's mirrored overhead in the dim light, where reflections of three full-breasted girls tangled with Hyung Gang Wa's oiled body—a mass of obese flesh.

The attendant drew near, bowcd to thc tall woman in a lacy gown who stood guard next to the bed. She tried to take the package, but Tree Trunk insisted on handing it over to his master himself.

The woman cleared her throat to gain her master's attention and parted the curtain. The attendant refused to back away under the tall woman's fierce gaze. He filled his eyes and nostrils with the revolting yet stimulating sight of the fat man trying to have fun.

The tall woman awaited the right moment as the three young girls continued to massage Hyung Gang Wa from his shiny scalp to the soles of his corpulent feet. He yawned. They escalated their movements, both in speed and intensity. The attendant failed to appear disinterested. The big man yawned again despite their steady manipulations.

Now noticing the gauzy veil had parted, Hyung Gang Wa jerked away from the trio of teenage girls whose breasts were too big for their age. He bolted upright, his face waxen, eyes heavy-lidded.

The morbidly obese man's voice gurgled and rasped as he spoke. "What has kept you?"

Tree Trunk said, "The boy was late."

"I'll have the pharmacist's head if it happens again." He extended a soft, plump hand. "Well, the package, you idiot. Give it here, quickly. Quickly!"

The attendant nodded, saying nothing, handed the gold pea over with a deferential bow. He then rushed from the room with visions of the three young maidens burned into his libido.

~

Hyung Gang Wa's puffy eyes flashed with desperation. Removed the gold foil. Popped the gray-white nugget into his jowled mouth. He swallowed without benefit of water or his ever-present cup of rice wine.

Two of the girls rubbed his back. The third employed her attention elsewhere. He leaned forward and sighed, revealing his yellow teeth and larger-than-life dimples in both jowled cheeks that pressed upward toward his adipose-encased eyes, they were little more than foggy slits.

A moment later, his enthusiasm swelled. The girls responded with fingers now exploring below his waist with slow rhythmic motions at first. Then, more vigorously. The fat man's smile grew wider and wider.

~

Friday,
September 30, 1988
Wedgewood, Massachusetts

The town's principal thoroughfare screamed *quaint.*

Its small stores and steepled churches looked like a Norman Rockwell painting. Farmhouses, barns, and fenced-in pastures normally as green as emeralds clustered around Wedgewood.

From above, a proud sun dappled grassy meadows through millions of gold, brown and yellow leaves that had been a dozen shades of brilliant green just a few weeks earlier. These meadows peeked out from folds in the earth like wrinkles in a blanket on a crisp and sunny day. In and around Wedgewood and its rolling hills, all seemed beautiful, serene, perfect.

A rusty Ford Bronco rumbled down a country road. The official state seals on the Bronco's doors announced this old four-wheel-drive truck belonged to the Massachusetts Environmental Police.

Sam Travis hunched behind the wheel listening to the strains of Robert Palmer's *Simply Irresistible* on the radio, and tapped his thumbs to the beat on the wheel. His threadbare uniform was a bit small these days. He wore it pressed—with pride. Well, sort of. He didn't not *love* his job, but could imagine doing nothing else. Naw, he was made for this gig. But there were days....

The Bronco rambled up the sloping driveway, stirring up the dust that was an artifact of this autumn's dry weather. Oak and birch trees stood at attention on either side of the curved drive, but they looked tired. He'd stacked three cords of dried oak, beech and white birch alongside the left end of the cape-style house weeks ago. Most of it was ready to generate some heat. The house's weathered cedar shakes and shingles held in that heat during cold winters.

Travis's heart fluttered. The Bronco's door creaked as he swung it open. The heady scent of pine sap all around the yard reminded him why he loved living out here. As he slid out of the truck, the tip of his holster always dragged on the seat to his right. The protruding hammer had long since worn a hole in the seat's back.

Patched with the wrong-colored vinyl repair tape, allegedly permanent—he just called it duct tape—was already peeling off. Travis swore he'd get his tired ass to a junkyard to find another seat. He'd scavenge another old truck to butcher. On behalf of the Commonwealth of Massachusetts, of course.

But that would take time he didn't have. Maybe he'd just wander down to Hank's hardware store. He'd find a suitable seat cover with elastic straps to hold it in place, and to hide the hole... at least to keep it from getting worse.

He checked the new leather retainer loop he'd had sewn into his old holster. Secure. Kept his trusty old revolver from falling out. A reflex. Time and weather had loosened that holster, but it was part of him. The old .357 Smith and Wesson sported too many scratches in its finish from dropping to the ground as he'd crawled out of that old truck the last couple of years. The gun showed some battle scars but was meticulously maintained. His life had too often depended on it.

Travis frowned at the grass growing up and around his old lawnmower in the front yard. Plus, most of a pile of garden hose was not visible in the tall grass—a.k.a. weeds. A rake leaned against the house, and the damn weeds held that old rake hostage, too, growing right through its blades. He'd take a day off....

Sam's frown of guilt turned into a grin. Spotted Brian, his twelve-year-old son, bottle-feeding a scrawny fawn he cuddled in his arms at the bottom of the porch's steps. Poachers had slaughtered the tiny deer's mom. Kind of how cancer slaughtered his own. They had adopted "Fawny"—Brian had named her.

This kid.

"Hi, kiddo. School let out early?"

Brian said, "Hey, Dad. Kinda."

"Waddaya mean, kinda?"

"I didn't know if you could make it in time to feed him," he nodded down at the little deer, "so I excused myself from the last period."

Travis stared down with clamped lips and one cheek puckered. After a shallow sigh of resignation, he said, "Excused? You mean skipped, don't you?"

"Jeez , Dad. It's not that." Brian wrinkled his forehead as if his next words were the most sincere he ever uttered. "Just trying to keep her goin' after all she's been through. We don't want to lose her now, do we?"

Travis hinted at a grin as the boy looked up at him, ruffled his son's hair as he climbed the first porch step.

"Okay. But remember, schoolwork comes first." He took a deep, cleansing breath. "Getting big, isn't she?"

"Yeah. Must be the vitamins."

Travis climbed the rest of the steps at a tired pace.

Saturday Morning,
October 1st
Glenville, Massachusetts

These woods always reminded Frank Murdock of Christmas. The pine and hemlock trees that loomed over the log cabin stained its brownish exterior to somewhere between a weathered gray and the black of neglect. But it always smelled like Christmas.

Out front, a sign nailed to a post announced,

Environmental Police
Regional Headquarters,
Glenville, Mass.

Frank swung open the cabin's screen door. It banged against its stops as he stepped out onto the porch and filled his lungs. Sometimes he felt stronger than he himself expected. The truth? He had grown too darn old and tired for the job. But he'd admit that to no one out loud, not even to himself.

He slapped away the cobwebs from the top corner of the screen door. They weren't there last night. A few clung to the sergeant's stripes on his right shoulder. Those stripes were less faded than the rest of his forest-green uniform. He scratched at the third-day stubble on his jowled neck.

The grizzled game service veteran hobbled side-to-side out to his Bronco, a clone of the one that his partner, the promising young Sam Travis drove, though rustier. But for the sweet fart of fate, he'd have lost one or more of that truck's Swiss cheese fenders behind him in a ditch on a country road.

His left knee gave him trouble most of the time. Today was one of those days. Not the only thing that irritated him, though.

These dents and all this grime? Past adventures, eh? If we get some budget, maybe the boss springs for a new fleet of Broncs... yeah, sure thing—come a hell a Sundays!

Frank grabbed the handle, swung open the driver's door with a screech from its pair of rust-dry hinges and hoisted his creaky carcass up into the driver's seat. His eyes had grown bloodshot from filling out forms for the last hour.

Blasted paperwork... two more years and I'm gone... gone... gone....

Twisted the ignition key.

Bam!

The Bronco sputtered and stalled. Murdock slammed his fist against the wheel. The muscles in his jaw rippled. Didn't mean to grind every single natural tooth left in his mouth. Probably chipped at least one, or worse. He was sure to put the dentist's youngest boy through his freshman year at Holyoke Community College.

Twisted the ignition key again. More sputtering.

Fire up, you son-of-a-buck!

Finally, the engine took pity on the old woods cop. After a quick J-turn, Murdock drove past the cabin in a cloud of dust with sparks shooting from the exhaust pipe—actually, from the hole in the pipe in front of the rusted muffler. One more backfire, and the Bronco disappeared, leaving a pall of blue smoke in its trail.

Murdock bumped along a remote dirt road that was more of a game trail than an actual thoroughfare. His chunky trail tires kicked out gravel. Clotted chunks of mud had caked inside all four wheel wells before the first freeze. Stayed all dried up in there, now, like gray concrete.

Intermittent static issued from his dash radio. Then, the sultry tones of their female dispatcher offered a welcome respite from the noise that the radio's antiquated squelch could not defeat. Murdock had been warned about his playful flirting. Like he had a shot!

"Unit twenty-one... unit twenty-one... please respond to a shooting complaint near the abandoned hotel at Wolf Hollow."

Shit. Means another hike to the top of that wretched ridge.

He tried not to sound pissed at that silky voice washing over him from his radio's speaker. Or too sarcastic. What was her name, again? "Unit twenty-one received. Thanks a lot!"

"Sorry, Frank. You're the only officer in that district. Complainant states she's heard shots fired there for over a week now."

"Received and en route."

A week-old complaint. Typical.

Murdock pointed his Bronc up into the hills on the winding road toward Wolf Hollow. Clouds of dust swirled behind, but a fair amount of it filled his Bronc, too. Swiss cheese wheel wells'll have that effect.

Coming around a curve too fast, he slammed on his brakes. Even denser dust engulfed him and the Bronc. Almost got jammed up on a fallen tree and half a dozen boulders.

Great. A landslide. Just what I need.

Murdock snatched the microphone from its hook on the dash. "Unit twenty-one on portable at Wolf Hollow."

"Received, twenty-one."

This trail's a cuss-ed mess!

Still muttering to himself, he climbed out of the cruiser, surveying the steep incline. Spotted the head of a foot trail he knew led to the abandoned hotel up top.

Murdock chose his steps with care. Didn't need a twisted ankle. Small rocks tumbled around his feet as he walked, rolling down the steep trail behind him, clattering in hardscrabble protest.

Frank stopped for a moment on the incline to do a quick three-sixty. A panoramic view of the countryside from the ridge reminded him why he chose this line of work. Breathtaking. He loved *his* Western Massachusetts mountains.

The wind had picked up. Or more likely, it hadn't, but felt like it up on the ridge. Leaves rustled as they took to the air, skittering across his path.

And there it was—the abandoned hotel. Not much left other than its foundation, a concrete slab, and two camouflaged tents pitched there, all organized like it was a professional operation of some sort. He could guess.

He approached the campsite, now on full alert, and still managed to step right into a still-steaming pile of dog crap.

Shit!

He dragged his soiled boot over a pile of dead leaves that had accumulated up against a rotten log. Still shaking his left boot every other step, Frank continued on into the campsite.

Off to his right hung camo pants drying on a clothesline. There was a wire run for dogs, and the remains of a fire. Just a bed of ashes within an impromptu rock circle.

Murdock soft-stepped up to the rightmost tent that was zippered shut like the other one. He unzipped it, bottom up, for a peek inside. Halfway up, he stooped, pushed aside the flaps, and faced a barking, snarling whirlwind of teeth, fur and blazing eyes, inches away.

He flew butt behind heels onto his ass, stunned by the attack.

Gee-ZEUS!

The big dog choked against his now ribbon-tight chain to get at him from inside that tent.

The hound relented, but continued to snarl in frustration as Murdock got to his feet. As he got to his feet, he noticed drops of blood glistening on the dried leaves near where he had stumbled back. He stooped to run a finger over it.

Still stooping, he sniffed—the drop smelled coppery. Eyeballed it up close. Rubbed it in a circular motion between his right thumb and forefinger. Slippery. Yup. Blood.

After his third three-sixty scan since entering the camp, he followed the intermittent blood trail. He often bragged he could track anything, anywhere, anytime. And he had.

The trail led him to a clearing surrounded by... camouflaged netting? And a game pole constructed of two straight hardwood tree limbs driven into the ground ten feet apart. Someone had strung a rope between the poles eight feet off the ground. Guy ropes outboard of the poles ensured they would support tremendous weight.

He saw four dead bears hanging by their necks. They'd cut off their paws at the wrists and stripped their hides down from their necks to reveal incisions deep into abdominal flesh. Still raw and bloody. And steaming.

What the hell? A crew of pro poachers!

The end of a rifle barrel poked out of the bushes just twenty yards away, brushing a limb and its dried leaves. The crosshairs of a scope centered on Murdock's back. A finger tightened, and....

Murdock spun around, reacting to a sound any *normal* sixty-two-year-old pair of ears would have missed. At that moment, a bullet struck Frank three inches above and four inches to the left of his chest's center. He sprawled backwards.

The poacher walked toward the fallen game warden. Leaves crunched beneath his boots in the now deadly silent forest.

Murdock's voice wheezed, "Help. Please."

A raspy laugh echoed in the silence. The poacher's response to Murdock's plea with the rifle pointed at his forehead? A blast that shattered the forest's silence.

The man with the mean eyes kicked the uniformed piece of meat at his feet as he drew in the sweet scent of cordite.

WHAT'S NEXT?

If you like what you've seen of
"Lethal Game: Bears Under Siege,"
the first book in my Sam Travis Adventure series,
please visit GKJurrens.com
or purchase a copy from your favorite online retailer.

Now, before you go...

Please ***subscribe at GKJurrens.com*** to be informed of my new releases. ***And don't forget to leave a brief review where you bought this book. Or email gjurrens@yahoo.com with your comments. I'd seriously love to hear from you.***

I gratefully read every review.

Thank you.

- GK

OTHER BOOKS BY GK JURRENS

~

Historical Fiction (Great Depression Era Crime)

- Black Blizzard: A Lyon County Adventure
- Murder in Purgatory: A Lyon County Mystery

Aubrey Greigh Mysteries

- Voodoo Vendetta - Culture That Kills
- Dancing With Death - Who Will Die? Or Disappear?

Sam Travis Adventures:

- Lethal Game - Bears Under Siege
- Lethal Trail - No Body Is Safe

Fictional Autobiographies (Drama/Thrillers/Intrigue)

- Dangerous Dreams: Dream Runners: Book 1
- Fractured Dreams: Dream Runners: Book 2

Future Fiction (Paranormal Mystery Thrillers)

- Underground, Mayhem: Book 1
- Mean Streets, Mayhem: Book 2
- Post Earth, Mayhem: Book 3
- A Glimpse of Mayhem: Companion Guide to the Mayhem Trilogy

Non-fiction

- The Poetic Detective: Investigate Rhyme With Reason

- **Why Write? Why Publish? Passion? Profit? Both?**
- **Moving a Boat and Her Crew**
- **Restoring a Boat and Her Crew**

BEFORE YOU GO

Please write and post a brief or email your thoughts to gjurrens@ yahoo.com.

Remember, other readers and I need to know what you think. **I read every single review with gratitude. Thank you.**

Also, feel free to browse or subscribe at GKJurrens.com for announcements and giveaways.

- GK Jurrens

DEDICATION

For the real Aubrey Gray and his lovely bride, my big sister.
Carol, I wish he could have seen this book, too.

DISCLAIMERS

This entire novel is certified to be *"AI-free,"* that is, the authors—*certifiable humans*—wrote all 85,167 words, *not* artificially intelligent software.

This is a work of fiction. Any similarity to actual persons, behaviors, places or events should be considered coincidental and fictional.

Research of this manuscript's period and its theme mandated judicious use of ethnic pejoratives and mild profanity and are not meant to offend the reader. Quite the contrary, the use of these literary devices is intended to demonstrate a commitment to authenticity.

ACKNOWLEDGMENTS

Many thanks to all my beta (pre-publication) readers for your unvarnished feedback on this manuscript, including my grammar police, my law enforcement experts, and my story flow guardians. But I offer a special thanks to my most brutal critic of all, my lovely bride, Kay, who always offers me a humbling experience.

You all helped me make this my *best book yet* (so I'm told).

Thank you!

- GK

ABOUT THE AUTHOR

~

GK Jurrens writes with undiluted passion. He's published sixteen fiction and non-fiction titles to date including twelve action-oriented novels across five series. He also teaches writing and independent publishing seminars nationwide.

With UpLife Press, GK has independently published:

- Outdoor Environmental Adventures
- Historical Crime Fiction
- Modern Murder Mysteries
- Contemporary Autobiographical Fiction
- Futuristic Paranormal Romantic Mysteries
- Science Fiction
- Poetry & Essays
- Writing & Publishing
- Nautical Travelogue
- Sailing Yacht Restoration

Gene and his wife have lived and traveled in a motorhome for almost a decade. They wander their beloved North America as a source of endless inspiration, having lived in forty-two states in the last decade for a few weeks to a few months each.

After studying Liberal Arts and Electronics Engineering Technology, Gene earned a Bachelor of Science degree in Business and a

Master of Science degree in Management of Technology from the University of Minnesota, USA.

Six years of government service (US Coast Guard Search & Rescue, Marine Law Enforcement) and a successful three-decade career in global high-technology (IBM) preceded more than a decade of voyaging on America's waterways, the Florida Keys, and the Eastern Caribbean from the British Virgin Islands to Granada, near the coasts of Venezuela and Trinidad.

And brief forays sailing around the Greek Cyclades Islands in the Aegean Sea as well as the San Juan Islands in the American Pacific Northwest offered Gene and his wife Kay more unique sailing challenges.

With multiple works always in process, Gene continues to write with a sense of urgency, and of course, passion. Always. He embeds contemporary social issues in each of his action-oriented stories.

www.ingramcontent.com/pod-product-compliance
Lightning Source LLC
Chambersburg PA
CBHW051956240626
47153CB00005B/1777